D0305489

THE DEVIL'S PACT

July 1943. With North Africa secured, the Allies launch an invasion of Sicily, and the 2nd Battalion, King's Own Yorkshire Rangers are in the van of the assault on the Italian beaches. Now B Company Commander, Tanner's promotion has brought him fresh problems. Not only has his new Battalion Commander decided to make his life as difficult as possible, but he and his men soon find themselves battling against some of the toughest troops in the Wehrmacht. In the bitter fighting that follows, Tanner witnesses a new kind of warfare where the end will justify the means.

THE DEVIL'S PACT

THE DEVIL'S PACT

by

James Holland

Magna Large Print Books
Long Preston, North Yorkshire,
BD23 4ND, England.

British Library Cataloguing in Publication Data.

Holland, James
    The devil's pact.

    A catalogue record of this book is
    available from the British Library

    ISBN   978-0-7505-3891-6

First published in Great Britain in 2013 by Bantam Press
an imprint of Transworld Publishers

Copyright © James Holland 2013

Cover illustration © Collaboration JS by arrangement with
Arcangel Images

James Holland has asserted his right under the Copyright, Designs
and Patents Act, 1988 to be identified as the author of this work

Published in Large Print 2014 by arrangement with
Transworld Publishers

LP

Magna Large Print is an imprint of Library Magna Books Ltd.

Printed and bound in Great Britain by
T.J. (International) Ltd., Cornwall, PL28 8RW

For my parents and for Ned,
who accompanied me to Sicily.

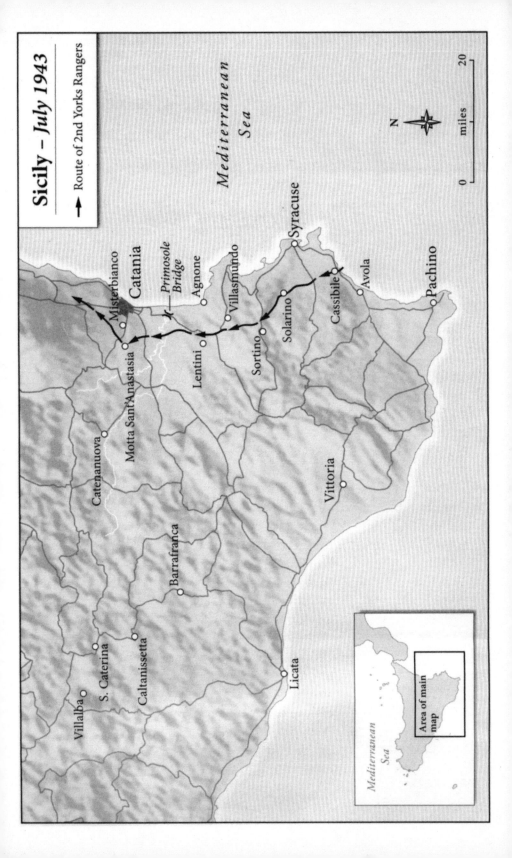

Sicily – *July 1943*

→ Route of 2nd Yorks Rangers

Mediterranean Sea

N

0   miles   20

Misterbianco
Catania
Primosole Bridge
Agnone
Villasmundo
Syracuse
Avola
Pachino
Cassibile
Solarino
Sortino
Lentini
Motta Sant'Anastasia
Catenanuova
Vittoria
Barrafranca
Villalba
S. Caterina
Caltanissetta
Licata

Mediterranean Sea

Area of main map

Glossary

2 i/c – second-in-command
angel, angels two – 1,000 feet, 2,000 feet
bandit – enemy (in the air)
basha – house
CP – command post
croaker – a wounded person
CSM – Company Sergeant-Major
cushy – easy
dekko, have a – take a look
DZ – drop zone
ENSA – Entertainment National
  Service Association
iggery – quick, hurry up
jaldi – quickly
KOYLI – King's Own Yorkshire Light Infantry
LCA – Landing Craft Assault
LST – landing ship tank
MG – machine-gun
M/T – motor transport
OCTU – Officer Cadet Training Unit
O Group – Orders Group – a group of key
  personnel gathered before an attack or
  operation
OP – observation post
OSS – Office of the Strategic Services
PIAT – Projective Infantry Anti-tank

(like a bazooka)
Red Devils – British Airborne Forces
(nickname)
Regia Aeronautica – Italian Royal Air Force
sitrep – situation report
SMLE – Short Magazine Lee Enfield .303 inch
calibre rifle
Spandau – Allied term for any German
machine-gun, dating back to the First World
War when some Maxim guns were made in
Spandau in the western suburbs of Berlin
stonk – sustained artillery fire, usually
concentrated on one area

1

Friday, 28 May 1943, around one a.m. The
Dakota droned on, a low, monotonous rumble,
the pitch of the two engines changing only
occasionally as the plane hit turbulence or the
pilot adjusted course. Captain Jack Tanner,
sometime of the King's Own Yorkshire Rangers,
but now, well, he wasn't so sure, closed his eyes.
The noise of the plane was so constant it had
become a kind of silence. He opened his eyes
again and glanced at his watch, the dials only
faintly visible despite the luminosity of the face.
Surely, he thought, it must be almost time. A
flight of one hour and five minutes, they had
been told, at a cruising speed of around 140
miles per hour. 'It's just a brief hop across the
Med.' The pilot had grinned. 'Piece of cake.'

Tanner had not reciprocated the smile as they
had left the briefing tent at La Marsa airfield,
nausea already stirring in his stomach. If he had
wanted to spend his life in the air, he would have
joined the RAF a long time ago. While others had
gazed enviously up at, first, biplanes, then Spitfires
and other modern aircraft, Tanner had been
grateful to have his two feet firmly on the ground.
Fortunately, during the more than ten years he
had been a soldier, he had not had much cause to
find himself airborne. Once or twice, that was all.
He understood the principles of flight, but it still

15

seemed unnatural to him that a large mass of metal, oil and high-octane fuel should travel high up through the sky, and he did not like having to place his life in the hands of someone and something else. On the ground, he was confident he could handle himself as well as any man. In the air, it was a different matter.

Tanner shifted in his seat and felt the canvas safety strap dig into his waist. The Dakota, or C-47, as the Americans preferred to call it, belonged to the 51st Troop Carrier Wing, and would, Tanner had learned, be transporting British and American paratroopers over to Sicily when the invasion was eventually launched. Either side, running down the long fuselage, there was a row of fourteen metal seats, then a space towards the tail for stores and the jump hatch.

Tonight, however, the seats were largely empty – Tanner alone on one side, Major Charlie Wiseman and Colonel Max Spiro on the other. Tanner glanced across at them, the three-quarter moon casting a pale glow through the windows behind him. Spiro was playing with something – a rosary? – his lips moving faintly, perhaps muttering to himself. There was a wedding band on his left hand. How old was he? Late thirties, Tanner guessed, probably with a family back home in Washington or wherever he lived. He looked short and fleshy next to Wiseman, who sat with his back straight, head against the side of the fuselage, eyes closed, a faint smile across his face. Tanner cursed him for looking so relaxed, but rarely in the past few months had he ever seen Wiseman more than slightly ruffled. Spiro now caught his eye, then quickly looked away. At least he could speak Italian, Tanner thought. Spiro looked Italian too: dark hair, slightly greying, dark brows, dark eyes, dark skin. 'He *is* Italian,' Wiseman had told Tanner. 'Leastways, his parents are. First-generation Sicilians.' Spiro had grown up speaking Italian, Wiseman had said. 'Half of all Americans speak some European lingo,' he'd added. 'Hell, about a quarter of us speak Kraut.'

'What about you?' Tanner had asked.

Wiseman had shrugged. *'Un poco Italiano. Grazie tante, Signorina.'* He had grinned. 'Put it this way, I know what a *flautista* is.'

'What is it?'

Wiseman had laughed and slapped Tanner on the back. 'Look, we'll be just fine. Don't you worry, Jack.' Even Wiseman had a Mediterranean look about him: the same dark hair and eyes. Tanner supposed he did too. Like Wiseman, he was tall – six foot and a bit – with almost raven dark hair and the kind of olive skin that looked out of place on Englishmen, even those brought up on the land as he had been. It was no wonder after two and a half years fighting in the Mediterranean and North Africa. The difference was his very pale blue eyes, but he had noticed a number of Arabs in Tunisia, especially, shared that feature. 'You look a perfectly convincing Sicilian,' Wiseman had told him.

'Look like one maybe,' Tanner had replied, 'but I've got more in common with a bloody Jerry than an Eyetie. And I can speak more Arabic and Urdu than Italian.'

He wondered how he had ever got himself into

17

this mad enterprise but, of course, as was so often the case in this war, he had had little choice in the matter. Since early March, after the débâcle of Kasserine, he had been attached to the US II Corps, assigned as a liaison officer on General Patton's staff. In Charlie Wiseman, one of Patton's senior aides, he had soon found a friend and ally. Together they had fought at El Guettar, at Hill 609, and at Bizerte, Tanner trying to pass on his experience to these green American troops fighting the Germans and Italians, while Wiseman had helped him to bridge the cultural gulf between the Americans and the British. And when General Patton had had his spat with Air Vice-Marshal Coningham, Wiseman had successfully kept Tanner out of it, saving him from finding himself horribly compromised. For this, especially, Tanner had been grateful. He was a soldier, not a politician. The argument, as most of Patton's staff had realized, was about tactical differences and the use of air cover; Patton, however, had not seen it that way. As far as he had been concerned, the Limeys had once again been sneering down their noses at their American allies. No one on Patton's staff had cared to mention that Coningham was a New Zealander.

Two weeks earlier, on 13 May, the fighting had ended. After what had sometimes seemed to Tanner like for ever, the Germans and Italians had been driven from North Africa. A quarter of a million troops and God only knew how many tanks, guns and aircraft had been captured. Tanner had seen them: long lines of dusty, exhausted enemy troops, tramping along in endless

18

columns down sun-drenched roads into PoW cages. Defeat had been etched on their faces, expressions of despair and relief in equal measure. Briefly, as Tanner had beetled around in his Jeep, passing messages and liaising with various units and headquarters within II Corps and First Army, he had been sure that the war would soon be over.

Now he rubbed his eyes, then felt the cool metal of the Beretta on his lap. Two weeks! That was all it had been. But in that fortnight those moments of hope had gone. There would be no end to the war – not for a long while yet. The Germans were not about to throw in the towel: they were still deep inside Russia, and so what if North Africa had been lost? Fortress Europe was still theirs. The fighting would continue, first with an Allied invasion probably, he supposed, of Sicily and then – well, then, they would have to invade mainland Europe. Where was anyone's guess, but it was as certain as day follows night. *Christ*, Tanner thought. All that fighting still to come. How could he ever have thought otherwise?

And an uncomfortable idea had crept in: that surely his luck was about to run out. The odds were massively against him, he knew. Jesus, it was something that he was still alive at all. Death was not a matter he liked to think about too much. One day at a time. That had been his philosophy ever since war had broken out. But now... Now he was about to jump out of an aircraft onto an enemy-occupied island. *Bloody hell*, he thought. He glanced at his watch again. By his reckoning there could not be more than five minutes to go.

Five minutes. Were these, he wondered, his last moments? Was this finally, after all this time, the end of the road?

Just two weeks – two weeks and one day – since the end of the fighting in Tunisia. They had all got drunk, swum in the sea, and watched the parades in Tunis. For so long, they'd been fighting for this goal: the end of the war in Africa. Then, after the euphoria, had come the realization of what still lay ahead. Even so, Tanner had expected a lengthy spell of inactivity. He'd even wondered whether he and some of the other old-timers might be sent home to England. There had been a time when he would have baulked at such an idea, but not now. In truth, he'd been in England barely three months in the past ten years; he had no family, no home. Nothing. Yet England was still home. He'd saved a bit of money over the years. Maybe he'd buy into a farm tenancy, not in Wiltshire, where he'd grown up, but somewhere else. Dorset, perhaps. Devon, even. For the first time since he had left home as a sixteen-year-old and joined the Army, Tanner had begun to think of a life beyond that of a soldier. A quieter life. A life of peace.

Wiseman had put paid to that three days ago – Wiseman and the brass with their unrelenting plans to grind the Axis into the dust. He'd been woken by Wiseman at II Corps headquarters in Bizerte and told they were both needed in Tunis. They'd driven down, reached one of the grand old hotels in the capital, now used by Eighteenth Army Group, and had been ushered in to see an American two-star heading up Allied intelligence in Tunisia.

It was a large, airy room on the first floor, with a view of the sea. A cool breeze floated in, while overhead, fans whirred. There were five of them: Wiseman and Tanner, Major General Carter, then another American, introduced as Colonel Simpson but wearing a neatly cut dove-grey civilian suit, and Lieutenant Colonel Max Spiro. Both Spiro and Simpson worked for the Office of Strategic Services.

'That's Washington-speak for secret intelligence,' said General Carter, as he walked over to a sideboard and poured large Scotches with soda for Wiseman and Tanner. He had passed them their drinks, then returned to his desk. Either side of him, Simpson and Spiro sat in wicker chairs, but with no further seating, apart from an old chaise-longue at the far side of the room, Wiseman and Tanner had remained standing, clutching their glasses. Wiseman had told him almost nothing on the way down; a sudden summons was not unusual. In any case, Tanner was not one to press for information if it was not forthcoming, and especially not since he had assumed it would be some instruction about training or another administrative directive. He had hoped it might be a posting back to his regiment. He liked the Americans well enough, but he had missed his friends. Seeing Peploe and Sykes had reminded him of this.

But no. It had been nothing of the kind.

'So,' General Carter had said, leaning forward in his seat, 'we need you two to accompany Colonel Spiro here on a little operation in Sicily.'

'Sicily, sir?' said Tanner, unable to keep the surprise out of his tone.

'Yes,' Carter replied. 'You'll be dropped by plane and then you'll rendezvous with a certain Sicilian gentleman called Don Calogero Vizzini. Spiro and Colonel Simpson here have been, er, communicating with Signor Vizzini and others in Sicily for some time. I won't trouble you with the ins and outs of it but, suffice to say, a large element on Sicily is sympathetic to the Allied cause or, rather, keen to see Mussolini and the Fascists thrown out – and that, gentlemen, is the Allies' current number-one objective. See the back of Mussolini and his buddies and that's Italy out of the war and a major headache for the Nazis. So Colonel Spiro is going to negotiate with Vizzini and you two are going to watch his back.'

Tanner cleared his throat. 'Why me, sir?'

'You're a Brit. We're the Allies, Captain, and we need to show Vizzini and his *amicos* that we stand together. You've served with us Americans, and you have a proven record – a most impressive one, if I might say so. And it's also, let's say, beneficial that you and Major Wiseman at the very least have a mutual trust and understanding. The major has already vouched for you, Captain.'

Tanner had shot a glance at Wiseman.

'You don't know Spiro, but he's a first-class officer and ideally placed to conduct an operation of this kind.'

Carter leaned back, lit a cigarette, then eyed Tanner. 'The hard work's been done, Captain. Long months of patient negotiation. I'm sure you understand that communications between the

US and Sicily are difficult to say the least. Fortunately, the ties between certain elements of Sicilian society and those across the Atlantic in New York and elsewhere are still strong, war or no war.'

'Excuse me, sir,' said Tanner, 'but assuming all goes well, how do we get back?'

'You're heading to a place called Villalba, Captain,' Simpson now said. He was a neat-looking man, with oiled greying hair and a clean-shaven face. 'It's a small town in the mountainous interior, but only thirty miles or so from the northern Sicilian coast. We'll drop you in at night. You'll be given instructions as to where to go, but once you're with Don Calo you'll be quite safe. The next night, you'll begin heading to the coast. The following evening, you should reach it. You will then signal to a British submarine that will be waiting off-shore. The crew will pick you up and take you home.'

'How will they pick us up, sir? A submarine can't approach the shore.'

'In collapsible canoes called falbots.'

'And what if the shore is mined, sir?'

'We're confident it's not. The Italians do not expect an attack along their northern Sicilian shores for obvious reasons. In fact, there is a long stretch of beach in that area which is largely uninhabited. As General Carter has said, the hard work has already been done.'

'So you see,' said Carter, exhaling a cloud of cigarette smoke, 'this is little more than an escort mission. I'm sure a man of your experience, Captain Tanner, has faced many more dangerous

situations than this. Sicily is not overly populated. Most of the inhabitants live huddled
together in towns and rarely venture out. You'll
be met by friends and will be travelling under
cover of night guided by Vizzini's men and away
from any towns. Do you think we'd be sending
you in if we thought there was a high risk of
compromise?'

'When do we go, sir?' Tanner asked.

'You'll be leaving in three days' time, when the
moon is a little more full.'

'And does this mean we'll be invading Sicily
next, sir?'

'Maybe, Captain, maybe. Our planning teams
are considering a number of options. But, as I
said, getting Italy out of the war is our main
objective. This mission could go some way to
achieving that. It's important. If it wasn't, we
wouldn't be asking you to do this.'

Afterwards Tanner had berated Wiseman. 'I
thought you'd enjoy a little adventure like this,
Jack,' Wiseman had retorted. 'Honestly, it'll be
fine. You heard those guys. I know it sounds crazy
but, really, the risks are quite small.'

'That's what's bothering me,' Tanner had
snarled. 'When people say something's going to
be a cake-walk, it's usually anything but.'

'Nothing you and I can't handle, Jack.'

'What if it's a trap?' Tanner had asked.

'Then we're screwed, and we have to use our
wits to get the hell out of there. But it isn't a trap.
D'you think I'd be willing to put my ass on the
line if I thought this was a sting? Sicily's not like
the rest of Italy, you know. I tell you, Jack, get this

right,' Wiseman had assured him, 'and the invasion will be a whole load easier.'

In the intervening three days, there had been parachute training, including a practice jump, briefings from Spiro and Simpson about Sicily and the current political situation in Italy, detailed ground briefs of Villalba, the villa there to which they were to proceed and the surrounding countryside, as well as their planned route to the coast. Maps were provided, with aerial photographs. Spiro instructed both Wiseman and Tanner in basic Italian. Tanner had been impressed by the thoroughness. He remembered heading to Norway a little over three years earlier and what a fiasco that had been; he wondered how different things might have been had they prepared with the same kind of thoroughness. The Allies had evidently learned something during this war.

And yet Tanner could not shake the unease that had been growing inside him these past few days. Over the years he had come to trust his gut instinct. His father had been a gamekeeper and had told him as a boy to regard instinct as a sixth sense. It was, he'd said, an essential attribute for any gamekeeper, and Tanner had found it even more important for the soldier in war. He'd never forgotten it and, he knew, it had saved his life on more than one occasion. Yet he also knew that instinct improved with experience. He was not one to criticize the inexperience of the Americans – some of the fighting he had witnessed on Hill 609 had been as brave as any he'd ever seen – but it worried him now that this venture had been planned by men who were all too new to war.

Carter was a major general, and Simpson a colonel, but their over-confidence troubled him. *These people know what they're doing,* Wiseman had assured him. *They know a hell of a lot more than you or I ever will.*

Maybe, Tanner thought. He hoped so.

The door to the cockpit opened and the crew chief emerged. Using the static line that ran down the centre of the cabin for balance, he felt his way towards the rear door. Tanner watched him remove it, a sudden blast of whistling air gushing in as he did so. Tanner's mouth had gone dry. The day before he had stood by the hatch as he had prepared for his first jump. A feeling of intense helplessness had swept over him, and then a hand had pushed him hard and he had been hurtling through the air, his body rigid and his mind unable to function, until somewhere deep within him he had ordered his hand to pull the ripcord. Moments later, the chute had un-furled and blossomed out, yanking his shoulders and enabling him to drift to earth. Relief at touching hard ground once more had been no greater than the momentary terror he had felt as he'd been pushed from the plane. This second jump, should, he knew, be easier. There was a static line that pulled the chute from its pack almost immediately; he would need to operate the ripcord only if his main pack failed, which was unlikely. Even so...

A red light came on.

'Stand and hook up,' said the crew chief.

Tanner did so, staggered as the Dakota hit turbulence, then, following Wiseman's lead,

26

clipped his ripcord to the static line and moved towards the open door. All three wore their normal uniforms; there was to be no pretence at being Italian, after all. For Tanner this meant denim battledress trousers, shirt and Denison smock, an item he had filched from the quarter-master's stores before Alamein. On his head he wore a dark wool hat. He had a pack of ammunition and explosives on his back, food and more ammunition in a pack on his front, and around his waist, a water bottle, a knife, and a Colt .45 semi-automatic pistol. A further handgun, a German Sauer, was in his pack. Around his neck was his Italian Beretta sub-machine gun. His rifle, which he had carried through mountains, across oceans and deserts and had never yet lost, he had been forced to leave behind for fear it would get tangled in his chute. He felt naked without it.

A glance out through the open door. Air rushing in. Mountains, hills, fields, olive and citrus groves bathed in dim, milky light. Wiseman looked at him, grinned, then clasped his shoulder. Tanner glanced around him. There was Spiro, next to him, looking sick. Ahead a town, a mile or two off. Then the green light went on, the crew chief shouted, 'Go!' and Wiseman flung himself out.

For a second, Tanner stood there, frozen. Then he saw the crew chief's hand rise to push him and jumped, felt himself tumble through the cool, sharp air and then, *thank God,* the parachute ballooned, he felt the straps yank his shoulders and he was floating, drifting, down. He looked up. There was Spiro above him, silhouetted against the moon, while droning on, away to the north, the Dakota was nothing but a dark shape, a moment earlier so big but now the size of a bird.

Silence from below, apart from a dog barking somewhere a little distance away. He saw Wiseman land, his chute crumple, then a few seconds later the ground was rushing towards him, and he bent his legs, felt them pound painfully into the ground, and rolled over, the smell of herbs and soil filling his nostrils and the cooling billow of the collapsing chute falling around him.

Quickly, he unclipped his harness and struggled free of the cords and silk. He had landed in a field of young green corn. No more than a mile or so to his left a town stood on a rising promontory, dark against the sky. Villalba? He hoped so. Where was Spiro? And Wiseman? He glanced up, saw Wiseman crouching, gathering up his parachute, then behind him spotted Spiro, tangled in the cord and silk and battling to free himself.

Tanner was about to hurry over to him to help when suddenly, away to their right, from where the dog was barking, he heard something and saw dark shapes moving. Instinctively, he gripped his Beretta, but it was too late: more than a dozen men, weapons silhouetted against the sky, were running to where Spiro was still desperately trying to free himself.

'*Eppure, ci sei!*' shouted one of the men.

'*Mani in alto!*' called another, now swinging around towards Tanner and Wiseman and bringing a sub-machine gun to his shoulder. Tanner thought for a moment. Should he open fire? He could probably hit them all with one carefully directed burst, and with the wooden butt of the

28

Beretta, which fitted snugly into his shoulder, that was easily achievable. But could he avoid Spiro? Probably not. And without Spiro, the mission would fail in any case.

'*Mani in alto o sparo!*'

Tanner did not need to speak Italian to understand that. *Hands up or I'll shoot.* Several men ran towards him. Tanner dropped the Beretta and, still kneeling, slowly raised his arms. 'Damn it,' he muttered to himself, lowering his head. 'Damn it to Hell.'

And when he looked up, he could see, standing above him in the pale moonlight, long black leather boots and the dark, perforated steel of a Beretta barrel pointing at his head.

2

Seventy miles away from Villalba, as the crow flew, lay the small town of Motta Sant'Anastasia. At one in the morning, much of the town slept, its streets still and quiet, the only movement from prowling cats and scurrying rodents. Perched on a hilly outcrop on the lower slopes of Mount Etna, the town stood out on a limb from the plain of Catania, which stretched below to the coast, on the eastern side of the island, and the ring of towns further up beneath the volcano.

Oil lamps still burned in the doctor's house. The doctor had died the previous year, aged only sixty-one, collapsing with heart failure. Most who had known him suspected that in fact heart-break had killed him. The house was both large and prominent, perched at the tip of the pro-montory on which the town had been built, and the townsfolk muttered to themselves that it was far too large for a young girl still in her twenties and her small daughter. Some supposed she was waiting for the right man; others blamed her solitude on the uncertainty of war.

That night, however, Francesca Falcone was not alone, for her brother, Captain Niccolò Togliatti, was visiting, and the two were talking late. Remnants of the evening meal still lay at the far end of the kitchen table, while at the other, brother and sister sat opposite one another. The high French windows were open, allowing not only an early summer breeze to flow into the room but also the fresh, sweet scent of earth, olives and animal dung.

Francesca watched her brother finish his wine, put the glass on the table, then lean back and sigh. 'Perhaps it is time for bed,' she said, after a moment's pause.

'No, stay up a little longer. Let's have some more wine.'

'Are you trying to make me drunk?' She laughed.

He shrugged. 'Why not?' He stood up and took another bottle from the tall dresser that leaned against the far wall of the kitchen. 'What could be nicer?' he said, swaying slightly before sitting down again. 'I've missed you more than you can know, my little Cesca. There were times in Russia when I thought...' He paused, straining to pull out the cork. 'That I'm here at all, my darling sister, is a miracle.'

Francesca said nothing, but took his hand.

'I have never felt so alone,' Niccolò said, lighting a cigarette. 'Or so cold or so full of despair. To die out there – to be left, frozen, for the dogs and the crows. My men were extraordinary. Their bravery was...' He tailed off, blinked and rubbed his eyes. 'Sorry.' He tried to smile. 'Look at me. A grown man and about to cry.'

Francesca gripped his hand. 'You're safe now, Nico.'

He smiled. 'Right now, yes.'

'I remember when we heard the news,' said Francesca. 'We'd had nothing from you for so long, and then the telegram arrived saying you had been wounded. Poor Papa – if only he'd known. He was never the same after we left Palermo, but he worried so dreadfully about you.'

'It's been strange returning here and finding him gone. I wish I'd had a chance to speak to him although, to be honest, I thought I'd never see any of you again. But I was lucky, you know. A graze, really, that was all. But it's a miracle you got any news at all. Russia – it's so vast, Cesca. We were all constantly amazed that any post got through. There were long gaps sometimes, but we always had our mail eventually. If it hadn't been for that – that link to home... It was very important to us.'

'And then nothing more until the fourth of April. What a happy day that was. You were back in Italy – alive and well.' She laughed, remembering.

31

'The fourth of April.' Niccolò smiled. 'I'm touched, little sister.'

'I prayed for you. I prayed so hard. Cara too.'

Niccolò drank some wine, then leaned back. 'Well, someone was watching over me. If not God, then who knows?'

They were silent a moment, then he said, 'But what about you, my Cesca? You've barely told me anything. Cara looks well – as beautiful as her mother. The same straw-coloured hair and blue eyes.'

'She's fine. We've been safe here. We can never escape the war but here we have carried on with life as best we can. Catania has been bombed but not us.'

'Seriously, Cesca, who could ever resist those eyes? She's going to break hearts, that one.'

'Beauty – that's all men are interested in. I fear for her, Nico. Having the kind of face and eyes a man likes is a curse.'

Niccolò frowned. 'What can you mean?'

She ran her hands through her hair. 'Ever since Papa died, there have been men, you know, sniffing around. Trying to get me to marry them. I know what they're thinking. That girl, she's pretty, she has a big house. She would be a good match.'

Niccolò smiled. 'But quite flattering?'

'No!' said Francesca. 'Annoying. Sometimes I feel I can't breathe.'

'But who are these people?'

'Oh, there's another doctor, but he's over fifty and I think he got the message. There's a young boy who was wounded and has come home, and there's Salvatore Camprese. He's the worst.'

'Camprese, Camprese,' said Niccolò. 'Do I know him?'

'He's the mayor. He's not quite forty and not bad-looking, I suppose, but he makes my flesh crawl. He thinks he's a big shot in town. I've heard rumours that he's part of the Society.'

'Not here, surely. What about Mori's reforms? I thought the "Iron Prefect" had all but stamped it out.'

'So now Salvatore plays the good Fascist. It's a game. Look,' she said, a note of irritation in her voice, 'I don't know. It's just a rumour I heard.'

'Maybe he really is a Fascist and when they go he'll go too.'

'No, men like him change with the wind.'

'Do you want me to talk to him? Ask him to leave you alone?'

'And be in even more hot water once you're back with your men? Don't you dare. He's harmless at the moment, I suppose, but I know what he would be like. He'd want to own me. He reminds me of Giovanni.'

'Giovanni?' Niccolò looked confused. 'I was so sorry when I heard, Cesca. You must miss him, though.' He leaned forward again and took her hand. 'Do you mind me asking?'

Francesca thought a moment. 'No, I don't mind. You never really knew him, did you?'

Niccolò shrugged. 'I suppose not. I was away so much. It's ten years since I left Sicily, you know. He seemed like a decent fellow.'

'He wasn't.'

'Cesca?'

'I've shocked you.' She ran a finger around her

33

glass. 'He wasn't interested in me at all. I barely saw him. I was nineteen and alone in Bologna, while he spent all day and night, it seemed, with his friends and God only knows who else.'

'He was unfaithful?'

'Aren't all Italian men?'

'Papa wasn't.'

'Perhaps not Papa. But few have his principles. His morals.'

'But Giovanni gave you Cara.'

'Yes. Yes, he did.' She sighed.

'I'm sorry, Cesca. I had no idea.'

'No one did. I've never told anyone what I've just told you. I often wonder if I ever loved him. I'm not sure I did. I think I loved the idea of him. I was young, he was handsome. His prospects were good.'

'A lawyer, no less.'

'And I so wanted to escape Sicily. To escape what had happened to Papa. To escape the filth and poverty of this town. My God, after Palermo! Remember what a backwater it seemed?'

Niccolò smiled.

'Goodness knows,' Francesca continued, 'it still seems that way. Fabia had already left – she had her prince in Rome. You had joined the Army. I wanted to escape too. This place...'

'And now it seems magical. I never want to leave. Papa may have been drummed out of Palermo, but Motta Sant'Anastasia seems the most beautiful place in the world to me. I don't care that it's backward and dirty. This house is not.' He stood up and went out of the French windows onto the balcony. Francesca followed.

The moon shone brightly, the landscape bathed in pale light. Etna, towering, magisterial, rose up to their left, while ahead lay folds of green, solid and undulating where once there had been flowing lava. Beneath them was their own small farmstead: the barn with the goats, the pigs and their cow, and beyond, the orange and lemon trees, the almonds and olives. This small domain had ensured they had never gone hungry like so many Italians since the outbreak of war; like so many Sicilians in their daily struggle with life.

'Look at this, Cesca,' said Niccolò, as she joined him. He was leaning on the balcony, the smoke from his cigarette blown into darting wisps by the faint night breeze. 'It's so beautiful.' He smiled, then kissed her cheek. 'I'm so glad to be back, to be home at last.'

Francesca hugged him tightly. 'I'm so happy to see you, Nico. Thank God you came back to us.'

Soon after, Francesca took herself off to bed but, despite the late hour and her tiredness, sleep eluded her. She thought about many things, her brain a whirl of activity. She thought of her brother when they had been children. He was three years older than her, and had teased her mercilessly when they were little. She remembered how she had prayed to the Virgin Mother to help her, to get him out of her life, but it was not until he was seventeen and gone to university in Rome that the teasing had stopped and she had grown to adore him; he was her beloved handsome older brother. She had cried when he had gone, and cried again when he came home one summer to announce that he was joining the Army. Even as a seventeen-year-old she had known what that would mean – that he would most likely end up fighting. She had seen the expression on her father's face too. And so it had proved, although never had she imagined Italian troops dying in Russia.

Her husband had escaped such a fate, but had been sent to North Africa. Given a commission, he had returned one day in the uniform of a lieutenant and, almost the next, that of a captain. When he had gone, she had felt relieved, free of his overbearing presence that had swept into their apartment in Bologna. There had been his drunken love-making – little love was involved: rather, she had grown to feel violated every time he climbed on top of her. He had hit her only once, a back-handed slap across the face, but he had bullied her long before then. It was the contempt he had shown her, his lack of interest in her life, her feelings, the way he had used her as an ornament, a sexual object... She felt tears well now as she thought about him, and about how miserable she had been. Giovanni had offered an escape: a handsome, clever man with a home and prospects in the northern city of Bologna. But she had been a mere girl, whose head had been too easily turned.

You're tired, that's all, she told herself, but her mind turned to the news that he had been lost. A prisoner of war, heading to Canada. The ship had been struck by a German U-boat and every single one of the prisoners had been killed. Had he drowned or had the torpedo done for him? She had often wondered. When the telegram arrived, the postman had put an arm around her shoulders and told her how sorry he was. Giovanni's family had been devastated, but Francesca had felt only relief. She had worn black, had maintained the charade of mourning, but the only tears she had shed were for herself and Cara, then just four years old. She had stayed in Bologna for a month, but the suffocating presence of Giovanni's family had been too much, so she had gone home, to the place she had tried to escape six years earlier: back to Sicily, her father, back to the misery and poverty of the island. The widowed daughter of a small-town doctor. And then her father had died and suddenly she was alone, with just Cara for company. What could she do? Sell the house? She would do nothing until the war was over. Better to wait, see out the war, then go. Maybe to Rome, maybe to America. Anywhere but here.

At least Cara was happy, she thought. She had friends, a mother who doted on her. Lots of children had no fathers. 'You must miss your father,' one of their neighbours had said to her just a week ago.

'I have my mamma,' Cara had replied.

Francesca sighed. Niccolò alive and well, her daughter happy, and yes, her brother was right: Sant'Anastasia might be a backwater, but at least they had a house and food on the table. And at least Francesca had something to do, teaching in the village school where Cara was also a pupil. She hated Camprese's attentions, but he would give up eventually – surely. What lay around the corner was in the hands of God. And what was around the corner? Niccolò had not talked about it that day and nor had she; neither had wanted to spoil his first day home with talk of war. She wondered whether the Allies would try to invade. And if so, what then? Francesca yawned and turned over. It was incomprehensible. She could not imagine it. Foreign troops and planes and tanks. But, surely, she thought, they would not be interested in Motta Sant'Anastasia?

It was nearing two in the morning. The three of them had been picked up, made to put their hands behind their heads and marched, the barrel of a Beretta pointed at their backs, up the winding road that led into Villalba. Every time Tanner had tried to speak he had been told to be silent, while Spiro's pleas had been met with scornful laughter. A building near the town centre – a glimpse of a small central square and church – and then they were pushed inside. Tanner saw the word 'Carabinieri' beside the door, but then they were being shoved down a corridor and through a thick, heavy door, where a row of cells awaited.

Spiro began talking again, but one of the men angrily spoke back. Another grabbed Tanner's shoulder and chuckled. 'Tomorrow,' he said in English, then raised his hand like a pistol and pretended to fire.

All three were pushed into the same cell, the door clanged shut and the key turned in the lock. It was dark, although a thick shaft of moonlight poured through a small window high above them. Tanner could just make out a single wooden board that was a bed.

'They mean to execute us in the morning,' said

Spiro. 'Jesus Christ.' His voice quivered.

'They might mean to,' said Tanner, 'but we're not dead yet.'

'Well said.' Wiseman struck a match and lit a cigarette. 'One hidden for emergencies,' he said, taking a deep draw, then passing it to Tanner.

'I don't understand it,' said Spiro. 'Everything was arranged. I just don't know what could have gone wrong. It's as though those guys were waiting for us.'

'I'm sorry, Colonel,' said Tanner, 'but I'm not interested in what's gone wrong. This always sounded like a sodding mad idea, but now we need to think about how we're going to get out of here. With a bit of luck, that submarine will still be there to meet us. If we can get out and to the coast, we might still be all right.'

'But how the hell *are* we going to get out? We're locked up in this Goddamn cell,' said Spiro.

'We'll leave it an hour or two,' said Tanner. 'Chances are, most of them will slope off to bed. Then we'll call the guard, and you, sir, can pretend to be doubled up in agony. I'll get the bastard as he comes in to look. Once we've got keys and a weapon, we'll be away in no time.'

'You make it sound so easy.'

'It should be, with this bunch of jokers. Crazy bloody Eyeties.'

'I knew it was the right call bringing you along for this, Jack,' said Wiseman.

Tanner grunted, sat down on the bed with his back to the wall, and sighed.

It was no more than ten minutes later when he

heard footsteps and talking, then a key being turned in the lock. Tanner sprang to his feet and stood beside the door. As it opened, he lurched forward and swung his right arm. He felt his fist connect with a man's head, heard a sharp groan as the Italian fell back into the man behind, then leaped through the door and jumped on both. The first, he now saw in the dim light of the corridor, was dressed in civilian clothes, while the man behind wore the same uniform he had seen earlier.

'Jeez,' said Spiro, as Tanner looked for the *carabiniere's* weapon.

Both men appeared to be out cold, but then the first groaned, put his hand to his cheek, and spoke.

Tanner heard the words 'Don Calogero' and stopped. 'What's he saying?' he said to Spiro, as he pulled the man to his feet. He turned to Wiseman. 'Charlie, grab that pistol,' he said, nodding towards the holster on the policeman's waist.

'He's from Don Calogero,' said Spiro. 'He's come to get us.'

Wiseman took the pistol.

The Italian spoke again, still rubbing his cheek and glaring at Tanner with fury, while behind, the *carabiniere* remained sprawled on the floor.

'He is one of Don Calogero Vizzini's men,' said Spiro. 'He said we should not have been imprisoned. He says we are to come with him now.'

Tanner wiped his mouth. 'Tell him I apologize,' he said. 'Tell him we were told we would be executed. I was just trying to get us out.'

Tanner listened as Spiro translated, then held

out his hand to the man.

The Italian eyed him suspiciously, nodded, and shook it.

'What about him?' said Tanner, gesturing at the unconscious policeman.

The Italian spoke.

'He says we should take him. Don Calogero will need to see him.'

'Brilliant,' muttered Tanner. He leaned over, grabbed the man by the scruff of the neck, then pulled him to his feet and flung him over his shoulder. 'So how far is this Don Calo bloke's basha?'

'He means house,' said Wiseman.

'Not far,' Spiro replied, after another flurry of words.

No one else was visible at the barracks; the front desk lay abandoned, a lone oil lamp hanging from the wall. Outside the night was quiet, but immediately two more men joined them. Tanner raised an eyebrow. *Keeping guard,* he thought. In silence they walked across the piazza, past the looming façade of the church and down a short side-street between two sizeable houses. Turning onto a street parallel to the square, they stopped beside a large villa.

'Very nice,' said Tanner.

The Italians signalled to them to follow, then climbed the steps to the front door, opened it and ushered them in. Lamps were lit to reveal a high-ceilinged hallway, off which there were a number of doors, and a stone staircase that led to a second floor.

Tanner heaved the policeman off his shoulder

and laid him roughly on the floor. 'What is this place?' he asked.

'Don Calo's house,' said Spiro, 'but keep your voice down. We don't want to wake him.'

'What?' said Tanner. 'We've got to wait for him to have his beauty sleep before you talk to him?'

Spiro nodded. 'That's what Bartolomeo said.'

'That's the feller you slugged,' added Wiseman.

Bartolomeo was talking to Spiro again. Tanner listened, then watched two other men pick up the policeman and lug him into a different room.

'OK,' said Spiro. 'They want us to get some rest. There's a room prepared for us. Bartolomeo says we'll be quite safe here.'

'Really?' said Tanner. 'We've just broken out of jail, kidnapped a policeman, walked no more than a couple of hundred yards, and we'll be safe?'

Spiro smiled. 'You don't understand. Don Calogero runs this town. No one would dare come here.'

'Quarter of an hour ago you were thinking we'd be shot at dawn, sir,' Tanner said, in a low voice. 'This makes it all OK again, does it?'

'The *carabinieri* won't dare squeal to anyone that we're here,' said Spiro. 'There was some kind of mix-up earlier, that's all. Don Calo's men were expecting us later and the *carabinieri* hadn't been warned off. That's all. Don Calo's the king of these parts. Hell, he's one of the most powerful men in all of Sicily.'

Tanner looked at Wiseman. *What do you think?*

Wiseman shrugged. 'That's what we've been told,' he said. 'It kinda stacks up. After all, Bartolomeo was about to get us out of there before you

KO'd him.'

'Very well,' he muttered. He followed Bartolomeo and the others down a long corridor and
into a back room, which looked as though it was
normally used as a store. Three palliasses had
been laid out, and there, beside them, leaning
against the wall, were their kitbags and weapons.
Tanner hurried over and grabbed his Beretta. He
had taken it from a dead Italian at Mareth and it
had become a favoured submachine gun.

'Happier now, Jack?' said Wiseman.

Tanner smiled ruefully. 'A little. But I'll feel
even better when we get aboard that sub. I don't
trust these Eyeties. Not one inch.'

As he lay down on his palliasse and lit a cigarette, retrieved from his pack, he prayed his
suspicions would prove unfounded.

3

Saturday, 29 May. It was shortly after seven a.m.,
and Tanner lay awake on his straw mattress, his
hands behind his head, staring at the ceiling.
Spiro and Wiseman slept – he could hear Spiro's
gentle snores. A rat or some other rodent had
woken him, scurrying in the corner. Beside him
lay his Beretta, while his Colt .45 rested on his
stomach. He had slept, but fitfully, and even now
felt on edge, vulnerable, irritated by his incom-
plete understanding of the situation he was in.

Colonel Spiro had told Tanner something about

Don Calogero Vizzini before they had left La Marsa: that he was one of the most powerful men in Sicily, that he was a man of honour, and that he had the authority to help overthrow Fascism on the island. Tanner had asked further questions but the shutters had come down so he had not probed further; he understood his role, and getting involved with Spiro's work was not part of it. Even so, he couldn't help wondering. He assumed an Allied invasion was likely, some time in the not-too-distant future. He also guessed that Vizzini was, on the face of it, a Fascist official on the island, but someone prepared to turn, if the time and price were right. Admiral Darlan, in Algeria, had been such a figure, he knew. A pro-Nazi admiral and governor of Vichy French North Africa. His friend John Peploe had told him about it – how the Allies had done a deal with Darlan before the Allied invasion there the previous November. According to Peploe, the US General Mark Clark had been sent by submarine and had paddled ashore for secret negotiations.

This time the Allies were sending a half-colonel, but Tanner supposed he should not read too much into that; after all, they would hardly parachute a general into the centre of an island as big as Sicily. He was surprised at the location for this meeting, though. Admittedly, he had not seen the place in daylight, but Villalba appeared to be a rather insignificant place: a small town in the middle of the Sicilian countryside, with dusty roads and, as yet, few concessions to the modern world. There was no mains electricity, no sign of any vehicles. The house they were in was large, but rather shabby, Tanner thought. He wondered whether Spiro had been horribly duped, or whether Vizzini had chosen this place precisely for its remoteness. But, then, why not meet somewhere discreet on the coast, as, according to Peploe, General Clark had done in Algeria?

He supposed all would become clear in time, but the sooner they were on their way the better, as far as he was concerned. Three months he'd been with the Americans; if and when they got back to Tunisia, he was determined to get a transfer – back to the Yorks Rangers, if he had anything to do with it, and if not, to some other regiment. *I'm a soldier,* he thought. *I'm not suited to this kind of work.* He thought about his time in Cairo, the previous summer, when he'd been briefly seconded to the Secret Intelligence Service. He'd hated it. Secrets, shadows, nothing what it seemed. Like this place. He sighed. Just what the hell was going on?

It was not until past eleven o'clock that they finally met Don Calogero Vizzini. Bartolomeo had taken them to a kitchen and given them bread, honey, coffee and oranges, which they had eaten with relish. Don Calo, it seemed, had 'business' to attend to in town.

Then, at last, at a quarter past eleven, with Tanner's impatience mounting, they had been led into a large drawing room. Old still-lifes, landscapes and poorly painted portraits hung on the walls, and a portly man, dressed in a short-sleeved shirt, braces and dark trousers that covered a bulging stomach, sat in a leather chair beside the fireplace.

His thinning grey hair was combed back, while he wore dark-rimmed spectacles over hooded eyes. A trim moustache covered his top lip.

Tanner wondered who he was and was surprised that someone so casually dressed did not have the courtesy to stand up.

'Don Calo,' said Bartolomeo, striding over to stand a little behind the man.

Tanner was dumbfounded. *This* was Don Calo?

Spiro stepped forward and introduced himself, shaking hands, then gestured at Wiseman and Tanner.

Don Calogero nodded, said, 'Signor Saggio,' to Wiseman and chuckled.

Chairs were offered. They sat down. 'Do as they say,' Spiro had briefed them earlier. 'We're their guests and there are strict codes of etiquette. If they offer a drink or food, take it.'

Tanner listened now, but understood little. The scene before him seemed so fantastical, so unlikely. He wondered whether Spiro and his colleagues in the *OSS* had been taken for a ride by the unremarkable-seeming man in front of him. He had seen Italian commanders before, even a captured general, and they were all cockatoos – bedecked in medals and braid, chests thrust forward. Here, though, was a man with no obvious vanity: an ageing Sicilian with a paunch and a cheap shirt. The paunch was, he supposed, the only sign of prosperity. Every other Sicilian he'd seen so far had been stick-thin. Occasionally, Don Calogero interjected; his voice was low and gravelly, and he spoke much more slowly than Spiro did. A confident man, Tanner guessed, and clearly in control.

After nearly an hour, Don Calogero paused, waved his hand in the air, then clicked his fingers. *'Caffe?'* he asked, looking at Wiseman and Tanner. *'Vino? Grappa?'* Then before they could answer, he said, *'Grappa.'* He had made the decision for them. One of his men – not Bartolomeo – disappeared, returning a minute later with a tray, a bottle, and four shot glasses. Don Calogero sat back and smiled, waiting for the *grappa* to be served. When all had a glass, he raised his and said, *'Salute. La fine di Mussolini e del fascismo.'* He chuckled again, then sipped from his glass.

'To the end of Mussolini and Fascism,' repeated Spiro in English. He glanced at Wiseman and Tanner and grinned.

Tanner drank and felt the liquid burn his throat. Don Calogero looked at him and signalled with his hand – *drink, drink* – so Tanner knocked back the rest in one gulp.

'E fatto qui,' said Don Calogero.

'He says they make it here,' said Spiro.

'Molto buono,' said Tanner. Very good.

Don Calogero smiled and nodded, then pointed at him and said something to Spiro.

'He's asking whether you were the one who knocked down Bartolomeo,' relayed Spiro.

Don Calogero spoke again, and Spiro looked embarrassed.

'What's he saying?' asked Tanner.

Spiro cleared his throat. 'He says if you'd been Sicilian you might not be alive today for doing what you did. But he also says he could do with someone like you working for him.'

47

'*Quando la guerra e finita,*' said Don Calogero, then laughed wheezily.

Tanner understood that. When the war is over. He smiled and nodded. *Fat chance.*

'Good,' said Spiro, turning to Wiseman. 'We have a deal.' He stood up and shook hands with Don Calogero, who smiled amiably. '*Grazie mille, Don calo. Tu sei un uomo d'onore,*' he said, bowing.

Don Calogero eased himself up out of his chair. '*Ora di pranzo!*' he said, clapping his hands and rubbing his palms.

'Lunch,' said Spiro.

They waited for Don Calogero to lead the way, the older man taking Wiseman's hand and patting him gently on the shoulder as he passed. '*Buono, buono...*' he muttered.

Tanner saw Wiseman smirk and raise an eyebrow – *God knows* – then followed the entourage out into the hall where the aroma of cooking had wafted through. It smelt delicious.

Later, around eight o'clock that night. Two of Don Calogero's men led them – Zucharini and Baldini. Like Bartolomeo, they were small, wiry and middle-aged. Tanner and Wiseman towered over them – at least a foot taller and even broader. Dark hair and skin wouldn't fool anyone, Tanner realized.

They left the town as dusk settled. No one was about; Villalba was like a ghost town. Although the sky was darkening, Tanner could still make out the surrounding countryside. He was struck by how empty it was: rolling hills and valleys, with endless fields around Villalba, then open pasture and scrub, but almost no other sign of life. Behind them, Villalba disappeared from view. There were no metalled roads, only white, dusty tracks winding over the folds of the land. Cicadas and crickets chirruped. The scent on the air was strong: soil, wild flowers and young corn. Early summer.

After around ten miles they saw another town away to their left, a collection of dark silhouettes, a church higher than the rest, but there were no villages, no farmsteads.

They had barely spoken. The two Italians up front occasionally murmured to Spiro, but now Wiseman said, 'Pretty empty, isn't it?'

'Where are all the farms?' asked Tanner.

'In the towns,' said Spiro. 'It was safer that way. Safety in numbers.'

'From who?'

'Bandits. We still need to watch out for them. They're more of a menace than the militia.'

Just before four a.m., they paused. Tanner was tired; they all were. They drank water and Wiseman handed around chocolate, which the Italians appeared not to have seen before. They devoured it hungrily, grinning at this new source of ecstasy.

'How much further are we planning on walking tonight?' Wiseman asked. 'My eyes are used to the light well enough, but night marches are not easy. We've all stumbled a fair amount.'

Spiro consulted with their guides, who began pointing and gesticulating.

'We have to get past Valledolmo,' he said. 'It's a couple of miles away on our left. Then the land rises and we enter a long valley below the Bosco Granzo. We'll lie up there for the day. There's a

49

cave they know.'

'How long?'

'An hour. Maybe a little more.'

They set off once more, the dusty track becoming noticeably more stony as they entered a narrow valley, walking alongside a rocky stream. The land either side of them rose up, towering over them darkly. Tanner felt as though they were being watched over by some brooding force of nature. Silence still, but for the gush of the stream.

Around five in the morning, the first hint of dawn spread along the eastern horizon. The darkness of night softened to pale blue and grey. The Italians muttered to Spiro, pointed, and they all began to clamber up the slopes to their left, towards a rocky outcrop, through baby oaks and scrub. They reached the rocks, their breath heavy, as the horizon behind them turned from pale grey to deep gold.

'*Ecco*,' said one of the Italians, looking up at the rocks. They jutted out into the sky, but between them, at their base, was an inlet, a shelter.

'Hardly a cave,' said Wiseman.

'It'll do,' said Tanner. 'It gives us cover, but we can look down into the valley below easily enough.' He peered inside and saw signs of an old fire: bits of charred wood and stones still lay in a rough ring. He wondered who had been there before them. 'I'll take first watch, if you like,' he offered. 'Three-hour shifts?'

'All right,' said Spiro. 'If you're sure.'

Tanner sat by the mouth of the rock shelter while the others settled. He felt tired, hungry, and his feet ached, but he wanted to see his surroundings for himself before he had any kip. There was certainly no visible sign of any habitation: no fields, no fruit or olive groves, not even livestock. Above them, the ground rose, covered with more scrub and stunted trees, although what lay beyond, over the ridge, he couldn't say. What a strange place Sicily was, he thought. It had surprised him by how backward it seemed, with its population apparently living in towns for fear of bandits, and with peculiar shabbily dressed men like Don Calogero ruling the roost. He looked at his map of Sicily, and reckoned they were no more than a dozen miles from the coast, yet here, in this quiet and apparently unoccupied valley, it felt as though they were in the middle of a vast wilderness.

He had fought against the Italians for more than two years. A lot of their kit had been poor. The tanks had been no match for British and certainly not the better German models. Much of their artillery looked as though it had been built in an earlier era. The Breda machine-gun was all right, and the Beretta sub-machine gun was a beauty, but whenever they had overrun Italian positions, he had been amazed to find, more often than not, several types of small-arms ammunition, different models of rifle and a lack of standardization that must have caused their quartermasters nightmares. The food they found was revolting; bully beef and hard-tack biscuits never seemed quite so boring after they'd overrun an Eyetie position. The prisoners they took were invariably poorly turned out, and missing key parts of their uniforms. What was more, he hadn't noticed any improvement over the course of the long North African campaign. British tanks had improved; so too their field and anti-tank guns – the new seventeen-pounder was an incredible piece – and no matter how monotonous the rations were, they always had enough to eat and char to drink; they might feel hungry at times, but never ravenous. God only knew, fighting in the desert was tough enough, with the millions of flies, the incessant heat during the day and the cold at night, the lack of home comforts, but to fight with half-baked kit, insufficient rations, and without the kind of replenishment of uniforms and weapons that he and his men had taken for granted was quite another matter. If some of the Italians appeared to give up all too easily, was it any wonder? And, as it happened, he reckoned the Eyeties could be as tough an opponent as any. In Tunisia, they had proved themselves doggedly hard bastards on a number of occasions, and as brave as any man.

It was true, he thought, that he had been in Sicily only a day and two nights, and he supposed the main cities were quite different places, but he'd always thought Italy was, well, a more sophisticated country. He had seen pictures of Mussolini and newsreels of Fascist soldiers goose-stepping through Rome, which had given the impression of a certain degree of strength and prosperity. This place, though – or this part of Sicily, at any rate – seemed to be the part of the country that did not fit. An island tacked onto the rest, poor and backward, where bandits lurked. And what of Don Calogero? He couldn't help thinking that Spiro and the intelligence bods had been duped by that man. How could some little old man wield such influence? Perhaps in Villalba he was the *bwana,* but what use was some back-arse-of-nowhere town in the big scheme of things? Spiro had said very little about the conversation with Don Calogero; he hadn't said very much about the mission at all. Nor had Wiseman, but then, Tanner thought, Charlie was probably as much in the dark about it as he was. Still, Tanner was not going to ask. The secrecy of the mission had been emphasized; he was there to protect, to demonstrate Allied solidarity; it wasn't his place to start asking questions about things he knew he'd get no answers to.

Tanner wished again that he could be back with his mates in the York Rangers: with Peploe, Sykes, Browner and the other boys. Englishmen, who called a spade a spade and with whom there was none of this cloak-and-dagger tomfoolery. *Jesus,* he thought. The sooner they reached that sub the better. The sun was rising, golden light spreading across the valley. From the small trees and shrubs he could hear birdsong, and smell a crisp freshness as he breathed in. A rock lizard darted in front of him, then disappeared behind a stone. Behind him, hidden in the crevasse in the rock, the others slept, one of them snoring lightly.

He was still thinking about the Rangers when he heard something – the sound was faint, but enough to make his body tense. Stones moving. An animal of some kind? What did they have in these parts? Deer? Wild boar? Foxes? He listened intently. Nothing. His heart had quickened. Still he listened, his hands gripping the Beretta, and slowly he began to relax, only to be gripped with renewed alarm when he realized the birdsong had stopped.

Crouching by the edge of the rock, he pulled back the bolt on the Beretta, then picked up a stone and threw it at Wiseman, then another towards the Italians. Wiseman sat up and looked at him– *What is it?* Tanner pointed towards the slopes above them and motioned to him to get up.

Another small clatter of stone. Distinct this time. The others were all up now. Tanner scanned the ground ahead but could see no one; the sound of footfalls had come from above them, but out of view. Could it be an animal? He thought not. Well, whoever it was would get a shock if and when they came into view. Wiseman was now beside him, Tommy gun in hand.

Tanner listened again and this time heard rustling; they were getting nearer, no more than twenty or thirty yards away, he guessed. Wiseman nodded to him – *I hear it.*

Then a rifle shot rang out, the bullet zipping past Tanner's head and fizzing off the rock. A tiny splinter struck his cheek as he instinctively ducked. *From ahead! Christ!* Tanner saw a figure dart between the trees, and now he heard a rush of footsteps – a number of men, hurrying down the slopes. He was about to spring out and open fire, when Baldini called, *'Basta! Che cosa vuoi?'*

'Siete circondati!' A rough voice from above.

'Banditi,' said Baldini.

'He says we're surrounded,' said Spiro. Tanner heard the catch of fear in his voice.

'Bollocks!' said Tanner. Another rifle shot rang

54

out, the bullet zapping past higher this time. A warning shot.

'*Mettere giù le armi!*'

'I think I got the gist of that one,' said Tanner.

'Well?' said Wiseman.

'Sod that,' said Tanner, 'I'm not laying down my weapon.' He pulled a grenade from his belt.

'*Mettere giù le armi!*' came the voice again, but now Baldini spoke out.

'*No! E mettere giù le armi,*' he said. '*Lo sono un uomo d'onore.*'

'I'm sure you are, mate,' said Tanner, looping his finger in the grenade pin.

'Wait,' said Spiro. 'Jack, wait!'

Tanner looked at him. *What?*

Baldini called out again.

'Look,' said Tanner, 'let's just shoot the bastards. I reckon we've a good chance. I'll throw the grenade, then on one, you and I stand up, Charlie, and open fire.'

'No, wait,' said Spiro, clutching Tanner's arm. 'They've stopped firing.'

Baldini spoke up once more, and this time, after a moment's pause, they heard one of the men say, '*Va bene, va bene. Pace.*'

Baldini stood up, Zucharini beside him, and stepped out into the open. Tanner could hardly believe what he was seeing.

'What the hell's going on, sir?' he asked Spiro.

A clatter of stones from above, and now a group of men appeared before them. One, clearly their leader, stepped forward. He was small, dark, and roughly clothed, with bandoliers crossed over his chest, a thick moustache and a week-long beard.

He eyed Tanner, Wiseman and Spiro suspiciously, then turned to Baldini and Zucharini.

They talked in low tones for a couple of minutes, then Baldini beckoned Spiro to join them. Tanner watched Spiro delve into his jacket pocket and hand something to the man with the thick moustache, who glanced furtively towards Tanner and Wiseman. Tanner gripped his Beretta, then stepped clear of the crevasse, Wiseman beside him. Once again, they towered over this rabble of poorly clothed and armed Sicilians. He counted a dozen, some with rifles, one with a flintlock blunderbuss, the others with knives. Only one had a sub-machine gun. Tanner smiled to himself. He reckoned he would have come off best, after all: the blast of the grenade, the smoke and confusion, the mass of bullets being sprayed. Feeling something trickling down his cheek, he raised his hand, felt and saw blood. Nicked by that piece of stone. It stung and he cursed.

Moments later, the bandits turned and began clambering back up the slopes. Tanner could scarcely believe it.

'We'll be safe here for the rest of the day,' said Spiro, relief on his face.

'If you say so,' said Tanner.

'What you just saw, Jack, is the power of Don Calogero.'

'I'm flabbergasted,' he said. 'But should we really have let them go? What if they report us? What about the Italian Army? And the police? There must be some on this island – not everyone can be beholden to Don Calogero, surely.'

'They're outlaws, Jack. Beyond the law. The

moment they make contact they'll be arrested, no matter what information they have.'

Tanner shrugged. 'All right. But if we'd opened fire, I reckon we'd have got the lot and saved you a few bob.'

Spiro smiled. 'But was it worth the risk?'

'It depends on whether the risk of letting them go proves less or more than opening fire on them.'

But it seemed Spiro had been right: they were not troubled for the rest of the day.

Later, once dusk had fallen, they moved off once more, tramping through a largely deserted landscape. Mountains loomed at either side of them, then fell away as they emerged into a wide, open coastal plain. Joining a road that led north towards the sea, they continued their journey, the going easier and faster now. Once an Army truck thundered by, but they had heard it coming from a long way off and were able to hide as it passed. By early morning they were within sight of the coast and the sea, the light of the moon twinkling benignly on the dark expanse of water.

They had been given a marker: a small spit that jutted out to sea to the east of the river mouth, five miles west of Campofelice. Following the river, they crossed the coastal railway – a single track, running dead straight. Empty, quiet and still. Beyond, down the shallow embankment, they paused, the smell of the sea strong on the air.

'I'm going to send another signal,' said Spiro.

'We should scout around,' said Tanner.

'Seems pretty empty to me,' said Wiseman.

'Best to be sure,' said Tanner. 'We should have

a look at the beach first. See if there's any defence obstacles. When we move, we want to move without any surprises.'

Wiseman nodded. 'All right. I'll come with you. Maybe hold off sending that signal until we're back, sir?'

'All right, but make it quick,' agreed Spiro. 'Baldini and Zucharini can stay with me.'

Tanner and Wiseman walked forward. The sea was only a couple of hundred yards further on, and by hugging the sandy, tufty grass of the riverbank, they soon reached the low dune that overlooked the beach and crouched among the grasses. Ahead, silhouetted against the sky, were coils of wire.

'Damn it,' whispered Wiseman. 'That wasn't there before.'

'Nor that encampment over there.' Tanner pointed across the mouth of the river. Half a dozen tents were dark against the moonlight.

'Shit,' muttered Wiseman. 'That's torn it.'

'Not necessarily,' said Tanner. 'Let's have a look at the beach. Maybe we can move along a bit – look, the shoreline is slightly concave. Three hundred yards on, no one in the camp will see us.'

'Although they might see the canoes.'

'They'd have to be crack shots, though, wouldn't they? Anyway, I don't see that we've got much choice.'

'That's true enough. It's been a cinch so far. We should have guessed there'd be some spanner in the works.'

'Good plans rarely go the distance in my experience.' Tanner grinned ruefully, then scrambled up and, crouching low, ran along the dunes a hundred yards, Wiseman following, then dropped onto the beach, the sand soft beneath him. Just a single coil of wire. *Good.* That would be easy enough to negotiate. They could probably get through without the need to cut it. But what about mines? He looked down and could see a mass of footprints along the beach. The work had been recent – in the past day or two, he guessed – and now that he looked more closely, he saw that every fifteen yards or so he could make out where the sand had been lifted and smoothed over, with more footprints around each site.

'Mines?' hissed Wiseman.

'Looks like it.' He squinted along the beach. 'A landmark,' he whispered. 'A landmark would be helpful.'

They hurried along the beach, still crouching low, a soft breeze blowing off the sea and rustling the thick dune grass. Behind them, the encampment had disappeared from view.

'There,' said Wiseman, pointing to a cluster of palm trees a short distance ahead.

Tanner nodded. As they reached the trees they paused. The sea was so peaceful, so calm. Above, the moon shone, and a billion stars twinkled, just as they had always done. Where was the sub? He wondered. Was it out there?

'This should do,' he said, then glanced to either side. Nothing – no house, no other trees – just the long expanse of the beach stretching away from them. 'How far is this from the river mouth?'

'Four hundred yards or so?' suggested Wiseman.

'And a little more to where those Eyeties are camped. It'll have to do. We'd better hope they don't have any sentries.' He glanced at his watch. It was after three. 'We need to get a shift on. Come on, Charlie, iggery, eh?'

'Iggery, Jack.' He grinned.

Spiro was far from happy when they rejoined him.

'Where the hell have you been? There are God-damn soldiers over there!' he hissed.

'Yes, we saw the encampment,' whispered Wiseman.

'Encampment?' whispered Spiro. 'I just saw two, rifles on their shoulders, walking down the opposite side of the river, then back again.'

'Damn it,' said Wiseman. 'We were hoping they were all getting in the zeds.'

'Bollocks,' muttered Tanner.

'Jesus! How are we going to be picked up now?'

'It's not over yet, Colonel,' said Wiseman. 'We spotted the encampment – half a dozen tents, no more – on the other side of the river, so headed along the beach a little and found a good spot. It can't be seen from the Eyetie camp. And there's a clump of palms right by it – a good marker for our sub.'

'All right,' said Spiro, 'but we need to get a move on. It'll be dawn in ninety minutes or so.'

'Where are those soldiers now?' asked Tanner.

'I don't know,' said Spiro. 'They wandered down, smoking and having a cosy little chat by the sound of things, then wandered back. But we need to watch our asses.'

'No, sir, I'll watch your backsides.'

'What do you mean, Jack?' asked Wiseman.

'Those Eyeties won't be able to see us, but there's a good chance the sentries will see the sub or the canoes paddling to the shore. You brought me along to protect you, didn't you?' he said, turning to Spiro. 'Take Baldini and Zucharini with you. We might need them to cause a diversion. In the meantime, sir, you head to those palms, send your signal, and I'll have a dekko at the sentries.'

'What the hell are you going to do?'

'Trust me, sir,' said Tanner.

'I'll come with you,' said Wiseman.

'Easier done alone,' Tanner replied. 'Now go. I'll catch you up.'

Spiro glanced at Wiseman, saw him nod, then said, 'All right. Good luck.'

Tanner watched them hurry off, crouching, out of sight, then keeping low, he darted to the riverbank. Thick, tufty grass grew down to the water's edge. Taking off his pack, boots and webbing, he slipped into the water, clenching his teeth at its chill. Still, he thought, not as cold as the English Channel. Silently, he swam to the other side, then feeling for the sand, carefully eased himself out of the water. There were low dunes here too, only a few feet high, undulating gently. He crawled forward through the grass until he reached a sand path through the dunes and saw, on a grass bank, thirty yards beyond, the encampment. He paused and listened. The gentle brush of waves on the shore, low snores from one of the tents and, *yes, voices*. Faint, but voices all right, coming from beyond the tents, towards the shore.

Tanner slid down onto the path and crawled forward until the cover of the grassy bank on his left lowered as it gave way to the beach. Cautiously raising his head, he looked across towards the tents, the nearest of which was now only ten yards away. A little further on, two men sat side by side on what looked like wooden boxes – dark silhouettes, shoulders hunched, rifles across their backs. Tanner watched for a moment, thinking. Silencing one was easy enough, but two, without waking the rest of the camp, was another matter altogether. *Go on,* he thought, *move*. A match sparked, causing a small halo of light, then was quickly cupped as the cigarette was lit. Tanner looked around him – a stone, or a stick, that was what he needed: something to distract them. He wondered whether Spiro had made contact with the sub. A glance at his watch. *Getting on for four.* Time was running out: the deep sleep of night would be replaced by the slow rousing of dawn.

Behind the tents he saw some shrubs– *Yes, that'll do*. He would creep over there and make a small noise, something that might draw one of the men to investigate, but as he was about to turn and move back up the sand path, he saw one of the men stand, stretch and walk away from the shore. Quickly, Tanner hurried down the path, the head and shoulders of the man still in his line of vision. By the bushes, the man paused and fumbled at the front of his trousers. Seeing this, Tanner grinned, took his clasp knife from his pocket, then put it back. *Not this time.* Lightly stepping up onto the grassy bank and crouching, he ran quickly and silently towards the Italian.

The man was still urinating when Tanner tapped him on the shoulder. A turn of the head, an expression of bewildered surprise, and a split second later, Tanner's clenched fist hit the Italian square on the side of the head, between eye and ear. He managed to catch the man as he toppled, gently laying the unconscious body on the grass.

He now walked back past the tents, the snores still rising through the dark canvas, and approached the second sentry. The Italian's back was towards him. *Don't turn yet, mate.* Just five yards now, and then as he drew almost alongside, Tanner cleared his throat. The Italian flicked away his cigarette stub, spoke and turned. As he did so, Tanner drove his fist towards the man's skull. A brief look of utter surprise, visible to Tanner in the moonlight, then the eyes rolled and the man slumped sideways.

Good. Tanner scampered quickly back to the river, slipped into the water once more, swam to the far shore, collected his kit, put his boots back on and, after pausing briefly to make sure all was clear, ran along the beach.

'You're wet, Jack,' Wiseman said.

'I went for a swim.'

'And those sentries?' asked Spiro.

'Out cold – only for an hour or so. I didn't think it a good idea to kill them. They'll struggle to explain it when they come to, but two dead bodies – well, we don't want the Eyeties thinking the Allies have been here spying on them.' He glanced at Spiro. 'Are they coming?'

Spiro nodded and pointed. 'Look.'

Tanner glanced out to sea. Faintly, some two

hundred yards away, maybe more, he saw a dark form resting above the surface and then, closer towards them, three shapes. Tanner watched as the figures became clearer. Three men, three canoes. He smiled.

'Time to catch our ride,' said Spiro. He turned to Baldini and Zucharini, spoke to them, shook hands, then waded into the sea.

'Good to see you, sir,' said the man, softly, as Tanner approached one of the canoes. 'Just hold her steady and get into the back. There's a blade for you there.'

'Thanks,' said Tanner. The canoe wobbled, but he managed to clamber in, and a moment later, the man in front was paddling again, the blade quietly slipping into the water and the small vessel surging towards the waiting submarine. Tanner paddled too, watching as the conning tower and long, dark hull of the sub loomed towards them. Then they were alongside and men were helping to haul him up.

'Quick,' said a man, 'let's move.'

Wiseman and Spiro were aboard now too, the collapsible canoes were being pulled from the water, and as Tanner climbed up the tower, he looked back. The coast was so peaceful. Not a sound. Nothing stirred. Away, far behind the beach, the mountains rose darkly. Tanner glanced at his watch. A little after four. *We pulled it off.*

4

Wednesday, 2 June. At the doctor's house at Motta Sant'Anastasia, Francesca Falcone was preparing lunch in the kitchen when she heard a motor engine rip into life below the balcony.

'Listen, Mamma,' said Cara, who was seated at the table drawing. She scraped back her chair and hurried to the balcony. 'Look!' she said. 'It's Uncle Nico!'

Francesca followed and saw, at the open doors of one of the barns, her brother squatting beside his motorcycle, screwdriver in hand. The engine was ticking over, then suddenly revved into a roar.

'He's got it working again!' said Cara. She jumped up and down as she peered through the iron railing.

'He's a clever man, your uncle,' laughed Francesca.

As though sensing he was being watched, Niccolò looked up, grinned, then switched off the engine. Quiet returned. 'Well?' he said.

'All right, I admit I was wrong. You did it.'

'Come down,' he said.

'I'm making lunch.'

'For five minutes.'

She smiled. 'All right.'

Cara came with her, hopping down the stone steps that led to the yard below the house. 'Can I sit on it?' she asked, running to her uncle.

'Of course,' said Niccolò. 'Shall I start it up again?'

Cara nodded, then screamed with delight as the engine burst into life.

'Now, remember what this is,' Niccolò told her, as he switched it off once more. 'A Benelli Monalbero Sport. One of the most beautiful motorcycles ever built.'

Francesca leaned against the barn door. Inside there was a workbench with a number of old tools, as well as several ageing cans of oil. The place smelt of oil, wood and rubber. It smelt of Nico, Francesca thought. As a boy, he'd always had oil on him somewhere – on his hands, under his nails, a smear on his trousers or shirt. The barn here had become a workshop, where old and broken motorcycles came back to life.

'Are you going to take it with you?' she asked.

'What – and let my men anywhere near it? You must be joking.' He grinned at her again. 'Anyway, it might get damaged, or worse. It might get hit by a bomb. No, I'm going to leave it here, locked up and safe, and keep it for when the war's over.'

'There's no fuel in any case.'

'That's true enough. A drop in the tank, but that's all. It wouldn't even get me as far as Catania.'

She watched her brother as he stood back and wiped his oily hands with a rag. 'Do you think it'll be long?' she asked.

'Will what be long?'

'Until the war is over?'

He straightened up and wiped his brow with the back of his sleeve. 'No – no, I don't. Well, our war at any rate. What Hitler and his Germans want to do is up to them, but I think for us it's almost over now.'

'You think the Allies will come?'

'Yes. Soon, I should think. I was talking to some people in Naples a couple of weeks ago and they still think Sardinia might be the Allies' target.'

'Sardinia? Could they?'

Niccolò shrugged. 'I suppose so. If they took Sardinia they could then make a landing north of Rome.'

Francesca's eyes widened. 'My God, Nico.'

'But I think they'll land here. Much closer to Tunisia, to Malta. And they will win. They have more aircraft than us, more ships, more guns, more men, more tanks and more fuel – especially more fuel. If we hadn't lost North Africa, well, who knows? But a quarter of a million men were taken in Tunisia, Cesca – that's a lot of soldiers. It's hard to recover from that, you know, and so much left behind. Aircraft, weapons. Trucks. We didn't have as much as the Allies before that, but now... We're finished. Mussolini's finished.'

'Thank God for that.'

'If it means the end of the war.'

Cara tugged at her mother's skirt. 'I'm going inside, Mamma.'

Francesca stroked her hair. 'All right, darling.' She watched her daughter climb the steps.

'She's a sweet kid,' said Niccolò. 'Happy too.'

'For now. But what about when the Allies come?'

'You'll be safe enough here. It's along the coast that the fighting will take place. With a bit of luck, you might miss it altogether. Catania might get a pasting, but stay here and you should have nothing to fear.' He smiled. 'You'll be fine, and so will Cara.'

Francesca's heart quickened. He sounded so calm, so reassuring, yet something close to panic gripped her. She felt a little giddy and lowered herself onto one of the wooden crates by the open barn door.

'To think Mussolini might go – that he might soon be no more,' she said.

Niccolò's brow creased and he looked up at the house.

'What is it?' said Francesca.

'Nothing.'

'What? Tell me!' Alarm in her voice.

'Well, I suppose the Allies will govern the island for a bit but then what? We don't want a return to the bad old ways: an island governed by bullies and henchmen. I don't want Fascism a day longer, but we have Mori to thank for one thing.'

'Mori is a brute,' muttered Francesca.

'Maybe, but where is the Honoured Society now? A return to those old days is unthinkable. It would destroy Sicily.'

'The Allies believe in democracy.'

'They believe in beating the Axis.'

Francesca put her head in her hands. She could feel tears welling. Niccolò was going in the morning, heading back to his battalion, leaving her with Cara and the pestering of her suitors. The future was unknown, uncertain, but one that promised war on their doorstep, danger for her brother – for all of them – and the prospect of the constant, inescapable shroud of fear when the fighting was finally over.

She felt her brother's arm around her shoulders. 'Why did you have to say that?' she asked. 'Isn't it bad enough that we might have tanks and soldiers pouring through our town?'

'You asked me.'

'Because you looked so serious.'

'I'm sorry. I'm probably wrong.' A rueful smile. 'It's hard to be optimistic when you've seen what I have. Come on,' he said, forcing a smile. 'Cheer up. At least we have today. Summer is here. It's a beautiful day. My Benelli is running again, and you are about to give me an incredible lunch. What is there to be glum about?'

Francesca laughed, even though tears were sliding down her cheeks.

The convoy had been late in starting, so that by midday, they had barely travelled forty miles, and now were being slowed again as they passed through the coastal town of Sousse.

'Will they never bloody learn?' muttered Corporal Brown, leaning on the steering-wheel.

'Is that Browner moaning again?' said Sykes, from behind. 'What are you on about this time, Browner?'

'Having to go through these sodding towns,' he said. 'Why don't we go round them? The trucks can cope. Going through just slows everything down.'

Tanner looked up. The column had ground to a

halt. Mules pulling carts and even cattle were ambling past them. The streets were busy with people and market sellers, and it smelt too: woodsmoke, animal dung, probably human dung as well, for all he knew. People were shouting. Why did Arabs have to bloody well shout all the time? Across the far side of the road he saw a dog, dead by the look of it.

Tanner pulled a packet of cigarettes from his shirt pocket and lit one. 'I'll admit, Browner, you've got a point,' he said, 'but what's the hurry? Ten days to get to Alex. Think of it as a holiday.'

'Can we go to the seaside, sir?' said Phyllis. He was sitting behind Tanner in the main body of the truck.

'You're at the bloody seaside now, Siff,' he said. He pointed lazily. 'It's over there.'

'I meant have a swim, sir.'

'Don't see why not. What time did Major Peploe say we were going to stop, Stan?'

'He said we're to aim to leaguer up at about five o'clock, sir,' said Sykes. 'Unless, of course, we get held up and fall behind schedule.'

'So there's your answer, Siff. No swimming today. But if we're ever by the sea, and there's time, you can have a swim. Fair enough?'

'What about ice-creams?' said Sykes.

'Oh, I'd die for an ice-cream,' said Phyllis.

'When did you last have one?' asked Sykes.

'On leave in Cairo, I think. Before Alamein.'

'What?' said Sykes. 'You mean you didn't have one at Suleiman's in Tunis?'

'No, sir,' said Phyllis. 'What's Suleiman's?'

'What's Suleiman's?' said Sykes, in a tone of

incredulity. 'Can you hear that, boys? Siff here's never even *heard* of Suleiman's. Blimey, Siff, I worry what planet you're on sometimes.'

Tanner smiled.

'Suleiman's had the best ice-cream you ever tasted, isn't that right, sir?' said Brown.

'Too bloody right, Browner,' said Sykes. 'Cold and creamy and sweet and more flavours than you can imagine. Christ, I reckon I must have spent five quid there on ice-cream alone. Siff, I can't believe you've never even heard of it. Where were you? I reckon Siff's just about the only Allied soldier in Tunis who never went there, don't you, Browner?'

'Must be,' agreed Brown. 'I can taste it now. Chocolate ice-cream, melting in my mouth, cooling my throat. Dee-bloody-licious.'

In the mirror, Tanner saw Phyllis scratch his head. Griffiths was asleep, but Trahair was awake, a big grin on his face.

'What about you, Kernow?' Phyllis asked him. 'Did you go there too?'

'Oh, yeah,' said Trahair. 'Several times.'

'Where was I, then?'

'Well, I went once when you had your hair cut that time. And then when you got drunk and fell asleep by the fountain, me an' Taffy went.'

'You never said.'

'No? I'm sure I did. Must have forgotten to.'

Phyllis was quiet for a moment, then said, 'So where was it?'

'Sort of in the middle,' said Sykes. 'Near the market.'

'Not far from that big mosque,' added Brown.

71

'I s'pose it was quite discreet, wasn't it, sir?'

'Now you mention it, Browner,' agreed Sykes, 'yes, I s'pose it was. But, really, Siff, you missed out there. Hmm – yum yum.'

'What about you, sir?' asked Phyllis. 'Did you go?'

'Didn't need to, Siff. I was with the Yanks. They have ice-cream for breakfast.'

They all laughed.

The column rolled forward again, trundling along at walking pace. A little further on, they passed a group of Arabs trying to right a large cart that had overturned. A number of watermelons – presumably its load – lay in the dust at either side of the road.

'What was it like, sir,' said Brown, 'being with the Americans?'

'All right,' said Tanner. 'Good lads, most of them. Patton ain't all there much of the time, but he's got spirit, I'll give him that.'

'I seen pictures of him,' said Brown. 'He was wearing cowboy pistols.'

'He always had them. Pearl-handled. A bit of a showman, is General Patton.' He pulled a shred of tobacco from his teeth. 'I'll say one thing for the Americans, though. They learn fast. Reckon they'll be pretty good before long.'

'Should make our life easier, then,' said Sykes. 'Maybe we really have turned a corner.'

Maybe, thought Tanner, but there was a long way to go. Of that he was sure.

'Well, sir,' said Brown, 'it's good to have you back.'

'Thank you, Browner. It's good to be back.'

'Funny to think you've been gone three months. You were with us all that time and then we have three company commanders just like that.'

'Captain Tanner's the luck of the devil,' said Sykes. 'I told you that before, Browner.'

'Speak for yourself, Stan,' said Tanner. He and Sykes had been together since the start of the war when they had been deployed to Norway in April 1940 with the 5th Battalion. People came and went in war – some killed, some wounded, some simply moved on. It was often sad yet inevitable, but he knew he had been lucky to have Sykes alongside him for much of that time. A bloke needed a mate in war, Tanner thought. A bloke to chat with, to sit in silence with, to share experiences with. A bloke you could trust. A mate who'd watch your back. He reckoned he'd have been killed several times over if it hadn't been for Sykes.

'You're still here, though, aren't you, sir?' said Sykes.

'As are you, Stan.'

'Unlike Captain Donald,' said Brown. 'He got blown up after Mareth.'

'He was being a bit careless, though,' said Sykes. 'He didn't have to walk off the road, but he got impatient.'

'Then Captain Troughton was killed at Wadi Akarit.'

'Lost a few lads there,' said Sykes.

'And Captain Henderson was wounded at Enfidaville.'

'And then they didn't give us another,' added Phyllis. 'Got merged with B Company instead, and C Company with D Company.'

'We were down to half strength then, sir,' Brown said, turning his head towards Tanner. 'Non-bloody-stop it's been since Alamein.'

'So we'd better enjoy this holiday now, Browner,' said Sykes, 'and I say that because I could sense you were about to start moaning again.'

Brown did not respond. He was a young man, like most of them: barely twenty, with a long, thin face and light brown hair. His hands gripped the steering-wheel, a tattoo newly etched on his right forearm, and a watch around his wrist – dirty white strap, the badge of an experienced Eighth Army man. The Aertex shirt bore the two stripes of a corporal, while his legs were covered with khaki drill trousers rather than shorts – Tanner had insisted upon that: trousers meant fewer cuts and insect bites and, he thought, looked better. Men in shorts resembled schoolboys. They had stuck with trousers while he'd been away.

He was glad to be back. Glad to be commanding his own company for the first time. It had happened very quickly, the letter waiting for Wiseman on their return: a request from Major John Peploe, acting Officer Commanding of the 2nd Battalion, the King's Own Yorkshire Rangers. Wiseman had shown it to Tanner immediately. 'You're wanted,' he'd said, passing him the typed letter.

'You don't need me any more,' Tanner had replied. 'The lads put Jerry to the sword at the end of this fight. I take it you've no more trips overseas planned?'

'Not me personally, no.' Wiseman had grinned.

He had slapped Tanner's shoulder. 'Well, buddy, I'm not going to stop you, although I'd have you serve with me any time. I hope you know that.'

And that had been it. A day later, one of Wiseman's men had driven him down to the Rangers' camp near Enfidaville and, to his delight and surprise, many of his old company were still there, Sykes, Brown and Phyllis included. Even Hepworth had returned, back in the company and now platoon sergeant. McAllister had survived, too, and was platoon sergeant under one of the new subalterns, Lieutenant Bradshaw. A good pairing, Tanner thought – Mac would look after Bradshaw, all right.

They rumbled on, past palm groves, citrus groves, through collections of ramshackle buildings. Despite the locust swarm of two armies fighting up this coastal strip of Tunisia, Tanner still saw the odd chicken and goat, mule and ox. It was a warm, sparsely populated land, but it was not the desert; despite the dark, jagged mountains that were never far away, Tunisia was a more fertile place. In many ways, it was not so very different from Sicily.

The dust was bad, though: seventy-odd vehicles trundling down the same road. He poured a small amount of water onto his handkerchief and wiped his face.

'You've got to admit, though, sir,' said Brown, seeing him do this, 'that this new truck's a great improvement. We're not coated in dust and sand like we used to be.'

Tanner glanced up at the olive drab canvas covering the cab. The Yorkshire Rangers were a motorized battalion, which meant they lived in and operated from their vehicles, rather than being deposited at the front by larger troop-carrying three-ton lorries. For more than a year, they had spent most of their time in either tracked carriers or the smaller fifteen-hundredweight trucks. It had meant smaller sections too: four of seven men in every platoon, rather than three of ten as was the case in other infantry companies. In the desert, their MWD Bedfords had been stripped down: no doors, no windscreen, no canvas. They had been basic as hell – an engine, four wheels, a few spare petrol cans and space for seven or eight men to sit – but these new ones, presumably freshly arrived from Britain, had all of the more normal fixtures and fittings, including a canvas roof over the cab and a further canopy over the body of the truck. The canvas had been rolled up so that Tanner could talk to Sykes and the others in the back, but it was, he knew, a sign of how fortunes had changed that they no longer had to worry about marauding Messerschmitts and Macchis spotting the glint of sunlight on glass.

'I'll give you that, Browner,' said Tanner.

'It's a wonderful thing having command of the skies, isn't it?' said Sykes.

Tanner smiled. It was good to be back with Sykes and the boys.

They left the coast road south of Sousse and stopped for the night near the airfield at El Djem. The more fertile north had given way to rocky desert once more, but they found a sheltered spot at the southern edge of the town and parked.

Tanner clambered down as Sykes was already ordering the men to begin brewing some tea. He found Captain Fauvel, his second-in-command in A Company. Fauvel had been a B Company man, but had been promoted and moved across to A Company in the reorganization of the battalion since the end of the North African campaign. Older than most at twenty-six, he was still a year younger than Tanner, with thick, mouse-brown hair, gentle features and a pleasant, soft-spoken manner. Fauvel was, Tanner knew, the kind of man who would never have worn a uniform had it not been for the war; he had admitted as much in the mess the previous evening. Tanner had pointed out that the same could be said for Peploe, yet since joining the battalion three years earlier, their acting OC had proved an outstanding soldier and officer. Fauvel wasn't a Yorkshireman, although he had been training as a manager on one of the larger West Riding estates when war had broken out. He'd told Tanner that he could have avoided war service, but had felt it was his duty to go off and fight.

'Good for you,' Tanner had told him. He instinctively liked Fauvel and they had much in common: both southerners – Fauvel from Hampshire, Tanner from south Wiltshire – and shared a love of the land. 'We're countrymen, you and I,' Tanner had said. He still had the faint Wiltshire burr he had been born with; it had softened over time, but had never gone entirely even though he had spent so many years overseas, first in India, then the Middle East and, these past few years, the Mediterranean.

'Everything all right, Gavin?' he asked Fauvel.

'I think so.' Fauvel took off his cap and scratched his head, squinting into the sun. At the airfield in front of them, a number of Dakotas were coming into land.

'Transport planes,' said Fauvel.

Around them there was now a flurry of activity. Men were clambering down from their trucks, the engines ticking as they cooled; some were hurrying off to pee, others, like Phyllis, hastily starting the process of brewing tea. Tanner breathed in the warm, dry air and the sudden smell of burning petrol as Phyllis poured fuel onto a sand-filled flimsie and lit it. Americans drank coffee, mostly heated on small stoves or from huge vats brewed by canteen staff. British soldiers brewed char.

'We'll be into the desert tomorrow,' said Fauvel. 'Past Wadi Akarit.'

Tanner saw him swallow hard. 'Heard it was a tough one.'

Fauvel nodded. 'It was the Italians. The Young Fascists. They fought bloody hard. I lost a lot of men there. I'll be glad to have it behind us, to be honest.'

Tanner said nothing, but took out his cigarettes, offered them to Fauvel, who took one, then pulled one out for himself.

'The chaps in my truck think it's Sicily next,' said Fauvel, as he exhaled.

'Maybe.'

'I remember when I first came out here everyone said the Italians were push-overs. They might have been then, but they weren't in Tunisia.'

'I'd agree,' said Tanner.

'I'm just hoping they've lost some of the will to fight with the surrender in Tunis. We've just got the battalion back to almost full strength. We can't go through that again. We can't keep losing so many men.' He looked at Tanner. 'Can we, Jack?'

'Maybe they're sending us home. Get on the boat at Suez, back round the Cape, and hello, Blighty.'

Fauvel smiled ruefully. 'You don't really think that.'

'No – no, I don't. We'll be all right, though. I think those Eyeties are almost done. No matter where it is next – Sicily or Sardinia or Greece or bloody Timbuktu – I'm sure we'll be fine. It's different now. More planes, more everything. More Yanks for that matter. You saw those Dakotas coming in. We're gathering strength. Don't dwell on it too much, Gavin. Enjoy this little breather we've got.'

As he was saying this, he heard his name called and turned to see Peploe striding towards him.

'Ah, Jack, there you are,' said Peploe. 'Can I borrow you?'

'Of course,' said Tanner.

'Shall I go around and check on the platoons?' asked Fauvel.

Tanner nodded. 'Thanks.' He turned to Peploe. His old friend's willingness to smile, Tanner thought, was one of his most endearing features. The grin spread across his round, affable face.

'How are you settling back in?' Peploe asked him.

'Fine. Like I've never been away. It's good to be back.'

'Good to have you, Jack.'

'Was there anything in particular?' Tanner asked, as he saw Phyllis stirring in sugar and condensed milk not ten yards away. His mouth was dry.

'Yes, as a matter of fact there was.' He glanced at Phyllis. 'Let's have a brew, but then I want to show you something.'

'All right,' said Tanner. 'I have to admit, I'm parched.'

Peploe grinned at him. 'You'd never know it, Jack. I saw those furtive glances at the brew can.'

Ten minutes later, they were climbing into Peploe's Jeep.

'We're going into the town,' said Peploe. 'Remember how we never quite got to look at Knossos properly?'

'I do,' said Tanner, as Peploe pressed the starter button and put the Jeep in gear. 'Jerry paratroopers spoiled the party.'

'Well, I promised myself then not to make that mistake again. When we got to Tunis, I went straight to Carthage, and I'm going to look at El Djem too.'

'What's at El Djem?'

'Only the best-preserved Roman amphitheatre outside Rome. There's not much to be said for regularly putting one's life on the line, but seeing some of the ancient world's finest is some compensation in my book.'

'You didn't see it on the way up, then?'

'No. Too busy chasing Italians and Germans for

that. Anyway, I thought we could look at the amphitheatre and have a chat while we're about it. The battalion can manage without us for an hour or two. There have to be some perks to the job.'

'Do you think you'll keep it? Being OC, I mean?'

'I don't know. No one's said a thing. "Right, you're acting officer commanding, Peploe," was all I was told. The word "acting" suggests temporary, don't you think?'

Tanner shrugged. 'Officers are getting younger and younger. You're perfectly capable of doing the job. You know the battalion and its men as well as anyone. Everyone respects you. Why risk upsetting the apple-cart by bringing in someone new?'

'Good of you to say so, Jack, but you know the Army doesn't work like that. I'd be honoured to take it on – of course I would – but I wouldn't be at all upset if I was stood down. It's a hell of a responsibility, you know.'

'I hope you do keep it, John,' he said, happy to return to first-name terms now that it was just the two of them. 'The last thing we want is some newcomer arriving and trying to throw his weight around.'

'He might be a brilliant man.'

'I doubt it. He's either going to have been promoted from another battalion, or brought in from somewhere completely different – a staff job, or another theatre. You're doing a fine job by the look of things. They should leave you to crack on with it.'

'Well, time will tell, Jack. Time will tell.'

The amphitheatre dominated the centre of the town. Parking the Jeep beneath its high, curved walls, they jumped out and passed through one of the archways into the arena. For a moment, neither spoke, as they looked around the giant ancient structure.

'It's bigger than Lord's,' Peploe said eventually. 'This place could seat thirty-five thousand people, you know.'

'It's incredible.' At that moment, the lowering sun struck one of the arches at the far end of the amphitheatre, casting a dazzling beam of golden light across them.

'There's been fighting here for millennia,' said Peploe, lowering his cap over his eyes. 'We're just another generation of soldiers.'

'But still fighting Eyeties,' said Tanner.

Peploe smiled. 'I suppose so, yes, although I wouldn't say Mussolini's Italy has much in common with Ancient Rome.'

'He wishes it did, though.'

'I'm sure. But the Roman Empire lasted centuries, more than a thousand years, if you include Byzantium. Mussolini's Italy has lasted twenty-one.'

Peploe produced a bottle of whisky and two tin mugs from his haversack and together they walked towards the high banks of stone seats that surrounded the arena. 'What were the Americans like?' Peploe asked, as he poured two large measures.

'A bit rough around the edges,' said Tanner, lighting a cigarette.

Peploe passed him a mug and they chinked them together.

'Cheers,' said Peploe.

'Cheers.'

'The attitude in Eighth Army was rather condescending, I thought,' said Peploe.

'They were green to start off with, no doubt about it, but they learned quick. Damn quick. On Hill 609, they bloody proved themselves, all right.' He exhaled. 'That was a bitch of a fight. Jerries dug in on the top. We'd take it, then be counterattacked, but the Yanks never gave up. Germany's on our doorstep and we're Europeans and we've been in it from the start, but those boys...' He shook his head. 'Most of them farm lads from God only knows where in the middle of America. What do they care about Hitler and Nazis and Musso-sodding-lini? And yet they fought and fought. The war will be a hell of a lot easier to win now they're alongside us. They're different – don't stand on ceremony so much – but they're good, John. Don't let anyone tell you otherwise.'

Peploe smiled again. 'Good. Glad to hear it.'

They were silent for a moment, then Peploe said, 'So, is it going to be Sicily?'

Tanner had not spoken a word to anyone about his mission to the island, but on the other hand, no one had ever told him not to; not Wiseman, not Spiro, not even General Carter. There had been no signing of the Official Secrets Act. Maybe the Americans didn't even have such a thing. Could he mention it to Peploe? Instinctively he thought not, but then again what did he know? Very little.

'I think so,' he said.

'You know what it's like in a battalion. Always the last to find out anything. But at a corps headquarters – well, there are rumours.'

Tanner took a sip of his whisky. No. It was not his place to tell Peploe or anyone else about what had been a highly secret mission. His silence, while not asked for, had been a given. It was a question of honour, as much as anything. *Honour. Those Sicilians and their bloody honour.*

'The rumour is Sicily,' he said at length. 'In any case, Sardinia would be out of fighter range. Now we've got command of the sky, no one's going to let us lose it, especially not while we're carrying out a seaborne invasion.'

'Because that's what it's going to have to be,' added Peploe, 'no matter where we land.'

'Yes,' said Tanner.

'Makes sense. But why send us back to Egypt?'

'Because we can't send the entire invasion force from Tunisia.'

'Of course. And Egypt is still Headquarters Middle East.' Peploe leaned forward, his elbows on his knees. 'It feels like we've been doing this a long time, doesn't it?'

'We have.'

'I had a few good days in Tunis and now we're on the road again, and I know we don't have to worry about enemy aircraft, or some Jerry strongpoint up ahead, but the prospect of what's to come is hanging heavy on me, Jack, I don't mind telling you. For so long it's been the war in North Africa. For a couple of days it felt like the end of the whole war, but now there's the knowledge that we've got to start all over again. I'm not sure I've got the stomach for it any more. So many good chaps have gone already. I heard that one of my oldest friends was killed just before the end – a chap I'd known since I was seven. Blown up at Medjerda.'

'I'm sorry.'

Peploe took another swig of his whisky. 'I keep wondering who's next. Whether it's my turn. It's this journey. Too much time to think.'

'Everyone feels that way at the moment. Gavin Fauvel does. I do. I'm sick of fighting. I've been a soldier for more than ten years. I just want to be left in peace. Go back to being a gamekeeper. Me, my dogs, the countryside around me.'

'Maybe a Mrs Tanner and some junior Tanners.'

Tanner smiled. 'Never say never, John.'

'Well,' said Peploe, 'here's hoping Sicily is a walkover and that they then decide it's time we had a breather. Perhaps they'll send us home.'

'Perhaps.'

'Come on,' said Peploe, getting to his feet. 'We should go back.'

Later, Tanner lay in his tent, wide awake, his thoughts turning back to the mission to Sicily. What a strange episode. He wondered what had happened at the beach defence encampment when dawn had broken and those two Italians had woken up. Would they have known that an Allied soldier had knocked them out cold? He remembered Wiseman asking him on the voyage back how he had managed to knock them out. Easy, Tanner had explained. Neither had been expecting any trouble. 'Catching people un-awares gives you a hell of an advantage.' Knock-ing out the second had been harder but, Tanner had gone on, he'd been expecting his mate to rejoin him. Instead, he'd had Tanner's fist driving into the side of his head.

'Quite the pugilist,' Wiseman had said.

'I wasn't Eighth Army boxing champion for nothing,' Tanner had replied.

Honour. It had been a matter of honour not to tell Peploe, and yet that word, *onore,* had been used over and over again by those Sicilians. Those *Men of Honour.* He thought of that first night back in Tunis, a drink with Wiseman in a quiet bar near the centre of the city.

'You haven't once asked me about what we've been doing,' Wiseman had said.

'I supposed you'd tell me if you thought I ought to know,' Tanner had replied.

'You're a good man, Jack.' Wiseman had chuckled. 'But aren't you curious?'

'A bit.'

Wiseman had eyed him, as though weighing up how much he should say.

'I heard a lot of talk about honour,' said Tanner. A smile from Wiseman. 'I like to think I'm a man of honour too,' Tanner continued, 'but it's not something I shout about.'

'Not in the Sicilian sense, you're not,' said Wiseman. 'A man like Don Calogero is...' He paused, searching for the right words. 'He's a pro-tector. He owns much of the land around there.

He is, I suppose, an unofficial governor, for want of a better phrase. Being a man of honour is like being part of a special society. Kinda like the Freemasons, or the Knights of St John. Men of honour look after one another, but of course there's a hierarchy, and Don Calogero is the man at the top.'

'In all of Sicily?'

'Yes.'

'Really?' said Tanner. 'He hardly seemed the type.'

'It's not about being showy' said Wiseman. 'In fact, the less ostentatious the better. Don Calogero doesn't need to strut about in fine clothes to show he's boss. He just has to blink and people do as he says. People respect his authority for what it stands for, not for how he parades about the place.'

'No wonder he hates the Fascists,' muttered Tanner.

'The Fascists have been trying to stamp out the Honourable Society,' said Wiseman. 'It's another reason why Don Calogero is so willing to help the Allies.'

'They haven't succeeded, then?'

'No – at least, not in the heart of Sicily. In the coastal regions it's a bit different. Their grip has been loosened a bit.' He paused, then said, 'Sicily used to be owned by knights and barons but they weren't interested in living on their estates, in a place like Villalba, miles from anywhere. So they had managers, overseers, who did it for them. Eventually the overseers became more and more powerful and bought the estates from the landlords. Don Calogero's family is one of those.

His brother is the priest of Villalba, you know. That makes him the second most important person in the town. So you see, Jack, Don Calogero's got it all sewn up,' said Wiseman.

'And those bandits?'

'He offers protection from men like them. And they know better than to take him on.'

'It's a protection racket,' said Tanner.

'Not exactly.'

'Sounds like it to me. All those Sicilians huddled together in towns, with men like Don Calogero keeping them safe, and in return, he rules the roost.'

Wiseman lit a cigarette, flicking open his brass lighter with one hand. 'But it's more refined than that.'

'If you say so.'

'Anyway, that's not our concern.' Wiseman blew out a cloud of swirling smoke. 'The point is, Don Calogero can make sure we have minimal trouble should we decide to invade Sicily.'

'Should?'

'All right. When. Jeez, it's not as though it's a hard one to guess.'

Tanner nodded slowly. 'So we help Sicily get rid of Mussolini and Fascism and put men like Don Calogero in power instead.'

'We get rid of Mussolini, then Italy drops out of the war. If Italy's outta the war, the Nazis have got to either fill Italy and Greece and the Balkans with Germans or hand them over to us. If they go for the former option, then those are troops that can't be fighting the Russkies or waiting for us when we invade France. And if they don't go for it, then we're a massive step closer to Berlin. Whichever way you look at it, Hitler's got a massive problem on his hands. So men like Don Calogero get to be a little more powerful as a result – so what? You saw what it was like over there. Fuckin' miserable. Who'd want to be a Sicilian peasant, no matter who's the boss man? Not me, I can tell you.'

Tanner turned his glass. 'This war,' he said. 'I've been fighting Jerry for more than three years now, and when I started I thought it was because we wanted to rid the world of Nazis. The waters are getting muddy, though. I know we're still trying to smash Adolf and his mob, but it's not so black and white now.' He looked up at Wiseman. 'You're a good bloke, Charlie, but keep me out of this cloak-and-dagger lark in future, will you?'

Wiseman gave a mock salute. 'All right, Jack. I'll try.'

Well I'm out of that game now. He was back in the battalion, with his own company, Sykes as CSM, and his old friend John Peploe as battalion commander. He smiled to himself. This was more like it. From what he'd seen in Sicily, he reckoned the invasion would be a pushover. One last effort, he told himself, and then, with a bit of luck, the Rangers might be given a rest.

Just so long as there were no more surprises lying in wait. But what surprises could there possibly be?

5

Monday, 14 June 1943, early morning. At the 76th Infantry Regiment's camp outside Sortino in south-east Sicily, Captain Niccolò Togliatti was taking a shower, the cool water trickling over his thin body. *Oh, to be fat.* He reached up and turned off the tap. The showers were rudimentary to say the least – a row of old fuel drums with holes in the bottom and taps attached – but they got rid of the previous day's grime and sweat. The showers, Togliatti reflected, as he stepped clear, were rather indicative of the Army's entire set-up in Sicily – or what he'd seen of it, at any rate. They had been under-equipped in Russia, but here, in Sicily, the situation was far worse. The 76th Infantry Regiment appeared to be short of just about everything: weapons, ammunition, vehicles, rations. Experience, too. He had not seen any armoured units although, according to Lieutenant Colonel Rizzini, the battalion commander, there were a few, both Italian and German. Training with these was clearly out of the question, though.

As Togliatti dried himself and dressed in his sand-coloured breeches and vest, his thoughts turned back to the Eastern Front. It was true there had been times when supplies had been short out there, too, but at least the men had known how to make the best of what they had.

Experience, he thought, counted for a great deal, and he reckoned that in Russia he and his men had become pretty good soldiers. The problem with the 76th Regiment and with the rest of the Napoli Division, as far as he could make out, was that very few of them had ever seen any action. Not for nothing had they been nicknamed the Ghost Division.

Reaching his tent, he finished dressing: a tropical tunic – *sahariana* – over his vest, then belt and pistol holster, socks, tall black leather boots, and finally his *bustina* side-cap. Once ready, he headed to the mess for breakfast. His stomach was rumbling painfully, but the two hard-bread crackers and mug of ersatz coffee were never enough – not when they were burning so much energy on endless route marches.

He was pleased to see Riccio already sitting in the canteen. As a newcomer, Togliatti had had little chance yet to get to know many in the battalion, and had lost so many in Russia that he was loath to build new friendships. Riccio, however, had proved an exception. He, too, was a combat veteran, although of North Africa, and had also been wounded, evacuated back to Italy, then posted to the Napoli Division. Although they were the same age, Riccio seemed older: he drank more than Togliatti, had a whore in Sortino, a weary cynicism and barbed wit that Togliatti found entertaining; it was such a contrast with their fellow officers, most of whom were as keen as they were naïve.

'May I join you?' Togliatti asked.

'At the morning feast? Be my guest,' muttered

Riccio. 'By the way,' he added, 'I've already heard today's training programme. You'll never guess.'

'A full-kit route march?'

'Ah, yes, but with a difference. We're also going to dig some communication trenches between the new bunkers our engineers are building, so there won't be gymnastics this afternoon. God forbid that we should actually train to fight anyone.'

Togliatti laughed. 'Colonel Rizzini wants us fit, you know that.'

'The good colonel wants us fit only because General Porcinari has said we're to be fit. And he's been telling us to get fit because otherwise what would we do all day? How do you keep an entire division busy when there's hardly any fuel and scarcely any ammunition? But now he's had a flash of inspiration – we can dig as well as march.' He pushed his mug away and rested his cheek in his hand. 'Argh,' he groaned. 'I do wish the Allies would get a move on. Get it over and done with.'

'Don't say that to D'Angelo or Del Boca. They think North Africa is nothing but a minor setback. They're planning personally to send the enemy back into the sea.'

'Mary, Mother of Jesus.' Riccio sighed.

Two hours later Togliatti was marching at the head of his company, the sun burning down on them, this latest march already eight kilometres long. He could feel the sweat mixing with the dust kicking up from the company in front, but although his mouth felt parched, he dared not drink any more water for a while. His canteen had to last all day and that meant careful rationing.

In truth, he did not mind the route marches as much as Riccio did. The initial frustration he had felt at the lack of proper training had quickly made way for feelings of more ambivalent *sangfroid*. The thought of the island being overrun by British and American troops hardly appealed, but on the other hand he did not believe they could possibly stave off an invasion. Allied superiority meant the enemy was bound to prevail. That being so, he reasoned, the sooner it was all over the better. What was the point in getting killed if they were bound to surrender sooner or later anyway? Rather, he had decided he would do what was asked and expected of him; he would look after his men, most of whom were little more than boys, try to help them survive, and then, perhaps, they would one day all go home.

Home. It wasn't so very far away – just thirty kilometres or so to the north. He wiped his brow as they climbed up the winding road towards the row of pillboxes still being constructed on the ridge ahead. He had been so glad to leave that house, to get away from Sicily to Rome, the vibrant, sophisticated capital. He still remembered the sense of shame he had felt when his father had been drummed out of Palermo, cut adrift from the Society and people he had served. Motta Sant'Anastasia had seemed so small, so backward – a terrible exile that cast a shadow of shame on them all. His father had become withdrawn and irritable, lashing out in anger at the slightest provocation. They'd all wanted to leave – even his darling sister, Cesca.

He smiled when he remembered his decision to join the Army. How young and foolish he had been, like many of the young platoon commanders under his charge now. He had been in Rome when Mussolini had declared war on Britain and France, and remembered the exhilaration he had felt. He and his friends had cheered, and raised their arms in salute, but then he had seen an old lady in black staring at them with tears rolling down her face. 'Why are you sad?' he had asked her. 'Italy is going to be great again!'

She had put a hand to his face. 'My boy, you have no idea what you are saying. May God protect you.'

Togliatti cringed now at the memory. What a callow, feckless youth he had been, falling for Mussolini's rhetoric and believing what the Duce had promised. 'We will win!' he had assured them. A new Rome, a new Empire, one that bound the Mediterranean and half of Africa. How hollow that seemed now. He thought of Giulio and Marco, his two greatest friends, dead in the snow in Russia. Russia! That had never been part of the plan, part of the new Italian Empire. He swallowed hard, a wave of emotion overwhelming him. Tears pricked his eyes. *Come on, pull yourself together.*

As they continued climbing out of the valley, his thoughts turned to his sister. She had been scared – not for herself, he knew, but for little Cara. A sweet kid, and as pretty as her mother. Cesca was an angel, he thought, a truly good person. He couldn't bear the thought of her being unhappy with Giovanni; he'd had no idea the man had treated her so badly. But Giovanni was gone, dead, like so many in this war, and Cesca had started to make something of a life again – a life that was now threatened. He cursed and gazed upwards, tears welling once more. Suddenly his heart was telling him to fight, to do everything he could to defend his family and home – and, yes, it was his home, a beautiful place that promised peace and happiness. He wanted desperately to help Cesca and Cara to live the life they deserved, yet his head was saying something quite different.

They reached the brow of the ridge and the first of the row of pillboxes overlooking the road. The harsh, gritty smell of fresh concrete filled the air. Engineers, stripped to the waist, backs glistening, were hard at work. As the column halted, Togliatti looked back down towards the valley. The land around, he knew, naturally lent itself to defence. Stretching away to their left was the sea, but the ground rose up a kilometre or so inland. The valley behind them was just one of many formed by ancient rivers that had scythed through one ridge after another. Anyone advancing north could be clearly seen as soon as they reached the ridge, but were they to gain that ground, they would then have to negotiate the valley beyond. Determined defence, Togliatti reckoned, would slow the enemy considerably. Instinctively, he thought of what might be achieved by carefully positioned mortars and machine-guns, then remembered the hopelessness of the situation. *Dear God, please let me get through this.* The end – it was nearly upon them. It had to be.

Later that day, more than a thousand miles away. The Yorks Rangers had covered almost two thousand miles in ten days, but at last the battalion drove into the tented camp at El Shatt on the south-eastern shore of the Suez Canal. Tanner had initially felt glad that the journey was finally over, that the men would soon be busy once more, training for the invasion that was surely only weeks away, but on crossing the canal and seeing the camp spread before them – row after row of tents, vehicles, flags and sand – relief quickly gave way to something close to disenchantment. For that ten-day period, they had talked, smoked, drunk tea, laughed, relentlessly taken the piss out of Phyllis and Brown, and almost daily swum in the Mediterranean. They had also passed a near-endless procession of battle debris – burned-out tanks, aircraft, trucks, petrol tins, blackened hunks of jagged metal that had reminded them of the long and bloody battle they had fought along the North African shores. But, Tanner realized, they had been together, the morale in the company as good as he had ever known it, and free of any bother from above. No red-tape-loving staff officer to stick his oar in, no over-officious brigadier or divisional commander telling them what to do. Here, though, as they saw the coils of wire that surrounded the camp and passed through the gates, guarded by Thompson-carrying sentries, their autonomy had been removed in the snap of a salute.

Following the procession of Battalion Headquarters and HQ Company, Tanner led his A

Company down the sand tracks, glancing out at the array of flags as they went. There was 5th Division, a khaki square with a single white 'Y' for Yorkshire stitched across it, and then, a little further, 13th Brigade and 15th Infantry Brigade. They turned off down another sand street and passed the 1st Battalion Green Howards, one of the infantry battalions they were to join in the brigade. At the Green Howards' camp area there was plenty of activity, with men cleaning weapons and preparing their supper, the familiar smell of paraffin mixed with bully beef wafting on the air. Soldiers looked up as they passed, then the vehicles in front were turning again and men with clipboards were directing them towards their allotted encampments. Several larger tents denoted Battalion Headquarters and the mess. At last Brown brought the vehicle to a halt.

'We're here, sir. End of the road.'

Tanner nodded, lit a cigarette and got out. *Back in the Canal Zone*. It was as though the past ten months had never happened.

An hour later, he had finished touring his platoons and was looking forward to some food when he saw Sykes approaching him.

'You heard the news?' Sykes asked.

'What?'

'We've got a new battalion commander.'

'Bollocks,' said Tanner. 'I thought Major Peploe was doing a grand job.'

'I couldn't agree with you more.'

'Jesus,' muttered Tanner. 'Who the hell makes these decisions? Who is he anyway?'

97

'You might know him, actually. Used to be with the 2nd Battalion out in India before the war. Name of Creer.'

Tanner stopped. 'Croaker,' he said. He looked at Sykes, then pushed back his cap and rubbed his brow. 'Croaker Creer. Please, God, no.' He moved a few steps away.

'Jack?' said Sykes.

Tanner had his hands to his head. Then, aware that some of the men were looking at him, he said, 'Come with me, Stan.'

Pushing open the flap of the bell tent he shared with Fauvel, he was glad to see it was empty. While he liked Fauvel well enough, he did not want his second-in-command hearing what he was about to tell Sykes.

'Here,' said Sykes, passing Tanner a hip flask. 'As bad as that, is it?'

Tanner nodded, then took a swig. 'Thanks,' he said, pulled out one of his American Camels and offered Sykes one.

Tanner sat down on the folding canvas chair next to his camp bed. 'He's a bastard,' he said.

'In what way?'

Tanner rubbed his face again. 'He was in the Second Battalion when I first joined out in India. I went out there as a boy soldier in 'thirty-two – but you know that, Stan. Christ knows why I'm telling you this.' He sighed. 'But I didn't join the battalion until a couple of years later, when I'd turned eighteen. Creer was a platoon commander then.'

'In your platoon?'

'No. He was in a different company, but then

our company second-in-command got ill and Creer was promoted. So I had Creer as company two i/c, and Blackstone as CSM.'

'Blackstone?'

'Remember him?' Tanner smiled wryly.

'That murdering treacherous bastard?' Sykes took off his service cap and smoothed down his hair.

'He made my life a misery,' said Tanner, 'and had Croaker wrapped around his finger. He wasn't a traitor then, mind, although he probably murdered a few. I certainly wouldn't have put it past him. He was always on the bloody scam. Thieving, up to no bloody good. And he protected himself with bribery. He'd draw people into his little gang. Promise to make their life easier if they'd just do one little thing for him – look the other way when he was nicking something, lend him a truck to pick up dodgy goods. That kind of thing. And, of course, when they'd done wrong once, he had them. There was no turning back. My problem was that I wouldn't ever dance to his tune. I don't like bullies, Stan.'

'And Creer?'

'Creer was in on it. Thought the sun shone out of Blackstone's arse. Blackstone gave him backhanders, made sure he looked good. He was called Croaker because he twice avoided action during the Loe Agra campaign. First he had dysentery, next he got himself wounded. Made out he was at death's door, but it was little more than a scratch. Both times Blackstone covered for him.'

'Couldn't you do anything about it?'

'I was only a youngster. You know what it's like. No one was going to listen to some nineteen-year-old private.' He shook his head. 'Jesus. I can honestly say I've not given Croaker a thought in years. I assumed he'd been found out and kicked out.' Tanner groaned. 'Sod it. Of all the bloody people, Stan, here he is, a bloody half-colonel and commanding the battalion. There's no justice in this world. There really isn't.'

Sykes eyed him. 'He might be different without Blackstone. Maybe he's changed.'

Tanner grunted. 'Oh, I'm sure.'

'And you're not a private any more. You're an officer and a company commander. A respected and decorated one, an' all. I don't see what he can do even if he wanted to play silly buggers. And don't forget the major. Major Peploe's not going to put up with any shenanigans, is he?'

'Stan, he can make life difficult,' said Tanner, 'that's what he can do. He'll make A Company lead the attack, send us forward under fire, do his damnedest to make me look bad. And he'll do so because he hated my guts and because he's a right bastard. Believe me, I'd love to be proved wrong, but a leopard doesn't change its spots. Not in my experience anyway.'

'Sir?' said a voice from outside, then the flap opened and Trahair, Tanner's batman, appeared.

'What is it, Kernow?' said Tanner.

'Sorry, sir, but Major Peploe's coming this way and he's got the new boss with him. Just thought you ought to know, sir.'

'Thanks,' said Tanner, putting his cap back on. He turned to Sykes. 'Here goes. Keep what I've just told you under your hat, will you?'

'Course,' said Sykes, standing up. 'Right,' he added. 'Let's have a look at this bloke.'

Stepping out of the tent into the warm evening sunshine, Tanner saw Creer and Peploe just twenty yards away. Walking towards them, he stopped and saluted.

'Ah, there you are, Jack,' said Peploe. 'I understand you've served under Colonel Creer before. Colonel Creer is our new officer commanding.'

'Yes, sir. The colonel and I were in India together.'

Creer took a step forward. 'Tanner,' he said. 'It's been a while.'

Tanner eyed him. The moustache had gone, but otherwise he was much as he remembered: the same ears sticking out, the wide cheekbones and the narrow chin, giving his face a slightly triangular shape. Dark eyes and thick brows. Tanner cursed to himself. Creer had not gone with the rest of the battalion to Palestine – what had it been? Polio? *No, something else.* Not as serious as polio. Of course it wasn't. *Croaker Creer. Christ. How did he get here?*

'It has, sir,' said Tanner.

'And now look at you.' Creer turned to Peploe. 'When I last saw Tanner, he was a mere private and now here he is, bold as day, an officer and a company commander. It's a funny old war, Peploe, it really is. ORs getting field commissions, native Indians getting commissions. What a changing world we live in.'

'There are, though, Colonel, plenty of cases of British soldiers rising through the ranks. It's a question of whether they're up to the job, not whether they were born with a silver spoon in their mouth. I would say most in those circumstances make excellent officers. After all, they've had to overcome more to reach that position.'

Creer turned sharply to Peploe, an eyebrow raised. 'An interesting thought, Peploe.'

'And, I can assure you, Tanner here is first class. His record speaks for itself.'

'Careful, Peploe – you'll make the man blush.' He turned back to Tanner. 'Anyway, Tanner. Here we are – reunited after, what? Six years it must be.'

'Yes, sir. Six years would be right. You left the battalion before operations in the Lower Shaktu area. You were ill, if I remember rightly.'

Creer eyed him carefully. 'Yes, yes,' he said. 'I was laid a bit low then.'

Spotting Sykes, Peploe now said, 'And this is A Company's CSM, sir. Warrant Officer Sykes.'

Sykes saluted.

'Tanner and Sykes have served together since Norway,' added Peploe. 'We're lucky to have him in the battalion.'

Creer chuckled. 'I'm surprised they haven't give you a commission as well, Sykes.'

'Me too, sir. It's criminal.'

Tanner winced inwardly as he heard Sykes stress 'criminal'.

'Maybe it's because of your lip, CSM,' said Creer.

'Sorry, sir. Just joking, sir.'

'Hmm,' said Creer. Then, his face lightening, he suddenly clapped his hands together. 'Anyway,' he said. 'Must get on. Do the rounds. I'll catch up with you later, Tanner. We can have a chinwag about the old days. Eh?'

Tanner watched them go, saw Peploe glance back at him, then turned to Sykes.

'Blimey,' said Sykes, 'he's a piece of work, ain't he?'

'He's an arse, Stan,' said Tanner. 'An absolute bloody arse. And to think we've got to bloody well go to war with him in charge. Jesus.'

And where they would be going to war was revealed later that evening by Brigadier Rawstorne at a gathering of battalion and company commanders, although he stressed that under no circumstances were they to tell their men. He was telling them now only because they were here in the desert and confined to camp. The rest of the men would not know until they were on ship and steaming across the Mediterranean.

It was, to no one's surprise, Sicily. Operation HUSKY would be the largest seaborne invasion the world had ever seen, two armies, the British Eighth and the American Seventh, side by side, supported by an immense aerial and naval armada. He could not tell them when precisely the invasion would be but he could assure them it would be soon. Training was progressing, he said, although the newly arrived Yorks Rangers would have to work hard in the ensuing weeks to catch up.

'I cannot stress to you enough,' Brigadier Rawstorne told them, outside Brigade Headquarters, 'the importance of what we are about to undertake. We are, after nearly three long years, re-entering Europe. The tide has turned. Hitler's gamble is backfiring, his Thousand Year Reich beginning to crumble after just ten. We will invade Sicily, defeat the Axis forces there and occupy the island. It is probable that Mussolini will fall, and with him Fascism, and that Italy will be forced out of the war with catastrophic and far-reaching consequences for Nazi Germany.' He paused and looked around at them all. 'I know many of you have already fought long and hard in this war, but the world needs you to fight some more. We are taking part in a moral crusade, a battle for freedom and a return to peace that our families, children and future generations will enjoy. Do not underestimate the rightness of our cause.'

Tanner wondered about that. He supposed the brigadier was right, and knew that men like Peploe and even Hepworth had joined not because they had to but because they had felt it was the morally right thing to do; they believed it was their duty to help rid the world of Hitler and the Nazis. But what was the price? Deals with men like Don Calogero Vizzini, who, it seemed to him, was little more than a vigilante. Deals with Russia. As far as he could tell, Communism was every bit as bad as Fascism, and Stalin hardly much better than Hitler. Peploe had told him about Stalin's purges: tens of thousands rounded up and executed. And yet Stalin was now an ally. He looked up at the sky, the endless, cloudless blue, Brigadier Rawstorne's voice, crisp and assertive, ringing out over the still desert air.

Then Fauvel nudged him. 'Psst, Jack,' he whispered. 'Over there.'

Tanner glanced to his left. 'What?' he hissed.

'Look at those Green Howards bods. See that one in the middle – the captain? That's Hedley Verity. I'll swear it is.'

Tanner squinted. A man of medium height, greying hair at the sides and a thin mouth. Tanner smiled. 'I think you could be right, Gav.'

'He's only the world's best spin bowler. What the hell is he doing here?'

'Even great cricketers have to do their bit in this war.'

'I suppose so.'

Brigadier Rawstorne had finished and the assembled officers were dismissed. As they began dispersing, the group of Green Howards officers moved towards them.

'Look,' said Fauvel, 'they're heading this way.'

Peploe drew alongside Tanner and Fauvel. 'Don't drag your feet, chaps,' he said.

'It's Gavin,' said Tanner. 'He wants to meet Hedley Verity.' He nodded in the direction of the Green Howards.

'Good God!' said Peploe. 'Why's he here?'

'That's what I said.' Fauvel grinned.

'I saw him take nine for forty-three against Warwickshire at Headingley in 1937,' said Peploe. 'I simply have to shake his hand.'

'That was rather what I was thinking, sir,' said Fauvel.

A moment later they were face to face with the Green Howards officers.

'Captain Verity?' said Peploe.

105

'Yes, sir?' said Verity, glancing at the crown on Peploe's shoulder.

'John Peploe, Yorks Rangers. May I just say what an honour it is to meet you?'

Verity smiled. 'Why, thank you, sir. Pleasure's all mine, I'm sure.' He spoke softly, with a pronounced Yorkshire lilt.

They shook hands, then Peploe said, 'And this is my A Company commander and his two i/c, Captain Jack Tanner and Captain Gavin Fauvel.'

'Tanner?' said Verity. 'I've heard of you.'

'Really?' said Tanner, surprised.

'You're the chap who did that raid on Tobruk,' said another. He held out his hand. 'Captain Bill Synge. How d'you do?'

They shook hands.

'Yes,' said Synge. 'I read about that somewhere. *War Illustrated,* I think.'

Tanner felt embarrassed. 'All exaggerated, I'm sure. It didn't come from me, at any rate.'

'Tanner's being modest.' Peploe smiled. 'He was given a DSO for that. His second. He has a DSO, MC and Bar, as well as a DCM and MM.'

'Brave fellow,' said Verity.

Tanner shrugged. 'I've been lucky. These things are a bit meaningless in many ways. There are lots of people who do brave things and never get given gongs.'

'I was telling my friends that I've seen you get a nine-wicket haul,' Peploe said to Verity, 'and I've enjoyed watching you play many times.'

'Thank you,' said Verity. 'I've been lucky too. To play cricket for a living is a great privilege.'

'I'll say,' said Peploe.

'Anyway,' said Verity. 'Now we know where we're heading. Do you think the Italians will have the stomach for much of a fight?'

'I hope not,' said Peploe.

'Well, I wouldn't mind some of your experience. You Rangers have seen it all, haven't you? We're all a little green in the First Green Howards. No pun intended.'

'You'll be fine,' said Tanner.

'Still playing any cricket out here?' asked Fauvel.

'A few games. There's talk of fixing up a pitch out here.'

'Out here?' said Peploe. 'But it's just sand.'

'They put coconut matting down,' said Synge. 'It's not too bad, actually. We've been challenged by the KOYLI.'

'Can we challenge you too?' said Peploe. 'The lads would love a game. Especially if you were playing, Captain Verity.'

Verity smiled. 'Tell you what. If you don't mind passing on a few tips about fighting to us new boys, I'll turn my arm over. We'll have to clear it with the colonel first, though.'

Peploe grinned. 'It's a deal.' They shook hands and went their separate ways.

'How about that?' said Peploe. 'This war really is extraordinary. I've seen ancient wonders of the world that I thought I'd never visit and now it seems I'll get to face the great Hedley Verity. It's not all bad, is it?'

The prospect of a cricket match against Verity and the Green Howards had lifted Tanner's spirits, but they were dashed again when he returned to find an order waiting for him to see Colonel Creer.

Cursing, he hurried off to Battalion Headquarters and reported to Creer's tent.

'Ah, there you are,' said Creer, as Tanner entered. The colonel was sitting behind a makeshift trestle-table desk, a hurricane lamp hanging from the central pole. He stood up and, from a bottle of Scotch, poured two measures into the tin mugs before him.

'A little *chota peg*, Tanner,' he said, passing him one of the mugs.

Tanner took it. 'Thank you,' he said.

Creer sat down, leaned back in his chair, eyed Tanner, then said, 'This is a friendly warning. Just between you and me, all right?'

Tanner sipped his whisky.

'I don't mind admitting, Tanner, that my heart sank when I discovered the arrogant little shit I had known out in India was now my A Company commander. I'm sure your heart sank too when you learned I was your new officer commanding.'

Tanner said nothing.

'I'd be within my rights to give you the chop if I so chose, but the men seem to look up to you and you have a supporter in Major Peploe. What's more, I understand you've only just rejoined the battalion. More's the pity, but there you go. So.' He clapped his hands together. 'For the time being we're stuck with each other.'

'So it seems, sir.'

'I should tell you that I don't approve of promoting people through the ranks. You may be an officer now, Tanner, but you're certainly no gentleman.'

'For God's sake,' muttered Tanner.

'I beg your pardon?' snapped Creer.

'We're trying to win a war, sir, not keep the peasants in their place.'

Creer sat back again. 'Still insolent. I wonder whether you've learned anything, Tanner. That's what I remember about you – your refusal to toe the line, and your insistence on making life difficult for others in the battalion.'

'You mean I wouldn't play to Blackstone's rules.'

'Blackstone was a very popular CSM, Tanner. A character, a real battalion man.'

'He was a bully. He was corrupt.'

'He ran the company smoothly and successfully. Everyone played the game in India – it was a way of life. Everyone but you, Tanner.'

'You're wrong, sir. He wasn't popular. The lads were just scared of him or went along with him because he had something on them. You know what peer pressure is like among young lads in the Army. He took advantage of that.'

'You're talking rot, man! Tell me what young rifleman isn't scared of their CSM.'

'Sir, in France he murdered German and British troops and two French civilians. He betrayed his men and his country. I'm glad I stood up to him all those years ago.'

'That will do, Tanner,' Creer snarled. 'You haven't changed, I see. Still as arrogant as you always were. And as disrespectful.'

'Not to those who deserve respect.'

109

'Now, listen to me,' hissed Creer. 'I want you to understand this, Tanner. I'm going to be watching you. Watching very carefully indeed. You might be the big hero around here, but I am the officer commanding now. If you cross me, or try to make life difficult, I'll see that you regret it. Is that clear?'

Tanner clenched his fists. One strike – that was all it would take: a clean, short, sharp thrust of his arm, his fist ramming into Creer's temple.

'Is that clear, Tanner?' Creer repeated.

'Crystal,' muttered Tanner.

'Good. Dismissed.'

Tanner saluted, turned and walked out.

He went slowly towards his tent, having pulled out and lit a cigarette. It was dark, but still warm, the sky bright with stars. He wondered what he should do. Request a transfer? Start again? No. That was running away from the problem and, in any case, he liked being around Sykes and Peploe and the other lads. He trusted them too. They were good soldiers – soldiers he could utterly depend on in battle. Tanner sighed and kicked the ground. *Bloody hell!* Stopping a moment, he looked around. A sea of tents, rows of faint shapes in the darkness. There was still the smell of cooking on the air, and low voices. No, he thought, he would stay. Stay and keep his head down. Look after his company, make sure they trained hard, and avoid Creer as much as possible; he would have to because he didn't trust himself with that man. And it wasn't like it had been in India. He'd been a boy, a private, the lowest of the low. Now he was a company commander, and while he did not think too much of medals, they did help. Decorated men were held in high regard by most. What was more, Peploe would always stick up for him – Creer had admitted as much. The thought cheered him. He paused to light another cigarette. So long as Peploe was second-in-command of the battalion, there was little Creer could do. Surely...

6

Friday, 9 July 1943, around seven p.m. Tanner sat on the forward deck of HMT *Dunelm,* an 11,000-ton former passenger ship, Dunkirk veteran and now troopship. On board were not only the entire 2nd Battalion Yorks Rangers but also a large number of supplies, engineers and support troops, making around twelve hundred in all. They had been at sea for four days.

Tanner was cleaning his weapons, not for the first time since leaving Port Said. It was something he had always done meticulously, no matter how bad the situation or conditions in which he found himself. His father had drummed it into him as a boy. Tanner had loved helping him clean the guns: the smell of the gun oil, the gleam of the dark metal, the sense of pride in doing a job well. And as, first, an NCO, then more recently as a commissioned officer, he had repeatedly impressed upon his men the importance of keeping weapons clean. Clean weapons, he knew, saved lives. If a rifle or Sten gun jammed, it was invariably because its user had not looked after it properly.

It was certainly true that Tanner had accrued more personal weapons than most. There was his rifle, which, now that he was an officer, he was not expected to carry; on the other hand, he had carried it, one of the pre-war Short Magazine Lee Enfield No. 1 Mark IIIs, since before sailing to Norway back in April 1940. He had had it specially fitted with mounts and pads for the Aldis scope his father had used in the last war. Having the option to snipe with accuracy from a half-decent distance had been a life-saver on numerous occasions, and he was damned if he was going to give it up now. So far, he had been careful to keep it out of sight of Colonel Creer – he felt sure that an officer carrying a rifle would be exactly the kind of thing to which Croaker would take exception. Fortunately, he reckoned there was little chance of Creer being anywhere near the front-line action so, once ashore, he could carry it on his shoulder without fear of being caught out. Until then, he had Trahair; he still felt uncomfortable having a batman, but he had to admit, a servant had his uses.

He was also reluctant to leave his MP40 behind. This was a German sub-machine gun he had picked up in Crete. Firing the same ammunition as the British Sten, it had been easy to maintain, and because the magazine could be simply removed and the metal butt folded back on itself, it could be stowed away in a rifleman's pack or, to be precise, Trahair's pack. He had thought of putting it in with his personal kit, which was wrapped up and tied with leather straps and kept with the B Echelon Administrative Platoon. Presumably, he thought, it was somewhere in the ship's hold; it would catch up with him eventually. But since they were heading into battle, what was the point of having weapons if they couldn't be used?

The rest he would carry himself. He had a small semi-automatic Sauer handgun, also German, which he liked for the ease with which the magazine could be replaced, and for its solid but light feel in his hand. That would go in his haversack. On his belt in its holster was an American .45 Colt. When he had been with the Americans in Tunisia, he had been amused by their seemingly endless fascination with German Lugers. To his mind, the Luger needed to pack a far bigger punch if it was to justify its size. It baffled him that they should be so desperate to get their hands on those German pistols when they had such a fine handgun themselves. The Colt was a little heavy, but packed one *hell* of a punch. When Tanner used a pistol, it was at close quarters, and when he fired, he wanted to make sure the enemy never had a chance to fire back. To his mind, there was no better handgun than a Colt for killing people. He'd managed to get two more – one for Peploe and another for Sykes; he now wished he'd got one for Fauvel too. The British-issued revolvers were hopeless – the last thing anyone wanted to do was fiddle about hand-loading every bullet into the chamber in the middle of a battle. Adrenalin, fear and anxiety

113

made fingers shake. A simple, easy-release magazine was far better.

Finally, he had his Italian Beretta. There was not a lot to choose between that and the MP40, but the Beretta did not pack away so easily, and Tanner preferred the more solid and comfortable wooden butt. Like the MP40 and the Sten, it also used 9mm rounds, so getting enough ammunition was not a problem. This he would wear slung on his shoulder as he stepped into the LCA, and would reclaim his rifle from Trahair the moment they were lowered onto the water. All were polished, oiled and very, very clean.

He was conscious of excited voices around him, and looked up to see men crowding on the prow of the ship and pointing.

'What have they spotted?' said Fauvel. He had been squatting next to Tanner, writing up his diary. On his other side, Sykes had been repacking his own kit.

'Sicily?' said Sykes, springing to his feet.

Tanner and Fauvel followed. There, on the distant horizon, they could see a mountain, a faint patch of white cloud around it – or was it smoke? Tanner wasn't sure.

'Etna,' said Fauvel. 'That's Mount Etna. Christ – we're nearly there.'

Tanner saw him swallow hard. 'Nerves?'

'A few.'

'We'll be fine.'

'It certainly won't be for lack of information.'

Tanner smiled. 'That's true enough.'

'Remember Norway, boss?' said Sykes.

Tanner smiled ruefully.

'A bloody shower that was,' continued Sykes. 'The bloody planners who thought that one up wouldn't have been able to organize a piss-up in a brewery. We've come a long way since then, I can tell you.'

'Glad to hear it,' said Fauvel.

Sykes was right, Tanner thought. The British Army had progressed in almost every regard. The training back in the Canal Zone had been thorough, with LCAs made available for practising beach assaults and plenty of live firing too. There had been tactical instruction, training with artillery and even armour, as well as the usual physical training, something Tanner considered important after the inactivity of the previous few weeks. He felt his men were ready. True, there were a lot of new lads – Trahair for one – but there were enough men with experience of battle to see them through. The only major disappointment, and one that had angered the men, was that they were losing their motorized status. The trucks and carriers would, for the time being, be left behind. On Sicily, in the opening moves at any rate, the Yorks Rangers would be ordinary infantry once more. Trucks would still ferry them up the line, but they would no longer live and fight in their own. It was inevitable, Tanner supposed. Sicily was different from the desert, as he well knew. On Sicily, the fighting would be different: closer, less manoeuvrable. Disappointing though it was, the decision, he knew, was the right one.

Prior to sailing, the officers had been briefed in detail. Aerial photographs of the landing beaches had been handed out, the operational plan relayed by division and brigade staff. 'You battalion and company commanders,' Brigadier Rawstorne had told them two days before departure, 'are responsible for making sure each and every one of your men knows exactly what they are supposed to be doing. Make sure you pay attention at your briefings.' Tanner had done so, largely because he understood the responsibility that rested on his shoulders and that he needed to do the best for his men, but also because he did not want to give Creer any cause for complaint; the two had kept a wary distance during their time at El Shatt Camp, but Tanner knew that Creer would welcome the chance to humiliate him.

Only once they were finally at sea were the men told their destination. No one had been surprised, despite the supposed secrecy. 'You don't say, sir! Well, there's a turn-up for the bleeding books!' The sheer scale of the enterprise, however, had dazzled them all. More than three thousand ships in two task forces, the British from Egypt, the American Seventh Army from Tunisia, had set sail, with more than four and a half thousand aircraft in support. Tanner had been staggered: in Norway, they had barely seen an Allied plane, in France only a handful. There had been Luftwaffe galore over Crete but no sign of the RAF; only in the last year had there been an obvious and growing number of Allied aircraft in the skies.

Over the ensuing three days at sea, in balmy summer weather, Tanner had done exactly as the brigadier had told them, briefing every single man

116

in A Company. Booklets, *A Soldier's Guide to Sicily*, had been distributed to each man, platoons allocated to their assault landing craft, while Tanner had also chosen the ten men who were to be Left Out of Battle. Accurately overprinted maps had been issued to all officers and senior NCOs. Sitreps had been given: the enemy forces opposing were likely to be of varied standard; six coastal divisions protected the main ports and were thought to be under-manned and poorly equipped. Four better-trained and -equipped Italian divisions, partly motorized, were based inland. There also appeared to be two German divisions. Enemy air forces were considered slight in comparison with the Allies', while British and American bombers were targeting ports and airfields in the south-east in the run-up to the invasion.

The Allied plan was to land the two armies side by side by sea in the south-east of the island, supported by two airborne divisions. The role of XIII Corps was to land on a two-division front, secure a bridgehead, advance north and capture the port of Syracuse, then the Simeto river, the larger port of Catania and the surrounding airfields. Their own role, Tanner explained to his men, was to land in the 15th Brigade sector at the small coastal town of Avola. Their part of the beach was codenamed 'How Green'. The beaches there, he told them, using aerial photographs and detailed maps, consisted of a small narrow sandy foreshore, enclosed by low cliffs leading up to grassy verges. Beyond were orchards of almond trees and the main road. Further beyond, about two miles inland, there was a high ridge, with a deep and obvious V-shaped cleft, directly west of their landing point at How Green. Capturing that would be the task of 50th Division on their left. Their own job was to get quickly off the beach, secure the road and advance north. They could expect wire and a few concrete pillboxes. These would have to be taken out. 'Learn your maps,' he told them. 'Study them and study them again.'

There were also repeated embarkation rehearsals. The men would be sent down to the bowels of the ship, then ordered up in their correct landing serials along the various companionways, narrow, hot and dimly lit passageways, and ordered to marshal alongside their allotted assault craft. Glistening, irritated soldiers grumbled but Tanner approved of such drill. It kept the men busy, but it also gave them confidence – confidence that they were prepared, trained and ready for their part in the biggest seaborne invasion the world had ever known.

For now, though, the training was over. The men had been given an extra tot of rum a couple of hours earlier, in the hope that it might help them sleep, but few could, judging by the number on deck. Tanner knew that he, for one, would not be sleeping: he was far too tense for that. He wandered away from Fauvel and Sykes and leaned on the ship's railing, staring first at Etna in the distance, then at the men around him. A number were sitting down, writing letters – to parents and girlfriends mostly, he guessed. There were a few older ones but most were boys. He wished he had someone to write to. His father had been dead eleven years now, and there was no other family; there had been a girl in Crete, but he had not heard from her since the day he had sailed away two years before. For a while he had lived with a half-French nurse in Cairo, but they had drifted apart too. She'd written a few times but the letters had dried up. What was the point? They had both known they would not see each other again. He sighed and thought of that farm in England he'd promised himself. Maybe then he'd find himself a girl – someone who would want to marry him and settle down. Perhaps then he could create a new family all of his own. Just so long as he survived the next day, then the days and weeks after that. How long would the campaign last? It was impossible to say. Perhaps he would be wounded. Perhaps he would be killed. *Christ,* he thought, it was about time. He'd cheated Death so often – one day his luck was bound to run out.

'You look wistful, Jack.'

Tanner turned to see Peploe beside him. 'Miles away,' he muttered.

'It's the waiting, isn't it?'

'Actually, I was thinking of home.'

'Feels a long way away.'

'I've had enough of fighting,' said Tanner. 'I'm beginning to want to go home.'

'You and me the same. Maybe we will after this.' Peploe paused, then said, 'Actually, Jack, I was wondering whether you'd mind coming down to my cabin a moment.'

'Of course.'

They walked back along the deck and down

one of the companionways to the officers' cabins, Tanner with his haversack and weapons slung over his shoulder.

'It's two letters,' said Peploe, as they entered his small, sparse cabin and closed the door. 'One to my parents and one to my sister, Jenny. Will you look after them? In case anything happens?'

'Of course.'

'I'm not being morbid, and I don't want you thinking I've had some ghastly premonition or anything, because I haven't. But you never know, do you? This invasion, it seems such an incredibly, overwhelmingly large enterprise, don't you think? I know nothing has been left to chance, but I've no idea what to expect. I've never been to Sicily before. Or Italy for that matter. I've looked at the photographs and read that silly little blue book they've handed out, but I still don't feel much the wiser. Do you?' He sat down on the narrow bunk and motioned to Tanner to take the single chair.

'Actually, I've been there,' said Tanner. 'To Sicily, that is.' After all, he thought, what did it matter now?

'You have? When?' Peploe looked surprised.

'Just before I rejoined the battalion. I parachuted in with a couple of Yanks – an agent and an intelligence officer.'

Peploe laughed. 'My God, you're a dark horse, Jack! What on earth were you doing?'

'I'm still not entirely sure, to be honest,' he said. 'Pre-invasion groundwork, I think.' He told Peploe about the mission: about Don Calogero, the emptiness of the countryside, the backwardness of the people, and about the escape on the

120

British submarine. 'It was only a small part of the island that I saw, but if the rest is anything like it, I'd say we haven't got too much to worry about.'

'That's good to know.'

Tanner rubbed his chin. 'Don Calogero was a strange bloke. The Yanks think he's one of the most influential men in Sicily, but looking at him you'd never think so. A Man of Honour, apparently.'

'Mafia,' said Peploe.

'You what?'

'Mafia – it's what they're known as. Mafiosi call themselves men of honour, but they're known elsewhere as the Mafia. There are strands of it in America too. Bugsy Siegel, Lucky Luciano. Gangsters, really.'

'What name did you just say?'

'Siegel. Lucky Luciano?'

'Luciano – yes, they mentioned him. Not to me, but I heard his name when they were talking. It was all Italian to me, but they definitely mentioned him. So he's a gangster, is he?'

Peploe nodded. 'Quite notorious. I have a feeling he's now in jail, though. The Mafia operate by running protection rackets. If he's head of the Mafia, your Don Calogero probably is one of the most powerful men in Sicily.'

'Jesus,' said Tanner. 'The things you have to do to win a war.'

Peploe smiled. 'To think I joined up with such strong ideals. But it's hard to keep the moral high ground when you're bombing cities, killing women and children, and cutting deals with racketeers. I still think Nazism is an evil, though,

121

that has to be wiped from the face of the Earth.'

They were silent for a moment, then Peploe said, 'We should get to the wardroom. They're serving dinner shortly. Be there early and you can choose who you sit next to.'

Tanner smiled. 'Anyone you're trying to avoid?'

Peploe grinned sheepishly. 'You know perfectly well.' He patted his legs, about to stand up. 'I do hope he behaves himself once we're ashore.'

'You'll barely see him. Croaker's a master at avoiding the action. I just hope he doesn't start issuing any stupid orders, because if there's one thing I'll put money on, it's that he'll give A Company the dirtiest jobs.' He stood up. 'I'm relying on you, John.'

'With a bit of luck, he'll just let us get on with it,' said Peploe. 'You've survived so far, Jack. I mean, it's clear as day the pair of you can hardly bear the sight of each other, but he's not actually interfered with your running of the company, has he?'

'Bastard gave me out the other day.'

'No disgrace being LBW to Hedley Verity.'

'I bloody hit it. Even Hedley said so. The only man to appeal was the bloke at mid-off. And me and young Hawke were going well. We might have won if I'd been able to stick around with him a bit longer.'

Peploe laughed. 'Jack, we'd have never won. What were Hedley's figures? Seven for eighteen. I'm sorry we lost, but to be honest, I was just happy to have the chance to play against one of the finest spin bowlers who's ever lived.'

'I suppose so,' admitted Tanner, then felt the

ship roll. Out in the narrow passageway, it rolled again. They stumbled and had to brace themselves against the wall.

'Christ, what's going on?' said Peploe. 'Is that the wind?'

Tanner shrugged. 'I suppose it must be.'

'Well, let's hope it doesn't get any worse.'

The ship seemed to be rolling more gently as they reached the wardroom. A few other officers were there, milling around the table that was freshly laid. Stewards in white coats were offering drinks when Creer arrived. He glanced at Tanner, then moved on. He had his favourites – Ivo Macdonald, the D Company commander for one, and especially Captain Masters, the battalion intelligence officer. All smiles, all charm, a gentle pat on the shoulder for Masters. Tanner sipped his tea. *Bastard.*

They sat down. The padre said grace, a mumbled 'Amen', then the chink of spoons on bowls as they began their soup.

'The Last Supper,' said George Ferguson, the C Company commander, grinning and looking around to see if others were smiling too. No one was.

Tanner sat between Peploe and Lieutenant Shopland, one of his platoon commanders.

'Funny to think that this time tomorrow we'll be eating rations again and on Sicily,' said Shopland. His expression changed as he looked around the table.

Tanner knew what he was thinking: that not all of them would be alive tomorrow evening. The ship lurched, and Creer cursed as he spilled his tea. The ship rolled again, and Tanner saw that Creer's face was now drained of colour. Staggering, the stewards managed to clear the soup bowls and reappeared soon after with plates of steaming stew. Tanner watched Creer. He could see the colonel was struggling. The ship was rolling and pitching, not violently but more than enough to make balance awkward and stomachs churn. A door banged open nearby, while the vessel creaked and groaned.

'It'll be fun loading into the assault crafts in this,' said Shopland.

'I'm sure it'll pass,' said Peploe.

'I quite like it,' said Tanner, tucking into his stew. 'There's a rhythm to it.'

Creer pushed back his chair and stood up, clutching the edge of the table. 'Excuse me, gentlemen,' he said, then rushed from the room, nearly falling as he stumbled out.

Tanner grinned, then felt Peploe's elbow in his side. 'Behave yourself, Jack,' he said quietly.

Tanner glanced at him and winked. 'He's not called Croaker for nothing,' he whispered. He wondered whether Creer would have recovered by the time they were due to get into their assault craft and head for the shore. He hoped not.

It was ten p.m. At their camp near Sortino, Captain Niccolò Togliatti sat at one of the long trestle tables in the mess tent playing cards with Riccio when he heard the faint drone of aircraft. Cocking his head, he listened. He was conscious of his heart beating faster once more.

'Not again!' groaned Riccio. 'The fifth night in

124

a row!'

Moments later, the camp siren droned. Togliatti and Riccio threw down their cards and hurried out of the tent, joining others already looking up at the dark night sky. The roar of engines grew, but it was not the camp at Sortino that these bombers were after. Nearby, anti-aircraft guns began booming, the ground pulsing with the force of the shots. More guns thundered, further away, towards Catania. Searchlights began flickering, then flares dropped from the sky and, moments later, bombs were falling.

'Cesca,' mumbled Togliatti, as the airfields of Gerbini to the west of Catania came under attack. They were not fifteen kilometres from Motta Sant'Anastasia. He was worried sick about his sister and niece. Night after night, enemy planes had bombed Catania and the Gerbini airfields. The cellars in the house were deep, he knew, but he felt so impotent, so unable to help them.

More bombers arrived, this time heading straight for Catania. The anti-aircraft guns continued to thunder, searchlights flickering across the sky, and the ground shook, even from twenty kilometres away. Orders were being shouted and men were hurrying from their tents to the slit trenches that lined the camp.

A despatch rider sped by, heading towards Colonel Rizzini's tent.

'An invasion alert?' said Riccio.

Togliatti shrugged. 'I don't know, but I'm going to check on the men.' He hurried over to the 2nd Company tents and found most of the men already taking cover in the trenches that ran alongside them. Spotting one of his platoon commanders, he was about to speak when a series of bugles sounded. The signal for immediate alert.

'All right, boys,' he called. 'Time to move. Out of the trench. Go, go, go!' He clapped his hands, urging his men to hurry, then ran to his own tent where he found Aldino, his soldier servant, hastily gathering his kit.

'Good,' he said. 'Thank you.'

'Is this it, sir?' asked Aldino.

'Your guess is as good as mine,' Togliatti replied. 'Now, let's get going.'

They ran to the parade ground at the edge of the camp. Away to the north, bombs were still exploding with faint red and orange pulses, while the anti-aircraft guns continued to pepper the sky.

Togliatti strode between his men, making sure each platoon commander and sergeant was present. *Good, all in order.* Another bugle sounded, then an officer from Battalion Headquarters hurried over to him.

'We're heading out,' he snapped. 'Taking up positions south of here.'

'When do we move?'

'Now. In company order.'

'Is this the invasion?'

'God only knows,' replied the headquarters man.

Saturday, 10 July, a quarter to two in the morning. Tanner lay on his narrow bunk in the cabin he shared with Fauvel. Despite the gnawing thought of what was to come, he had been asleep, lulled by the rolling of the ship and the decent supper inside him, but for some reason had woken suddenly. Across from him, Fauvel was reading, the light in their blacked-out cabin still on.

Fauvel, noticing Tanner, put the book down with a sigh. 'I think I've read this page eight times,' he said.

'What is it?'

'A John Buchan. I thought it might take my mind off things.'

Tanner looked at his watch. 'I reckon we'll be off soon. Best get ready.' He sat up. He was already dressed: denim battledress trousers, a map stuffed into the large pocket on the thigh, rubber-soled desert boots, ankle gaiters and khaki drill shirt. Some of the men carried the serge battle blouse, but Tanner preferred the denim version: it was lighter, for summer wear, but still plenty warm enough if need be. He put it on now, with its curved shoulder tabs, green writing on black that said, 'Yorks Rangers'. Beneath was a square black patch with a single white 'Y', the 5th Yorkshire Division symbol. Above the left breast pocket were his medal ribbons, not worn on the shirt, but the jacket only: his DSO, MC and Bar, DCM and MM, the latter two given when he had still been in the ranks. Then came the webbing: two straps through the epaulettes, ammunition pouches, belt, haversack, binoculars and his Colt .45. He grabbed his Beretta and slung it over his shoulder.

'I'm ready,' he said. 'You?'

Fauvel swallowed and nodded.

Tanner looked at his watch. *0156.* He tapped his

127

feet on the floor. His mouth felt a little dry so he took a swig of water from the mug beside his bunk. The ship still rolled and groaned, but not as much as it had earlier. It would still be uncomfortable, Tanner thought, in the flat-bottomed assault craft, pitching and lunging on the swell. He had never suffered from sea-sickness, but others did. *Not the best preparation.*

The Tannoy now blared several sharp notes, then a voice broadcast, 'Serials one to thirty, move to your waiting area. Take up position by your assault craft.'

Tanner glanced at his watch once more. *0200. Bang on.* 'Right,' he said to Fauvel. 'Let's go.'

Fauvel smiled weakly, his face ashen. They stood up, steadied themselves, and left.

The ship was in blackout so only pinpoint lights guided them along the passageways. The rolling made them bang into the walls. Men were cursing. As Tanner and Fauvel reached the door to the deck, they heard the clatter of boots on the companionways.

'Make way to your sally ports,' blared the voice over the Tannoy.

Outside, men were shouting orders. More aircraft were thundering high above them. Faint lights could be seen on the distant horizon – *fires?* – while all around them, in the moonlight, the great hulking outlines of the Allied armada, Force A of the Eastern Task Force, could be seen, one after another. *Put yourself in the shoes of the enemy,* thought Tanner. This show of might would put the fear of God into them. Surely.

Reaching the assault craft, he found Sykes and

Trahair. 'Have we got everyone, Stan?' he asked, clutching the side rail as the *Dunelm* rolled again. The rigging clanged above them as the wind gusted across the ship.

'They were all there down below, sir, but I'll do another head count.'

Tanner turned to Trahair. 'All right, Kernow?' he said. 'Got my rifle safe?'

'Yes, sir.'

'Here,' said Tanner. 'Give it to me.' He could see no sign of Creer; it was too dark in any case.

Navy personnel were handing out tots of rum. Tanner took his gladly, feeling the spirit fire his throat. Orders were now given for the men to clamber into their assault craft, which hung from the ship's side. During the repeated rehearsals, both at day and night, these steel vessels had been calmly level with the ship's deck, but now swung heavily; the men had not been prepared for this. Rope netting had been slung across, but even so, as Tanner was the first to clamber aboard, he cursed as he clutched the netting and felt his holster catch. Untangling himself, he was then swung violently against the side of the LCA, so that he gasped with pain.

The others in his Company Headquarters were clambering aboard too, cursing as they clung to the rope, then were dropped into the belly of the assault craft. Tanner moved to the bows, urging his men to find a seat on the benches that ran along each side and down the centre of the vessel. 'Come on!' He saw Brown stumble, weighed down by his heavy pack and other gear. 'Here,' he said, offering a hand and pulling the

129

corporal to his feet.

Men shouted and swore as the assault craft filled and hung there, suspended on its davits from the side of *Dunelm,* swinging precariously.

'Jesus,' muttered Sykes, stumbling down beside Tanner. 'It's not the bloody Eyeties we need to worry about it, but getting this thing into the sodding water.'

Another wave of bombers roared overhead; from the shore, still some miles away, anti-aircraft guns were pounding into the sky, gun blasts and bomb explosions mixing in a deep, dull cacophony that could be easily heard over ten miles out to sea.

Tanner counted the men. All sixteen of Company Headquarters present, plus a dozen sappers, several carrying mine-clearing explosives, and a three-man mortar crew from the Battalion Support Company. Several men clutched the cardboard cups they had been given to vomit into. Minutes passed. Impatience creeping in, the LCA still swinging in the wind. But the wind was dying down.

'That's something,' said Sykes, sitting next to Tanner at the bow. 'Admittedly, it's still blowing, but it's not a storm, is it?'

Barely had he said this than *Dunelm's* engines stopped and the LCA was lowered unsteadily to the water. Tanner saw Taffy Griffiths cross himself, and Brown clutch his rifle, his head lowered. With a smack, the LCA hit the water, clanking chains were released, the coxswain opened the engines and the craft began to move away from the ship. For a further ten minutes, they circled *Dunelm,* waiting for the other LCAs to join them, and then, at last, they were off, speeding the eleven miles towards the shore.

The invasion of Sicily had begun.

7

Saturday, 10 July, around 2.30 a.m. In Motta Sant'Anastasia, Francesca Falcone sat in the cellar of their house, clutching Cara. Opposite, Salvatore Camprese was watching her. Why had he had to come, she wondered, banging on the front door, just as the air raid sirens had sounded? She had been on her way in her night-clothes to the cellar, Cara in her arms, when she had heard him.

'Francesca! Francesca!' he had yelled. 'Are you all right? Let me in!'

'Go away!' Francesca had replied.

'Please, Francesca, let me in!' A bomb crashed nearby. 'Please, Francesca! I came to make sure you were all right. You can't turn me away now!'

And so, reluctantly, she had let him in. 'All right, but only until the raid is over. Understand?'

'Of course.'

So now she was stuck with him.

'I wish you'd let me look after you, Francesca,' he said. 'It's not right, you being here on your own with Cara in this big house. If you were to marry me, I'd be a good husband to you. I'd look after you, I'd–'

'Stop this talk, Salvatore. Not here, not in front

of Cara. I don't want to marry you. Please understand that, and don't come here again in the middle of the night.'

Several bombs seemed to land nearby, the building above them shaking as they exploded. Small bits of grit and plaster fell from the walls. Another, much louder, much closer, crash followed and Francesca felt Cara clutch her ever more tightly.

She wondered whether anything of Catania would still be standing, or any aircraft at Gerbini in flying condition.

Another crash, this time to the north of them, within the town, by the sound of it. Francesca closed her eyes, hugged Cara and felt more grit and dust fall on her. She coughed and spluttered, then Cara and Camprese were coughing too.

'Quick,' he gasped, 'put this over your mouths.' Taking a large handkerchief, he poured water from a small ewer onto it and passed it to her.

'Thank you,' she said grudgingly.

Slowly, the dust settled, and the explosions faded away. They waited a few minutes, and then the all-clear sounded.

'It's over,' said Francesca. 'You can go now.'

They dusted themselves down, then climbed the stone steps to the main part of the house.

'I only wanted to make sure you were all right,' said Camprese. 'You know how much I admire you, Francesca.' He took her hand and kissed it.

'Good night, Salvatore,' she said, opening the door. Once he had gone, she closed and bolted it, then took Cara upstairs to bed. After she had settled the little girl, she went back downstairs into the kitchen and opened the French windows onto the balcony. The air was thick with the stench of smoke and explosives. Away, towards the coast, she saw fire burning in Catania, an orange glow throbbing against the sky.

She wished the Allies would come. The waiting was so terrible. *I just want this over.* It was funny, she thought, how Niccolò cherished this place. He could have it when the war was over, if that was what he wanted, but she would not stay. She was here with Cara because she had no choice, but later, when peace returned, she would leave Sicily and small-minded men like Salvatore Camprese.

She wished her father was still alive. She had Cara, but she was lonely. She missed him. She missed Niccolò. What a terrible time to be alive, she thought sadly.

4.10 a.m. They had put to sea further out than expected – the coxswain reckoned about eleven miles – and at seven knots per hour, that meant at least ninety minutes to the shore. It was true the wind was dropping, but in a flat-bottomed assault craft even the slightest swell could be felt. Fountains of spray rained over the men as the vessel buffeted through the waves. They were all soaked. Tanner prayed his weapons would still fire; he had covered the end of his Beretta with the condom issued earlier to each man, and wrapped an oily rag around the breech of his rifle, but whether these measures would suffice, he had no idea. A number of men had vomited as the flat-bottomed boat had lurched and rolled, not into the cardboard cups but over the wooden floor. The stench of vomit, oil and salt spray was overwhelming. From where he stood, Tanner had been able to see little – only the clouds scudding across the moon – but now, more than ninety minutes into their journey, he could see the dull outline of the coast in the first thin light of dawn.

From inland, enemy artillery was firing, the shells hurtling over them. Stabs of tracer were criss-crossing from the shore and the approaching LCAs. How far now? Four hundred yards, Tanner guessed. He glanced around – assault craft either side of them, white furrows trailing behind, and way back, out at sea, the dark, distant shapes of the armada. The naval gunner in the machine-gun shelter opposite the coxswain opened fire, the sound loud and tinny. Columns of water were erupting around them – mortars, Tanner guessed. *Come on, come on.* He ducked instinctively as tracer zipped above his head. *Let's just bloody well get there.*

He turned to the men. 'Make sure your buttons are undone on your battledress.' He looked at Griffiths. 'All right, Taffy? Ready to throw your kit off if you have to?'

Griffiths nodded. Tanner couldn't decide whether he was sick or scared. Or both.

A burst of bullets clattered against the edge of the boat. Everyone ducked. Tanner looked up again. From the shore, a searchlight was switched on, but as a dozen machine-guns opened fire from the advancing LCAs, it went off again.

Two hundred yards. The first assault craft now landing, men pouring out onto the beach. Guns booming, shells screaming, the roar of the LCAs' engines. Another plume of sea-water. Tanner gasped, wiped it from his face. *One hundred yards.* More firing from the shore. Ahead, two LCAs collided, one slewing around. Tanner glanced around. Fauvel at the back, Sykes beside him. Also ready at the front were the sappers. Coils of wire on the beach and, *yes*, there was the shallow cliff. A lurch as the assault craft hit sand, the coxswain looked around, the doors swung open, the ramp dropped and Tanner ran out, dropping into water that came up to his knees.

'Come on! Come on!' he yelled, standing there, urging the men to get out. A bullet fizzed overhead, then a roar as two Italian fighter planes appeared from nowhere, no more than fifty feet above them, machine-guns clattering. Lines of bullets spat across the beach, and Tanner was conscious of several men falling. Then the planes were past, lines of tracer following them as the assault-craft gunners opened fire. Another LCA had drawn up alongside them, men pouring out. Who the hell were they? Not Rangers. Tanner now ran forward onto the beach, then yelled at his men to crouch down as the sappers fitted anti-tank mines to the wire, ran fuse back down the beach, then detonated them. A loud blast, sand and grit spewing into the air, spattering onto Tanner's helmet, and then he was on his feet again, urging his men forward, through the blasted gap, onto the shingle and clambering up the small cliff onto the ground beyond. It was flat, but small trees and bushes dotted the land in front. *Good cover.* Occasional bullets were fizzing

135

and zipping overhead, but it was hard to say where they were coming from. He held out a hand and pulled several men up, then urged them forward. 'Come on!' he shouted. 'Keep going!'

He ran forward himself, conscious of the river to his right that he'd seen on his map, and of the cleft in the ridge several miles up ahead. *Good. We're in the right place.* Somewhere to his right, guns were booming. *Where are they?* To his left, someone cried out and fell. Who was it? *Donaghue.* Not dead, but there was firing from up ahead – a farmhouse, he saw, through the trees, as Phyllis, with the radio, and Sykes scrambled down beside him, followed by two more, unfamiliar, figures.

'Who the hell are you?' said Sykes to the two men, as Tanner felt inside his haversack for his Aldis scope.

'Gulliver and Loader, sir,' said the first. 'We're from the Wiltshires.'

Tanner froze. He had known families of those names back home. *Bollocks. Not now.* Quickly, he fastened the scope. It was zeroed at four hundred yards, but no matter: at this range it would do what was required. A bullet whined overhead. Then he saw a faint orange spurt as an enemy machine-gun opened fire from a first-floor window. He glanced around: most of the men had stopped, taking cover behind the trees and shrubs. Away to their right, guns were firing again. Where the bloody hell were they?

'See him?' asked Sykes.

'Yes,' said Tanner. He lay down, and inched forward, pulling his rifle into his shoulder. Another burst of machine-gun fire, bullets spraying in a wide arc, but too high: twigs and foliage snapped as they zapped above them. Tanner peered through the scope. He could see two men beside the machine-gun, heads just showing above the windowsill. Another spurt of orange and the head juddering as the gunner fired a three-second burst. Tanner lined up his shot, cross-lines on the Italian's helmet. A small intake of breath. *Steady.* Finger around the trigger. Squeeze. The rifle cracked, Tanner felt the bolt jerk into his shoulder and saw the gunner collapse. The other man ducked as Tanner drew back the bolt, and lined up a second shot. *Show yourself.* Sure enough, a moment later, the top of the Italian's helmet reappeared. Another short intake of breath, then Tanner pressed the trigger a second time, saw blood spray into the air, then was on his feet and urging his men forward, running, then sprinting towards the house. He fired a burst from his Beretta – *thank God, it still works* – then, as he neared the house, pulled a grenade from his haversack, ran to the wall, crouched beneath a window, pulled the pin, waited two seconds and threw it in. An explosion, a cry from within, and Tanner was up, kicking open the door and spraying the room with a burst of his Beretta.

Silence. Then groaning. One Italian was crying out.

Tanner was conscious of someone beside him and half turned to see Sykes. He stepped forward, saw an Italian, coughing and spluttering but with his hands on his head. Tanner grabbed him by the shoulder and pushed past him, then walked on through into another room. Chairs and boxes lay upturned. He took the stone stairs and climbed up to the first floor.

'Anyone here?' he called. Silence. 'Stan, send a couple of lads up.'

Cautiously Tanner walked onto a landing, then into the room where the machine-gunners had been. Two men lay dead, large pools of dark blood flecked with dust spreading around their heads. A third man crouched in the corner, hands around his head. To the north, the guns were firing again. Tanner glanced out of the window. Beyond the house there was a grove of trees, then the river, but he could not see any enemy artillery. He could only hear it. He glanced down at the soldier.

'All right, son,' said Tanner, lowering his Beretta and offering a hand. The soldier looked up. A boy, thought Tanner. *Christ*. He offered his hand again. Startled, the young man got to his feet.

'It's all right,' said Tanner.

Brown now stood in the doorway. 'Jesus, sir, you nailed them all right.'

'Browner, get this lad out of here, will you?' He looked at the boy and saw the damp stain at his crotch, then went over to the two dead men, rifled through the jacket of the first, and in the breast pocket found his record book. *122nd Reggimento Costiero. 1 Compagnia. Carbone, Luigi Augusto*. Tanner looked down. Dead eyes stared up at him, so he crouched, lowered the lids, then walked out and headed back down the stairs.

The shooting had stopped and a number of his men now stood around the house. A group of

Italians was outside, hands on their heads, watched by Griffiths with a Sten gun pointed at them. As Tanner stepped out of the house, he saw Lieutenant Shopland and the rest of 1 Platoon approaching from the shore.

'We heard the shooting,' said Shopland. Sergeant McAllister was with him.

'Seems you've got it in hand, though, sir.'

'Where are the others?' Tanner asked.

'Three Platoon have landed, but I haven't seen Two Platoon yet.'

Tanner nodded, then noticed a dozen Wiltshiremen standing around too. 'What the hell happened to you?' he asked.

'The coxswain on our LCA said his compass was broke. We circled the ship, but it was dark and he lost track of the others. We ended up landing next to you,' said the man who had called himself Gulliver. Tanner saw the sergeant's stripes stitched to his shirtsleeves.

'And your platoon commander?'

''E got hit. He's being looked after down by the beach.'

Tanner grunted. 'All right. You'd better stay with us for the moment. We can get you back to the rest of your battalion later.' He looked at Gulliver. 'Where are you from, Sergeant?'

'Salisbury way, sir.'

'Yes, but where exactly?'

'Village called Alvesdon.'

Tanner pushed his helmet back and rubbed his brow. *Alvesdon.* Of all places.

'Do you know it, sir?' said Gulliver. 'Your accent, sir, doesn't sound very northern, if you

139

don't mind my saying. You're not from round there, are you?'

Tanner scowled at him. 'Never you mind.' He turned, looking for Phyllis, then spotted him squatting by a tree, wearing a headset, the radio before him. Sykes stood over him. Nearby, a short distance to the north, a volley of artillery boomed. The ground pulsed. Small arms could be heard to the south.

'Where the bloody hell are those guns firing from?' he said. 'We need to get them, Stan.'

'Agreed,' said Sykes, rolling a cigarette.

Tanner crouched beside Phyllis. 'What's going on, Siff?'

'B and C Companies are ashore, sir,' he said.

'Ask them about those guns. Suggest we take them out before pushing north towards Cassibile.'

Phyllis spoke into the radio, listened, nodded, then turned back to Tanner. 'Brigade want us to destroy the gun position, sir. Three or four one-oh-twos. Attack to go in at oh five thirty.'

Tanner looked at his watch. It was five to five and now light, the sun just appearing on the horizon out to sea. The stench of smoke and cordite still hung heavy on the air, but it felt cool and crisp. 'Have you co-ordinates?' he asked.

'Yes, sir. 700124.'

Tanner took out his map and marked the spot with a pencil, then called Shopland, McAllister and Fauvel to join him. 'We're going to take out those guns,' he told them. 'One Platoon can have this particular honour.' He looked at McAllister and Shopland. 'But Sykes here and I will be

140

coming with you.' He turned to Fauvel. 'Gav, I want you to stay here. Get these Eyetie prisoners sorted out, and try to find out where Two and Three Platoons are. When you've gathered them together, come and find us.'

'All right,' said Fauvel.

Tanner now showed them the map. There was a curving railway line a couple of hundred yards ahead and a wide river valley to their right, then a series of groves and fields. The guns were, it seemed, dug in there. 'First we've got to get past the railway. There's a bridge, but I think we should approach by heading down the river valley. We'll work out a plan of attack when we get there and see where the guns are. All right?'

'What about those Wiltshire boys?' asked Sykes.

'We'll take them,' said Tanner. 'That gives us the best part of fifty men. Should be plenty.'

They set off, spread out wide from the edge of the river valley with the groves as cover. As they neared the railway embankment, machine-gun and rifle fire sputtered, forcing the Rangers to drop down. They responded with the Bren, so Tanner, with Sykes beside him, was able to creep forward to within thirty yards of the embankment. The Bren fire seemed to have pinned the defenders down, but then a head and a barrel appeared and the enemy machine-gun opened up once more. Tanner could hear them talking, the voices rapid and urgent.

'They're panicked,' he whispered to Sykes. He glanced around. Trahair and Griffiths were on his right, while further to their left were McAllister and a section from 1 Platoon.

'Grenades?' Sykes grinned.

'I reckon,' said Tanner. He felt in his haversack and pulled one out, then held it aloft for the others to see. McAllister nodded. Bren fire chattered once more. Tanner held up his right hand. *Three, two, one.* Pull the pin, pause, then throw. Half a dozen Mills bombs flew through the air, dropped behind the embankment and then, a moment later, exploded. Already, Tanner was on his feet, charging the embankment, his Beretta at his hip. Clambering to the top, he fired a short burst, then scrambled down the other side.

Several Italians lay dead, one with a severed leg, which lay some yards away; more were wounded. One pointed his rifle at Tanner but, seeing his comrades raising their hands, lowered it hastily. Others were running, disappearing into the groves. Most, however, stood there with hands raised. More Rangers arrived, cresting the railway embankment. Ammunition boxes and weapons lay on the ground; an abandoned mortar stood a little further on. The position, Tanner reckoned, had been held in company strength at least – some hundred and more men – but they had shown little stomach for a fight. It was hardly surprising, he thought, to look at them: shabby uniforms, most either middle-aged or young boys, and clearly poorly trained – their shooting had been high, there had been little sign of any fire support, and the panicked chatter had suggested a lack of clear thinking. He wondered what was going on to the south, and further along the railway embankment, where small-arms fire could still be heard. Well, he thought, that wasn't his concern just now; his priority was those guns, which were still firing. And it was now after five.

'Jesus, will you look at this lot!' Sykes whistled.

'Come on, Stan,' said Tanner. 'We need to get a shift on. Iggery, eh?' He strode along the top of the embankment. 'Jesus,' he said, looking at all the prisoners. 'Just what we bloody well need.' Then he saw more Rangers emerging into the clearing before the embankment. 'Good,' he said. 'They can deal with this lot. Now let's go. Jaldi.'

Sykes put his fingers into his mouth and blew a short, sharp whistle, then signalled with his arm, urging the men towards them. Tanner had already set off, running at a jog towards the river. Pausing briefly at the bank of the shallow valley, he looked around, heard the guns firing again in turn, and this time saw smoke and dust rising from beyond a dense citrus grove that stood on the far side. How far? Four hundred yards? Five? No further, at any rate.

The valley was no more than fifty yards wide, and he scrambled down to the water's edge. The river gurgled over a rocky bed, easily fordable. Having waved to his men to follow, Tanner waded across, then ran along the far bank. After a couple of hundred yards, he clambered up it and saw he had reached the edge of the citrus grove. The guns fired again, the din much closer now so that he could smell the whiff of cordite on the air. Half crouching, half running, he moved from orange tree to orange tree until he could see the guns clearly. They were dug in across a grass field that was interspersed with patchy groups of almond trees. They had been sited well, Tanner had to admit, with netting around them and making good use of the trees. No doubt they were well hidden from the air. With his field glasses, he examined the site carefully. There were three of them, about fifty yards apart, pointing south-east, back towards the invasion beaches, rather than out to sea. Gun crews stood around each, and although there were no obvious communication trenches connecting them, there was a forward screen of slit-trenches manned by infantry. He also counted four machine-guns. The field, however, was lined by a dry-stone wall; the newly risen sun was gleaming off the limestone. Tanner smiled to himself. *Good*.

Sykes was now beside him. Tanner signalled to the others to push back, well out of sight. Then, beckoning to Sykes, he moved back to the edge of the river valley, well out of view of the guns. The men were all there, clutching their weapons, their uniforms already beginning to dry.

'Right,' he said. 'It's getting lighter by the minute and that sun is now shining directly in those Eyetie gunners' eyes. We're going to split. Lieutenant Shopland, I want you with One Section, and the Wiltshires, to spread along the front edge of the grove here and fire at forty-five degrees across the front of the site. There are at least four Eyetie MGs screening forward, but if the others we've seen are anything to go by, they tend to fire high. So you keep low, all right? Your job is to draw the fire. The rest of us will skirt back along the river. Then, using the wall behind the guns, we'll take them out in turn.'

He glanced at his watch. It was twenty past five.

144

'Questions?' he said.

'When should we start firing?' Shopland asked.

'At oh five thirty,' said Tanner. 'In ten minutes. Now let's go. Iggery.'

8

Fifty miles away, as the crow flew, Lieutenant Colonel Charlie Wiseman was coming ashore in a DUKW amphibious vehicle, conscious that the last time he had been on Sicilian soil he'd left the north coast in virtual silence in the early hours of the morning, slipping away in a canvas canoe to a waiting British submarine. Now it was D-Day, on the south coast, and he was part of the largest seaborne invasion the world had ever known. And he was landing in anything but silence as shells hurtled over and exploded, engines roared, and small-arms fire chattered.

That he was there at all seemed like something of a miracle after the previous day's storm. Wiseman had been on USS *Monrovia*, Admiral Hewitt's flagship for the Western Task Force, but even that vessel, a large, solidly constructed attack-transport ship, had rolled and pitched in the storm. Wiseman had watched from the bridge, the normally still and tranquil blue of the Mediterranean transformed into dancing white tops. The flat-bottomed LCTs, the larger landing craft carrying the invasion force's tanks and motor transport, had bounced on the bucking waves like corks. They had been nicknamed 'seagoing bed pans', which had seemed a neat joke, but on that crossing of the Mediterranean, Wiseman had wondered whether 'barely seagoing coffins' might have been a better description.

The mood on board *Monrovia* had grown increasingly tense as the afternoon had worn on. General Patton had repeatedly grilled Lieutenant Commander Steere, his meteorologist, for updates. 'Still convinced this storm's going to blow through, Steere?' he had growled, at around five in the afternoon, as Steere had once again laid out his weather charts.

'It will calm down, sir,' Steere had said.

'It'd better,' Patton had replied.

And so it had, but not before the airborne troops had been flown over. Wiseman had watched them, alongside Patton, Admiral Hewitt and General Lucas, a vast stream of Dakotas and gliders, dark against the moonlit sky. Wiseman had wondered how successful the drop would be. He remembered parachuting into Villalba from one lone aircraft on a clear and windless night. But what effect would this wind have? Steere had recorded gusts of up to thirty-seven knots, and while it had died down a little by the time the airborne troops went over, it was still plenty strong enough to scatter those paratroop divisions – one American and one British – to the four winds. Those boys had a key role: to secure vital road junctions to the north of Gela in an effort to block any Axis counterattacks, and to capture two key bridges along the east coast on the British invasion front to the south of Catania and Syracuse. Whether they would or not, only time would tell, but Wiseman's earlier confidence had been dashed somewhat. He knew he could rely on Don Calogero Vizzini to ensure Sicilian resistance was limited, but he could not control the first forty-eight hours of the invasion – and that was the critical part. So long as both British and American forces were able to establish firm bridgeheads, the Axis would never hold the island. Fate, however, had dealt them a cruel hand: who would have thought there could be such a wind in the middle of summer?

At least Patton had remained resolute, just as he always did. The general had given a rousing speech a minute after midnight, when, in *Monrovia's* stateroom and before his entire staff, the First Armoured Corps flag had been lowered and replaced by the new Seventh Army standard.

'Gentlemen,' Patton had said, 'I have the honour to activate the Seventh United States Army. This is the first army in history to be activated after midnight and baptized in blood before daylight.'

Wiseman had always reckoned he wasn't easily moved, but at that moment he'd felt pretty damn proud. A freshly promoted lieutenant colonel, he was a key member of the new Seventh Army's G2 Intelligence team with a vital role to play as Allied forces landed in Hitler's Fortress Europe. It was an historic moment and he was at the very heart of the invasion, a witness to great events.

Patton had insisted on radio silence. He had wanted surprise. Admiral Hewitt, on the other hand, had argued for a heavy naval bombardment first, pointing out that not even the dopiest Italian could fail to suspect an Allied invasion after the aerial battering they had received the previous week.

'Horseshit,' Patton had replied. 'The enemy can't keep alert all the time. We're going to land and all of a sudden we'll be at their necks.'

Patton had got his way, but radio silence had meant that as dawn had begun to break it had been hard to know what was happening. Patton had no idea how the airborne troops had fared, or whether the 1st Division were securing a toe-hold on the beaches. Earlier, they had watched fields of ripening corn burn, the flames visible from *Monrovia* six miles out at sea. But now that day was dawning, they could not see what was happening on the beaches. Patton had sent Wiseman, one of his senior intelligence officers, to find out.

As he came ashore, Wiseman marvelled at the din. Guns boomed, shells exploded, trucks and tanks rolled onto the beach, small arms rang out and, above it all, men were yelling orders that few had much chance of hearing. 'Get your ass to Gela, Wiseman,' Patton had told him, 'and then report back to me exactly what the hell is going on.' *Complete chaos is what's going on,* thought Wiseman, as the DUKW drove, with a grinding of gears and a belch of thick smoke, out of the water and onto the sand.

He had never seen anything like it. Enemy mines had closed Yellow and Green Beaches directly in front of the town, so that at Red Two, where he had come ashore, there was appalling congestion. The sea was thick with LSTs milling about, unable to get close enough to the shore, and overturned landing craft floating or jutting out of the shallow surf. Debris floated on the surface: boxes, packs, dead Americans. On the beach itself, troops hung about in the dunes, unsure what to do. As Wiseman jumped onto the sand, an explosion erupted not fifty yards away on the beach. He ducked instinctively, saw a rolling ball of flame and bits of dark metal being hurled into the sky – another DUKW being blown to pieces on an anti-tank mine. Further along, a large part of the town's pier had been destroyed, while a number of the houses that lined the seafront had been reduced to rubble. Out at sea, ships were still bombarding the coast, the shells screaming overhead and landing with shattering explosions.

An LST was now grounded and lowering its ramp. Wiseman watched as Sherman tanks rumbled forward. Elsewhere a number of rubber dinghies were ferrying troops from a grounded assault craft. Desultory small-arms fire rang out, mostly from GIs in the dunes taking pot-shots at imaginary and real Italians. He saw a dead GI on the sand, the man's guts spread out underneath him, then spotted a group of medics tending several men.

He walked on, up into the dunes, where he found a number of troops from the 16th Infantry looking anxiously towards the town and occasionally taking shots.

'What the hell's going on?' he said, standing there, above them.

'Eyetie snipers, sir,' said one of the men, a young lieutenant. 'We're pinned down.'

Wiseman could see plenty of houses, many now destroyed or damaged but no sign of any Italian troops. 'Don't you think you ought to lead your men forward, Lieutenant?' he asked. 'Get them off the beaches and take the town.'

At that very moment, Wiseman felt something strike his helmet and the next thing he knew he was on the ground, lying on his back, staring at the sky and conscious of something thick and wet running down the side of his face.

'My God, sir!' shouted the lieutenant. 'Medic!' he yelled. Several pairs of eyes were now staring down at Wiseman. Someone was fumbling at the strap of his helmet, then pulling it clear. A field dressing was ripped open and placed against his head.

I've been shot in the head, Wiseman thought, but he could still see, could still hear. Or was he dead already? Was this what it was like when you died? With his right hand he pinched his leg, felt it clearly, and realized he was not dead. But how could that be? He started to push himself up.

'Steady, sir,' said someone. 'Take it easy.' A hand was still pressing a bandage to his head.

'It's all right,' said Wiseman. 'I'm OK. Someone tie this bandage around my head, then let me get up.' He sat up, conscious of a medic hurriedly wrapping the bandage around him, then picked up his helmet. Sure enough, there was a hole, just to the side, and as he turned it over, something fell out, something small and dark. Dropping the helmet, he picked up the small object. It was the remains of a bullet. Now he looked at the inside of his helmet and took out the liner. A line had

150

been scored all around it, like the thread of a screw.

'I'll be damned,' he said, and began to laugh.

'What's so funny, sir?' asked the lieutenant.

'A minute ago, son, I thought I was dead. But it seems I've been shot in the head and lived to tell the tale. That bullet hit my helmet, went round and round between the steel and the liner, then ran out of steam. Cut me bad, but I can live with that.'

The lieutenant whistled. 'You've the luck of the devil, sir.'

The medic shook his head in wonder. 'God was smiling on you, sir. He saved you for something, all right.'

I wonder. Maybe He did. He wiped his bloodied brow with the sleeve of his jacket, then glanced at his watch. It was 5.25 a.m.

Tanner led his assault group of some two dozen men back along the river, then crouching, hurried along the far side of the wall. The guns were still booming at intervals. The dense orange grove in front of the battery had given way to patchy olives and gum trees, which extended beyond the field where the 102s were dug in, offering further cover.

Pausing, Tanner glanced at his watch again – just three minutes until Shopland's men opened fire. Then he turned to McAllister. 'Take one of the Brens and head on until you're level with the second gun. The other we'll set up here.' He looked at the rest of the men, squatting around him. 'When the others on the far side open up,

151

give them several long bursts. I'll try to take out the officers. Then, using the trees as cover, we'll charge them. All right?' Nods from the men. 'Good,' said Tanner. 'Now go.'

He watched McAllister's men scurry off as he gripped his rifle, and then looked around for a good spot from which to see the enemy. His Aldis scope was still attached to his rifle but, with the sun still low in the sky and shining directly at them, he had to make sure that the lens did not glint and give them away.

Moving a few yards along, he stopped by a thicket of broom bushes, which he hoped would offer some cover. The nearest gun was about seventy-five yards away. His rifle at his shoulder, he scanned for any obvious officers or NCOs. It was hard to tell, thanks to the cover of the netting and the trees, but he could see one man standing to the right of the gun, wearing knee-length leather boots and what looked like a smarter uniform than the others.

Got to be an officer. He lined up the shot. The man stood stock-still. Two loaders were putting a shell into the breech of what Tanner guessed was a 102mm anti-aircraft and coastal-defence gun. The officer raised his hand, then brought it down. As the gun fired, Tanner squeezed the trigger, felt the kick of the butt into his shoulder and watched the man drop to the ground. For a moment, none of the gunners noticed, the sound of the rifle shot blotted out by the blast of the big gun, but then they spotted him lying there. Tanner watched them hurry over, looking around frantically – as Bren and rifle fire opened up from the far side of the field. Several men fell. He heard the reply from the Italian machine-gunners and then, close by, bursts of more Bren. Tanner found another target, squeezed, saw the man twist and drop, then fired again, this time missing. Another long burst of the Bren, and now Tanner swung his rifle across his shoulder, grabbed his Beretta, brought a spare magazine from his pouch and leaped over the wall, glancing either side of him briefly to see the others were following.

A bullet fizzed nearby, but he kept sprinting towards the gun. Several men already lay sprawled beside it, but as he neared them he opened fire with a second's burst. He was conscious of an ammunition pit, of upturned wooden boxes. Netting spread between the trees, the morning sunlight pouring through it; bullets spat, twigs and branches snapping. A figure appeared. Tanner opened fire, feeling the Beretta judder. Pulling a grenade from his haversack, he ran to the front of the gun, pulled the pin, dropped it down the barrel and ran clear. A moment later, a dull crack, smoke poured from the end of the barrel, and suddenly he was conscious of men either side of him, Sykes with his Thompson, and Brown, his rifle raised to his shoulder.

Tanner ran on, changing his magazine as he did so. Suddenly he was into the clear, out of the trees, the light bright. Figures running, but then cut down by fire from the almond grove. He saw an Italian bring a Beretta to his hip, but Sykes got him with a burst from the Thompson. A volley of machine-gun fire zipped by, too high, but Tanner still ducked and ran on, and then they were at the second gun. One dead – no, two. The rest had fled.

Tanner paused, crouched by the wheels of the gun, gasping. The firing had suddenly lessened and then he heard voices shouting, '*Ci arrendiamo! Ci arrendiamo!*'

'I think they're throwing in the towel, boss,' said Sykes, peering around the edge of the gun. Tanner got back to his feet and, with his Beretta drawn into his shoulder, carefully moved around the gun. Ahead, in the slit trenches screening the guns, men were standing with their hands in the air. Shopland and the others were emerging from the grove, while McAllister and several other Rangers hurriedly approached the third 102mm. Several Italian gunners emerged into the clear, hands on their heads.

Tanner slung his Beretta onto his shoulder, pushed his helmet back and wiped his brow, then took his water bottle and drank.

'Job well done.' Sykes grinned.

'Any casualties on our side?' Tanner asked.

'Didn't see any, although it would be a miracle if not. A fair amount of lead flying around.'

Tanner took out a bar of chocolate and snapped off a chunk, then walked towards the third gun. 'I put a grenade down the first,' he said to Sykes, 'but we'll leave the other two. They might come in useful.'

He walked into the open, bathed in warm sunlight, took out a cigarette and lit it. It occurred to him he should report in so he beckoned Phyllis over. 'Can you give me a sitrep, Siff?'

'Yes, sir,' said Phyllis. He was carrying the No.

154

46 set strapped to his back. He bent down, eased it off his shoulders and onto the ground. With the headset on, he called up the battalion.

'Hello, Buster, this is Charlie,' he said. A pause, then his face brightened. 'Roger,' he said. 'All three enemy guns captured, repeat, all three guns captured.' Another pause. 'Roger, understood. Roger. Over and out.'

'Well?' said Tanner.

'A, B and C Companies all safely ashore, sir. D Company landing shortly.'

'What about Battalion Headquarters?'

'Not sure, sir. We're to advance on Cassibile.'

Tanner nodded. Cassibile. One of the day's objectives – a small town a couple of miles north of How Green where they had landed. He glanced at his watch and saw it wasn't even six o'clock. It felt like it had been a long day already. They had landed, overrun enemy resistance, captured at least a hundred prisoners and taken out three 102mm coastal guns.

And now they had to capture Cassibile.

9

Saturday, 10 July, around six a.m. Captain Niccolò Togliatti took the cup of coffee Aldino offered him and gazed out at the tranquil sea. It seemed scarcely possible after the high winds of the previous day. Dust had whipped into their eyes, several tents had been blown away, and branches had split from the trees, yet now the sky was clear, the sea as smooth as glass, the air dry and still. Surely, he had thought last night, the invasion alert would prove yet another false alarm, but there, out to sea, clearly visible though his binoculars, was a monstrous Allied fleet.

The sight confirmed his worst fears. How many ships were out there? Hundreds, if not thousands. He wondered what General Guzzoni and those running Italy's war really believed. Could they honestly think it possible to throw the Allies back into the sea? There were some quarter of a million in the Italian Sixth Army, but while that was no small number, a large proportion were either too young or too old to be front-line soldiers. Many men in his own 2nd Company were twitchy. Twitchy and under-equipped. There were only nine Bren light machine-guns across the three platoons, not the twelve they were supposed to have. The Support Company was, on paper, supposed to have eighteen 45mm mortars, but there were only twelve. The rifles issued to the men were mixed: some were 7.35mm calibre, others were 6.5mm, underpowered. There were not enough of either, so three men in each platoon had been given 6.5mm carbines, which were even less effective than the longer-barrelled rifles. Two sizes of ammunition caused problems, and were easy to mix up, but Colonel Rizzini, the battalion commander, had insisted that both calibres be spread across each section and platoon rather than allocating one platoon the 7.35 and another the 6.5. 'It is not fair to leave any one platoon underarmed,' he had said.

'It would be bad for morale.'

Togliatti reckoned the colonel had a point, but on the other hand, accidents involving the wrong ammunition – as had happened, fatally, a week earlier – did little to improve morale. It did not help that most of his men were reluctant soldiers with no combat experience – the majority of those who had fought in North Africa had been forced to surrender and were now languishing in Allied prisoner-of-war camps. Most of those in Russia had been killed or captured. Only a lucky few, like himself and Riccio, had been wounded and evacuated home. Spared to fight another day.

The position they had taken up in the night was, however, a good one. Straddling the winding road that led north, towards Catania, they were perched on a low ridge that overlooked the coast, a few kilometres to their left. A number of concrete bunkers and blockhouses had been built on either side of the road and above, as the ground rose to a high and imposing rocky ridge. These were connected by zigzagging trenches. There were machine-gun nests and mortar pits, while in front were coils of wire and even a few anti-tank and anti-personnel mines.

Togliatti stood beside one of the blockhouses and glanced to the sea, then back down the road, to the south. The line of fire was clear, while the blockhouse tucked in behind a small jutting promontory a little way above had even clearer views of the advancing enemy. All in all, he reckoned, this was a good defensive position. But so what? What could they do? Hold off the enemy's advance forces. And then what? The enemy would bring in reinforcements, call in the guns and their overwhelming air power, which Riccio had told him about and which Togliatti had seen this past week. Something was still smoking near Catania, a vivid reminder that Allied bombers had pounded the city yet again. He could hear naval guns booming in the distance and aircraft engines from somewhere to the south.

So they would fight, for an hour, a day, maybe even two, holding off the Allied advance, only to retreat, or even surrender, the dead and wounded lying all around. Togliatti rubbed his eyes. What was the point? Wouldn't it be better to hoist the white flag as soon as the first Allied troops arrived? *Yes, of course it would.* And yet he knew he would not. Honour would not allow it.

6.20 a.m. A Company of the 2nd Battalion, Yorks Rangers, was now approaching the small town of Cassibile. Captain Fauvel, with 2 and 3 Platoons, had joined them at the enemy gun site and they had cut across a series of large, dense orange groves to join the road clearly marked on their maps that led from How Green beach directly to the town.

Tanner had expected to find a column of Rangers already marching down the road, but it was empty; from the direction of the beaches, distant shell and small-arms fire could be heard, but it seemed unlikely that the Rangers were still caught up in the fighting.

'Where the bloody hell is the rest of the battalion?' he said to Fauvel and Sykes, as they reached the dusty road that led to Cassibile.

'Maybe they're already there,' said Fauvel.

'No,' said Tanner. 'Look at the road. You'd see a mass of boot prints if they were.'

'Fair point.' Fauvel looked back down the track as the platoons emerged onto the edge of the road.

Tanner was gazing towards Cassibile. Citrus groves lined either side of the road, which ran dead straight for about two hundred yards and then veered sharply to the right, heading directly into the town. He signalled to the men to continue and they marched on. All seemed quiet, apart from occasional birdsong, the air still between the dense groves. Not a soul could be seen. Tanner gripped his Beretta.

Suddenly an Italian fighter plane swooped over them from the north, low, and opened fire, machine-gun bullets peppering the ground in two lines. Tanner dived into the trees, then, as it passed, hurried back out again and saw it climbing and banking towards the ridge away to the west.

'Bastard!' he muttered, then ran down the road. 'Anyone hit?' he called. 'Anyone hurt?'

A number had been struck by stone splinters, but only two had been hit by the Macchi's bullets. One, a private in 3 Platoon, was already dead, while the other lay bleeding by the side of the road, his mates desperately trying to staunch the flow of blood from his stomach.

It was Corporal Baxter, one of Lieutenant Harker's section commanders. Blood was trickling from his mouth and his hands were red where he had clutched his wound. His eyes were wild, his lips trembling.

'All right, Bill,' said Tanner. 'Steady there. We'll have you sorted in no time.'

Sergeant Hepworth squatted beside him, ripping open another field dressing.

'Mother,' called Baxter. He suddenly gripped Hepworth's arm. 'I don't want to die, Hep. Not here. Don't let me die.'

'Course I won't, Bill,' said Hepworth.

Tanner heard the sound of an aero engine and then the Macchi was over them again, but this time heading out to sea. They all ducked, but the Italian fighter was swiftly followed by two Spitfires, blazing machine-gun and cannon fire. A loud crack, then an explosion. The men cheered.

'He's gone into the sea, sir,' said one of the men.

'Serves him bloody well right,' muttered Tanner, then looked down at Baxter. The colour had drained from his face, replaced by a waxy white that Tanner knew only too well. Baxter began to spasm.

'All right, Bill, all right, lad,' said Hepworth. Baxter's hand released its grip, his arm dropping to his side, then he gurgled, let out one last gasp and died.

'Damn it all!' Hepworth cursed. 'He was a bloody good man, was Bill.'

Tanner patted Hepworth on the shoulder. 'I'm sorry, Hep.'

Hepworth stood up, walked away and kicked the ground. 'I've seen too much of this, sir. I'm

160

sick of it. Christ, I'm only bloody well twenty-two. I should be out chasing girls, not watching me mates bleeding to death in front of me.'

Tanner put an arm round his shoulders. 'Come on, Hep. It's hard, I know, but you're a sergeant now. You've got your men to think about. They look up to you.' He took out one of his American Camels and handed it to him. 'This will all be over soon enough. You'll still have plenty of time to chase all the girls you ever wanted.'

Hepworth nodded. 'Sorry, sir.' He drew on the cigarette.

'And here,' said Tanner, passing him his hip flask. 'Yankee whiskey. Have a sip.'

'Thanks,' said Hepworth. 'I'm all right. I'm just sorry about Bill. He was a pal.'

Tanner left him and hurried back down the road, urging the men to their feet as he passed. He saw the two Wiltshiremen, Gulliver and Loader, nudge one another and nod in his direction. *Jesus, that's all I need.* The last thing he wanted was them gossiping. He hoped that Cassibile would be easily taken, that they might then get the Wiltshiremen back to their own unit without delay. At the head of the column, he found Fauvel and Sykes waiting for him.

'We've had a dekko,' said Sykes. 'The town's just around this corner up ahead. A straight road heading right through it, houses and buildings either side. An old-fashioned linear town, boss. Seems quiet enough.'

'Too quiet?' asked Tanner.

'I wouldn't say so. If I was an Eyetie, and there was an invasion on my doorstep, I reckon I'd get

161

inside and lock the door.'

'What about either side of the town?'

'Fields,' said Fauvel, 'with stone walls. A few olives, but no more citrus groves. Enough cover, though.'

Tanner nodded. 'All right. But we're going to do this by the book. Call the platoon commanders, will you, Stan?'

Sykes hurried off and returned a few minutes later with Shopland, Harker and Braithwaite.

'Right,' said Tanner, clutching his map. 'Cassibile looks quiet enough, but we're doing this properly. One Platoon will go around the left-hand side of the town, Two Platoon the right. Three Platoon can approach the main road through. I want each platoon split into covering groups and clearing groups. Company HQ can provide the fire section. We'll set up at the edge of the town covering the main road through. Any idea where the church is?'

'About seventy-five yards on the left once you enter the town,' said Fauvel. 'You can see it from just around that corner up ahead.'

'Good. That's got to be One Platoon's priority.' He turned to Shopland. 'I'll lead with you, Jim.' To Sykes, he said, 'Company HQ will also provide an ambush group. Stan, you can lead that. Take Griffiths with the Bren and the Wiltshiremen. Head around the town and set up at the far end covering any line of retreat.'

'Yes, sir,' said Sykes. 'I'll get going right away.'

'Stan?'

'Sir?'

'Keep those boys from the Wiltshires in order,

all right?'

'Of course, sir.'

Sykes whistled to Griffiths, called over the dozen men from the Wiltshires, then looked at his watch. 'What time?'

'Oh six fifty,' said Tanner. 'We'll go in then. That gives us fifteen minutes. Enough time for you?'

'Should be. It's not far.'

'Good. Now get going.'

He watched Sykes's group hurry off into the groves, then turned back to the others. 'Now, listen,' he said. 'Chances are, the town's undefended. So don't let your men start hurling grenades about and firing at anything that moves. Civvies are civvies, not enemy soldiers.' He turned to Fauvel. 'I want you to stay with the fire group.'

'Right,' said Fauvel. 'There's a two-storey barn right at the edge of the town. Looks right down the main street.'

'Perfect. Get that covered. That will be the killing ground if it comes to it.'

Leaving his rifle with Trahair and the fire section, Tanner led 1 Platoon into the town, split into sections spaced apart and on either side of the street. The first houses were low, one-storey buildings. There was graffiti written on the wall of one: a painted stencil of Mussolini with the word 'Vincere' underneath, but a cross had been splashed across it in red paint and the words 'Cazzo Mussolini'.

'What does that mean?' said McAllister.

'I'll tell you one day when you're old enough,'

163

Tanner replied.

They walked on cautiously. Up ahead, a dog wandered into the road, paused, barked a couple of times, then trotted out of view. Another low building. The shutters were back and Tanner saw an elderly couple cowering inside. Suddenly a door opened, and a middle-aged man stepped out almost in front of Tanner. He pointed his Beretta at the man, who immediately thrust his hands into the air.

'*Non sparare! Non sparare!*' exclaimed the man. '*Noi siamo gente pacifica qui!*'

'What's 'e saying?' said McAllister.

'Don't shoot,' muttered Tanner, then looking at the man he said, '*Soldati? Italiano soldati?*'

'No, no!' He pointed repeatedly towards the far end of the town, stabbing the air for emphasis. '*Nella caserma.*'

'What?' said Tanner, irritation in his voice.

'*Caserma,*' said the man again. '*Nella caserma. Soldati. Ca-serm-a.*'

'It's bloody Eyetie gibberish,' said McAllister.

'He means the barracks, I think,' said Tanner. '*Kaserne* is German for barracks. Is it the same in Italian?'

McAllister shrugged. Tanner looked across at Shopland, whose section had halted on the other side of the street and was watching the exchange. He turned back to the Italian man. 'What about the church? The *chiesa? Soldati in chiesa?*'

'No, no,' said the man, then jabbed his hand towards the far end of town once more.

Tanner sighed, then called Shopland across, who glanced up the street, and hurried over.

164

'This bloke is saying there are troops at the far end of the town. I think he said there are some barracks.'

'How do we know he's telling the truth?'

'We don't. But we've got this place covered, and if he is, Sykes might not have enough men so I'll hurry up the road with Mac, Three Section can clear the church, and you can get the rest of the platoon to move smartish down this street.'

'All right. It certainly seems quiet enough.'

Tanner patted him on the shoulder, then said, 'Come on, Mac, iggery, all right?'

They hurried off, past the church, half walking, half jogging, turning and watching carefully. Behind them, more Italians were emerging from their houses as the Rangers passed. Not a shot had been fired. Inexplicably, Tanner felt his heart beating faster. He gripped his Beretta tightly. He could see the end of the town, the last of the buildings. A small place, just a few streets wide, like something out of a western he'd watched at the cinema in Cairo. A few shops, still shut before the day's trade, some houses and a church and not much more. *Too quiet.* Where the hell was Sykes?

They were now at the end of the town, level with what appeared to be the last house. There was an alleyway, then just one more long, low building, boarded up, covered with dust, just a few yards ahead, and what appeared to be open country beyond. Tanner looked down a narrow alley and movement caught his eye. Immediately crouching, he looked more carefully. It was Hepworth, lying on the ground. Tanner whistled softly and saw him turn, then point. *Up ahead.*

'What?' Tanner mouthed.

Suddenly there was a loud explosion. Tanner jolted, instinctively pressing himself against the wall. Recovering his composure, he glanced at Hepworth again, saw him rise and, with several others, move forward.

'Bloody hell!' called McAllister, behind him. 'What's going on, sir?'

'Follow me and we'll find out,' Tanner called back.

He ran on to the end of the low building, then paused and peered around it. Smoke was rolling upwards into the air, debris and grit clattering down. Faintly, through the smoke, Tanner could see several rows of wooden huts, then figures emerging, dark shapes escaping the smoke. Bren and rifle fire opened up and now the men were shouting, stumbling and falling.

'Come on,' said Tanner, waving McAllister and the others forward. He ran, then saw more men staggering out as the smoke cleared, their arms held high.

'*Ci arrendiamo!* We surrender!' shouted an Italian.

'Cease fire!' yelled Tanner. He waved to McAllister to fan out with his men. 'Cease fire!'

An Italian officer stumbled towards him, coughing, hands still raised.

Tanner waited, watching. He could not understand why the barracks had not been marked on their maps, not picked out by those examining the stream of detailed air-reconnaissance photographs. How many men were based here? There

166

were two rows of low wooden huts; a company at least.

The Italian stood before Tanner, straightened his tunic, saluted, then handed over his pistol.

'I am Captain Angelo Brasco,' he said, in faltering English. 'I have the honour to be commander of the Third Company of the 207th Coastal Regiment.'

'Honour,' muttered Tanner. 'It's all you bloody Italians ever talk about. Didn't fancy much of a fight, then?'

'I see no point in needlessly wasting the lives of my men, Captain.'

'All right,' said Tanner, conscious of Shopland standing beside him. 'Your surrender is accepted. Please order your men to lay down their weapons, then form up here. Detail a party to attend to the dead and wounded if you wish.' He turned to Shopland. 'You're in charge of watching over them here, Jim, all right?'

'Yes, sir,' said Shopland.

Tanner turned back to Brasco, who saluted.

'Carry on, Captain,' Tanner said, still holding Captain Brasco's pistol, a semi-automatic Beretta, then turned. Where the hell was Sykes? Two of the huts were burning fiercely, while a gum tree overlooking the barracks had also caught fire. Spotting Hepworth, he walked over to him. 'Seen the CSM, Hep?'

'He's rounding up Eyetie prisoners, sir.'

'So what the hell happened?'

'It was the CSM, sir.'

Sykes was now walking towards them, grinning.

'I'd never have guessed,' Tanner replied. 'All

right, Hep, tell Lieutenant Harker to take his platoon back through the town and inform Captain Fauvel what's going on. And well done. Good work here.'

When Hepworth had hurried off, Sykes approached Tanner and said, 'Some of those Eyeties were still in bed!'

'I suppose it is quite early.'

'How can they not have heard what's going on, though? D'you think it'll always be this cushy?' He pushed his helmet to the back of his head.

Tanner shrugged. 'God knows. We were told these coastal divisions were likely to be a bit piss-poor, weren't we? What happened, Stan?'

Sykes had begun rolling a cigarette. 'Well, we got here without being spotted, no problem. Plenty of cover – walls, shrubs, trees. Then we spotted these Eyetie bashas here. To be honest, I thought they might be some kind of farm, but then we saw some guards out front. They was watching some planes and occasionally pointing out to sea, but otherwise just standing out front doing sweet Fanny Adams. So I dug out a stick of dynamite, got the boys ready, and lobbed it towards the end of the huts. Then, whoomp! The Eyeties have the worst wake-up call of their lives and we nail the lot.'

'You made me nearly jump out of my skin.'

'Sorry, boss.'

Tanner grinned and patted him on the back. 'Well done, Stan. Good work.'

'So what do we do now?'

'Not sure. Where are bloody B and C Companies? I thought they'd landed just behind us.'

'Busy corralling prisoners?'

'Well, I wish they'd get a shift on.' He looked at his watch. It was only a little after seven. 'I'd better find Captain Fauvel and get Siff on the radio again.' He scratched his cheek as one of the burning huts collapsed. 'To be honest, I want to get rid of those Wiltshire boys, too.'

'Actually,' said Sykes, 'I was going to talk to you about them.'

'Oh, yes?'

'There's two that know you.'

Tanner sighed. 'Gulliver and Loader.'

Sykes nodded.

'I thought they'd recognized me earlier. Bollocks.'

'They knew you by your other name, though. Scard.'

Damn it, damn it. Tanner pulled out a cigarette and lit it. 'I really ought to get back to Fauvel,' he said. 'Do me a favour, will you, Stan? Keep an eye on them. Don't let them start talking to any of our lads.'

'That's not all, though, sir,' said Sykes.

Tanner's heart quickened. He drew on his cigarette.

'They said you killed a man,' said Sykes, in a low voice. 'That you killed him, then ran. Never to be seen again. Until now, but with a different name.'

Tanner turned on Sykes. 'And what do you think, Stan, eh? That I'm a murderer?'

'No, of course not. But you're always so bloody mysterious about your past. How long have we known each other? Three years? I still don't know why you left home, or why you're called Tanner and not Scard. And I've never asked either. None of my business.'

'You're right there,' Tanner snapped. 'It isn't.' He flicked away his cigarette. 'Do as I ask, please, Stan. Keep your eye on those Wiltshire boys. I don't want them blabbing to the men, all right? I'm heading back to see Captain Fauvel.'

Tanner walked down the main street of Cassibile, cursing his misfortune. People were coming out of their houses. Through a window, he saw a young man hastily changing out of his uniform and into civilian clothes; he froze, but Tanner walked on. He didn't care that one Italian should avoid becoming a prisoner of war; as it was, there were already too many. His own company had captured several hundred, and he could only guess how many more had been taken that morning. The town was shabby: dusty, poor and charmless. It was already getting hot, and the summer heat would be intense in this part of the world. No doubt plenty of mosquitoes too; certainly, they had all been given malaria pills. He spotted a thin, mangy cat skulking on a wall. What a place to live, he thought, and once again he found himself filled with thoughts of home, its green, lush, curving chalk hills, little streams, brick and flint cottages. Cattle, sheep and crops. The call of a cock pheasant in frosty autumnal undergrowth.

And then he thought of Gulliver and Loader and what they had told Sykes. *Curse them.* Of all the rotten luck. He could rely on Sykes to keep his trap shut, but he knew only too well how soldiers liked to gossip. Like bloody housewives. He had to do something about them. Have a word with Gulliver and Loader. Threaten them, maybe. Tanner wiped his brow. *Damn it.*

Fauvel greeted him cheerily outside the company command post. A runner and 1 Platoon had already told him about the capture of the barracks at the far end of town. Several of the men stood around a small stove.

'Char?' he said.

'Thanks.'

'Curious that the barracks hadn't been marked up,' he said, as he handed Tanner a mug.

'I thought so too,' agreed Tanner, 'although I suppose it was quite well hidden by the gum trees there. Mistaken for farm buildings, maybe. Anyway, hardly made much difference. Sykes had it covered.'

Fauvel smiled. 'He's a fine soldier.'

'He is.' He looked towards Phyllis, who sat on the ground, leaning against a wall, his radio set beside him. 'So, what news? Where the hell are the others? I really thought they'd be here by now.'

Fauvel rolled his eyes. 'Seems B and C Companies *had* landed, but not at How Green. They ended up at Jig Sector.'

Tanner laughed. 'All the best-laid plans, eh?'

'I suppose it was dark, the water choppy.'

'One Eyetie beach looks much like another.'

'Something like that.' Fauvel grinned.

'So what do we do?' He took out his map again. 'There's Case Nuove on the coast to the east of here. Should we take that too, or keep going towards Syracuse?'

Fauvel shook his head. 'No. Seventeenth Brigade are on our flank and have been given Case Nuove. We're to head a short way north of Cassibile and set up a roadblock until the rest catch up.'

'All right. Where are Battalion Headquarters?'

'They landed at How Green, as planned. They're co-ordinating the arrival of supplies and B Echelon, and waiting for D Company to come ashore and for B and C Companies to catch up. They're expecting to join us before midday.'

'When we'll be one big happy family once more.' Tanner drank his tea. 'Right. Let's get going.'

Back at the far end of the town, the Italian prisoners had been disarmed and corralled. Tanner had decided he would give the task of sending the prisoners back to the beaches to the dozen Wiltshiremen; it would, he hoped, kill two birds with one stone.

He found them drinking tea and chatting with some of the Rangers. Much to his annoyance, there was no sign of Sykes. He noticed Gulliver and a couple of 3 Platoon men look up furtively as he approached.

'Where's the CSM?' he snapped.

'Gone for the call of nature, sir,' said Corporal Cooper, a section commander in 3 Platoon.

'Gulliver,' said Tanner, looking at the man. 'A word.'

Gulliver looked around – *What, me?* – then stepped forward, following Tanner a short way from the others. 'What is it, sir?' he asked.

172

'Come with me.' Tanner walked on, back towards the main road through the town and to the alleyway before the last building. When they were out of earshot and sight of the others, he stopped and turned to face the other man, eyeing him coldly. Tanner could see the fear in Gulliver's face: eyes darting, the heavy bulge of his Adam's apple as he swallowed, the slight movement from one foot to the other.

'What, sir?' he said, trying to avoid Tanner's gaze.

'What you told Sykes,' said Tanner. 'Jesus, Gulliver – how old were you back then? Twelve?'

Gulliver nodded.

'Too young to have a bloody clue about what happened that night. Gossip, Gulliver, that's what it was, bloody gossip, and now you have the nerve to start prattling to my men about something you know absolutely nothing about.'

'I'm sorry, sir. I – I was so surprised to see you. It was just chatter, you know. I meant no harm.'

'Who else did you tell? Eh? Have a cosy little chat about it with the lads, did you?'

'I'm sorry – honestly, sir, I'm sorry.'

Tanner wiped a hand across his mouth. 'Jesus, I ought to bloody knock you to a pulp.' He took a step closer, saw Gulliver swallow hard again, then grabbed the man's crotch. Gulliver winced. 'People like you, Gulliver, make me annoyed, very, very annoyed,' Tanner hissed. 'There's enough crap in this war without your bloody loose tongue. Do you realize what it's like being an officer when you've come up through the ranks? It's tough, Gulliver, that's what it is, but I've earned the respect of my men, and I've earned it the hard way. I don't need people like you turning up and cocking things up. Do you understand?'

Gulliver nodded. Tanner stared at him for a moment more, then released his grip, and took out Captain Brasco's pistol from his gas-mask bag. Gulliver recoiled. 'No!' he said. 'I'm sorry, sir, really, I didn't mean anything, I–'

'Christ,' muttered Tanner, 'I really ought to give you a hiding. What did you think I was going to do?' He handed over the pistol. 'Take this, Gulliver, and now I want you and your men to march the Eyetie prisoners back to the beaches. I can't have you with us any more. Someone there will help you rejoin your unit. Understood?'

Gulliver nodded.

'Get those prisoners, Gulliver, and then get out of my sight,' Tanner snarled. 'And pray you don't cross my path again.' He watched Gulliver wince and limp away, then took out a cigarette, lit it, leaned against the wall and sighed. For a moment he closed his eyes. He could rely on Sykes, and with a bit of luck, the men would soon forget about it. Hopefully, he'd scared Gulliver into silence. They would be in battle again soon, and those who'd heard the story would have other things to think about. Soon enough it would be forgotten.

But as he walked out of the alleyway and back towards his men, instinct told him that this was wishful thinking. There was a lot of hanging about as a soldier. Much of the time, it was pretty boring. Gossip enlivened those moments, and really good gossip was gold dust. Really good gossip like the news that A Company's commander had once murdered a man, then fled to join the Army.

Soon all the men would know. And then Creer would find out. *Bloody hell. This is all I need.*

10

Later, early evening, the same day: D-Day. The battalion was in fields to the west of Syracuse, manning another roadblock along a dusty track that loosely headed north. Two companies on one side, two on the other. Nothing had stirred since they had moved there, and now only one platoon from each company covered the approach. Behind, among the trees and shrubs and crumbling stone walls, the men rested, prepared food, drank tea and smoked.

Tanner sat at the foot of an olive tree, cleaning his weapons. It was, he thought, a pretty good position: the ground rose steeply from the port of Syracuse so that even a couple of miles west of the town, where they now were, they could look down on the town and the sea beyond from quite a commanding position. He wondered why the Italians had not sited some guns here or, at the very least, some men. Or perhaps they had, but had moved back – or forward. Maybe they were the men A Company had encountered earlier that afternoon while manning their roadblock north of Cassibile. They had still been waiting for the rest of the battalion to catch up when a column of Italian armoured cars, ammunition lorries and staff cars had suddenly appeared and driven straight towards the waiting Bren guns. Moments later, as the Brens opened up, some vehicles had run off the road, an ammunition truck had exploded, and then, as enemy soldiers had dived for cover, a brief firefight had ensued. Tanner had lost one man dead and four wounded, the Italians several more, before a white flag had been produced and waved from behind a wall. Tanner had been saddled with yet more prisoners.

Early in the afternoon, 17th Brigade had passed through, the rest of the battalion had finally caught up, and were ordered to continue their march north, this time helping to protect the western flank of 17th Brigade's assault on Syracuse.

That attack was still going on now, the sound of small-arms, light-artillery and tank fire crackling and thrumping a couple of miles away. 'Extraordinary, isn't it?'

Peploe was walking towards him, Tanner realized, his head turned towards the town.

'I mean, really, this is a lovely spot,' he said, sitting down beside Tanner. 'Crickets and cicadas chirruping away, olive trees and tamarisk dotted about, the ancient city of Syracuse spread before us, and beyond that, the wine-dark sea. Yet here we are, watching a battle. You can actually follow its progress.'

'It's almost ours,' said Tanner.

'I'd say so. And isn't it amazing to think we've already got guns and tanks and other vehicles ashore? I take my hat off to the planners, I must say.'

A sudden dull boom resounded from the port.

'That's a Sherman,' said Tanner.

'I rest my case.' He passed Tanner his hip flask, then looked around. They were some yards away from the men, something Tanner had understood about being an officer: it was important to create a little distance, to be slightly apart from the rest.

'Er, where are Sykes and Fauvel?' asked Peploe.

'Fauvel's doing the rounds, checking on the platoons. Sykes is watching the road, making sure Two Platoon is on its toes.'

'Good, because I need to talk to you about something, Jack.'

Tanner took a swig from Peploe's flask, but said nothing.

'There's a rumour going round,' said Peploe, 'that you murdered a man, then ran away and joined the Army. Tell me it isn't true.'

'That was quick,' said Tanner, handing back the flask. 'I thought this might happen. Didn't think it'd be quite as quick as this, though.'

'Well?'

'It's gossip, John. Tittle-tattle. There was a lad in the Wiltshires who ended up with us earlier. A young sergeant called Gulliver. He came from the same village as me when I was a boy. But he was a kid at the time I left. He knew nothing.'

Peploe sighed. 'Sometimes rumours like this aren't such a bad thing. When I was at OCTU, we had an instructor who was said to have done time for murdering the man who cheated with his wife. The word on the street was he'd avoided the gallows because it had been considered man-slaughter. Then he'd been let out to join the Army. God knows whether it was true, but we were all a little wary of him. A little scared, even. If he was ever in a particularly bad mood, we'd all remind ourselves that if we weren't careful we might end up getting the chop – literally.' He turned to Tanner. 'Everyone looks up to you, Jack. The men think the world of you, but you know as well as I do that the colonel is a notable exception.'

'Does he know about this, then?' asked Tanner.

Peploe nodded. 'But I'm afraid it's worse. The sergeant from the Wiltshires–'

'Gulliver?'

'He's dead. Apparently you gave him the Italian captain's pistol. One of the Italians saw him with it and tried to take it off him. In the scuffle a shot was fired and he was killed.'

'I'm sorry to hear it, but what's that got to do with me?'

'Creer says you planned it deliberately to get Gulliver out of the way. That you put the Italians up to it.'

'That's madness!'

'Of course it is. But Creer is looking to under-mine you, Jack. He doesn't want you in his bat-talion but knows that while the men think so highly of you his hands are tied.'

'He's a bastard. A lily-livered bastard. I curse the bloody day he showed up here.'

'Look, don't worry. So long as I'm in this bat-talion, I'll back you up all the way. If he tries to sack you, I'll resign too. He'll have a mutiny on his hands. But you need to watch it. He's out to get you, Jack.'

Tanner lit another cigarette. 'Christ,' he muttered. 'It's bad enough having to fight Eyeties and Jerries without having to battle against men like Croaker.'

'And he knows the men call him Croaker, Jack. And he also knows you're the only person who could have known it was his nickname in India.'

Tanner rubbed his face wearily. 'Ah, to hell with him. I've not got in his way, I've not made life difficult for him. Back in India, I never snitched on him and Blackstone – I just didn't play their game. I didn't want to be sullied by the kind of corruption they went in for. Creer was a coward, but I never accused him of cowardice. Jesus, he should be bloody thankful, for God's sake. A Company have done well today, and that reflects well on the battalion. *His* sodding battalion.'

'But you know perfectly well that it's not about that. It's because he feels threatened by you, Jack. And by me, to a certain extent.'

'Well, I wish someone had turned a pistol on him, not on poor bloody Gulliver.'

They were silent for a moment, then Peploe said, 'You still haven't told me, though, Jack.'

'Told you what?'

'That you didn't kill whoever it was you're supposed to have killed.'

Tanner turned and looked at his friend. 'Do I have to, John?'

'Look, Jack,' said Peploe, 'I trust you implicitly. You know I do. But when I defend you against Creer, it would be nice to know that I have your word that this is just gossip and nothing more. You've always been so mysterious about your past. About why you changed your name from Scard to Tanner. I've never pressed you about it. I respected your privacy. But now this has happened, it seems rather important to know. Forgive me, but can you understand that?'

Tanner was silent for a while as he smoked his cigarette and looked down towards Syracuse. 'There's a battle going on out there and we're talking about something that may or may not have happened a long time ago back home in Blighty. It's ridiculous.'

'Jack, please.'

'I'm sorry, John. I made a vow eleven years ago that I'd never talk about it. I gave a man I respected my solemn word. I've kept it all this time, and I'm a man of my word, as you well know.'

'So that's it? You're not going to defend yourself?'

'Oh, I'll defend myself all right. I'll just not betray an oath.'

'You're a stubborn bastard, Jack.' He stood up. 'So be it. I'll do what I can. But he wants to get you, and he'll use this against you.'

Tanner saw he was about to leave, then said suddenly, 'I never murdered anyone.'

Peploe turned. He smiled. 'You don't know how glad I am to hear that.'

Tanner flicked away his cigarette. 'But that's all I'm saying. Maybe one day, John, I'll break the vow I made to David Liddell – he was the man I promised. My father was his gamekeeper, and he

180

was a very fine man. Perhaps one day I'll tell you everything. But not here, not in the middle of this sodding war with people dying as we're talking about...' he searched for the words '...ancient history.'

Peploe patted Tanner's shoulder. 'All right, Jack. You win. But one day, it would be nice to know the whole story.' He turned and walked away.

Sunday, 11 July, six a.m. Lieutenant Colonel Gerald Creer felt a flash of irritation as his batman, Private Stainforth, shook him awake.

'Mug of tea, sir,' said Stainforth.

Creer rubbed his eyes, heaved himself up and took the mug. 'Thank you,' he muttered.

'Major Peploe and Captain Masters are waiting for you in the office, sir. At your convenience.'

Creer nodded.

'There's some hot water in your basin, sir,' added Stainforth, then disappeared.

Creer sat up, wriggled out of his sleeping-bag and swivelled his legs around. The bed was huge and high off the floor, the centrepiece of a large, high-ceilinged room that spoke of former grandeur. His trousers and shirt lay on a gilt-edged Louis XIV chair, which, with a small desk and a lone cupboard, was all the furniture the room possessed; all that had been added was a standard canvas fold-away British Army washstand.

Creer washed and dressed. A Company had come across the place the previous afternoon after a shoot-out on the road: a villa, in the lee of an outcrop of rocky rising ground, but with views down towards Syracuse and the sea. By all accounts, the place had been the headquarters of an Italian regiment, and it had amused Creer to think that one lot of officers had been kicked out and replaced immediately by another. The perks of victory.

As he shaved, he peered into an ornate gilt mirror hanging on the wall. He was thirty-eight, clean-shaven, with a lean, tanned face, and fair hair that was rapidly receding. There were a few lines now, across the brow, from his nose to the edge of his mouth and around his eyes. The lips were thin, the eyes pale grey. Creer had always rather liked the way he looked: there was, he thought, in his face and bearing, a kind of urbane intelligence. The receding hair line was a source of irritation, but otherwise, he felt he was ageing quite well. Certainly, he was not as obviously middle-aged as some; he had yet to spot a single grey hair.

Nonetheless, sleeping poorly was soon going to take its toll. Sleeping on the move was all well and good when one was young, but he'd got used to the comfortable bungalow in Quetta and the hotel digs in Cairo. Thank God that, as battalion commander, he had had first dibs on the rooms in this villa, a prerogative he believed he'd earned, but which he also felt laid down a useful barrier between him and his men. He was the boss, and while it was important to win people over, it was also necessary to maintain an aura of superiority.

Despite this, he felt tired and not a little irritable. The last day of the journey across the sea had been hellish. He had never been a good sailor but his insides had felt as though they'd been boiled in acid. It was true that he had had no intention of ever going ashore in the first wave, but as he had left dinner in the wardroom that night he had seen Tanner look at him with a degree of contempt that had added humiliation and anger to the pain in his stomach. 'Croaker', Tanner called him. It meant a man badly wounded or at death's door, except that in Creer's case the term was used ironically. He had never heard Tanner say it since his return, but he had overheard it being used by other men, and how else could it have resurfaced if not spread by that man?

Tanner Tanner, Tanner... What was he going to do about him? He remembered the horror he had felt when he discovered that the once trouble-some private had become the battalion hero, much decorated, commissioned and a company commander. For a moment, he had even considered resigning and returning to Cairo. Admittedly, he had not entertained the idea for long: to command the regiment one had joined as a junior subaltern was a singular honour, and while he would have been content to remain a desk-wallah for the rest of the war and his career, to cut and run would have been tantamount to suicide.

Perhaps, he had told himself, Tanner had changed. Perhaps the two could get along after all these years. This, however, had soon proved very wishful thinking. Tanner had not changed one iota: he was still the same stubborn bastard he had always been, the unbending, proud and utterly incorruptible pain in the backside he had been in India. The implacable and defiant stares, the undisguised contempt, the air of superiority. Christ, it made his blood boil. Now he nicked himself and saw a small globule of dark blood appear. He closed his eyes, cursed silently, then dabbed his jaw.

But what to do about him? One thing was absolutely clear in his mind. One of them would have to go and he was damned if it was going to be him. That some country-yokel upstart should come out on top was unthinkable. The previous day had initially set him back as Tanner's blasted A Company had landed on time and in the right place, had captured hundreds of pathetic Italians and taken out an important gun position and the town of Cassibile, an early D-Day objective. But then had come the news that Tanner had once murdered a man and run away. Even better, his accuser had been later killed. There were no charges that would ever stick, Creer knew that, but it was a question of chipping away at Tanner's prestige; of slowly but surely eroding his position. Creer would use this to undermine him; to humiliate him.

And there was no doubt that war was dangerous. So Tanner had proved miraculously impervious to enemy bullets, shellfire, or mines so far but his luck might run out. The Italians had to make a better fist of things soon and there were German troops on Sicily too. They were unlikely to roll over. And here was a cheering thought as he sluiced away the shaving soap and cream: as battalion commander, it was his decision as to which company would lead an attack. A Company, he thought, would find itself in the van of every battle the Rangers fought. By the law of averages, Tanner would surely find himself either wounded or, even better, dead. *Surely.*

It was with his mood somewhat lifted that Creer trotted downstairs and out to the driveway at the front of the villa. The 'office' was not in the house, but in the back of a fifteen-hundredweight truck, so that Battalion Headquarters could move at a moment's notice. On board were field telephones, wires trailing over the edge and down the drive, and a radio set, with a small desk along one side for the battalion signalmen, waiting to pass on incoming messages or relay orders to the companies up at the front. Peploe and the intelligence officer, Captain Jerry Masters, were leaning against the truck, drinking tea and chatting with Lieutenant Warbrook, the adjutant. Several chairs, brought out from the houses, had been arranged on the driveway, which was round and revolved around an ornate but dry fountain. Palms and eucalyptus trees rose around the side of the drive and the front garden, shielding the house from where the rest of the battalion were dug in five hundred yards further up the road.

'Morning, sir,' said Peploe, with a cheery smile. 'A beautiful day.'

'Morning,' replied Creer.

'Best part of the day if you ask me,' said Masters.

'It's going to be hot, for sure,' agreed Peploe.

'Sleep all right?' asked Creer.

'Got bitten alive,' said Masters. 'Bastards buzzing about my ear all night. I'll be happy when our kit catches up and I can retrieve my net.'

'You obviously haven't been drinking enough gin and tonic, Jerry,' said Creer. 'Quinine, that's the key. I'm immune to them now.' He clapped his hands together. 'Anyway, what's the news? Have we got the latest sitrep?'

'Yes, sir,' said Warbrook, clutching a thin piece of paper. 'This is from Division at oh five forty-five. Syracuse taken, but we knew that, and also Ponte Grande. However, the good news is that the Italians were in such a hurry to flee Syracuse, they failed to blow any of the harbour installations first. So it's intact.'

'Yes, that's bloody good news,' said Peploe. 'It'll really help with the unloading process.'

'Er, first German opposition has been encountered,' continued Warbrook, 'and Thirteenth Brigade have now taken Floridia and are advancing on Solarino.' He scanned the sheet of paper once more. 'Unloading continuing well. At Gela, the Americans have established a bridgehead but opposition has been stiffer than in Eighth Army's area. The German Hermann Göring Division counterattacked heavily yesterday but were beaten back. The Americans are expecting further heavy counterattacks today. Bridgehead holding, though. The airborne drop has not been a success – the high winds caused huge problems, as one can well imagine. Gela airfield taken, and probably Comiso this morning. Air forces struck Catania and Gerbini airfields again last night.'

Peploe looked up. 'So, all in all, situation encouraging. I've also been up to see the men, who seem in buoyant spirits after yesterday's suc-

186

cesses. I think they're happier now that they're here and off the ship.'

'Good,' said Creer. 'I'll head up in the Jeep shortly. And what about today's plans? Where are Brigade?'

'Brigade at Avola but moving up to Syracuse. Seventeenth Brigade advancing on Augusta, Thirteenth on Solarino.'

'And what are our orders?'

'Await supplies for the time being,' said Peploe, 'and be ready to move up through Thirteenth Brigade.' He grinned, and said, 'Apparently, a German anti-aircraft unit pushed north out of Syracuse yesterday afternoon and prompted panic among the Italians there. Hundreds deserted, guns were put out of action, and Syracuse more or less abandoned. A bit of fighting to the north of the town, but that was more or less it. Incredible, isn't it?'

'How the devil d'you know all this, Peploe?' asked Creer.

'I went down there about an hour ago, sir. Took one of the Jeeps and spoke to an officer in the Seaforth Highlanders. I told him we'd heard the battle going on last night and he said it had been the easiest fight he'd ever been in. It's a beautiful town. A bit bombed, but not too badly.'

'Must have a look,' muttered Creer. He disliked Peploe almost as much as Tanner. Always smiling, always cheery, and incredibly efficient with it. Peploe was one of those types who would never have worn a uniform had it not been for the war, but whose obvious intelligence, charm and manifest good sense made him an excellent officer. Creer was well aware that, while the men admired Tanner, there was great affection for Peploe; most, he knew, would have far preferred Peploe to remain OC of the battalion. And he was so damn keen. Getting up at the crack of dawn and heading into Syracuse! *For God's sake.* It was as though Peploe was deliberately trying to show him up.

'Anything else to report, Warbrook?' Creer asked.

'Not at the moment, sir.'

'Good. I'll take the Jeep and go up and see the men.'

He had just pushed back his chair and was lighting a pipe when a motorcycle turned into the drive and headed towards them.

'A DR for us by the look of things,' said Peploe.

The despatch rider stopped and Creer stepped forward, took the note and read it alone.

'Anything important?' asked Peploe, as the motorcycle roared off again.

'We're being temporarily attached to Fifty Div and to Sixty-ninth Brigade,' he said. 'We're to pass through Thirteenth Brigade at Solarino and advance on Sortino.'

Peploe took out his map. 'Sortino,' he muttered. 'I've got a number of pillboxes marked up to the south of there. We might have a fight on our hands at last. When do we leave?'

'Immediately,' replied Creer.

'In that case, I'll follow you up to see the men, sir.'

'See to the clearing up of this place first, will you, Peploe?'

Peploe smiled affably. 'Of course, sir. Right away, sir.' He stood up, saluted theatrically and hurried into the house, calling to the men.

And that was another thing that irked, Creer thought – the way no slight, no put-down, ever seemed to ruffle Peploe. As he got to his feet, Stainforth clambered down from the office.

'Where to, sir?'

'Where d'you bloody think?' he snapped. 'To see the men.'

'Very good, sir.'

They drove off in silence, a cloud of dust following in their wake. It was only five hundred yards up the track to the battalion's main positions, and as they climbed the slight rise, Creer saw Tanner standing at the tail-gate of a fifteen-hundredweight truck that had been driven off the side of the road and parked under a tree. He seemed to be examining something with CSM Sykes and another of the men. Creer was still trying to see what it was, when suddenly he heard the roar of an aero engine and looked up to see a fighter plane hurtling low towards them.

'Christ's sake!' he yelled, as Stainforth yanked the steering-wheel sharply and veered as the enemy aircraft opened fire, spurts of bullets bursting along the road. A moment later, both men had leaped from the Jeep, but as Creer dived onto the ground, he was conscious that a figure up ahead stepped onto the side of the road and opened fire with a Bren gun.

In a trice, the plane was over them, so low Creer could see the black crosses on the underside of the wings, and the oil streaks across its pale belly. It sped on past but then the engine seemed to catch and falter. An audible crack, and black smoke belched from the nose. Cheers from the men, and the Messerschmitt climbed and banked over the high ground to the west, a trail of smoke following behind.

A shadow fell across Creer and he looked up to see Tanner standing over him, Bren slung across his shoulder. 'Not hit, are you, sir?' he said.

'No, no, I'm fine,' muttered Creer, hastily getting to his feet.

'And you, Stainforth?' asked Tanner.

'No, sir.'

Tanner looked at the Jeep, then at the road. Creer saw that the line of bullets pockmarking the surface veered to the right fifteen yards before the Jeep. For a moment the three stood there in silence, watching the Messerschmitt, which had swooped, engine spluttering, low in the sky before disappearing from view.

'Good shooting, sir,' said Stainforth.

'Always worth a pop when they're that low,' said Tanner. 'As much as anything, it puts them off their aim.' He winked at Creer, then saluted lazily and ambled back towards his men.

'A moment, Tanner,' Creer called.

Tanner stopped and turned. *Yes?*

'We're moving out. We're to pass through Thirteenth Brigade and take Sortino.'

Tanner nodded. 'Transport?'

'Only with supplies. We're to advance on foot. Get your company ready.'

Tanner saluted again and continued walking.

Curse you, thought Creer.

Behind him, Stainforth was getting back into the Jeep. 'Blimey, that was a close one, sir!' he said. 'Did you see the line of bullets? They were heading straight for us.'

'They were heading for the Jeep, Stainforth, not us. Don't get carried away. Now drive on. We need to get the battalion moving.'

As they drove on, Stainforth said, 'You have to admit, that was very impressive shooting, sir.'

'Hmm, perhaps, but it's a pity there's such a dark stain hanging over him.'

'Really, sir?'

'I suppose I shouldn't be telling you this, Stainforth,' said Creer, 'but there's fairly strong evidence that Tanner murdered a man a few years ago. Killed him, fled, and joined the Army.'

'You're joking, sir? Really?' said Stainforth, as they drove on towards B Company's positions.

'I'm afraid so. To be honest, he was always a little tricky out in India. Rather sly. Good at manipulating people. One of those types.'

'Well, I hardly know him, sir. Major Peploe thinks the world of him, though.'

'I wouldn't trust him as far as I could throw him, Stainforth. Between you and me, I've been having to keep a pretty tight watch on him since I took over. I often wonder if that's why they brought me in over Peploe.'

Stainforth whistled. 'Blow me, sir, I had no idea.'

'And yesterday a man from the Wiltshire Regiment somehow ended up landing alongside A Company. He recognized Tanner from back home,

191

and later that morning, he was shot. All rather convenient for our Captain Tanner, wouldn't you say?'

Stainforth shook his head. 'Incredible, sir. So what will you do about it, if you don't mind me asking?'

'It's a tricky one. It's all circumstantial, but having a possible murderer among our number, and a company commander at that, Stainforth, is clearly not acceptable.'

'No, sir.'

'I'm going to have to do something about it, but as to what, I'm not quite certain yet.'

Stainforth glanced at his OC. 'You never know, sir, the war may take care of it for you. It's a dangerous business, after all.'

Creer did not answer, but his mind was whirring. An idea had entered his head. An idea that might not only solve the problem of Tanner but that of Peploe too.

11

Sunday, 11 July, around 9.25 a.m. The admiral's barge landed on the 1st Division's beaches to the east of Gela, grinding gently as it came to a halt on the sand. The ramp was lowered and the general's Dodge command reconnaissance car and one Jeep rumbled off, Patton sitting up front beside Major Alex Stiller, his aide, who was driving. In the back sat Major General Hobart

192

'Hap' Gay, Patton's chief-of-staff, and Lieu-tenant Colonel Charlie Wiseman. Behind them, in the Jeep, four soldiers were acting as body-guards to the US Seventh Army commander.

Wiseman was glad of the chance to get back on land, although he had been reading the sitreps coming in with mounting concern. He wondered whether Patton should be risking coming ashore so early. Although German and Italian counter-attacks had been beaten back on D-Day, there were already signs that there would be heavy fighting this second day too. Reports had come in of enemy troops massing to the north of Gela; the naval guns had been booming since dawn, and even now, as they drove onto the beach, Wiseman could hear the crackle of small arms and shelling from a short way inland. He had not voiced his concerns – General Gay had done that, but Patton had swept them aside.

'That's precisely why I'm going ashore,' he had responded. 'A commander needs to command. Can't do that sitting on your arse six miles off-shore.'

Before they could go anywhere, the Dodge and the Jeep had to be de-waterproofed, so Patton stepped down, face set, helmet low over his nar-row eyes, boots shining and a pearl-handled revolver on each hip. The scene was one of chaos and the aftermath of carnage. The build-up of supplies was impressive, with more tanks, vehicles and crates of ammunition rolling off the LCTs as they waited. Those killed the day before had been taken away, but there were helmets in the sand, upturned boxes and a number of wrecked vehicles. Wiseman followed Patton as he looked at two DUKWs that had been destroyed by mines, then a Higgins boat with a huge hole torn through its side.

'An eighty-eight,' he said, 'or a one-oh-five. Pity the poor sons-of-bitches in that one.'

Shells continued to whistle overhead. Wiseman looked up and even saw the dark shape of one hurtle by, sucking the air from its path with a deafening whine. Moments later he felt a tremor as it landed, then heard the explosion. *Thank God for the Navy guns*. He wondered how they might have fared without them. Not too well, he guessed.

They were soon called back to their vehicles. Patton had originally wanted to see Terry Allen, the 1st Division commander, whose head-quarters were now a few miles further south-east along the beach, but having heard the sound of intensifying small-arms and mortars from north of Gela, he ordered Stiller to head towards the town instead.

'We'll go and see how Colonel Darby's Rangers are getting on,' Patton told them. 'I want the gap between the Rangers and First Division closed up right away, but until we see the situation for ourselves, we won't know what forces we need to allocate to achieve it.' Wiseman had to concede the general had a point. A path off the beach had been bulldozed, so they drove up the sand and onto the rough coast road, then headed west.

A group of Rangers met them at the edge of the town, hastily saluted, then, two clinging to the side of the Dodge, led them to Colonel Darby's

CP, through streets in which battle debris was all too evident. A number of buildings had been hit, the rubble tumbling down into the road. Telegraph wires lay strewn across another, blocking their path. Wiseman spotted a number of dead Italians, and a few nervous faces watching from the windows; the civilians were keeping low indoors. *Poor bastards*. The stench of death and smoke was heavy on the air.

They were led to a restaurant at the base of an apartment building near the northern edge of town. A Rangers captain saluted smartly as they drew up and Patton stepped down.

'At ease, Captain,' Patton said. 'Where's the colonel?'

'At the top, sir,' the captain replied. 'It's our OP.'

They followed him up the stairs to the top floor. The doors were open and inside they found Colonel Darby and a handful of other men, including a radio operator.

'General Patton, sir,' said Darby, saluting with snappiness. He wore his helmet at an angle, his Thompson slung across his back. Binoculars hung around his neck.

Wiseman followed them out onto the balcony. Ahead he could see open countryside, and a wide, gently rising plain of dense fields. The main arteries, the three roads leading towards the town, were clearly visible, while away to the right, running towards the sea, was the river Gela that gave the town its name. Beyond, maybe ten miles away, mountains rose, grey and dusty in the morning sunlight.

'Show me the enemy counterattack, Colonel,' Patton said, bringing his own binoculars to his eyes.

'Which one, sir?' Darby replied.

Patton lowered his binoculars. 'So it's like that, is it? I think you ought to put me in the picture, Colonel, and double quick.'

Wiseman listened as Darby explained that they had held the town the previous evening even though enemy tanks had reached the main square. There had, he told the general, been a number of Italian troops, but they had all been killed, captured or driven out. They were doing their best to withstand what they expected to be another heavy counterattack. He pointed out the enemy columns approaching. Now that Wiseman looked carefully, he saw clouds of dust along the track that approached the town from the north and another from the north-east.

'Those are Italians, sir,' said Darby, pointing north, 'and those are Krauts approaching from the direction of Ponte Olivo airfield. The Hermann Göring Division.'

Wiseman scanned with his binoculars. He could see Italian troops crossing open fields a couple of miles away and, further to the east, what appeared to be German tanks. He swallowed hard. Guns still boomed offshore, shells exploding inland, clouds of smoke mushrooming into the sky.

'I've got a perimeter of 4.2 mortars, sir,' added Darby, 'which I'll have open fire any moment at two thousand yards from the enemy. And I know every last man will keep firing until we've chased those sons-of-bitches out of here.'

Patton allowed himself a faint smile. 'Good,' he said. 'Take me down there, will you?'

'Of course, sir,' said Darby, but at that moment a pair of German bombers appeared, swooping in at just a few hundred feet. A second later, they heard the whistle of falling bombs, a deafening crash, and suddenly the street outside was enveloped in smoke and dust. Masonry was crumbling and crashing down on itself. Everyone had ducked, but while their own building was unscathed, the small one across the street had been hit and now a woman was screaming.

Patton coughed, straightened his belt and tie, then said, 'Let's go.'

The woman was still screaming as they got down to the street and into their vehicles. Choking dust and smoke filled the air, but soon they were through it and speeding towards a Rangers mortar position facing the Italian thrust from the north. There were four 4.2-inch mortars spread out in good positions behind stone walls at the edge of the town. Stacks of boxes of mortar shells stood around each. The men looked hot, sweat darkening their backs and running down their faces. Mortar rounds were bursting from the tubes in quick succession.

As the general and his coterie once again got out of their vehicles, they brought binoculars to their eyes. Wiseman watched the battle unfolding. He could see the enemy clearly, Italian infantry spread out across the fields, hurrying forward, scaling the walls that barred their way. How far were they now? About twelve hundred yards, Wiseman guessed. He glanced towards one of the mortars to see Patton himself placing a shell down the tube.

'What the hell kind of mortar shells are we using here, Sergeant?' he asked a Ranger.

'Phosphorous, sir,' came the reply.

Patton grinned. 'Mighty effective.'

He loves this, thought Wiseman. He had never met anyone who so obviously enjoyed the adrenalin rush of combat as Patton; that energy, the glint in his eye, at the smell of cordite and the sound of artillery, was extraordinary. He relished it. That was the word. Patton relished battle.

Still the Italians came forward. Wiseman watched the mortar shells explode, saw men flung into the air and falling to the ground, the line disappearing behind clouds of smoke and grit, then emerging again. He was conscious that the heavy naval bombardment had stopped and now Patton growled, 'Where the hell is the naval forward observation officer?'

The Navy FOO was, apparently, watching from a building a little way behind them.

'I want his ass down here now,' said Patton.

Five minutes later, the FOO appeared, saluting sharply.

'What's your name, son?'

'Lieutenant Cramer, sir.'

'Then tell me, Cramer, why the hell have your guns stopped?' Patton demanded.

'They're worried they're going to hit our own men, sir,' said the officer.

'Horseshit,' said Patton. 'Those Eyeties are still a good thousand yards ahead of us. Get on to Hewitt and tell him I want fire poured down on them. And jump to it.'

'Sir!' replied the FOO, who immediately called up on his radio set.

A few minutes later, shells were screaming overhead once more, so that naval and mortar shells were now bursting along the advance of the Italians. Wiseman watched what appeared to be a ripple of explosions, a line of rolling, erupting smoke and dust. He could not help feeling impressed. Italian artillery was firing in return, but the shells were intermittent, infrequent and inaccurate.

Machine-guns were chattering and rattling between the din of the guns, but Wiseman was conscious of an intense sound of battle now further to the east. Tank rounds punctured the racket, booming above the mortars and small arms and occasional blast of an American anti-tank gun.

'What's going on over to the east?' Patton asked Darby, who was talking on a field telephone.

'Kraut tanks and infantry, sir. They're getting close. I've got Captain Lyle holding the road with A and B Companies.'

'Let's go there,' he said and, to Cramer, 'You too.' They got back into their vehicles and drove off. They found Lyle easily enough, at a CP in a building on the very edge of the town. Mortar crews were firing, but so too were two 37mm anti-tank guns that had been set up either side of the main road that led from Gela to the airfield.

'Captain, your chinstrap is unbuckled,' said Patton, as Lyle saluted.

Wiseman smiled to himself. *Jeez*. The general was such a stickler. Who gave a damn about chin-straps in the middle of a battle? Well, obviously Patton did.

'What's the situation here?' Patton now asked, binoculars once more to his eyes.

'We've got a mixture of Eyetalians, sir, and Kraut armour. One tank broke through, but it withdrew again.'

Patton rubbed his chin thoughtfully. 'Let's get some naval help over here, too, then get ready for a counterattack.' He turned to Cramer. 'Lieutenant, I want five hundred six-inch rounds on this axis too. Kill every one of the Goddamn bastards.'

Soon after, shells were hurtling over, screaming through the air. Wiseman had watched the enemy only around nine hundred yards away. He spotted several tanks – Panzer IVs by the look of them – moving into positions of cover. A tank shell whumped into a building behind them, but while others ducked at the impact, he noticed Patton did not flinch. There appeared to be some kind of shallow ravine in which the enemy troops were trying to shelter. *Fools,* thought Wiseman. Mortar shells soon found their range, the phosphorous exploding with a bright white flash. Moments later, they heard the screams and now a number of Italian troops were running out of the ravine, their hands on their heads, others staggering around in shock. A machine-gun opened fire and Wiseman watched a number topple over.

'They're surrendering,' he said.

'Now's the time to go and get the bastards,' Patton told Lyle. 'Beat this rabble back and we can concentrate on the assault in the Twenty-sixth Infantry's sector. I want this gap closed up, Goddamn it.' He glanced at his watch, then turned to his radio man in the Jeep. 'What news of Truscott at Licata?'

'Situation stable, sir. Bridgehead secured, and no major counterattack.'

'Good,' said Patton, then turned to Colonel Darby. 'And the situation is now under control here, Colonel.'

'The enemy advance appears to be stalling, sir, I agree.'

'How many men do you have here, Captain?' he asked Lyle.

'Around one-twenty, sir,' Lyle replied.

'It's good to know that a few over a hundred stout and resolute American soldiers can halt a major counterattack by an Italian division. Now, take your men, Lyle, and complete the rout.'

'Sir!'

'I'm going to find Allen. I want this enemy counterattack beaten off and the bridgehead secured.'

Into the vehicles again, back through the ghost-town of Gela. Enemy aircraft overhead, and anti-aircraft guns pumping shells into the sky. Wiseman watched black puffs exploding, peppering the azure blue. Shells screamed over from the ships out at sea. Noise, noise, noise. The stench of bodies rotting in the heat. Some dogs feeding on one, tugging at a limp leg. *Jesus.* Out onto the coast road. LCTs lying offshore, the beaches busy with activity. More sounds of battle to the north and further east, where they were headed.

They were now alone, two vehicles beetling

along the rough road. *If the enemy suddenly burst through here...* But nothing, and six miles down the coast they finally reached 1st Division Head-quarters, an *ad hoc* scattering of vehicles, camouflage nets and foxholes. A limp flag, a green shield with a single red '1' emblazoned upon it, had been erected. Roosevelt, the divisional executive officer, was there, but not Terry Allen, the divisional commander, who was conferring with 2nd Armored Division a little further along.

Roosevelt gave the party a brief assessment of the situation. The German HG Division appeared to be carrying out the main thrust against them. German artillery was shelling their positions, and both tanks and infantry had made several attacks, but so far had been beaten back. American anti-tank guns and artillery were now dug in, while naval shelling continued.

'We're standing firm, sir,' said Roosevelt.

'I want you to do more than that, Teddy,' said Patton. 'I want the enemy killed and I want the gap between here and Gela closed. What the hell stopped you doing that last night?'

'We didn't have enough of our artillery and anti-tank guns ashore.'

'You should have seen to it that they were given priority.'

'They were, sir, but there was confusion on the beaches. Delays. The enemy counterattacked stronger than we expected.'

'All right,' said Patton, 'but keep them firing at those bastards now.'

A brief pause for some lunch from the stash of 1st Division rations already ashore, and then they were off once more, driving further along to 2nd Armored's Headquarters. Wiseman was impressed by the number of Shermans, tank destroyers and half-tracks already ashore. More LCTs lay ramp-down on the beach, with piles of rations, ammunition and other supplies stacked up ready to be moved off. A German gun began desultory shelling of the position, but it was wildly inaccurate, most falling into the dunes between the American positions and the beach. General Allen was not there but they eventually met him soon after and had a roadside conference. Allen had sent anti-tank guns, tanks and infantry forward to meet the latest counter-attack; a number of enemy tanks had been turned back. Earlier, he told Patton, he had been concerned, but now the situation was stabilizing once more.

'Get that Goddamn gap closed, Terry,' Patton told him.

They were still conferring, maps spread out on the front of the Dodge, when a formation of bombers came over. Wiseman counted fourteen. Anti-aircraft gunners opened up, bombs fell on the beach, and Wiseman felt sand and grit patter on his helmet. Neither Patton nor Allen looked up. A moment later, the bombers were climbing and droning on, out of the fray.

They headed back to Gela, pulled onto the beach and waited for a boat to collect them and take them back to *Monrovia*. They arrived, drenched from sea spray, at around seven o'clock, and went immediately to the wardroom, which had been set up at Patton's CP. The latest sitrep was delivered and read out. Gela had held, and the gap between the town and most of the 1st Division was finally closed. More than two thousand prisoners had been captured. Truscott's bridgehead was not only secure but expanding. Further east, General Middleton's 45th Division had taken the all-important Comiso airfield and already Allied aircraft were landing there and harrying the enemy.

'I am well satisfied with command today, gentlemen,' Patton announced to his staff.

'I'm certain your presence had much to do with restoring the situation, General,' said Gay.

Patton nodded in acknowledgement. Wiseman felt sure Gay was right. Patton was a curious man in many ways, but his leadership had been exemplary that day.

Patton now leaned forward on the map table. 'So now we start advancing.' He put a finger on the road that led north. 'Here's our axis of advance. The Brits can take Catania and we push north to the west of Etna, cutting off any enemy retreat through Messina.' Now he turned to Wiseman. 'And this is where your feller comes in, Colonel.'

'He's ready and waiting, sir.'

'Good, because we need to get our asses up to Messina just as soon as we can before Adolf starts sending reinforcements across the Strait. Sooner we're there, sooner we have this campaign sewn up.' He looked at the map again. 'General?' he said, turning to Gay. 'What's the latest intel on Eyetie forces in the west of the island?'

'The four coastal divisions are still there,

General, the 207th, 202nd, 208th and 136th. So too are the Assietta and Aosta, although there are signs that the German Fifteenth Panzer Grenadier Division is on the move.'

'Let those Krauts come,' said Patton. 'The more Germans we kill here the less we have to worry about later, but we expect the Italians to melt away, isn't that right, Wiseman?'

Wiseman cleared his throat. 'General, Don Calogero Vizzini has told us he has the power to ensure this happens.'

'Well, if he can, he'll have done the cause of freedom a great service.'

'It's something of a gamble, sir, as was explained during the briefing we gave on our return from Sicily just over a month ago. To many he is the unofficial head man here on Sicily.'

'I think we should be wary of depending too heavily on Vizzini,' said Gay. 'The Fascists have stamped down hard on the Mafia.'

'With the greatest respect, sir,' said Wiseman, 'the Honourable Society is still very much a part of life on Sicily. Fascism may have made it more, er, discreet, but it has done nothing to eradicate it. Vizzini is head of an organization that reaches into every corner of Sicilian life.'

'How can you be so sure?' asked Gay.

'I saw it with my own eyes, sir. I'll admit I can't speak for the coastal regions, but in the central interior through which we travelled, Vizzini reigns supreme. He assured us Palermo would come over to us, too, once he gave the signal.'

Patton nodded. 'We'll take Vizzini at his word. If his promises turn out to be hollow, we'll just have to kill a whole load more Italians and that'll mean diverting men and resources. But getting the Mafia on our side will make our job easier, and it's a gamble we should take.'

'Vizzini is waiting for our signal, sir.'

'And what is the signal, Colonel?' asked Admiral Hewitt.

'We're to fly over Villalba and drop a yellow flag with an L stitched onto it.' He smiled. 'Somewhat theatrical, I know, but it was Don Calogero's suggestion. It's something we knew we could deliver, so we felt obliged to agree to the request.'

Admiral Hewitt chuckled. 'And why L?'

'L for *libertà*, sir.'

'Freedom.' Hewitt smiled. 'Very good, Wiseman.'

'Freedom from the Fascist yoke,' said Patton. 'Amen to that. Good. As soon as we have our bridgehead firmly secured, you get onto it, Wiseman.'

'Yes, sir,' said Wiseman. *An alliance with the Honourable Society.* He wondered which was better for Sicily: Fascism or the return to power of the Mafia. He knew Patton liked to view the war as a moral crusade in which the Allies had God on their side, but he wondered about that. Still, it wasn't his job to concern himself with such matters. His job was to help make sure the Allies won. Whether God was with them or not.

12

Around 8.30 p.m. Tanner crouched low beside some jutting rocks and peered through his binoculars. He was overlooking a narrow valley, maybe some two hundred yards wide, he guessed, and perhaps seventy-five deep. The road snaked down, ran along the valley floor, over a stone bridge, and then up the other side, dog-legging once before climbing on up the far slope and disappearing over the ridge. A mile or so beyond that was Sortino, but barring the way, as he could clearly see, was a row of defences. He could see at least six pillboxes, one tucked into the rocks on the dog-leg at the far side, one more on the road directly above, and four below the crest.

Beside him, Sykes and Peploe peered through their own field glasses.

'Mortar pits, MGs, wire,' said Sykes. 'Probably mines too. D'you think we might have a fight on our hands here?'

'God knows,' muttered Tanner. 'They look prepared for a scrap, though.'

'How wide do you think this position is?' said Peploe. Tanner followed his gaze up the rising ground to the west. Above them ran a high, mountainous ridge. 'How far is that? A mile or two?'

Tanner looked east. They could no longer see the sea, which was now some six miles or more to their right. Between their current position and the coast, another road headed north, a route taken by 17th Brigade. 'My guess is that this line is being held pretty consistently from the coast to that mountain ridge,' he said. 'Outflanking's not going to be an option here.'

'Night patrols to make sure?' suggested Peploe.

'Maybe, although they'll know we're here then. You get useful intelligence but someone always gives the game away. Personally, I'd go for surprise.'

'Dawn attack, then,' said Peploe.

'I suggest we go in just as first light is creeping over and hammer them,' said Tanner. He had taken out his map and was busily marking up the defences with a pencil.

'And no barrage,' said Peploe.

'No,' agreed Tanner.

'What about enemy recce planes?' said Sykes. 'There've been a few over this afternoon.'

'But they were flying pretty high,' said Peploe. 'There's been nothing low over us and it's getting dark now.'

'All right,' said Sykes. 'Just thought I'd mention it.'

'I think the major's right, Stan,' said Tanner. 'If we strike at dawn I reckon we'll have a good chance of catching them on the hop. Even if they know we're here, they won't know when we're going to strike. You know what it's like that time of day – horrible to be fighting, with your eyes struggling to adjust. In any case, if we go in with a barrage, we'll have to wait for the artillery.'

'All right,' said Peploe. 'Are we agreed, then? Stan, you're happy?'

'Happy, sir?' grinned Sykes. 'I wouldn't say that, but I agree with the plan.'

'Good man,' said Peploe. 'Better report back to Creer, then.'

The vanguard of the battalion was a mile back from the ridge of the valley, well clear of the view of the Italian positions. All along the sides of the road, the men were sitting or crouched, some brewing tea, but otherwise eating dry rations only, for fear that the smell of cooking would waft towards the Italians. They looked tired and hot and most were covered with dust, having marched all the way from the landing beaches the day before. None had much enjoyed the march, especially in the heat, loaded with packs, haver-sacks and webbing. Flies had been a constant pest, attracted to the sweat, and most had spent the day with dark damp patches on their shirts. The dust kicked up by their boots had got every-where – up noses, into eyes and hair. Tanner's throat had been as dry as sand. The battalion had taken badly the withdrawal of their vehicles, and the men were still grumbling about it. Tanner was on their side: he'd enjoyed having the fifteen-hundredweights.

They found Creer a few hundred yards back, at the side of the road, Battalion HQ vehicles parked up beneath the shade of the tree. And that was another thing that annoyed Tanner: Creer and Battalion HQ had vehicles when the rest of the battalion did not. It was as though Creer was rubbing their noses in it.

'Well?' said Creer, when he saw them.

'The enemy seem fairly well dug in on the far side of the valley up ahead, sir,' said Peploe, as Tanner hung back. Cicadas and crickets were chirruping loudly in the rapidly fading light. 'Pillboxes, wire, possibly mines.'

'Strength?'

'Probably battalion, although I'd say only a company watching the road. We believe an infiltration assault at first light is probably the best option.'

'What about artillery?' asked Creer.

'We thought without a barrage, sir.'

Creer stroked his chin. 'Hmm,' he said. 'I'd feel happier having artillery.'

'It takes away any surprise, though, sir.'

Creer nodded thoughtfully, then spread out his map. 'Why don't we go in at first light as you suggest,' he said, 'but have the artillery supporting us in case we should need them?'

'But do we have any artillery, sir?' asked Tanner.

'They'll be here, Tanner,' said Creer. 'We're temporarily attached to Sixty-ninth Brigade and they're sending us two batteries of twenty-five-pounders. And we have our own mortars, of course.'

'And they'll be here by first light?'

'Yes, Tanner,' snapped Creer, impatience entering his voice.

'What size attack, sir?' asked Peploe.

'Company. No time for broad-front attacks. Our objective is Sortino. The road is what we need to clear, so a frontal attack in that sector. A Company to lead.'

'Again, sir?' said Peploe. 'Don't you think they deserve a rest?'

'No favouritism here, Peploe,' said Creer. 'You're always telling me A Company is our best, so it's only right they should lead the attack. We want this position taken swiftly. B Company will be in support.'

'Can I suggest we use a third company to offer fire support, sir?' said Peploe. 'We position riflemen and some MGs on the ridge.'

Creer nodded. 'Yes, all right. D Company. C Company can be in reserve. And you can lead the attack, Major. Need someone with experience up front.'

Peploe glanced at Tanner. 'Of course, sir,' he said.

'Good,' said Creer. He clapped his hands together.

'Hold on a moment, sir,' said Tanner.

Creer looked at him with a flash of irritation. *What now?*

'What about sappers?' said Tanner. 'We'll need the support of engineers to get through the wire and blow the pillboxes.'

'I can put a call through to Brigade,' suggested Peploe.

'Yes, yes, you do that, Peploe,' said Creer. 'Anything else, Tanner?'

'Are you happy for us to brief the plan of attack?'

'A Company's leading, isn't it?'

'Very well,' said Tanner.

'Inform the respective company commanders, please, Peploe, and Tanner, you work out a plan of attack with Peploe. Then I suggest you get some sleep.'

They both saluted and left him.

'I'm sorry, Jack,' said Peploe, as soon as they were out of earshot. 'It's a bloody shower. I honestly don't think he's got the slightest idea what he's doing. If he's going to leave everything to us, I wish he'd do just that rather than dipping his oar in purely to prove he's still in command.'

'Trust me, John, he knows exactly what he's doing. Trying to get rid of us, that's what.'

'No, he isn't. He just knows A Company's most likely to get the job done. You do the hard slog, Croaker gets the credit.'

Tanner chuckled mirthlessly. 'Croaker. Jesus. Whoever decided the battalion needed him wants his head examining.'

'He's vile, Jack. I honestly think I might have to ask for a transfer soon. Everything about him makes my blood boil. I've a mind to write to the brigadier, you know. Make an official complaint.'

'What would you complain about? He's done nothing that would get him the chop. It would look like sour grapes for not being given the battalion permanently. I can't bear the man, but he's canny, John. Always has been.'

Peploe kicked at the ground. 'You're right, of course.' He sighed. 'Let's get through tomorrow, and then see.'

Tanner grunted. 'If we get through tomorrow.'

Nine p.m. At A Company Headquarters, Tanner and Peploe briefed for the attack. In a clear patch of ground just to the right of the road, near several gnarled olive trees, a ring of officers and platoon sergeants stood around the two men. A

212

rough map had been scored into the ground.

'This is to be a silent attack,' said Peploe. 'We'll move off at oh three hundred hours, and be in position to launch the attack at oh four ten, at very first light. We're expecting to have some sappers, who will blow holes in the wire, which, from the look of things, is no more than twenty yards in front of the pillboxes. We'll have D Company and our own mortars dug in on the ridge. They'll fire smoke bombs and mortars to start the attack. The infantry will then assault the pillboxes, using grenades, PIATs, MG and sub-machine-gun fire. D Company will also offer MG and rifle-fire support from the ridge. A Company will make the main assault, with B Company ready to follow through, but surprise is key, and we need to take those six pillboxes swiftly. Break the crust of the position, and the line should crumble.' He turned to Tanner. 'Captain?'

'Thank you, sir,' said Tanner. 'We're expecting a tougher fight here, boys. The Eyeties we've been up against so far have been bloody useless coastal divisions, but this lot are the Napoli Division and supposedly better-quality troops. Nothing we can't handle, but we can't expect them to throw their hands in the air at the first rifle shot. Our objective is to make a breach in the enemy defences either side of the road to Sortino, then take the town,' he said, 'so it's the three pillboxes either side of the road that we need to take out. Now, I know they might look like a tough nut, but remember this: the blokes holding them have nowhere to go. It's a rigid defence and those blocks of concrete are also pretty restrictive in terms of what the men in them can see. It's going to be barely light and all they've got are those narrow slits. We, on the other hand, will have adjusted to the light and will be able to see all around us. That's a big advantage.' He paused and looked at them all, then said, 'These pillboxes have been built to be mutually supporting, so it's important we smash 'em all at once. If so, in the smoke and confusion and firing, they won't be able to help one another, and then they'll be easy pickings.' His voice, which normally held only a trace of his Wiltshire burr, was more accented now that he was speaking urgently. He crouched down, pointing to the pillboxes circled in the dirt with his sword bayonet. 'I've called them Able, Baker, Charlie, Dog, Easy and Fox, from west to east. So for the initial assault, each platoon will be attacking two. The key two are Charlie and Dog, here,' he said, pointing to the pillboxes next to the road, at either side of the hairpin, 'but as I say, we need to hit them all together, at the same time. Everyone needs to aim at the loopholes – D Company's Brens on the ridge, and those in the assault in A Company, all right? The more bullets you send through the loopholes, the less likely they'll be able to fire back. And you lot in my company,' he said, looking at McAllister, then Hepworth, 'remember you can move and fire from whatever position you want, but those Eyeties can only do so from their slits in the pill-boxes. Everyone clear so far?'

Nods from the men around him.

'So this is the plan,' he continued. 'Each platoon is to take two pillboxes, one section on each, with Platoon Headquarters and Three Section bypassing and taking care of any loose troops beyond. Those attacking the pillboxes will have sappers with them to lay charges. From the ridge here, mortars will be set up to the left of each pillbox. The attacking infantry need to keep wide on the right as they approach so we don't get hit by our own mortars. Once you're at the wire, and have blown a hole, the mortars will fire further beyond the pillboxes.' He stood up now. 'But listen, make sure you hit 'em strong, all right? No dithering, no hitting the deck and going to ground. We strike together and we strike hard, and this will be over in a flash.' He eyed them again. 'And one other thing. We go in with plenty of ammo and not much else. No spades, no packs. Stuff your haversacks with ammo and your belts with grenades. Fill your gas-mask bag with ammo and sling it across your shoulder so that it can rest on your back if you need to lie down, but so you can grab stuff from it easily when you need to. Field dressings in your pockets. I wouldn't even take water bottles. Drink beforehand. All you want is your weapon and ammo, and for it to be easy to get to. And nothing that can chink together. Bayonet on your weapon, not flapping against your haversack.' He allocated the platoons to the pillboxes they would be attacking. 'Which section does what is up to you, as is the approach you take. You all know what you've got to do and how to do it.'

Peploe stepped forward. 'Make sure your weapons are clean, then try to get some rest,' he said. 'And good luck.'

Monday, 12 July, around 3.45 a.m. Captain Niccolò Togliatti awoke with a start.

'Sir! Sir!' said Lieutenant Ranieri. 'Wake up, sir!'

'What is it?' said Togliatti, sitting up immediately. He pulled off the cape that had been covering him and sat up on his camp bed. Inside the bunker it was dark, apart from the glow of the night sky through the loophole.

'We think we've heard something, sir.'

'Where?'

'From across the valley.'

'All right,' said Togliatti, getting up. He hurried out of the bunker into the cool night air. It was not yet light, but above the stars twinkled and the quarter-moon shone brightly. After a few moments, his eyes adjusted and he began to make out the dark shape of the valley, the pill-boxes and the connecting trenches.

He stepped out and moved towards the edge of the wire, Ranieri following him. The night seemed still.

'It was from up there on the ridge,' said Ranieri. 'Just faint sounds.'

'Sssh! Let me listen,' Togliatti whispered.

For a few moments there was silence, apart from the sounds of his own men. Someone was snoring gently nearby, another shuffling his kit in the slit trench.

Togliatti cursed to himself. He could hear nothing above those noises.

'It's all quiet again now,' whispered Ranieri, beside him.

Togliatti moved further forward. All was still. Then he heard it: a small chink or scrape, followed by another. His heart began to thump. Was that a Tommy he'd heard? It was certainly a good time for an attack. Or was it just an enemy patrol? He paused, listened again, but heard nothing. Then another chink, faint, but unmistakable. He froze. That was no animal. That was the sound of men – soldiers.

'What do you think, sir?' asked Ranieri. 'A patrol? Shall I send some men out?'

Togliatti shook his head. His sixth sense told him there was more than a patrol out there. There was something about the stillness, and about the pattern of small noises, how spread out they seemed to be, that made him certain an attack was coming. *Dear God.* It was still dark, but soon they would be under fire. It was inevitable. It had been inevitable since the invasion two days before. Long days of waiting, knowing that soon the enemy would be upon them. He wondered whether he should fire a couple of flares up over the valley, but dismissed the idea: it would light up their own positions as well as any enemy. Bile filled his stomach and his mouth felt tight and dry. Togliatti swallowed hard.

'Ranieri,' he said, 'wake the men. Get them up. Quick.'

3.50 a.m. On the ridge above the valley, the men were ready. Mortars in place, D Company's Bren gunners lying between scrub and rocks overlooking the enemy positions. Tanner had walked between his men, reminding them to attack hard, to keep moving, to keep firing. The sappers had not arrived – God only knew what had happened to them – but Sykes had enough dynamite: he always did. Inveigling his way into the quarter-master's stores was one of Sykes's many skills, as he liked to remind Tanner, and frankly, Tanner thought, thank God for that, or the attack would have been in trouble before it had even started.

Sykes had given each of the assault sections a crash course in the use of American half-pound blocks of TNT. Detonators in the plastic, fuses crimped into the detonators, then lit, rush to the wire, place it, and everyone duck. Having recced the Italian defences, Sykes told them he reckoned each small block of explosive would clear a good twenty-yard gap in the wire.

The men began to move forward, to their start positions on the valley floor before the mortars and Brens opened up. Thank God the old standard-issue hobnail boots had gone, the men now wearing the rubber-soled desert boots they had adopted in North Africa. But there was barely a breath of wind. That was not so good, as a breeze could hide noise. Even so, he was pleased about how quiet the men were. It was the benefit of having experience in the ranks. All attacks held risks, he knew that, but he preferred the silent infiltration, particularly when attacking up or down sloped ground where there was little chance of being silhouetted against the night sky. Of course, some of the enemy might hear them, but they would have no idea what numbers were out there or what levels of fire-power were about to be directed against them. The key was for his men to get as close as possible to the start position before the mortars opened up, or before the enemy opened fire. Before flares were shot into the air and lit the place up. Even then, though, there was enough cover in the valley – trees, shrubs, rocky walls – and long, dark shadows caused by any light from a flare. So far, though, the enemy had kept quiet.

3.55 a.m. It was still dark, but the light from the stars and the moon was enough to see features and men and objects close by. Away to the east, the very first streaks of dawn lit the sky: a faint, lightening grey on the far horizon. Tanner smiled to himself. As far as the light was concerned, Peploe had judged it perfectly.

He found Peploe beside him now. They had agreed to follow the assault platoons: two small sections, Fauvel leading one, Tanner the other, Peploe next to Phyllis with the radio set linked to Battalion HQ. Their task was to urge the men forward, with Sykes to go to the rescue of any assault section struggling to clear the wire. Tanner had attached his scope to his rifle and had his Beretta around his neck, his Enfield on his shoulder.

'Ready?' whispered Peploe.

Tanner nodded.

'I've just seen Ivo,' said Peploe. 'D Company are ready. If the enemy send up flares they'll open fire early.'

'Good,' said Tanner. 'Let's get moving, then.' He looked around at his men, who were standing waiting patiently for the order to move off. Sykes

219

was beside him, and Brown, Trahair and Griffiths. He counted them all, then realized one was missing: Phyllis.

'Where's Phyllis?' he hissed.

'Here, sir,' said Phyllis, suddenly appearing. He turned not to Tanner but to Peploe. 'I've just had a message from Battalion HQ, sir,' he said. 'Artillery's not ready. The colonel's ordered us to wait.'

'What?' said Peploe, his voice incredulous.

'Jesus!' spat Tanner.

'He says we're to wait until he gives the order.'

'How bloody long is that going to be?' asked Peploe.

Phyllis shrugged.

'Well, get on the bloody radio, Siff, and ask,' said Tanner.

Phyllis squatted down with the radio set.

Peploe stood over him, clutching his chin, but Tanner pulled him away. 'This is madness,' he said. 'The men have already set off. If we wait they'll be exposed in the open in half an hour.' He looked at his watch. *0359.* 'D Company will be opening fire in eleven minutes. It's too bloody late and we don't need the artillery anyway.'

'Ignore it, sir,' said Sykes, beside him. 'The lives of the lads come first.'

Phyllis now rejoined them. 'He just says stand by until further notice, sir.'

Peploe took off his helmet, ran his hands through his hair, walked around in a circle, then said, 'Sod it. We go in. I'll tell him the order arrived too late. Phyllis, send a message back. Say, "Too late, men in position, D Coy about to fire. Arty not needed."'

Tanner gripped Peploe's shoulder. 'You've made the right decision, John.'

'That man,' hissed Peploe. 'Maybe you were right. Maybe he is trying to get us killed.' He put his helmet back on. 'Now, let's go.'

4.08 a.m. They had silently followed a path away from the road that led below a low outcrop, then cut back down towards the valley, so as not to be silhouetted against the night sky as they dropped below the ridge. Now, just a couple of minutes later, they were near the valley floor. It was still dark – too dark to distinguish much – but from their position below the low cliff of the riverbed, Tanner could see the outline of two pillboxes against the ridge of the northern valley side. The assault sections were ahead, he hoped, in the shrub twenty yards in front; he still could not make out any men. He glanced around him. Sykes, then next to him Trahair and Phyllis.

'Stick to me like glue, Siff,' he told Phyllis. He wanted his radio man beside him at all times. Brown was there, too, and Griffiths, and further along, Peploe with Fauvel and five others from Company Headquarters. The rest had remained on the ridge, Left Out of Battle.

Still no sign of life from the Italians. Perhaps, he thought, complete surprise would be achieved, after all. He lay there, rifle at his shoulder, thinking how still, how calm, *how silent*, it all seemed. The night air was heavy with the scent of wild flowers. He glanced at Sykes beside him and, in the pale light, saw his friend wink.

Tanner looked down at his watch. *Ten past four.*

Suddenly he heard a mortar whoosh into the sky, then the stutter of a machine-gun from one of the pillboxes and faint orange stabs of tracer arcing across the valley. A moment later several mortars exploded and in a split-second the dawn was alive to the din of battle.

13

Mortar shells crashed around the pillboxes, sending huge spumes of rock, grit and dust into the air, while the smoke bombs detonated and enveloped the Italian positions. Tanner was on his feet now, Sykes and Brown either side of him, following the assault sections as they emerged from their hiding positions and rushed towards the wire. Through the smoke, bullets and tracer hissed and fizzed. Tanner saw one man jerk and fall backwards, and two others drop to the ground.

Running up behind them, he yanked them back to their feet.

'Get up! Get up!' he yelled. 'Keep moving!'

He hurried on, following McAllister, who led the assault section on pillbox Charlie, the first bunker on the hairpin. He saw McAllister run forward with the TNT, then scurry back. A few seconds later there was a further deafening explosion, then the men ran forward again, towards the smoke. Another man was hit – *Who was that? Saundby?* – but the wire had blown as planned.

Half crouching, Tanner ran forward, ducking, weaving, scrambling through the gap in the wire. Through the swirling smoke, the pillbox suddenly reappeared, the muzzle flash of a machine-gun vivid through the haze. Bullets scythed above him, as McAllister and two others ran low towards the embrasure, ducking underneath. Tanner followed them, watched McAllister throw an anti-tank grenade through the port hole, then cover his ears. Shouts from within, then screams as the grenade exploded.

Tanner's ears rang shrilly, but he was conscious of Sykes beside him, and together they ran on, past the side of the pillbox to the rear. Startled Italians manned the slit trench that ran from the bunker. Tanner saw them instinctively try to bring their weapons to bear but both he and Sykes beside him opened fire, with Thompson and Beretta, and the men jerked backwards. Tanner ran along the top of the trench, which zigzagged up the valley side towards Baker and Able pillboxes. Baker lay above them, to their left, emerging through the rapidly thinning smoke. A machine-gun was still firing wildly and the assault section appeared to have ground to a halt, lying low in the scrub on the wrong side of the wire.

'Damn it!' cursed Tanner, crouching beside Sykes. Which section was that? *Hepworth's platoon.* He'd bloody well murder them later. Speed was of the essence; he'd told them that. *Hepworth should know better.* The mortars had already moved on, firing beyond the pillbox past the ridgeline. The sky was lightening already.

'He's firing wild, though, Jack,' said Sykes.

Tanner quickly looked around him. Smoke gushed from the embrasure in Dog pillbox; it appeared to have been silenced, but Able was still active, as was Fox. Fire from Able was supporting Baker. The chance to knock all of them out at a blow had passed.

'We've got to get Baker,' muttered Tanner. It stood about fifty yards above them.

'Agreed,' said Sykes.

Tanner glanced around and found Brown and Trahair behind them, looking nervously up towards pillbox Baker. Phyllis. Where was Phyllis?

A figure scrambled up behind them and collapsed on the ground gasping. 'Blimey!' said Phyllis, breathlessly. 'This is a bit bloody hot.'

'Put a sock in it, Siff,' muttered Tanner, then said, 'Right, we're going to have to do this. We're already inside the wire, but Hepworth's mob over there are not.'

'Look out, sir!' said Trahair.

Tanner ducked and felt a bullet hiss over his head as Brown lurched to his right and let out a short burst from his Thompson.

'You're all right now, sir,' said Brown, as Tanner looked back towards the trench. 'Got 'im. Some Eyetie poked his head up and took a pot-shot.'

'Thanks, Browner,' said Tanner. A burst of MG fire from Baker scythed over their heads. They ducked, then Sykes rolled over and pulled a stick of dynamite from his haversack, lit it with his American lighter, then hurled it up the slope. A pause, another burst of bullets whistled over their heads, then came the explosion.

'Now!' said Tanner. 'Get up! Brown and Trahair, move wide and give us cover. Stan, Siff, you follow me!'

They scampered on up the slope, the orange muzzle flash of the enemy machine-gun bright through the still swirling smoke. Bullets pinged onto the ground to their right, ricocheting off the rock. Tanner darted from side to side, ducking, gasping, then glanced at Sykes, who had produced two more sticks of dynamite. Together they dived behind a low rock, just twenty yards from Baker, flinching as more bullets pinged and hissed nearby. A glance behind, yes, there was Phyllis, clutching his helmet to his head. Grimacing, Tanner saw Sykes light first one stick of dynamite, then the other. The fuse fizzed, he passed one to Tanner, then they both rolled clear of the rock and threw the sticks. Another brief pause, then a double explosion. Smoke and dust and grit spewed into the air, but as it began clattering down on their tin helmets, Tanner and Sykes were already on their feet and rushing the last twenty yards to Baker, Tanner fumbling for a grenade as he did so.

4.15 a.m. At D Company's fire-support positions on the southern ridge of the valley, a Jeep skidded to a halt and a lieutenant from the Royal Artillery jumped out and ran over to Major Ivo Macdonald, D Company commander. Following him was a gunner with a radio set.

'Colonel Creer sent me,' he said to Macdonald. 'Lieutenant Stokes.' He saluted briskly.

Macdonald nodded. 'Better late than never. We

were expecting you chaps an hour ago.'

'Sorry, sir, but I don't know what you mean. We're here right on time. We were told you would be going in at oh four thirty.'

'Really?' said Macdonald, looking surprised.

'But I see it's already begun.'

'The start time was oh four ten,' said Macdonald. 'Never oh four thirty.'

Stokes shrugged. 'Chinese whispers, I suppose.'

'A signal taken down wrong,' agreed Macdonald. 'Anyway, it doesn't really matter. It was always going to be a silent attack, anyway.'

'Colonel Creer asked for artillery support, sir,' said Stokes. He looked around. A row of mortar teams were firing. Boxes of ammunition lay strewn around them. Up ahead, the ground rose slightly so that the opposite side of the valley was out of sight, but Stokes could hear the battle raging beyond: the sound of mortar shells exploding, of small arms, and distant cries over the din.

'Yes,' said Macdonald. 'I know.' He glanced at his CSM, Spiers, who raised a wry eyebrow.

'My orders are to see whether the attack needs our support,' said Stokes. 'We've a battery of twenty-five-pounders two miles back.'

'You'd better have a look, then,' said Macdonald. He led Stokes forward towards the valley's edge. As they approached the ridge, they crouched down and hurried towards some bushes beside a lone fig tree, where a Bren team was firing.

'How are we doing, Carter?' said Macdonald, squatting beside the gunner as he changed magazines.

'Looks like the attack's stalled a bit, sir,' said Carter.

Stokes glanced at Macdonald, waved over his radio operator, then lay down on his front and peered through his field glasses.

'There are six pillboxes,' said Macdonald, beside him, 'running left to right called Able through to Fox.'

'The two middle ones, Charlie and Dog, appear to have fallen,' said Stokes, 'but I can't see that any others have. All I can see are lots of men lying down among the rock and scrub.'

'Early days,' said Macdonald. 'They've only just gone in. I'll order the mortars to drop back a bit. Target the pillboxes overlooking the valley.'

'Our twenty-five-pounders will sort those out in a trice,' said Stokes. 'Let me contact Colonel Creer.'

'Wait,' said Macdonald. 'And that's an order. If you start shelling now, there's a good chance you'll hit our own. Give them a chance. The attack's only been going a few minutes.'

Stokes nodded.

'Good,' said Macdonald. 'Let me see what our mortars can do to help first.'

He left Stokes, who peered again through his binoculars. He could see Rangers on the far side of the valley, but they still appeared to be stuck. The orange flash of machine-guns and small arms flickered from the pillboxes. Stokes thought for a moment. Macdonald had just given him a direct order, but then so, too, had Creer, and he was a colonel and the officer commanding the Yorks Rangers. Macdonald was only a major.

Creer had demanded artillery support and it looked to Stokes as though the attack needed it.

Turning to Carter, his radio operator, he instructed him to call up the battalion's net. A few moments later, Stokes had on the headset and was speaking to Creer himself.

'Yes, sir,' said Stokes. 'It's hard to say... There's a lot of smoke as you would expect... Yes, all right, sir... Yes, Major Macdonald ordered me to wait... Of course, sir... Yes, sir... Right away, sir.' Taking off his headset, he turned to his radio operator. 'Contact the battery.' He pulled his map from his case.

'Are we going to fire then, sir?' asked Carter.

'Yes, Colonel Creer's orders. He wants us to stonk those positions.'

'Won't we hit our own men, sir?'

'No, I don't think so, Carter. They're still some way from the pillboxes. We'll start generously and creep down.' He quickly calculated the co-ordinates, double-checked he had them correctly, then relayed them to the battery. A five- or ten-minute stonk by eight twenty-five-pounders firing a mixture of high explosive and armour-piercing would soon sort out those pillboxes, he thought.

Two explosions from the valley made him look up. Beside him, the Bren opened fire again. Stokes peered through his field glasses. Smoke and dust swirled around pillbox Baker, but away to the left and right, below the domed roofs of Able and Fox, he saw the men still in the rocks and undergrowth.

With a gasp, Tanner felt his shoulder ram into the

228

edge of the concrete pillbox. He sank onto his backside and pulled out a grenade, a No. 74 anti-tank bomb. Inside, men were shouting, and then an arm appeared, waving a pistol vaguely towards the ground.

'Jesus!' muttered Tanner, as Sykes, under the second peephole, ducked away as the pistol fired close by him. Pulling the pin of the grenade, he counted three seconds, then lobbed it into the embrasure. More shouts from inside and then, a second later, the grenade exploded. Tanner was already on his feet, but jolted at the sound of a large explosion from pillbox Easy, some sixty yards to his right. Glancing across, he fleetingly saw Peploe and Fauvel urging the men forward. *Good.* He ran around the pillbox and fired two one-second bursts at the communications trenches behind. His ears still rang, his heart pounded, the smoke and the bitter stench of cordite made his eyes smart and his throat sore, but he was conscious of Italians raising their hands in the air and of a man calling, 'Don't shoot, don't shoot,' in English. More of his own were around him now. Brown and Trahair, and there was Sykes, Tommy gun pointed at the Italians.

Tanner stepped forward, towards the Italian officer, who still had his arms in the air.

'You speak English?' said Tanner.

The Italian shrugged. 'A little,' he said. Machine-gun fire rang out from the direction of pillbox Able. 'They won't shoot at us,' he said, turning his head towards Able. 'They won't shoot on their own. It is over.' He lowered his arms and reached into his holster. He handed Tanner his pistol. 'Captain Niccolò Togliatti,' he said. 'Thank God it's over.'

'The battle or your war?' asked Tanner.

'Both.' He smiled wistfully.

'Were you in the desert?' asked Tanner.

Togliatti shook his head. 'Russia. You captured our armies in North Africa, remember.'

'I do, as it happens,' said Tanner.

'Sir,' said a voice behind him. Tanner turned to see McAllister and some of his men from 3 Platoon.

'What about Able, sir?'

Turner looked up towards the pillbox away to their left on the ridge.

Following their gaze, Togliatti said, 'I will tell them to surrender. It's over.'

As he spoke, a noise made them both pause. An intense sucking noise, a terrific rush of air, then a dismal whine.

'Oh, no,' muttered Tanner. A split second later, the shell hit the ground twenty yards above them. Tanner felt the air sucked from him and a great force lift him from his feet and hurl him backwards. Pain shot through his back as he landed, sprawled, upon the bank of a trench, the recently dug soil cushioning his fall.

No! No, no, no! More shells were falling now, so he quickly rolled over and into the trench alongside two dead Italians. Others, who had moments before surrendered, now cowered beside him, hands clutching their helmets. Where the hell was Sykes? Where was Phyllis? He had to get to Phyllis and that radio set and stop this.

'Siff!' he yelled, over the din. 'Siff!' Where had Phyllis been? By Baker. *Get back to the pillbox.* A shell landed close by, sending a mountain of grit and debris high into the air. Metal and stone zipped above him, then the shower of stone clattered down on his helmet and shoulders. Keeping low, Tanner turned and moved along the low trench towards the pillbox. He reckoned he'd been flung a good ten yards or more. More shells crashed into the Italian positions. The ground pulsing, the screams of men. Dust, smoke, debris. Tanner could hear almost nothing now, his ears ringing, his head and back thumping with pain. The stench of burned flesh from the entrance to the pillbox. Crouching, he moved forward. More dead – an Italian with a leg gone, just a raw stump. Tanner picked him up, and heaved him over the edge of the trench as two more shells whumped into the ground above him. Stop, cower, wait for the shower of debris, then move on. *Where are you, Stan?* A man groaning, an Italian, clutching his stomach. He was half leaning against the door of the pillbox, his head tilted strangely.

'Siff!' Tanner yelled again.

'Mother,' murmured the wounded man. 'Mother.'

Tanner looked at him again and felt his body go cold. The man was not an Italian at all. *No. Please, God, no!*

'Mac,' he said, 'it's me, Mac. Tanner.' He tried to straighten McAllister, cradling his head.

'Sir?' he said. His eyes flickered. 'Think I've had it this time.'

'No, you'll be all right, Mac. I'll look after you. You'll be just fine.' Tanner looked down. *Oh, Jesus.* McAllister's stomach had been ripped open, leaving a dark, glistening mass. The boy was clutching it, vainly trying to keep his guts together. Coils of blood-soaked intestine had unravelled down his side.

'I've had it, haven't I, sir?'

'Sssh,' said Tanner, feeling inside his gas-mask bag. Where the hell was that morphine? Gone. He cursed, overcome by his inability to help his friend. 'You'll be all right, Mac.' *What am I saying? He's not going to be all right.*

Tanner held him there, but then McAllister looked down. 'Oh, God,' he mumbled. 'Oh, God, look at me! I don't want to die, sir. Please don't let me die!'

Tanner turned McAllister's head into his chest and rocked him gently. 'You're not going to, Mac, you're not going to.' He swallowed hard, and felt his throat catch. So many men had died in this stupid war, he thought, some good friends among them, but he had never let himself dwell on such things. Of course people died – that was what happened in war. But McAllister had been with him since Norway. Three long years. In that time he had grown from a cocky young Bradford guttersnipe into one of his most trusted men. And a fine soldier too. How old was he? Twenty-one. No older. *Twenty-one.* Tanner briefly closed his eyes. It was no age. Here, as he lay cradled in Tanner's arms, his body torn apart, he looked like a boy again.

McAllister began to sob, and although Tanner

232

tried desperately to control himself, he felt a tear run down his cheek too. He'd not wept in years – not once since his father had died – and yet here, beside this pillbox reeking of smoke, cordite and death, he felt overcome.

'You'll be all right, Mac,' he mumbled, but McAllister was dying and knew it, and was weeping because his young life was about to end. How could it be any other way, with blood soaking both their uniforms and with half his innards strewn on the ground?

Another shell hurtled over, smashing into the ground not thirty yards from them. Tanner ducked down, pulling McAllister tight towards him with one arm and with the other, feeling for his Colt at his hip. As the soil and stone and grit fell upon them, he raised the Colt towards McAllister's head and fired. 'Goodbye, Mac,' he said, holding the now lifeless body and then resting it against the wall of the pillbox. He wiped his eyes on the back of his arm, then clenched his fist and brought it to his mouth, felt his body tremble, then yelled, 'Siff! Siff!'

'Here, sir,' said a faint voice.

Thank God. Tanner scrambled to his feet and clambering out of the trench, leaving McAllister's lifeless body. He ran around the edge of the pillbox and there found Phyllis, huddled against the wall below the embrasure, knees tight up against his chest, hands over his ears.

Reaching him, Tanner gripped his shoulder and shook him. 'Siff!' he said. 'Bloody get that radio set of yours working!'

'You all right, sir?' said Phyllis as, with fumbling

fingers, he pulled the pack off his back.

'Just get on with it,' Tanner snarled.

Phyllis slipped the headset from around his neck onto his ears, and began calling up Battalion.

'Hello, Sunray,' he said, as another shell hurtled into the ground away to their right. 'Stop shelling. Repeat, stop shelling.'

'Here, give that to me,' said Tanner, snatching the mouthpiece, then yelling, 'Stop the bloody shelling now! Repeat, now!' He handed back the mouthpiece. 'Jesus!' he said. 'Keep going, Siff, until the shelling stops.'

More shells rushed over, exploding near pillbox Fox. Small-arms firing had stopped entirely. Smoke and haze covered the valley slopes. *Christ,* thought Tanner, *why are they still firing?* The battle was won, but at what cost? He wondered how many of his men were now dead or wounded, killed by their own artillery fire. How many more good men like McAllister? *If this is Creer's doing, I'll kill him. I'll bloody kill him.*

From D Company's positions on the ridge the other side of the valley, Major Ivo Macdonald had scarcely been able to believe what he was seeing when the first of the shells started whistling over. Lieutenant Stokes had struck him as a rather inoffensive sort of fellow, but taking him to the ridge edge had been little more than paying lip service to Colonel Creer. He was well aware that Creer had demanded artillery support, but it had not occurred to him that it would ever be needed. Nor had it been. Yes, A Company's attack had briefly stalled, but never critically so,

234

and no sooner had he left Stokes than he had watched two of the pillboxes fall. He had no doubt the battle would have been won soon after.

Instead, the air had been filled with howling shells from the eight twenty-five-pounders – shells that were falling on both the enemy and their own men.

Macdonald had felt sick – physically sick – as he had yelled at his radio man to call up Battalion immediately, then had run across to Stokes.

'What the bloody hell do you think you're doing?' Macdonald had barked. He was a tall, lean man with a gentle face and smooth dark hair. He was not a man to get easily riled, but right now, he had never felt angrier in his life.

'Carrying out my orders, sir,' Stokes had replied. 'I was told to direct our fire onto the pillboxes.'

'What about my bloody orders? Jesus, stop the shelling, Stokes! For God's sake, stop the shelling now!'

'But Colonel Creer ordered me–'

Macdonald had his pistol in his hand and now pointed it at Stokes. 'Stop the shelling, Stokes – now! My God, man, did you not see the men attacking just before the shelling began?'

'No, sir,' said Stokes. The colour drained from his face. 'I was watching the targets.'

'You bloody idiot!' shouted Macdonald. 'Both Charlie and Dog had been silenced before the first shell landed. You're a forward observation officer, aren't you?'

Stokes nodded.

'Then bloody stop this shelling now. You're

235

killing our own men!'

'Oh, my God,' said Stokes. He glanced at his signals man. 'Carter, tell the battery to cease firing with immediate effect.'

More shells whistled over as Carter tried to make contact with the battery.

Macdonald watched them explode, flinching as they did so. 'Good God,' he said, 'what have you done?'

'I – I was just carrying out orders, sir,' said Stokes. 'The colonel asked for a ten-minute stonk.'

'He wouldn't have done if he'd known he was hitting his own men.'

Macdonald continued to stare ahead. A pall of smoke hung over the valley. The two explosions settled, then a strange silence descended. No small arms could be heard; no more shells came over. Only a low groan – the groan of wounded and dying men.

Tanner found Sykes taking cover in one of the trenches that ran off pillbox Charlie just as the last of the shells had thumped into the Italian positions some sixty yards away. He was smoking a cigarette, his helmet and shoulders covered with earth, grit and debris. Either side of him lay two dead Italians, one with a large chunk of his head missing.

'Stan! Are you all right?'

'I think so,' he said. 'More than can be said for these two. Can't hear much, but otherwise I've not got a scratch.'

Tanner heaved one of the dead Italians out of

the trench and crouched beside him, gripping Sykes's shoulder as he did so. 'Mac's dead.'

'Oh, no.' Sykes drove his fist into the wall of the trench. 'He was a diamond, was Mac.'

'And how many more of our lads have been killed? That bloody murderer.'

'Croaker? You reckon this is his doing?'

'I'd put money on it.'

'Reckon it's over?'

Tanner nodded. 'Better be. Any rate, we need to take control here. Round up the prisoners, see who's still alive, get B Company down. Mac's by the entrance to Baker. We need to get him covered up. If you see him, brace yourself.'

Sykes grimaced. 'All right, Jack.'

Tanner climbed out of the trench and ran around to the front of pillbox Charlie, where he found Phyllis still crouching with his radio set, Brown now beside him.

'We need B Company down here and as many RAMC wallahs as possible. Get on to it now, Siff.'

Men were now emerging once more. Tanner strode along the top of the trenches, his Beretta in his hands.

'Come on, get up! Get up!' he called. Along the top of the ridge, he saw a number of Italians fleeing their positions. Raising his Beretta, he was about to fire, then lowered it again. What was the point? Glancing around, he saw Lieutenant Shopland and Sykes lifting McAllister. Tanner sighed. Then, as more Italians stumbled towards him with their hands raised, he saw a body lying against some rocks a little distance from the pillbox.

'Sir?'

He turned and saw Trahair and Brown, their faces covered with dust, and a small streak of blood on Brown's cheek.

'Why were we being shelled, sir?' said Brown. His eyes were wide and disbelieving.

'God only knows,' muttered Tanner. 'At least you're both alive. Look after these Eyeties, will you?'

He left them and walked over to the prostrate body by the rocks.

The man lay on the ground without an obvious wound on him. His officer's uniform, although covered with grit, was unmarked. Tanner squatted beside him. What had been his name? He couldn't remember, but he'd been talking to him just as that shell had rushed in. The man's face was calm: eyes closed, a faint smile on his face. Tanner had never seen a dead man look so much as though he were merely asleep. He leaned forward and felt for a pulse on the neck, but there was nothing.

What was his name? Tanner undid the man's top breast pocket and felt inside. His fingers touched a collection of papers and booklets, just as he knew they would. Soldiers the world over kept their most personal documents there, close to the heart. A pay book, another booklet, blue, with 'Libretto Personale' printed on the outside. And inside an identity photo and his name, place of birth, date of birth and other key pieces of inform-ation. *Niccolò Togliatti. Yes, that was it.* He rifled through the booklets and some photographs dropped out. A group of men in uniform, arms around each other's shoulders. Another, a family picture: a father, a teenage boy and girl and a younger girl. Then two more pictures, one of a mother and daughter, a very beautiful mother, and a second of the same woman: fair-haired, like Togliatti. Tanner whistled. She was lovely. Wife? Sister? He looked at the earlier photograph of the family group. Were the younger girl and the blonde woman one and the same? He thought maybe, but it was hard to tell.

Tanner stared at the photograph again, then slipped it into his own pocket before closing the booklet and putting it with the rest back where he'd found it. He stared at the dead man again, then pulled out a cigarette, lit it, and inhaled deeply. The sun was rising, the valley now bathed in light. A pall still hung along the valley floor but here on the ridge the smoke had cleared, even if the stench had not. Tanner stood up and inhaled deeply. *What a fucking morning.* Mac gone, this decent Italian too. *God knows who else.*

'There you are,' came Fauvel's voice.

Tanner turned. 'Gavin. Good to see you in one piece.'

'And you, Jack.'

'McAllister's dead,' he said.

'I heard. And a number of others beside. Harker's bought it, and so, too, has Griffiths, I'm afraid. We're sixteen dead and twenty-two wounded.'

Tanner rubbed his brow. 'Christ,' he muttered. 'That's more than an entire platoon.'

'But I'm afraid that's not all, Jack,' said Fauvel.

'What?' said Tanner. 'What is it?'

Fauvel sighed, then said, 'It's Major Peploe. I'm sorry, Jack.'

14

Tuesday, 13 July, around 1.30 p.m. War, as Lieutenant Colonel Charlie Wiseman had been discovering these past nine months, never went entirely to plan. Take the airborne drop, for example. The 82nd Airborne Division had been supposed to capture the high ground and road junctions around six miles north and north-east of Gela. This, it was hoped, would prevent enemy counterattacks down those routes as the main American invasion force landed. However, to do that, Colonel Gavin's 505th Regimental Combat Team had to be dropped in a pretty tight DZ, and that was the last thing that had happened.

Sitting in a tent at the new Seventh Army Command Post, Wiseman was reading through the sitreps barely able to believe just how far and wide those paratroopers had landed. Over most of southeast Sicily, as far as he could tell, including a fair number in the British sector. Had they taken the key nodal points north of Gela, the bridgehead might have been established more quickly, but as it was, the Rangers and the 1st Infantry had beaten off counterattacks by the Livorno and Hermann Göring Divisions with far greater losses to the enemy than themselves. It had been what Patton called a 'hard fight' but their boys had prevailed. Meanwhile the paratroopers, spread far and wide, had caused may-

240

hem. They were trained to use their initiative and to think on their feet, and so they had. Newly taken prisoners repeatedly claimed having been harassed and attacked by marauding paratroopers, while intercepted signals suggested the Axis command reckoned some four airborne divisions and fifty thousand men had been dropped. This had clearly hampered Axis plans and sown seeds of doubt and confusion. In fact, just one regimental combat team had been dropped, Colonel Gavin's, which amounted to just under three and a half thousand men.

Maybe, Wiseman thought, they were using airborne troops all wrong. Maybe the scattergun approach was more effective. When he had parachuted into Villalba, the C-47 had managed to drop them pretty much where they intended, but it was quite another matter accurately dropping men over an active battle front with flak pumping towards you, in high winds, all surprise gone. So maybe they shouldn't even try in future. Maybe spreading mayhem and confusion, ambushing supply lines, shooting up any enemy that moved was a better use of such highly trained and resourceful troops. Perhaps he would write a few notes about it and hand them to Patton or Gay.

He wondered how Patton and Gay were getting on with General Alexander and his delegation. The Allied Army Group commander had arrived just after one, while Patton was having his lunch. He'd not been best pleased to be disturbed, even by Alexander, although he liked and respected the British general. Alexander, Patton had told him, had seen action at every rank of command, and was the most experienced battlefield commander the Allies had. Patton liked fighting soldiers, not pen-pushers; he admired courage, and respected the kind of battlefield experience Alexander evidently held.

Wiseman liked to think Patton had gained Alexander's respect too. In Tunisia, Patton had done all that Alexander had asked of him. He had taken command of a demoralized II Corps and given it self-belief and a new fighting edge – which had been only too evident these past few days on Seventh Army's front. He hoped Patton would be given the free rein he deserved to push north right away, slicing up through Sicily, around the western side of Etna and to Messina before more reinforcements arrived. He knew that was Patton's plan and hope. Confidence at Seventh Army was high. The Livorno had been badly mauled, the HG Division thrown back. More and more supplies and vehicles were reaching the beaches with every hour. The feeling in the camp was that the worst was over, that the moment of danger, when the bridgehead had been threatened, had passed. Now the roads were open. Success, as Patton never failed to remind them, should be exploited.

Since Alexander's arrival, the commanders had been shut away in the map tent. Wiseman had not been invited to join them but now got up and stepped outside his own tent. Another bright, beautiful and scorching day. He pulled out a cigarette and lit it. The CP had been set up around the remains of an ancient Greek temple overlooking Gela. Not much remained – just a lone column and a few stones on the ground – but it held a good position. It was close to the edge of the town where Patton's personal digs had been established, but with views back down to the beaches and to the hills beyond. A good spot.

Wiseman had not even finished his smoke when Alexander emerged from the map tent, looking as dapper and unruffled as ever, followed by Patton and others. Alexander chatted amiably, made some amusing remark, at which the others laughed, then stepped into his waiting command car and, moments later, sped off. Wiseman watched Patton punch his hand a couple of times, then turn back into the tent. A moment later, one of the general's aides strode towards him.

'Colonel,' he called. 'The general wants you.'

Flicking away his cigarette, Wiseman walked up to him.

'What's going on?'

'Brace yourself,' said the aide. 'New boundaries.'

'Bad, then?'

The aide nodded.

Inside the tent, Patton, Gay and Major Stiller stood around the map table.

'Sir!' said Wiseman, saluting.

'Gay, put Wiseman in the picture, will you? I'm still too mad to speak.'

'Of course,' said Gay. He cleared his throat. 'It seems the British are doing pretty well, almost no resistance to speak of, so General Montgomery believes Eighth Army can wrap up this show in double-quick time. A matter of days, apparently.

He's suggested to Alex that we hold the HG Division here, that Leese's XXX Corps then cut in behind them, wedging them between us and the Brits.' He pointed this out on the giant map spread across several trestle tables. 'Meanwhile, Eighth Army's main thrust pushes on north along the coast and east of Etna, and then, with the Krauts isolated and cut off, XXX Corps attacks north around the west of Etna.' Gay sighed heavily. 'So, in other words, XXX Corps will be advancing down this road here. Highway 124.' He pointed to the road that ran north from 45th Division's sector. 'Through Caltagirone, Enna and Leonforte.'

'The road Forty-fifth Division was to use,' said Wiseman.

'Exactly. Or, rather, Seventh Army's main artery of advance north.'

'And now it's been handed to Monty,' thundered Patton, bringing his fist down hard on the table. He leaned forward, his jaw set. 'They take us for Goddamn fools. Alexander came here with no Americans in his team. Not one. What fools we are.'

'I'm sorry to hear this, General,' said Wiseman.

Patton raised himself up again. 'Orders are orders. That's what we do in the Army: we obey orders. When Alexander orders us to hand over Highway 124, there is nothing we can do but accept it. But we don't have to like it, and let me tell you, gentlemen, this makes me only more determined to show those sons-of-bitches a thing or two. Monty thinks he can steal our thunder. He thinks he can relegate us to a side-show. We're going to prove him wrong. Alex has agreed to let us advance west and take Agrigento.' He pointed to the port some thirty-five miles to the west.

'He has agreed to a reconnaissance force to attempt to take it,' interrupted Gay.

'We'll Goddamn take it, Gay.' There was a glint in his eye now. 'We take Agrigento, we don't need Syracuse, which saves us a turn of around 140 miles over bad roads, and having to share it with Eighth Army. It also means we can abandon the beaches as a means of unloading. With Agrigento in our hands, we can speed the build-up of forces, and with more forces and especially more vehicles, we can operate both more quickly and with a hell of a bigger punch.' He looked at them all in triumph. 'Bradley won't like it, but Forty-fifth Division will come in behind First Division and advance north through the interior. But this is where you come in, Wiseman.'

'Yes, sir.'

'I told you I wanted your man in Villalba to keep the Italians out of our hair. I still do, but we're now going to use the main road that crosses the island. I want your man to make sure we have as little trouble as possible. We're going to rush Palermo, take it, then cut back along the northern coast road and take Messina before Monty does. It's a hell of a lot longer, but these are the best roads this Godforsaken island's got. Our magnificent Seventh Army, gentlemen, will have the last laugh.'

Wiseman grinned. It was a brilliant plan. Whether or not the British XXX Corps managed to trap the Germans was another matter, but it was surely the case that Eighth Army would now draw the bulk of the island's defenders. If Don Calogero Vizzini could deliver on his promise, the road to Palermo would be virtually open. In Monty's plan, Seventh Army was the anvil, and Eighth Army the hammer. In fact, it would be the other way around.

'But, Wiseman,' said Patton, 'we need your man to deliver on his promise. We've invested a lot in this little venture of you intelligence fellows. Be sure you make good that promise. We need Signor Vizzini to demonstrate this influence of his. If he does, his organization can have the whole Goddamn island as far as I'm concerned. If he helps us get rid of the Fascists and Nazis, we'll help him get his kingdom back.'

Wiseman smiled. 'Yes, sir,' he said. 'I'll get on to it right away.'

Over to the east, in Eighth Army's sector, the Yorks Rangers had reached the town of Melilli, and were now leaguering in olive groves to the south, taking over positions from the 1st Green Howards, who were pushing north along with the King's Own Yorkshire Light Infantry. Tanner sat down beneath an old gnarled olive tree and pulled out a cigarette.

'Kernow, make us a cup of char, will you?' he said to Trahair.

'Now, sir?' he said, as he pulled his rain cape from his pack.

'Yes. Tea first, then bedding arrangements.'

The sun beat down, dappling brightly between the dark leaves. Tanner breathed in the smell of earth, sweat, tobacco and gun oil. It was the smell of life: of the Sicilian countryside, of soldiers. McAllister came into his thoughts: lying there in his arms, his blood-slicked guts trailing from the open cavity of his shattered stomach, the life seeping out of him. And now gone, no more. Nothing. Hastily buried that morning in a temporary grave. Later, his rotted corpse would be dug up, the bones and what flesh remained taken away and reburied in a newly marked-out cemetery. A stone would be added, just like those of all the dead from the Great War. McAllister would never return to Yorkshire. He wondered whether his parents and siblings would one day make it out here to see where their boy was buried. Unlikely. Mac's family were working-class folk. There wasn't much money. The Army shipped you out here for nothing when there was a war on, but when it was over the cost would be dear.

He closed his eyes, listening to the hubbub going on around him. Men talking, calling out, the crump of distant shelling to the north, and the faint sound of small arms. Then the familiar voice of Sykes.

'Well done, Kernow. That for me?'

'No, sir, it's for the captain.'

''E's asleep. 'E won't mind.'

'No, I'm not,' said Tanner, 'and I would.'

'That's all right. I'll take yours, Kernow. You don't mind brewing up some more, do you?'

'Would it make any difference if I did, sir?'

'No, it wouldn't.' Sykes grabbed the tin cup, then raised it. 'Cheers.' He came and sat down next to Tanner. 'I've checked on the men. Captain Fauvel's still with Battalion.'

'How are they?'

'Pissed off. Knackered. Sore feet. Wishing they had their vehicles back. Gutted about Mac and the others, and gutted about the major too.'

Tanner rubbed his eyes. 'You think he'll be all right?'

'Peploe? Yes, I'm sure he will.'

Maybe, thought Tanner. Wounded in the leg, head and shoulder. The piece of shrapnel in his leg had still been sticking out when he'd found him lying on the side of the hill, his head propped against a rock. It had hit an artery, and looked bad. Tanner had seen plenty of people die from loss of blood when an artery had been hit; Peploe's trouser leg had been soaked. And how much cloth had gone into the wound? It was such things that ensured a wound turned bad, that gangrene or septicaemia set in. The shoulder wound appeared less severe, as was the gash in his cheek; he'd be scarred for life, that was for sure.

Tanner had stood over the medic, watching him tighten the tourniquet around Peploe's thigh. His friend looked in a terrible way: bloodied and battered. Unconscious.

'What do you think?' he had asked the medic.

'We got to him quickly,' he said. 'He's still alive. If we can get him to a hospital quickly he might make it.'

'He might?' said Tanner. 'Only as good as that?'

'With a bit of luck he'll pull through.'

Tanner had walked with the stretcher-bearers

back to the far side of the valley. B Company were still following through, small-arms fire resounding from beyond the valley towards Sortino. He'd seen Ivo Macdonald, who had hurried over to him. 'Jack, I'm so sorry. I don't understand it. I ordered the FOO not to open fire. I specifically ordered him not to.'

'We know who was responsible for this,' Tanner had snarled.

He'd not seen Creer. Not then. It had been just as well. Rage had consumed him. He'd told Peploe the truth: he'd never murdered before, but he would have done then, gladly.

And so his great friend had gone, patched up, taken away by stretcher-bearers, and bundled into an ambulance. Was he alive or dead? With a bit of luck... *With a bit of luck,* he was out of the field hospital and on a ship back to Malta, away from the war, away from Creer. *Safe.* Three years they'd fought together, been friends, confidants. He would miss Peploe. He would miss him terribly.

At least he still had Sykes. He glanced at him now, watched him smoking his cigarette in the way he always did, almost cupped in his hand between thumb and finger.

'We're all going to miss him,' Sykes said, reading Tanner's thoughts. 'Him and Mac. I try not to get sentimental when blokes get the chop, but it's hard with them two. Mac was a hell of a good lad, and the major – well, they should have kept him as OC. God knows what the desk-wallahs were thinking.'

'I just hope he's all right.'

'He'll be fine. He's a fighter.' Sykes began making himself another cigarette. 'The battalion's changed, hasn't it? You remember when we first joined? You and me were right outsiders, weren't we? Me from London, you from the country down in the south. Surrounded by Yorkshiremen, we were, but now look. All sorts. Hey, Kernow, whereabouts in Cornwall are you from?'

'Bohortha, sir. It's near Falmouth.'

'Didn't fancy joining the Navy, then?'

'No. We're farmers, not fishermen.'

Tanner smiled. 'It's not just the battalion that's changing. Everything is. Better kit, plenty of air cover, soldiers being promoted through the ranks. They'll be giving you a commission next, Stan.'

Sykes laughed. 'No chance. Wouldn't take it anyway. I like where I am now. Best of both worlds, if you ask me. I was never in it for the money.'

'And you think I was?' Tanner grinned.

They were silent for a moment, and then Sykes said in a low voice, 'So what we going to do about Creer?'

'I was all for lynching him yesterday,' said Tanner, 'but you and Fauvel stopped me.'

'And with good reason. I know what you're like when you get the rage. You probably would have bloody killed him and then you'd have been strung up too. The captain and I kept you away for all the right reasons, let me tell you that, Jack.'

Tanner said nothing.

Sykes picked a bit of loose tobacco from his teeth, then said, 'I don't want to add to your woes, but that story's still doing the rounds. You murdering that bloke. It's now moved on so that you murdered Gulliver too.'

Tanner sighed. 'Do you know what, Stan? I'm not sure I give a toss any more. Yesterday, maybe, but not now. They can think what they bloody well like.'

'Yes, but I've been nosing about a bit. Turns out Croaker told Stainforth, his batman.'

'Bastard.'

'And, of course, Stainforth told his mates, who told their mates and so on. Chinese whispers.'

'He's doing it to undermine me,' said Tanner.

'Of course, but two can play at that game, can't they?' He looked at Tanner, a twinkle in his eye.

'Yes, I suppose they can.'

'The blokes like me, Jack, and they know me. I've been with the battalion for bloody ever. And, unlike Blackstone and Creer and their sort, I don't win them over by running some kind of battalion protection racket. That counts for something at times like this, I reckon.'

'What are you thinking? We need to be careful. Start blaming him openly for what happened yesterday and it could damage the whole battalion. That's not the way.'

'I agree. You need to deal with that. Major Macdonald knows the truth, doesn't he? He ordered that FOO not to fire, but was overruled by Croaker. You need to write to the brigadier, and get it signed by Macdonald and maybe some of the others. I'll put my name to that. So would Captain Fauvel and Mr Shopland.'

Tanner nodded. 'And send copies to General Dempsey and even Alexander. Don't get mad, get even, as my American pals would say.'

251

'Exactly. So you leave the rumour-mongering to me, and you get on with writing that letter. We'll play that bastard at his own game and he'll be gone soon enough.'

'Just so long as he doesn't kill us first.'

'I won't let that happen, and nor will you.'

Tanner smiled. 'Thanks, Stan.'

Another brief silence arose. Tanner glanced at Sykes. 'Come on, what is it? Spit it out.'

'Don't take this the wrong way, will you? I mean, I know you've been hit hard by Mac and the major. But we all have. The lads – they're pretty low. They've fought bloody well since we landed but yesterday's victory doesn't feel like one.'

'You're right,' he said. 'I've neglected them.'

'We've lost almost a third of our strength and mostly because of our own shells. I've done what I can, and so has Captain Fauvel, but they need you. You're the boss.'

Tanner got to his feet. He suddenly felt ashamed. He'd been wallowing in self-pity, which was not the behaviour of an officer and company commander.

Sykes stood up too. 'I'll come with you.'

Tanner nodded, then gripped his friend's shoulder. 'Thanks, Stan,' he said. 'That bastard's not going to win.'

Sykes winked. 'That's the spirit. Don't get mad, get even. I like that. That's exactly what we'll do.'

At Brigade Headquarters in Syracuse, Colonel Creer listened to Brigadier Rawstorne outline the plans for the next stage of the campaign. German

252

troops had arrived – information was a little hazy, but from a couple of prisoners, it seemed they were facing a German battle group known as 'Group Schmalz'. This, Rawstorne told him, was probably brigade strength and made up of troops from the Hermann Göring division.

'But we have two divisions against them, us in the Fifth, and the Fiftieth, so we mustn't be cowed. We've faced sterner opposition than this Schmalz Group before.' Rawstorne leaned on the map table. 'Anyway,' he added, 'Monty's got an ace up his sleeve. This bridge, here, over the river Simeto is the key.' He pointed to a river some seven miles south of Catania. 'Primosole Bridge. We've got an airborne drop going in tonight. The Paras are going to land north and south of the bridge and take it intact. They'll establish a blocking position half a mile to the north in case of any counterattack. Our job is to make sure we smash through Villasmundo. We've got Thirteenth Brigade pushing on towards Lentini and some commandos are being landed at Agnone as well. Monty's bullish. Reckons we'll be in Catania before the weekend.'

'Sounds like a good plan, sir,' said Creer. 'What will our role be, sir?'

'You chaps will be in reserve for the time being. We're pleased with the Rangers' performance so far, but what the hell happened yesterday?'

Creer cleared his throat. 'A rather inexperienced FOO, I fear,' he said. 'When I spoke to him, he told me the attack had become bogged down. He said he could fire ahead of them. The situation was compounded by Major Peploe disobeying my direct orders in attacking without artillery support.'

'Doesn't sound like Peploe. In any case, you'd decided to launch a silent assault, hadn't you?'

'Yes, sir, but we had been allocated a battery of twenty-five-pounders and it seemed prudent to have them in support in case we needed them.'

Rawstorne eyed him. 'All right. These things happen in war, I know. And maybe your FOO wasn't quite up to it. But I want a written report on this.'

'Of course, sir.' Creer's stomach churned.

'And who's going to be your new two i/c?'

'I thought Major Mallinson, sir. B Company.'

'What about Tanner?'

'I don't think so, sir. There are a few question marks over Tanner, sir.'

'Really? I hear his company have led the way so far. Led the assault on D-Day, took that gun position and Cassibile and led the attack yesterday.'

'That's true, sir, but Mallinson is a major and deserves his chance.'

'So does Tanner. He's the most experienced soldier you've got and the most decorated for that matter. It would reflect well on you, Creer. A man who has risen through the ranks like that.'

Creer felt the blood draining from his face. 'I'm not sure how far Tanner can be trusted, sir. There are rumours going around the battalion that he murdered a man.'

'Rumours? Any facts?'

'A man from the Wiltshires was caught up with our lot in the landings. He recognized Tanner.

Apparently, Tanner murdered a man, fled, changed his name and joined the Army, sir. Later in the day, this man was killed.'

Rawstorne raised a hand. 'Sounds like poppycock to me, Creer. Rumours and nothing more. The chaps thrive on such tittle-tattle. Have a quiet man-to-man with Tanner and ask him straight. In any case, the British Army has always been full of murderers, thieves and disreputable types. As long as they fight well and don't thieve or murder our own, who are we to care?'

Creer smiled weakly. 'I suppose so, sir.'

'Don't tell me you haven't met any bad hats before – all that time out in India you must have run into a few, eh?'

'One or two, sir, yes.'

'There you go, then. You're to make Tanner your second-in-command, Creer, and he's to be promoted to temporary major with immediate effect. Captain Fauvel will take over A Company. We'll get replacements to you just as soon as we can, but in the meantime, the Rangers will remain in reserve.'

Soon after, Creer was dismissed. Driving back to Melilli with Stainforth he stared out at the passing scenes. Syracuse had been only lightly hit, but there were still collapsed houses, rubble spilling onto the streets, and even a burned-out Sherman tank. Italians watched them speed by.

'I have to admit, sir,' said Stainforth, 'I'd no idea these Eyeties were so poor. You'd never have thought it from the newsreels of Mussolini before the war, would you? I mean, look at 'em. Most of the kids haven't got any shoes. Skin and bone.

Terrible, really. What beats me is why old Mussolini went to war in the first place, cos he clearly weren't up to it.'

Creer glanced at him. 'What's that?'

'Nothing, sir. Just saying how the Italians all look half starved.'

'Their bloody fault for allowing that imbecile to take charge.' He turned his head away, and began chewing one of his fingernails. *Bloody Rawstorne,* he thought, then cursed himself. He'd been foolhardy. The A Company attack on the Sortino position – he hadn't thought it through properly, he realized now. So Peploe had been taken out of the equation – might even be dead by now – but Tanner was still alive, turning up like the bad bloody penny he always had been. And he hadn't reckoned on Ivo Macdonald being there with that idiot Stokes. He would have to ensure Stokes took the rap when it came to writing the report. He'd have to talk to Macdonald too. *For God's sake!* He tapped a hand on his leg. And now Tanner was his new second-in-command. He groaned inwardly. *Tanner, Tanner, Tanner.* What was he going to do about him?

He thought hard. Perhaps it wasn't such a bad thing. *Better the devil you know.* He would be taking Tanner away from A Company, and Sykes and Fauvel and those NCOs he appeared to have known since the start of the war. What was more, when the Rangers next went into battle, he would be able to make sure Tanner went too, which was more than could be said for A Company. Having faced the brunt of the fighting so far and, thanks to yesterday, now much depleted, he knew he could not send them into the van of an attack again – not until the other companies had had their turn, at any rate.

Creer smiled to himself. Next time the Rangers went into action, they would be led by Major Tanner.

15

Tanner couldn't sleep. The ground was hard, his bedding simple, but these were not the reasons. A rubberized canvas rain cape that doubled as a ground sheet and two blankets, one for a pillow, the other to wrap around himself, were hardly the lap of luxury but he, like the rest of the men, was well used to sleeping rough. A few hours at night was all he needed, with a handful of cat-naps, if possible, during the day, to recharge his body's batteries. That night, though, his mind refused to find the sleep that usually came all too easily.

The air was still. No breeze, just the faint snores and coughs from the other men. He could hear Fauvel, sleeping nearby, breathing heavily. Tanner sat up, drank some water from his bottle, then lay down again on his back, staring up at the branches of the olive tree above him and the twinkling stars beyond.

His thoughts turned to McAllister once more. The fear in the lad's eyes haunted him, as though Mac, so hardened after three years of war, had become a boy again. Tanner tried to banish the image; it was unlike him to dwell on death like this. After all, he'd seen a lot worse. War rarely killed people cleanly; the Italian officer had been fortunate in that regard. Modern war, with its shards of white-hot jagged metal hurtling through the air at lightning speeds, made human flesh and bone seem very soft indeed. A head might be ripped off as easily as the stalk of a tomato, or a body sliced in two as if a knife had passed through soft butter. A bullet could cause the most horrific, deforming exit wounds.

He closed his eyes and told himself to think of something else, but found Mac's dying form replaced instead by an image of his father, lying there in the wood. It was dark, lit only by the moon, and, like McAllister, his father's stomach was a dark, sticky mess of blood. Tanner was lying beside him, his father's head in his lap, urging him to stay alive.

'They've got me this time,' his father was saying.

'No, Dad. You'll be fine.'

'Listen to me, Jack,' his father was telling him, 'you'll be all right. You're smart, you're strong, you know how to look after yourself.'

'Shush, Dad. Please.'

'Listen to me. Promise me this, Jack. It's an unequal world we live in, but you must always stand by your beliefs. Stick up for yourself. Do what you think is right. Understand? Do what is right.' He had spluttered and Tanner had seen blood pour from his mouth. His father had gripped him. 'Promise me.'

'I promise. Dad, you'll be all right.' His father's grip had loosened. 'Come on, wake up, hold on. You've got to.' But it was over. His father had gone. Murdered at almost point-blank range by the poachers he had been trying to catch for weeks. He'd survived three years of the trenches, only to be cut down by a bunch of local thugs he'd known since they were boys.

There hadn't been a day since then when Tanner hadn't thought of his father. He'd tried to keep the promise he'd made him too. *Do what you think is right.* Earlier, Creer had summoned him and offered him promotion to major and Peploe's old position as second-in-command. Tanner had been completely wrong-footed. After a brief moment when he had wondered whether he had heard right, he had refused.

'I'm offering you an olive branch,' Creer had said. 'I did when I first joined the battalion and I'm doing so again now. I'm trying to put our differences from the past behind us. For the sake of the men.'

'For the sake of the men!' Tanner had laughed incredulously. 'But you're a murdering bastard. You ordered the shelling of your men. Of me and my men.'

He had watched Creer visibly wince. 'No, Jack. If you remember, Peploe went in with the attack against my direct orders–'

'Because the orders were completely impossible to carry out! We had agreed a silent attack, but that attack had to go in at very first light. If we'd waited any longer it would have been too late.'

'And yet the attack became bogged down.'

'Hardly. We'd taken four of the six pillboxes before the stonk began.'

'Then the fault was the FOO's. He was my eyes and ears. I gave the order to fire on the advice of an experienced artillery officer.'

'That's bollocks. Major Macdonald has vastly superior experience to any gunner subaltern. He had all the fire support we needed and he specifically ordered the FOO not to fire. You countermanded that.'

'I did what was best for the attack. After that ten-minute stonk the position was won. In command one has to make tough decisions. I understand that, Jack.'

'I can't believe I'm hearing this. It was already won. That stonk wiped out a third of my company. If we'd needed extra fire support, we'd have called for it. At best, sir, you showed gross incompetence, at worst, you were willingly firing on me, Peploe and my men.'

Tanner could see the fury in Creer's face, his jaw muscles twitching, his fists clenched.

'Careful, Tanner. I could have you court-martialled for slander and insubordination.'

'Go ahead. But you wouldn't dare,' Tanner hissed. 'I'll not be your second-in-command, sir. Right now, my company is still reeling from what happened at Sortino. The last thing they need is a new commander.'

'You're angry, Jack, I know. You've lost some good men. But one day you might be faced with a difficult decision like the one I made. Maybe then you'll understand. Perhaps you'll be more forgiving too.'

'Jesus Christ!' muttered Tanner. 'Is that all?'

'Yes. But sleep on it. You might change your mind by the morning.'

No chance, thought Tanner now, as he replayed the conversation in his mind. Arriving back at A Company, he had immediately taken out some paper to begin writing his full report on the attack at Sortino, just as Fauvel and Sykes had suggested. He had spoken to Macdonald earlier, who had promised him a report of his own, but as Tanner had sat there under the olive tree, pen poised, he had found himself unable to commit words to paper. Writing did not come naturally; Peploe had, over the years, taught him a thing or two about grammar and spelling, skills he had never really learned during his all-too-brief schooldays, but it was more than that.

'I can't do this, Gav,' he'd told Fauvel.

'Why?'

'I don't know. It's like running to Teacher. Telling tales.'

'Hardly, Jack. He killed and wounded lots of very good men. I wouldn't call that a schoolboy snitch.'

'But I'll write a report, he'll write a report. His will be worded better. Neither of us will come out well. It'll achieve nothing. Peploe's disobeying of Creer's order will be scrutinized over and over, and because we're in the middle of a battle for this sodding island, he'll take the blame and it'll all be smoothed over. Creer will get away with it. You know what the Army's like.'

'I don't know. I'm not so sure.'

'It's not me, Gav. I prefer to fight my battles the way I know how. If Ivo wants to write a report, that's his affair, but there are certain things Creer will have to admit to in his own write-up. Any soldier worth his salt will see he's a blackguard with or without anything from me.'

Fauvel had nodded. 'Maybe. A dignified silence reflects better on us all, you mean?'

'Exactly. I can't stand the man. I wish he'd never darkened my life. I wish he'd never been given command of the battalion. But unless I'm directly ordered to give my version of events, I'm not going to say a word. I'll get him for what he's done, you have my word on that, but in my own way.'

Tanner lay there now, eyes wide open, staring at the branches above. Had he done the right thing? *What a mess.* But in his dying words, his father had been saying something more: that gut instinct should be trusted. It was something Tanner had adhered to religiously, however unpleasant the course of action might be. And his gut instinct had told him that sending off finger-pointing reports would come back to haunt him.

Wednesday, 14 July. At Ponte Olivo airfield, Lieutenant Colonel Charlie Wiseman was waiting for the 60 Squadron Mosquito that was due in from Monastir. It was another baking hot day, but after the bombing meted out by the Allies in the build-up to the invasion, and the subsequent heavy fighting at nearby Gela, there was not a building still standing, only a few hastily erected tents. The airfield looked a wreck, Wiseman

262

thought. Mangled, burned-out Italian aircraft were strewn around the edge, while the ground was pocked with hastily filled-in bomb craters. An atmosphere of destruction pervaded.

The Regia Aeronautica had made way for the US 86th Fighter Group. American fighter planes lined the perimeter in squadron groups. Wiseman had been sent to the 309th Fighter Squadron, on the southern side of the airfield. Hastily built blast pens had been constructed, a vast workshop tent erected, plus a number of pup, mess and chow tents.

Captain Tooley, the Fighter Group's intelligence officer, had been assigned to look after Wiseman.

'You been flying much, Colonel?' he asked.

Wiseman shrugged. 'A little.' He looked at his watch. Around 1100 hours.

'I'm sure he'll be here soon, Colonel,' said Tooley.

'You waiting for the Mossie?' said a pilot, emerging from the mess tent.

'Yeah.'

'They're beauties. Boy, we could do with some of those. Fast, powerful and kicking ass.'

'What about your A-36s?'

'Well, they sure manoeuvre OK, but I wouldn't call it the finished article yet, sir.'

'We've lost more Apaches to accidents than to the enemy,' added Tooley.

'Sorry to hear it.' He pulled out a crumpled packet of Camels, offered them around, then lit his own.

'Here she is now, sir,' said the pilot.

Wiseman paused and listened. Yes, there was the faint whirr of engines. 'It works every time.' He grinned. 'I light up and something happens.' He raised his hand to shield his eyes. 'There she is!' he muttered to himself, as the Mosquito banked and turned in to land.

A minute later, it had touched down in a cloud of swirling dust and was bumping across the rough 'drome.

Wiseman watched it taxi towards them, the roar of the engines deafening as it neared. Dust and grit were whipped into the air, but at last, after one final surge of revs, the engines were cut and the machine was suddenly silent, apart from the furious ticking of the cooling engines. Moments later, two men climbed down, both wearing flying helmets, Mae Wests, shorts and shirt sleeves, socks rolled down to their ankles.

The pilot was South African, Flight Lieutenant Keith Hammond, his navigator English, Flight Sergeant Les Greaves. Introductions made, Tooley led them back to the dispersal tent. 'Can I get you fellers anything?' he asked. 'A cold drink?'

'Cheers,' said Hammond.

Tooley clicked his fingers and an orderly scurried away.

Hammond turned to Wiseman. 'You're going to have to be navigator, sir. You OK with that? The Mossie's pretty cramped, I'm afraid.'

'Sure. I've been there before – in fact, I've jumped on this place.'

'And this time it's daylight, so should be even easier.'

Wiseman shot him a grin. 'Right.' He pulled

out a series of maps and aerial photographs. 'This is where we're going. Villalba. Actually, to be precise, we're going here.' He pointed to a large house near the centre of the town.

'Who lives there, if you don't mind me asking?'

'He's called Don Calogero Vizzini. A man of honour and influence.'

Hammond looked nonplussed.

'He's a man who can help us,' said Wiseman.

'Shall I have a look at those maps, sir?' asked Greaves.

'You bet.'

'Greavesie'll make some calculations, sir, although if you can map-read we should be all right.'

'A bearing might be helpful, though,' said Greaves.

'Right,' said Wiseman.

The orderly reappeared with four chilled bottles of Coca-Cola. Hammond and Greaves's faces lit up. They chinked their bottles together.

'Here's to our American allies,' said Greaves.

'I love you Yanks,' agreed Hammond.

'Amen to that,' grinned Wiseman. 'Now – shall we go?'

Wiseman had already been lent a flying helmet, Mae West and parachute pack so, leaving Greaves with Tooley, he and Hammond headed towards the now silent Mosquito. A small metal ladder hung down from an open hatch to one side of the cockpit.

'You go first,' said Hammond.

'Sure,' said Wiseman. He pulled himself up into the cockpit, which was as confined as Hammond had promised. His seat lay on the starboard side and a little back from that of the pilot, so he had to get in first. There was a window panel beside it that opened and was already slid back. Wiseman sat down and buckled his straps as Hammond appeared alongside him.

'All right?' he asked. 'Got what you need?'

'Yep,' said Wiseman. 'Right here.' He patted a small canvas haversack. From his folder he took out his maps and aerial photographs.

'And we're dropping a flag? Is that right, sir?'

'Absolutely.'

'Well, this is a first. I'm sure there's a good reason for it.'

'Oh, there is. I'd hardly be wasting your time if not. Tell you what, when this is all over, look me up and I'll tell you about it over a beer or two.'

Hammond laughed. 'You're on.'

Cockpit checks, Hammond following a familiar mnemonic; then, with a thumbs-up to the ground crew, he watched them pull away the chocks and pressed the starter button on the port, then the starboard engine. The propellers began to run in turn, the airframe shaking with increasing violence as he opened the throttles.

Then they were off, rolling bumpily along the rough airfield, until at the far eastern end they turned, paused, then sped down the dirt runway, swirls of dust following in their wake, faster, faster, the wings shaking and bouncing until suddenly the shaking stopped and the distance between the wing and its shadow below widened. Airborne, and speeding away over the hills to the north-west.

'OK, I'm heading on a bearing of three-five-zero,' said Hammond.

'It's about sixty miles away,' said Wiseman.

'So, ten minutes, then. I'm going to stay low, around angels two, and fly fast. I need you to keep your eyes peeled, though. There are still bandits about.'

The sky was vast and bright and, to Wiseman, seemed empty. Below him, the Sicilian country-side sped by. It looked dry and sun-scorched. Mountains, silvery grey valleys, small towns. He recognized Butera and Riesi and was content they were on the right track. Then, away to the west, he saw Caltanisetta and the main road that bisected the island.

And then there it was, Villalba, just as he remembered it from that moonlit night. 'There!' he said.

Hammond scanned the skies around him, throttled back, and flew lower. 'I'll circle the town first,' he said. 'It's near the church, isn't it?'

'Yeah,' said Wiseman. 'There's a main square. It's to the south of there.' He pulled out a tri-angular yellow flag with a black L stitched on it, and opened the side panel. Refreshing air gushed in.

They circled low, at just a few hundred feet. Wiseman could see people below, peasants, like those he had noticed back in May, but no obvious sign of any troops. Was Don Calogero really down there? Were his men waiting for this moment?

'OK,' said Hammond. 'There's the church, there's the square.'

Wiseman placed an aerial photograph in front

267

of him. 'See the house now?'

'Yes. Got it. I'll turn east, then fly a slow, low run from south-east to north-west so that we go directly over it.'

Moments later, they were speeding over the town, the main road and the church just on their starboard.

'Ready?' said Hammond.

'Sure,' Wiseman replied, holding the first of the flags out of the window to his right. Just as they neared the villa, he let go and saw it flutter down, but with the turbulence caused by the wake of the Mosquito it appeared to be heading towards the town square, not Don Calogero's villa.

'Damn!' he said. 'I'm not sure I got that right.'

'Want me to go around again?'

'Yeah, and this time I'll throw the entire haversack. That'll be heavier.'

'Good idea.'

Around they went again. Below, people were pointing, staring up, hands shielding their eyes. There was the main street on their right. The church up ahead. Seconds now. *One ... two ... three.* Wiseman let go, saw the haversack plummet, and this time he knew he'd dropped it well. Hammond flew on, climbed and banked. They were passing over the town one more time when Wiseman saw a man running in the garden of Don Calogero's villa, then watched him pick up the haversack, turn and wave.

Mission accomplished. But would Don Calogero honour his promise? Would the Italians now help the Americans?

But he's a man of honour. Of course he will.

At Motta Sant'Anastasia, the Germans had arrived, just three to begin with, in a requisitioned Italian car. At a light knock on the door, Francesca had opened it to see a German officer standing there, with two of his men behind. They looked rough, unshaven, and wore dirty cotton uniforms. The men's helmets were low over their eyes so Francesca could barely see their faces, but the officer had only a peaked cap on his head, which he took off on seeing her and gave a small bow.

'Sorry to bother you, Signora,' he said, in fluent but rough Italian. 'I wonder whether we might come in.'

'Why?' said Francesca.

'It's all right,' he said, with courtesy. 'We mean no harm. But I have a feeling your house may be an ideal observation post.'

'An observation post? You want to take over my home?'

'It is ideally situated.' He looked apologetic. 'We will try not to get in your way too much.' He peered around her. 'May we?'

'Do I have a choice?'

'I regret, no. I assure you, Signora, I am very sorry. But your ancestors built this house for its wonderful views, which is why we need it now.'

Francesca, her heart quickening, stood clear of the door.

'Thank you, Signora,' he said.

She followed them as they toured the house, Cara close beside her. The lieutenant gave the child a small bar of chocolate. 'She's a credit to you, Signora. A very pretty girl. One day she will be as beautiful as her mother.' He smiled, and despite herself, Francesca could not help smiling too.

'Your house is ideal,' he said to her eventually, having examined each room and the yard outside, below the kitchen. His name, he told her, was Leutnant Albert Kranz. He would do all he could to ensure any disruption was kept to a minimum.

Soon after, Kranz and his men left. They had not been gone long when there was another knock at the door and there was Salvatore Camprese, accompanied by two *carabinieri*.

'Are you all right, Francesca?' said Camprese. 'I heard the *tedeschi* had been bothering you.'

She sighed. 'They want to use the house as an observation post for their guns.'

'Then why not come and stay with me? I have room. You don't want Germans interrupting your life.'

'You must be joking,' said Francesca. 'At least this way I can keep an eye on them.'

'All right, but if you have any trouble, any trouble at all, you come and see me, OK?'

'Goodbye, Salvatore,' she said, closing the door.

Leutnant Kranz returned later that morning, this time with five others, and several boxes. He was once again apologetic but explained that they would need to use the kitchen with its balcony and the bedroom above.

'But that is my room,' she said. 'Is there no other you can use?'

'I regret, no,' said Kranz. 'You see, the view

across the Plain of Catania is perfect from those two rooms. The sun is above and behind us, so there will be no reflection from it in our field glasses, and this promontory juts out to a really very pleasing degree. Below in the yard, you have the ideal storage sheds. My men can sleep there too. Really, it was as though this house was built as an artillery observation post.' He smiled. 'It will not be for long,' he told her. 'And we are not asking you to leave.'

'Very well,' she said. What else could she say? Kranz had been polite but firm. She supposed she should be grateful that these Germans, at least, were courteous.

'My men will move anything for you,' said Kranz.

'Thank you,' said Francesca. She took Cara with her to her room. It was simply laid out: a chest of drawers, a wardrobe, two bookshelves and a large bed. The latter, she thought, could stay, but the rest could be taken into the spare bedroom, where Niccolò had stayed, and which was sparsely furnished.

As Kranz had promised, the men moved the furniture, so that all Francesca and Cara had to do was make the spare bed, and ensure her things were in order, that the photographs and trinkets she kept on top of the chest of drawers were put back as they had been. There was the framed photograph of her mother, looking young and beautiful and full of hope. There was another of all the siblings, which used to live in her father's room, and one of Nico just before he had left home to join the Army. Francesca held it and

271

looked at it. He'd not changed much – a few lines had been added, perhaps, but that was all. The picture caught the essence of her brother well, she thought: the intelligence, the kindness, the sense of fun.

She was just placing the picture on the chest of drawers when she turned to see Kranz in the doorway.

'Excuse me, Signora,' he said. 'But you should come downstairs.'

'What is it?'

'The postman.'

Panic gripped her. Glancing at Kranz, she hurried from the room, ran down the staircase and there, in the hallway, saw the postman's frame silhouetted in the light of the open doorway, like a sinister messenger from Hell.

Her insides felt crushed as she stepped towards him. Her heart hammered, and her head felt light. There was his hand, holding the telegram. Her eyes were drawn to the small buff envelope.

'What is it, Mamma?' said Cara, behind her.

Francesca felt a tear roll down her cheek. *Please, God. Please let him be all right.*

Then her hands were on the envelope and she was opening it and pulling out the simple, folded sheet of thin paper.

'I'm so sorry, Signora,' said the postman, then took a step backwards.

With shaking hands, Francesca stood there and read:

WITH DEEP REGRET REPORT CAPTAIN NICCOLO TOGLIATTI REPORTED MISS-

ING IN ACTION BELIEVED KILLED 12
JULY.

'Mama?' said Cara, but Francesca barely heard
her daughter. Staggering, she felt her way along
the hall towards the kitchen. The table. She
needed to sit down at the table. But the table –
the table she and Nico had sat talking at just
weeks before – was now being used by a German
listening on his radio set.

'No!' said Francesca. 'No!' And then she
screamed, a long, deep wail of despair and grief
that made the German push back his chair and
stumble to his feet.

When she stopped, Francesca felt the last of her
strength leave her. Her legs seemed to buckle and
her head felt as heavy as lead. Suddenly she was
on the floor, her head in her hands and convulsed
with deep, uncontrollable sobs.

16

Later that afternoon, a Jeep pulled up beside the
house on the southern edge of Melilli newly
requisitioned by A Company Headquarters, and
out stepped a corporal from Brigade Headquarters. It was Tanner he wanted to see.

'Sorry, sir,' he said, in a thick North Yorkshire
accent. 'Brigadier's orders. You're t'come wi' me.'

Tanner did not demur. 'Any idea what it's
about?' he asked, as they sped along the dusty road

273

towards Syracuse.

'I wouldn't know, sir. I just do as I'm ordered. You'll find out soon enough, though.'

Tanner smiled to himself. He liked the plain speaking of Yorkshiremen. You knew where you stood. They were all like that when he'd first joined as a boy soldier – the men, at any rate – and even at the start of the war he and Sykes had been about the only outsiders. Now, there were men from all over. Cornishmen like Trahair, or Welshmen, as Griffiths had been. Sykes wasn't the only Londoner any more. He wasn't the only Londoner from south of the river, for that matter.

A quarter of an hour later he presented himself at Brigade Headquarters, a palatial baroque villa at the heart of the town. Trucks and Jeeps lined the main square.

In the hallway, tables had been set up, behind which were clerks with typewriters. Telephone cables ran into a makeshift exchange. 'This way, sir,' said the corporal, leading him into a modest, but high-ceilinged room off the main hallway.

'Captain Tanner, sir,' said the corporal.

Brigadier Rawstorne was sitting at the side of an ornate dining-table, with a telephone, an in-tray, an overflowing ashtray and various papers before him. The smell of tobacco was strong.

'Ah, Tanner, there you are,' said Rawstorne, looking up. He smiled amiably. 'The man who would turn down a promotion from his brigadier.'

Tanner was surprised at this. 'From you, sir?'

'Yes, from me. I told Colonel Creer that you should be his new second-in-command.'

'I didn't realize that, sir.'

274

'Hmm. You imagined it was Creer's decision, did you?'

'I – I thought– In truth, sir, I wasn't sure what to think. But I had just lost a third of my company. I didn't think it was right to leave them to a new company commander.'

'Worried about morale, eh?'

'Yes, sir. And I thought it was wrong for a captain to leapfrog a major.'

Rawstorne sat back in his chair. 'I can't decide whether that's modesty or arrogance, Tanner.'

'Sorry, sir,' said Tanner. 'It wasn't meant to be arrogant.'

'Well, let's have a think about this. You were company second-in-command under Major Peploe, then seconded to the Americans. You returned to the battalion in June, so have been in command of those men for a single month. You don't think they might be able to cope with a new company commander now?'

'Of course, sir, but I didn't think it was the best moment. They've had enough upheaval as it is.'

Rawstorne leaned forward, resting his elbows on the table and bringing his hands together. 'Look, Tanner, I have no idea when the battalion will receive more replacements, but the fact is, A Company is out of the action for a while. You're the most decorated soldier in the brigade, let alone the battalion. Strictly *entre nous*, Creer is a good administrator, but lacks fighting experience. With Peploe gone, the battalion needs you as two i/c. So, please, take the bloody promotion and do as you're told.'

Tanner was silent for a moment, then said, 'Is

that an order, sir?'

'If you like, yes. Do you think I haven't got better things to do than waste time arguing with you?'

Tanner said nothing.

'And that's not all, Tanner. It seems we're in for a bit of a tougher fight than we'd first thought. Last night our airborne troops were dropped on a key bridge over the Simeto. Corps HQ had high hopes for this little operation. The Red Devils were to take the bridge intact, and then the road to Catania would be open. I don't mind telling you it was thought Catania would be ours in a couple of days.'

'So what happened, sir?'

'Jerry got there first. MGs and mortars set up either side of the bridge, artillery trained on targets to the south and our airborne chaps scattered too wide. Airborne troops are all very well, Tanner, but not good at digging in for the attritional battle.'

'We've got the force to deal with a few Jerries, surely.'

'But how to keep the bridge intact? It's an awkward crossing. And every day we're held up there, so more Jerries are pouring across the Strait of Messina. They're preparing a defensive line west of Catania along the lower slopes of Etna. It's a hell of a position. Views right across the Plain of Catania – a plain riddled with rivers, dikes and other unmentionable obstacles.'

'So we're going to have to slog it out the hard way?' Tanner sighed and ran his hands wearily through his thick but unkempt dark hair.

'Yes. I'm rather afraid we are. And in that fighting the Yorks Rangers are going to have to pull their weight.'

Tanner closed his eyes, then nodded. *I understand now.*

'Now, I still don't know what happened the day before yesterday – it sounds like Creer got a little jumpy. But these things happen in the heat of battle. An accident of war.'

'An accident of war?' said Tanner, sitting up. 'Sir, it was–'

Rawstorne held up a hand to silence him. 'I don't want to hear it, Tanner. I've asked Creer for a full report, which I will receive in due course. What happened happened. I'm sorry some of your men were killed. I'm sorry we lost Peploe. But war is dangerous. People do get killed. Thank goodness you were not one of them.'

He looked at Tanner and his face softened. 'Look, take this job, and grasp the battalion by the scruff of its neck. The Rangers need you. Damn it all, I need you, Tanner. If the brigade can do a good job here, then there's every chance the rest of the campaign will take care of itself. We will win. It's merely a question of time. But the sooner we do, the sooner this battle, and indeed the entire war, will be over.'

He patted his hands on the table in a show of finality. 'So do we have a deal, Tanner?'

'There is just one problem, sir,' said Tanner, slowly.

Rawstorne looked at him. *Yes?*

'Colonel Creer and I do not exactly get on.'

'Oh, for God's sake, man!' Rawstorne exclaimed. 'Then start getting on! Sort it out! You're both adults, damn it! Whatever differences you have, patch them up and in double-quick time. I've got more pressing concerns than the petty squabbles of two subordinates. Think of the battalion and the brigade and all the young men who look to you, Tanner, for leadership, and for experience. "I don't get on with Creer, sir." Good God, man. I don't want to hear another word about it.'

Tanner stood up and so did Rawstorne.

'So, *Major* Tanner. Let's hear no more about any contretemps with Colonel Creer, all right?'

Tanner swallowed. 'Yes, sir.'

'Right. Congratulations on your promotion and good luck.'

'Thank you, sir,' said Tanner. He saluted, and Rawstorne leaned across the table and offered him his hand. Tanner gripped it and looked into the eyes of his brigadier.

'Don't let me down, Tanner. I'm relying on you.'

Later, around seven that evening. Tanner had gathered most of the headquarters staff including the intelligence officer, Captain Jerry Masters, and the RSM, Tom Spiers, in the garden of the Villa Cortese, a baroque townhouse of faded glory near the town square in Melilli. There were around forty men in all, mostly administrators: clerks, the quartermaster and his team, the battalion MO and the adjutant. The men who made the battalion function as a whole. Tanner had chosen his moment carefully, waiting for Creer to disappear. 'He'll be visiting an Italian bint,'

Spiers had told him. Favours rendered in return for rations.

He stood under the large fig tree, the chirping of cicadas loud around him, and wiped his brow. Christ, he thought, but it was still hot. The brows of the men glistened, dark patches of sweat marked their shirts. A mosquito buzzed near his ear and he waved it away, then cleared his throat.

'I won't keep you long,' he said. 'I'm sorry you've lost Major Peploe. He's a fine man and a fine friend and the battalion will miss him. But I'm going to do my best. I've served with this battalion for most of my career and in that time we've repeatedly proved ourselves. We're good, bloody good, and experienced too. I saw the brigadier earlier, and he made it quite clear that he's looking to us to show the way in this brigade. It's up to us to justify that faith. People come and go, but the spirit should never be allowed to die. The spirit of a battalion is what binds it, what keeps everyone going even when things are tough.' He paused. Were they all listening? *Yes. Good.* 'We need to work and fight together. All of us. I know what you've heard about me, these rumours that have been doing the rounds.' Several men now shuffled their feet sheepishly, but Tanner continued to stare them down. 'They're to stop,' he said, 'before I do kill someone. Is that clear?'

A few nods.

'Yes?' said Tanner. 'You all got that?'

'Yes, sir,' muttered several.

'Right,' said Tanner. 'In the days to come, we're going to have some hard fighting. We're not facing ill-trained Eyeties any more, but well-trained and motivated Germans. Men who know how to fight. We all need to work together, to make sure we keep the strong spirit that's served us so well through France, Greece and Crete, through the Desert War. Spirit that's seen us lead the way in the days since we've been on Sicily. And know this: I'll not ask any of you to do anything I'm not prepared to do myself, but I'll also not put up with any muttering behind my back. You have a problem, you tell me, or the RSM here. Is that clear?'

'Yessir.'

'Good. Dismissed.' He watched them leave, until only Spiers and Masters remained.

'Well done, Jack,' said Spiers. 'It was needed.'

'The boss won't be happy,' said Masters.

'To hell with him. I don't give a damn what he thinks. I care about the battalion. And I'm not going to have my authority undermined by these stupid rumours. Rumours, I might add, that were peddled by Croaker.'

'You can't know that.'

'Can't I? Look, I'm not going to speak ill of Croaker to the men, but I am going to do this job my way. Be straight with people, and usually they'll be straight with you in return.'

'I agree,' said Spiers.

'Well, it'll be interesting, I'll admit that,' said Masters. He turned to Tanner. 'And now how about a drink in the mess?'

'All right,' said Tanner. *Why not?*

His first afternoon in the job had gone better than he had imagined it would when he'd left the brigadier some hours earlier. On arriving back at

Melilli, he'd first gone to see Ivo Macdonald, one of the company commanders he liked and respected. It had, of course, been too late to back down, but clearing his promotion with Macdonald was a courtesy he had been determined to make.

'Mind?' Macdonald had said. 'My dear fellow, that's very noble of you, but no, I most certainly don't mind. I'm delighted!'

'Really?'

'Of course. If anyone can keep Creer under control it's you.'

'I'm conscious I'm jumping past you other majors. This time last year I was still an NCO. Now I'm a major, albeit a temporary one. I don't want to piss off you and the other company commanders. We've got enough to worry about as it is.'

Macdonald had smiled. 'I don't want to run the battalion and I'm not sure Ferguson and Mallinson do either. I think you know full well what I think of the colonel. I'd be out on my arse in no time if I had to be two i/c. I know I wouldn't be able to stick it. The man's a half-wit.'

Tanner had then gone to see Creer and told him he had accepted the brigadier's promotion.

Creer had laughed. 'The most stubborn man I have ever met has finally climbed down. A miracle!'

'Orders are orders,' Tanner had said.

'You didn't seem to think so the other day.'

'It was an order impossible to fulfil. If you'd been at the front, you'd have realized that.'

In that moment, Tanner understood that everything had changed. Up until then, he had been wary of the officer commanding's influence and authority, but as he had stood before him, he had felt strangely empowered. Creer could order him into battle, but he could not push him around. He couldn't bully him. Not any more. The days when he had been a powerless private and Creer a platoon commander had long gone. Creer's efforts to undermine Tanner's reputation and authority might have worked perfectly in India, but had been less successful out here.

It had occurred to him there and then that later, that evening, he would stop the rumours once and for all; and he was now confident that his pep-talk had done just that. In India, where the most action they had seen was an occasional skirmish with natives, an arch-manipulator like Creer could thrive. But in the full fury of war, actions spoke a lot louder than words. Tanner knew he had never had much of a gift for the gab, but he could handle himself on the battlefield. Creer knew that too. What was more, he was now second-in-command because the brigade commander had demanded it. That, too, gave him considerable authority. It had given him confidence as well.

Finally, he had been to see A Company. Fauvel had been given command in his place, while Shopland had become 2 i/c. For the time being, they were down a platoon, but they would recover. He would miss having Sykes to watch his back, but at least they were unlikely to be committed to battle any time soon, unless the situation became desperate. His friends there would be safe for a while.

Tanner now followed Masters into the mess, which, until the battalion had requisitioned the villa, had been a reception room on the first floor. A number of cases of wine had been found in the cellar and 'liberated'.

'Actually, it's not at all bad,' said Masters. 'My people used to ship over Italian wine before the war, but I've never had Sicilian until now.'

'It's a shame Peploe's not here,' said Tanner. 'He'd appreciate this. He always fancied himself as something of an expert when it came to wine.'

'I wonder if he's still alive,' Masters said.

'Course he is,' muttered Tanner. 'He'll be fine.'

He left Masters soon after, and went to his new room on the second floor, but although he felt suddenly tired, sleep once more eluded him. Instead, he sat by his window and, with a paperback on his lap, listened to the sounds of the night: the crickets and cicadas, distant booms, the crackle of guns and small arms a few miles to the north. *Primosole Bridge.*

He wondered what had happened to Peploe, and wished he'd not mentioned him in the past tense. If he'd survived the first couple of days, the chances were he would be all right. He wished he could find out, but so many people passed through the casualty clearing stations and then the various and hastily set-up field hospitals that he knew there was no chance of that. All he could do was wait. The battalion would be informed in due course if he had died, and he was sure Peploe would write if he was recovering. Then he thought of the Italian officer, lying there so peacefully, apparently unblemished, killed by the concussion of the blast. He delved into his shirt pocket, pulled out his ID card and looked at the photograph of the young woman he had taken. He now felt rather bad about it; he wasn't sure why he had kept it. He supposed he'd been struck by the image of a pretty girl in the middle of that carnage.

At some point, he must have fallen asleep because suddenly he jolted awake. There was someone down below, out on the street, talking.

'...and don't say a bloody word.'

Creer. Grabbing his torch, he left his room.

Creer was halfway up the stairs when Tanner switched on his torch. The officer commanding wore nothing but his underwear, a pair of cotton briefs.

'Who the hell's that?' he barked. 'Turn off that bloody torch.'

'Oh, it's you,' said Tanner, feigning innocence.

'Tanner,' said Creer. 'What the bloody hell are you doing prowling about?'

'I heard something, so came down to see what it was. More to the point, what are you doing?'

'I fell asleep and the stupid bitch stole my clothes.'

'How embarrassing.'

'And now you're here. For God's sake,' he muttered, as he continued walking up the stairs towards him. 'Always turning up when least wanted.'

As Creer now reached him, on an impulse, Tanner drew up a hand, and brought it tight around his neck, then rammed him against the wall. Creer choked. 'Yes,' said Tanner. 'I am.'

'Tanner!' he croaked.

'You're a bloody disgrace.' He loosened his grip and stepped away.

Creer gasped. 'I'll court-martial you for this.'

'You wouldn't bloody dare. Jesus, look at you! How did you ever get this job? Peploe's a hundred times the man you are.' He shone the torch in Creer's eyes. He saw fear in them.

'Tanner,' said Creer. 'Don't do anything rash now...'

Christ, he really is scared. 'Look at you,' he said again, 'Jesus.' Then, switching off his torch, he turned and climbed back up the stairs.

17

Monday, 19 July, five a.m. The sun was already well above the horizon, beaming brightly, the sky a deep and cloudless blue. It was going to be another hot one. On the edge of the ancient town of Agrigento, Lieutenant Colonel Charlie Wiseman sat in his Jeep alongside two G2 junior staff of the US 3rd Infantry Division, and marvelled at the sight before him. Stretched out ahead along the winding dusty road that headed north was a vast column of vehicles: tanks, half-tracks and trucks, part of Patton's spearhead for the drive on Palermo. Truly, thought Wiseman, this was the might of America. From Agrigento's position on the hill, he could see the mountainous interior up ahead, while behind lay the dark blue sea and the harbour of Porto Empedocle, still thick with ships and landing craft.

The port had become operational only the day before, but most of the 3rd Division had been landed at Licata, twenty-five miles further south-east down the coast. Porto Empedocle would come into its own from now on, as Patton began his drive north and west.

The Italians had put up stiffer resistance than expected and it had taken three days to clear the coast to Agrigento and capture the port, but when Truscott's men had reported that both were now in US hands, Patton had been delighted. Some six thousand Italians were now in the bag, along with more than fifty artillery pieces and at least a hundred vehicles, all of which the Italians could ill afford to lose. Most importantly, however, the port was only lightly damaged. Clearing mines in the waters around it was the biggest task.

Now they were ready to go. Patton had outlined his plan to Alexander, had been given approval, and had created a new corps, consisting of the 3rd Division, 2nd Armored and 82nd Airborne, specifically for the task. The 82nd would drive west, along the coast, the 2nd Armored would remain in reserve, while General Truscott's 3rd Division would drive straight towards Palermo.

And Wiseman would be there to witness it. This, he knew, was the test of his negotiations with Don Calogero Vizzini. Don Calo had promised him that the Italians would melt away. He had assured him that his influence was strong enough. This, Wiseman knew, was the moment of truth.

As the column rumbled forward, Wiseman's stomach knotted. If Vizzini had been bullshitting him, his ass would be on the line.

Around the same time, in Motta Sant'Anastasia, the German gunners were beginning their daily shelling of British positions. Every morning it was the same: the clatter of the men getting up, the smell of rations and ersatz coffee, then the low murmur of orders, and the dull voice of someone sending the latest co-ordinates over the field telephone. Moments later, a dull boom from one of the guns dug in nearby in the lava hills, then another, and another. Others, further along the lower slopes of Etna towards Misterbianco, would also fire, the pulses of each shot felt throughout the house. A slight shake. Glass would chink.

Francesca lay in bed, Cara alongside her, her eyes wide open, staring at the ceiling. Another boom of a gun, the shell whistling out over the plain below. She wished they would all go away, that she could be left to grieve on her own. It was impossible to think that he was dead, gone, no more. Or perhaps he was still alive. Perhaps he had been taken prisoner after all. Perhaps another telegram would arrive telling them he was safe. Then these brief moments of hope would give way to despair once more. MISSING BELIEVED KILLED. That meant he almost certainly *had* been killed. There was no point in raising hopes to the contrary. If someone had seen him alive and well, they would have written 'missing believed taken prisoner'. But they hadn't.

The thought of never seeing him again was tearing her heart in two. Death was so final, so absolute. Nico, she knew, had not believed in God, and although she had always tried to, had gone to mass and confession every week, she could not, in her heart of hearts, believe that one day she would see her mother, father and brother again in Heaven.

Another boom. The room shook. Moments later, the distant crump of the explosion. She felt Cara hold her more tightly. *And these Germans.* She hated them, especially Leutnant Kranz. Always bowing respectfully, always asking after her health. He had brought her a bunch of flowers the day before. *Eurgh!* He repulsed her! 'I think he wants to marry you, Mamma,' Cara had told her. 'Like Salvatore.' Francesca didn't think that, but she knew he wanted her, and that every time he looked at her he was undressing her with his eyes. It was horrible. She felt debased. He always seemed to be there, just when she least expected it, putting her on edge all the time. At least she could send Camprese home when he pestered her, but Kranz – my God, there was no escape. And although so far he had not so much as laid a finger on her, she had no idea whether he would always be so restrained. He was a German officer: he could do what he liked. If he decided to have her, she was defenceless.

At around six, she got up, dressed and went to the dining room, now doubling as a kitchen, to prepare some breakfast for Cara. Before the arrival of the Germans, she would have gone first to the yard to the chickens, but the men took all the eggs so there was now no point.

'Good morning, Signora,' said a voice behind her.

Francesca started, then turned to see Kranz in the doorway.

'You have enough to eat?' he asked.

'Yes, thank you,' Francesca replied. There was a baker in town. The loaves were rationed – everything was – but with a bit of care, they could be eked out easily enough. A small slice each for breakfast was enough to keep them going through the morning.

'If you need anything, you have only to ask.'

A quickly flashed smile. 'Thank you.'

He remained there a while longer, watching her.

'Was there anything else?' she asked at length.

'It worries me, Signora, you being all alone here. A beautiful young lady like yourself.'

'I'm not alone. I have my daughter.'

'Even so, perhaps you might like to enjoy some company with someone your own age.' He took a step closer. 'I wonder, Signora, whether you might allow me to...' He paused. 'I wonder whether we might take a walk together. I have a very nice bottle of *sekt*. I had been saving it for my birthday, but–'

'That is very kind of you, Leutnant, but not today. I have so much to do!' Another quickly flashed smile.

Kranz nodded. 'Of course. Another day perhaps.' He bowed and left.

Francesca breathed a sigh of relief, then went to the dark wood dresser and rummaged through one of the drawers. She soon found what she was looking for: a small switchblade that folded in on itself, like a razor. She put it into the pocket of her skirt.

A little after 6 a.m., the battalion concentration area south of the Primosole Bridge. The Yorks Rangers had moved there the previous evening, having marched from Villasmundo earlier, and from Melilli the day before. Tanner had been much happier; as far as he was concerned, sleeping out in the open, with just his rain cape and a blanket for a bed, with the men around him, was preferable to that ornate villa in Melilli.

The battalion had stood-to at 0430, and just before six, orders had come in from Brigade for them to liaise with 13th Brigade in the Simeto river bridgehead area.

'I'll go myself,' Tanner said, taking the paper orders from the signaller.

He left the farmhouse where the battalion had established headquarters, and went to A Company, who had taken positions in an olive grove not far from the farmhouse. He found Sykes and Shopland sitting on a half-collapsed dry-stone wall drinking tea.

'Morning,' he said. Then, to Shopland, 'Mind if I borrow Sykes? I've got to head up to the bridgehead to liaise with 13th Brigade.'

'We're not going anywhere, are we?'

'Not in the next hour or so, no,' said Tanner.

'That's fine, sir,' said Shopland.

Sykes finished his tea, shook out the dregs and winked at Tanner. 'Won't be long, then, sir.'

'Thank Gavin for me, won't you?' said Tanner.

'No M/T, then?' asked Sykes.

'No,' said Tanner. 'Kicks up too much dust. We'll walk. It's only a couple of miles.'

'I miss our trucks, don't you?'

'Too right. Still, better to have sore feet and be alive, I suppose.'

'What's all this about, then?' said Sykes, as they walked towards the road to the bridge. German guns were shelling the bridgehead, occasional shells hurtling across from the Etna foothills and exploding a mile or so up ahead.

'It looks like the Green Howards are going to be placed temporarily under 13th Brigade command. I think there might be an attack going in shortly.'

'And why do you need me?'

'I don't, really. A bit of company, Stan. I want to hear what's going on.'

'Missing us, are you?'

'You think I'm happy spending my days with Croaker?'

'I wonder whether he's got his trousers and shirt back yet.' He grinned.

'You heard about that, did you?'

'Heard about it? Me and Browner half inched them!'

'He told me it was some Italian girl.'

'Well, it was, strictly speaking, but we put her up to it.'

Tanner laughed. 'How the hell did you manage that?'

'We followed him the other night. Browner and me was negotiating with some Eyeties when we spotted him.' He had been looking a bit 'furtive', Sykes told him. When they realized he was following a girl, they followed Creer in turn. 'So this girl goes into this house, down a little side-street, and Creer goes in after her.'

'You didn't watch, did you, Stan?'

'No, no, nothing like that. But we waited down below a little while, heard him giving her one, then it all went quiet and we wondered what was going on. To be honest, we weren't quite sure what we were going to do, but we thought there might be an opportunity for a little sport. Anyway, after a while she came out onto the balcony, so we reckoned old Croaker must have nodded off.'

'Tiring business. Then what?'

'We whistled to her and beckoned her down.'

'And she did?'

'Too right. I reckon she thought her boat had come in. Now my Eyetie ain't too clever, and Browner's is even worse, but we got along with sign language all right. She was a smart girl. She understood. Five minutes later, there she was with Croaker's shirt, trousers, boots, the lot. Wallet an' all. We gave her the wallet, another note or two for good measure, and ran off with the rest.'

Tanner laughed. 'And I caught him coming back in. He thinks it's me that's been telling everyone, but I've sworn blind it wasn't.'

'Nah, it was us. Told you two could play at that game. You won't tell, will you?'

Tanner laughed again. 'He tried to find the girl. Of course he couldn't, though, and then we were on our way again.' He chuckled again. 'Brilliant,

Stan. Good work. Everyone knows about it, that's for sure.'

'I'm surprised you haven't killed him yet. I don't know how you can bear to speak to him after what he did.'

'I nearly did – the other night, when he came in wearing just his drawers.'

'Oh, yeah?'

'I suddenly snapped. I don't know why then and not before. I suppose it was seeing him there, just wearing his underwear after a night whoring. He made some gibe and I grabbed him by the neck. I very nearly decked him.'

Sykes whistled. 'What did he do?'

'Threatened to court-martial me. He hasn't done anything, though.' He chuckled. 'He was scared. Maybe he still is. He's been keeping out of my way since then.'

'Good.'

'But it's no way to run a battalion, is it?'

'No, Jack, it isn't. It certainly isn't.'

Soon after, they reached the vineyards south of the river. Many of the vines had been wrecked and the stench had become suddenly overpowering: the sickly sweet smell of rapidly rotting flesh.

'Oh, Christ, this is bloody awful,' said Sykes.

'You're not wrong,' said Tanner, spotting several horse carcasses at the side of the road. He took out a handkerchief, wetted it in water from his bottle, then wrapped it around his nose and mouth. Signs of battle lay strewn everywhere. A wrecked glider stood mangled amid the shattered vines a little way to their right. Lying by the side of the road were a number of blackened vehicles, including a Jeep, two trucks and a carrier.

Small arms suddenly rang out from up ahead and away to their left. Then came the sound of engines revving, followed by the report of tanks firing.

'Jesus, this really is the hot spot,' said Sykes, as they approached the Primosole Bridge. It had been hit by shells at least twice, and there were shell-holes on the riverbank, while bullet marks littered the metal-frame bridge.

They were quickly waved across.

'I'd hurry if I were you, sirs,' said the corporal from the 2nd Wiltshires.

They did so, Tanner glancing at the open sea just a few hundred yards down the river on their right. Another crumpled glider lay broken on the far bank. Once they were across, the sound of battle intensified. A couple of miles to the north-west, smoke was rising into the sky and the chatter of small arms still rang out. More shells whistled over, although none landed near them. They hurried on and found the 2nd Wiltshires holding positions directly to the north of the bridge. A subaltern pointed them in the direction of 13th Brigade Headquarters.

'It's just after the dog-leg in the river. An old building with half the roof caved in. You can't miss it.'

They found it easily enough, although there was a flap going on. The chief of staff was yelling into a field telephone, while clerks and signallers were hurriedly taking down messages and tapping out orders on typewriters set up on makeshift trestle tables.

The brigadier hurried in, lean face, trim moustache.

'I remember him,' said Sykes. 'Got a VC at Wadi Akarit. Campbell.'

'I'll be with you in a moment, chaps,' said the brigadier, seeing Tanner and Sykes. More tank guns boomed to the north-east, then came the sound of mortar shells bursting.

'Sir! Sir!' Someone passed the brigadier a telephone.

'What?' said Campbell. 'Damn! Then make sure they don't lose the other. We need the other bridge kept intact... Yes... Not another inch.' He handed back the phone. 'Buggeration!' he said. 'Jerry's got Lemon.'

'What about Grapes?' asked his chief of staff.

'Still standing, thank God. I've told the Inniskillings they need to hold firm.' He turned to his air liaison officer. 'Some Jerry tanks are causing the problem,' he said. 'Can you get some air onto them?'

'I'll ask, sir.'

Brigadier Campbell now turned to Tanner and Sykes, who both saluted. 'Sorry, gentlemen,' he said. 'Anyway, thanks for coming. I was only expecting a subaltern. Who are you two?'

'Major Tanner, sir, second-in-command, Second Yorks Rangers.'

'Splendid. I'm afraid we need your help here. Brigadier Rawstorne has loaned me your battalion and also the First Green Howards. We have to try and expand the bridgehead, not least because we're going to need some heavy guns in here and we badly need the cover of the railway embankment, which is about three thousand yards to the north.'

'How far does the bridgehead extend at the moment, sir?' asked Tanner.

'About two and a half thousand yards. It's not enough. We need your two battalions as Brigade Reserve, so I want you up and in position here, along the Simeto, by thirteen hundred hours. Can you do that?'

'Of course, sir.'

'Excellent. We'll have you chaps on the left, Green Howards on the right. Cross the Primosole Bridge, but then push through the Wiltshires and take up positions in front of Grapes Bridge.' He showed them on the map, where the Simeto looped to the south, then forked. Grapes Bridge was just before the fork.

'All right, sir,' said Tanner.

'And we'll have an O Group here at eleven thirty. Tell Colonel Creer.'

Tanner and Sykes saluted again, then left.

It was Tanner, not Creer, who attended the Orders Group.

'You go, Tanner. You've already been to Brigade HQ, so it makes more sense. In any case, we're only in reserve. It doesn't need me there, does it?'

'Whatever you say, sir.'

There was quite a gathering at Brigade HQ. Tanner recognized Colonel Shaw from the Green Howards, and the air liaison officer he had seen earlier. The brigadier introduced everyone: Watson, his chief of staff, the officers commanding the Inniskillings, Wiltshires and Cameronians. Also there were the brigade medical and intelligence officers, as well as majors from the artillery and engineers.

'And this is Major Tanner from the Second Yorks Rangers,' said Campbell. 'No Colonel Creer?'

'No, sir. Colonel Creer is, er, indisposed.'

Campbell raised an eyebrow. 'I see.'

The men glistened in the heat, and slapped themselves as flies and mosquitoes buzzed around them. Headquarters felt sheltered with endless groves and vineyards around them, but it was impossible to see more than forty yards ahead. Looming over them, as it had been since they'd first landed but now even closer, was the giant volcano, Etna.

'I'm sure you've all seen the sitreps,' said Campbell, 'but let me bring you up to date briefly.' He had a standard 1:25,000 map pinned to the wall, with coloured-pencil lines drawn over it. 'The situation here is somewhat precarious. Taking Primosole Bridge, as you all know, took a hell of a lot longer than we expected. It was only two days ago that the Durhams finally secured a bridgehead to the north. But at least we've got it and at least it's still in one piece – just. Jerry has been tenacious – we're up against well-trained men from the Hermann Göring Division reinforced by paratroopers. In terms of positions, they now hold all the aces. They've got heavy guns dug in along the lower lava slopes of Etna.' He pointed to the map. 'Here, in a line from Misterbianco. This is Jerry's main line of defence.' He nodded to his chief of staff, who handed out a series of aerial photographs.

'These were taken yesterday afternoon,' Campbell continued. 'You can see that north of here runs a railway line, roughly east-west from Catania. It's on an embankment, and Jerry has his forward positions behind it. Mortars, Spandaus and so on.' He paused, looking at the photograph, then the map. 'Our corps is going to attack, and smash this enemy defensive line, but before that happens, we need our own heavy guns in here and, more to the point, we need them behind that railway embankment. So it's our job to extend the bridgehead. Get ourselves the railway and those dikes. In any case, Jerry's already too close for comfort. The Inniskillings had a bit of a scrap this morning. Jerry got lucky on Lemon Bridge too. Fortunately, we think it'll be repaired soon enough, but the point is, we need to extend our bridgehead, and it's going to be up to us to do it.'

A gun boomed from the lava hills, and they heard the shell screaming across the plain. Campbell paused, waiting for it to land. It came down a few hundred yards to their left. 'Any questions?' he asked.

'Presumably this will be a night attack,' said the colonel from the Cameronians.

Campbell nodded.

'Will we have artillery support?'

'Yes,' said the gunner major. 'We're moving them up today, although I'm afraid they'll be in rather open positions on the southern edge of the plain. That's why we need you to get that railway line.'

'So, a creeping barrage,' said Campbell. 'The

attack will go in about midnight on a three-battalion front, with the Rangers and Green Howards in reserve. The RAF are going to soften up targets through the day as well.' He glanced at the air liaison officer, who nodded in agreement.

'Now,' said Campbell. 'Shall we go forward a bit? Get the lie of the land. About two thousand yards north of here, there are a number of cornfields. This will be the start point.'

They set off, the entire Orders Group, making their way northwards along an old track. Desultory shelling continued, but none landed dangerously close. Away to their right, from the area around the Primosole Bridge, they heard a roar of machine-gun and cannon fire and then four Me109s were climbing out to sea, a Bofors gun pumping shells after them. None hit.

'I hope that wasn't your boys taking the brunt,' Campbell said to Tanner and Colonel Shaw.

'My thoughts exactly, sir,' said Shaw.

They reached the edge of the vineyards. Directly in front of them was another water channel and dike. Troops dug in there had made rough wooden footbridges, which they crossed, then climbed the dike. With the sun now high above them, Tanner knew there was no chance of using any binoculars. Even so, as he peered across the fields in front of him, he pitied the men who would be attacking there that night. He could picture it all too clearly: an artillery barrage that was never quite as accurate as it promised to be, flares crackling in the sky above, lighting up the advancing infantry like daylight, mortars bursting around them and withering enemy machine-gun fire pumping thousands of bullets towards them. Taking those German forward positions would be quite possible, but it would need a hasty advance, no dithering, and the knowledge that men were going to be hit in the process.

Shelling continued all day, the Germans and Italians lobbing 105s and 150s onto the British positions on the plain, the British returning with their own 5.5-inch and even some heavy 3.7-inch anti-aircraft guns. Twice, a gaggle of Messerschmitts and Macchis came over to strafe the road north across the Primosole Bridge, the Bofors guns defending either end pom-pomming after them. British medium bombers droned over in the afternoon and pasted both German forward positions and the heavy guns in the lava hills. For a while, Etna's lower slopes disappeared in a long, rolling cloud of smoke and dust, but when it eventually cleared, the desultory shelling continued once more.

Then at around half past five a signal arrived at Battalion HQ that they were once more to revert to command of 15th Brigade.

'What about the attack tonight?' said Tanner.

'Probably cancelled,' said Greer. 'Don't worry your pretty little head about it.'

Ignoring him, Tanner turned to one of the signallers. 'Find out where Brigade HQ now is, will you?' He stood behind the signaller, chewing at one of his nails. *Christ, it's hot still.* He wiped his brow with his sleeve. A mosquito landed on his arm, but he smacked it before it could fly away.

'It's a farmhouse half a mile north-east of

Grapes, sir,' said the signaller at length. '886705 is the reference, sir.'

Tanner looked at his map, found the spot, then hurried out. It did not take him long – a ten-minute walk cutting across the southern-curving bow in the Simeto river.

He found Rawstorne there, talking to Captain Verity of the 1st Green Howards.

'Major Tanner!' said Rawstorne.

Tanner saluted and acknowledged Verity. 'What's going on, sir? I thought Thirteenth Brigade were leading an attack tonight.'

'Change of plan, I'm afraid,' said Rawstorne. 'The Inniskillings took a bit of a hammering this morning and it seems half the brigade are struggling with malaria. I saw Campbell earlier and, of course, he was insisting on going ahead, but our chaps are fresher. So we're going to lead the attack.'

'That doesn't give us much time, sir. When's the O Group?'

'We'll have to do without. You were there earlier, weren't you, at Campbell's O Group?'

'Yes, sir.'

'And so was Colonel Shaw. First Yorks and Lancs are reconnoitring now, as I was explaining to Verity here. D'you know I once faced Captain Verity when he was still a boy? The rascal clean bowled me with one that dipped late.'

'The brigadier played a few games for Lancashire, Jack,' said Verity.

'Really?' said Tanner.

'I wasn't bad, but never quite cut it. Not for want of trying.' He smiled as though remembering. 'Anyway,' he continued, 'got a pencil and a piece of paper?'

Tanner nodded.

'Take these orders down then. Bridges Grapes and Lemon being re-bridged by CRE Fifty-one Div approaching Paterno. Recce forces in touch with Five Div, which will attack to break through existing bridgehead and advance to high ground to deny enemy observation and approaches from Catania.' He paused. 'Got that?'

'Yes, sir,' Tanner and Verity said in unison.

'Good. Fifteenth Infantry Brigade will attack under barrage and will occupy high ground south of Misterbianco. Seventeenth IB to follow up. Armour to move in between. On right, First Green Howards, in centre, Second Yorks Rangers, on left, First Yorks and Lancs, First KOYLI in reserve. Start line to be the road 9071 going west to 8572. Your objective is the road running 9075 to 8573.'

Tanner looked at his map and found both roads. 'So that's the road behind the railway line, sir?'

'Exactly. Those are Jerry's forward positions.'

Tanner looked again and saw a snaking dike to the south of the railway embankment. It was marked up as the 'Massa Carnazza'. 'What about this feature, sir? Do we know if Jerry's here?'

'Probably, Tanner. There will undoubtedly be MGs along there.'

Christ, thought Tanner.

'What time do we go, sir?' said Verity.

'We're aiming for a half-hour barrage from twenty-three thirty, but I will confirm timings later. Any other questions?'

'No, sir,' said Tanner.

'Good. You'd better get going. Move up into positions before last light.' He smiled at them amiably. 'Good luck, gentlemen. Knock 'em for six, eh?'

Outside Tanner paused, looking at the map, and scratched his head.

'What are you thinking, Jack?' Verity asked. 'Are we in for a tough fight tonight?'

'It's these dikes that worry me a little,' said Tanner. He held out the map. 'See this one here, south of the railway line? The Massa Carnazza?'

'Yes.'

'When you're defending, a nice curve is what you want. It means you can have interlocking fire. From the start line to the Massa Carnazza is about a mile, give or take, but the last half-mile is open country. There's corn there, which will give you some cover, but you need to push hard. Keep going and get that southern bulge of the Massa Carnazza just as soon as you possibly can. Get that and work around behind it and take out any other Jerry MGs. Then head for the railway.'

Verity nodded.

'Have you been under enemy fire, Hedley?'

'Not much. I've never been in an attack like this. None of us have, to be honest.'

Jesus. 'All you need to do is keep your head. There'll be lots of noise, and it'll seem disorienting, but just keep heading straight. Their MGs, particularly the new one, the 42, have a terrific rate of fire, but that's a problem for them too. They get hot very quickly, and when they get hot

303

they lose accuracy. They'll invariably fire high, so keep low and you'll be fine. You know, they don't tend to fire more than a three-second burst at a time, so keep low when they're firing, then run in between. Also, they frequently have to change ammo belts and barrels, so you'll never come under continuous fire. There will always be opportunities to move forward. Just don't let your men get bogged down. Keep 'em moving.'

He looked at Verity, who was nodding thoughtfully. 'You'll be fine,' said Tanner.

'I hope so.'

'Do you know who will be leading the attack?'

'Not yet, no.'

'But probably three companies and one in reserve?'

'Probably.'

'Then just make sure you all keep up. Problems occur when one company gets ahead of the others. Suddenly flanks are exposed. Stick together.'

Tanner could see Verity was nervous. Christ, he was nervous himself. Who wouldn't be? 'This must seem a long way from Headingley.'

Verity smiled. 'It does rather. But it's what I joined up for. I never wanted to be treated with kid gloves, just because I play a bit of cricket.' He held out his hand to Tanner. 'Thanks for the advice.'

'Good luck,' said Tanner.

At ten to one in the morning on 20 July, the battalion began moving forward to the start line. Timings had reached them late, around nine p.m. They were to cross the start line at 0200 behind the barrage. Most of XIII Corps' guns were now in the plain, on the southern side of the Simeto; the movement there had gone better than expected. That was something. It would be noisy.

Creer had insisted on belatedly forming a battalion Orders Group. With the adjutant, the RSM, the battalion intelligence officer and company commanders in tow, they had reconnoitred forward, to the edge of open ground. Ahead, around six hundred yards away, the railway line bulged south as it curved around a low spur in the Etna foothills. The spur was covered with citrus groves, by the look of it. Beyond that, maybe two miles further north, was the village of Motta Sant'Anastasia, jutting out on a promontory. To the east, and perhaps another mile to the north, lay the town of Misterbianco. Between where they stood now and the railway embankment, however, there was a series of cornfields, already high and ripe. They were crisscrossed by rough tracks, and the road that cut south-west across the line of their advance. Getting over that embankment and onto the spur would be the key. Tanner was conscious, though, as he looked at the ground ahead, that their objectives were more straightforward than those of the less-experienced Green Howards: the Massa Carnazza veered north, behind the railway line, in their sector, so that there was no double-line of defences to overcome.

'We'll attack with B Company on the right,' Creer had told them, 'C Company in the centre and D Company on the left, with A Company in reserve. Major Tanner will lead the attack.'

Tanner rolled his eyes.

'Where will you be, sir?' asked Macdonald.

'At the battalion CP at the start line with the signals section.'

'How about that hut, sir?' said Spiers, pointing to a small tiled barn by the side of the track thirty yards behind them.

'Ideal. Yes, that will be the CP.'

'Fine,' said Tanner, 'but you see that bulge in the railway line up ahead? That's where we all need to head for. Straight across this open ground. Take that railway embankment and get into the hills, and we'll be in a good position to exploit either side.'

He had made it sound so simple. Already, as they moved forward towards the start line in darkness, the ground looked very different. Ahead, the mass of Etna loomed, but it was a dark night. Tanner glanced at his watch. *Nearly one a.m.* An hour of waiting, of getting used to the faint light of the night. Pockets and ammunition pouches filled. Kit stripped to the minimum. Rifles, Bren and sub-machine guns cleaned, oiled and ready. Tanner walked along the companies, whispering encouragement to the platoon commanders and sergeants. 'Keep going, don't stop, head for the bulge.' With him were Spiers and Private White, with the portable No. 18 set.

He paused by Ivo Macdonald, took a swig of water, then peered out into the inky darkness. It was still warm, but mercifully cooler than it had been earlier. This attack had been set up too hastily, he thought. XIII Corps' artillery, a hurriedly put-together barrage and the cream of 15th Brigade attacking on a three-battalion front. It was the current thinking, he supposed; Eighth Army had the fire-power, these days, so they might as well use it to overwhelm the enemy. Even so, he couldn't help thinking there was a better way: a stealth attack to neutralize the MG outposts, followed by a heavy bombardment of the enemy main positions while the infantry assaulted in force. True, they had portable radios, these days, but infantry following creeping barrages smacked of old-school Great War tactics to him, and from what his father had told him, they had rarely worked. They hadn't worked much in this war, either, as far as he could tell. Alamein had been a fiasco as far as he was concerned.

Perhaps it would be all right, but he could feel the dull weight of nausea in his stomach. He thought of Creer, waiting at the CP, hovering behind the signals team. *The bastard. Hoping I'll get the bloody chop. 'Tanner will lead the attack.'* Said so nonchalantly. This attack and every other attack until some Jerry bullet or stray piece of shrapnel struck him down.

Tanner sighed, and gripped his Beretta tightly.

18

In Motta Sant'Anastasia, Francesca and Cara lay on the rough bed in the cellar, listening to the sounds of battle outside, beyond the house. Several bombs had fallen on the town earlier in the afternoon, and the noise of the aircraft and guns had not stopped all day. An old chandelier had fallen and smashed; bits of plaster had dropped from the cornicing. The house had been repeatedly shaken.

Nothing, however, had prepared Francesca for the onslaught that had begun ten minutes earlier. She had been asleep when the guns had opened up but, waking instantly, had rushed to the window. Flickers of orange fire could be seen from across the plain. Shells screamed and whined, then exploded. The vibration was unlike anything she had experienced before. It was as though an earthquake had begun.

Francesca had rushed to find Cara, who was crying, and led her to the cellar. It didn't feel safe now. The building continued to shake. Dust sat heavily on the fetid air, while showers of grit and plaster rained down, getting in their hair, going down their backs, in their eyes and clogging their mouths. What if the whole building collapsed? They would be entombed there, trapped for ever.

She was wondering whether she should take

Cara back upstairs when the cellar door opened and Kranz was coming down the stairs towards them.

'Are you all right, Signora?' he asked. 'We think you would be better in the sheds out in the yard. They are strong, and there is less chance of the house collapsing on top of you there.'

'We are safe here,' she said.

'Please, it would be better. We can look after you.' He held out his hand.

'I don't like it here, Mama,' said Cara. 'I'm frightened.'

'You see?' said Kranz. 'Cara has the right idea. You should listen to her.'

He held out his hand again. 'Signora,' he said, this time more firmly. Francesca felt in her pocket, but the knife was not there. *Of course.* It was not in her dressing gown but still in the pocket of her skirt.

'Very well,' she said, lifted Cara and began to climb the steps. A shell screamed over and landed nearby, shaking the house once more and making Francesca slip. She gasped, but Kranz caught and steadied her. She could feel his hand run across her back, and clasp her close, very close, to her breast.

'It is all right,' he said. 'I've got you.'

Francesca hurried on up the steps and out of Kranz's grasp, Cara's arms tight around her neck. Taking the outside stairs this time, they hurried down to the sheds by the yard – where Nico had kept his motorcycle. It was still there – she had to give Kranz credit for that – hidden underneath a tarpaulin.

'Inside,' said Kranz, behind her. 'Go on, Signora.'

Uncertainly Francesca sat on one of the wooden crates the Germans had brought with them. A team of artillery directors were still operating from the kitchen, but five men were here, taking shelter from the bombardment.

Francesca looked around at them, then at Kranz in the open doorway. Nico had said they would be safe; he had said it would soon be over. But it was not over yet, not by any means, and nor were they safe, no matter what he had promised. Rather, they were living on the front line, with shells falling around them and surrounded by strange German soldiers. She wanted to bury her head in her hands and cry, but instead she stroked her daughter's hair and stared at the stone wall opposite, praying that they would survive the shelling, that Kranz and his men would soon leave them alone.

Across the island, the US 3rd Division's lead units had leaguered for the night to the north-east of the small town of Casteltermini. It had been a good day for Patton's spearhead, and Charlie Wiseman was enjoying a few bottles of beer with his new friends in the 7th Infantry Regiment. Colonel Sherman had allocated a small *ad hoc* group to Wiseman for the advance on Villalba: four Sherman tanks, a couple of Jeeps and three half-tracks, which amounted to one platoon of tanks and one motorized infantry platoon.

It had been Colonel Sherman and his boys who had taken Agrigento and Porto Empedocle a few

310

days earlier, and Wiseman recognized in them the confidence of troops who now felt invincible. Forty-five miles they had advanced that day. Forty-five miles! In a day! Resistance had melted away.

'Hey, Colonel,' said Lieutenant Blake, the tank platoon commander. 'Geisler just picked up on the net that the Big Red One have taken Enna. D'you hear about that?'

'Yeah,' Wiseman replied. 'You know, a while back, that town held out for thirty-one years against the Saracens and now our boys take it with barely a fight.' He grinned.

'Might not always be this easy, though,' said Lieutenant Hartwell, the commander of the infantry.

'Well,' said Wiseman, 'it's certainly true that there's a fair few spaghetti benders in those hills up ahead. The Assietta Division are supposedly dug in on Monte Cammarata and around. And they've got blocking positions along all our main lines of advance.'

'You reckon they might just call it quits, though, sir?' asked Blake. 'I mean, what's the point? They know they're beat now, surely.'

'Maybe,' said Wiseman. 'But that's why we need to get our asses over to Villalba tomorrow. There's a man there we need to see, just to make sure everything's in order.'

'Who?' asked Blake.

Wiseman lit a cigarette, and smiled. 'Someone who's been helping us all along. A man of honour.'

2.10 a.m. Shells continued to hurtle over, blocks

of iron and explosive, screaming as they flew across the sky. The Rangers were already at the edge of the open ground, lying along a grassy track at the edge of a wheat field. The wheat was ripe and tall, nearly five feet high, but at six foot, Tanner could see over the top and, from the lights of the explosions, to the curve of the railway embankment no more than three hundred yards ahead. Most of the shells, though, were falling behind, onto the lower lava slopes that rose off the plain. That was where the enemy's guns were, but not where his forward positions were sited.

'Bollocks,' Tanner muttered beside Spiers. 'Those forward positions are almost untouched. I bloody hate barrages. Just holds everything up, tells the enemy we're coming and invariably hits the wrong target. We should be storming those positions now.'

'Some are landing short, though.'

'A few, but not many. Where are the bloody mortars? That's what we want. I'd suggest moving out further into the corn, but I know the other company commanders would never agree to it.'

'Especially after what happened to your lot the other day.'

'That was different,' muttered Tanner. He glanced at his watch. He wished he knew what defences the enemy had. A bit of wire up front, a few hastily sown mines. Schu-mines, most probably. He hadn't mentioned that to the men because he knew that if he did they'd never reach that embankment. Speed was what counted, and to hell with any mines. They had to get through the field and get through it quickly. He had impressed it upon the company commanders and to the men. Repeatedly. 'A moving target is a difficult target,' he'd told them. Another worry was that if they went to ground in the cornfield, the Germans might decide to set it on fire, in which case either the men would be flushed out and mown down by MGs or they would burn.

'We've got to run to that embankment, Tom,' he said to Spiers. 'Everyone knows that, don't they?'

Spiers grinned. 'They do.'

Tanner glanced to either side of them. Men crouched, waiting. He had a platoon from B Company on his right and one from C Company on his left. Along with Spiers, he had brought Chalkie White, his wireless operator, and Trahair, his batman, who had followed him from A Company. Also beside him were two sappers, Lieutenant Tummins and Private Selby. The engineers had been dispersed among the companies.

He hurried now along the front of the C Company men. 'When the barrage lifts, run for it,' he told them, above the din of the guns. 'Make sure you keep up. And if you get disoriented, follow the North Star.' He pointed up to the sky. 'Head north and you can't go wrong.' He repeated this line again – and suddenly their mortars opened up, mortar shells landing with what appeared to be good accuracy around the embankment ahead.

0220. Ten more minutes. Ten more minutes of shells screaming, of mortars whining, of the ground shaking. 'When the barrage lifts, run!' he

313

urged the men again, as he hurried down B Company's line. 'Keep heading north! Make sure you don't lag behind. Follow the North Star!'

He saw Mallinson. 'Men all ready?' he asked.

'I think so.'

'They've got to keep up. If they stall, they're in trouble. Got to keep 'em moving.'

Mallinson nodded. 'I know. Good luck, Jack.'

Tanner hurried back towards Trahair and White, and found Spiers there too. He looked at his watch again. *0228.* Any moment now. Another flurry of shells whooshed over, and then the mortars were dropping smoke bombs. The embankment up ahead disappeared in a fog of swirling smoke. Tanner felt his mouth go dry, quickly took a drink from his bottle and noticed his hands were shaking as he refastened the cap. Suddenly the barrage lifted and it was time to move.

He ran headlong into the corn, then veered off to push some C Company men forward.

'Come on!' he yelled. 'Move! Move! Move!' He saw Spiers doing the same and then through the smoke up ahead came the rapid *brrrp* of MG fire, harsh and grating like a saw, and arcs of tracer were spitting around them. Tanner ran, heard someone cry out and fall, heard bullets hissing and zipping above his head.

A glance around – *Yes, there's White and Trahair* – and others making swathes through the corn. Mortar shells were still falling – then two flares fizzed into the air above them, began to drop and, with a crackle, burst, casting a glow of light over them. Men were loosing off rifles as enemy

314

machine-gun fire criss-crossed the field in a series of bursts. Tracer sped towards them, and Tanner ducked, crouching. *One, two, three.* He rose again and sped forward. Was anyone still with him? *Yes, good.* Another burst of fire, Tanner crouched and ran, and heard more men falling. A hundred and fifty yards to go. *Two, three, and up,* and through the dispersing smoke, Tanner saw just three MGs, one at the apex of the bulge and two further round to the sides, each firing enfilades across each other. *Take out one and there'll be a gap and we'll be through.* Another glance around – *Trahair and White still there, and Tummins and Selby* – but shots were now coming from behind him on his right. 'Come on,' he muttered, 'keep up.' The noise was deafening, and Tanner's ears were ringing sharply. His heart was hammering, as another arc of tracer pulsed towards them. He crouched again, heard bullets snap the tops off the corn, looked around, saw the men were still with him, then urged them on again.

Just fifty yards now, the embankment looming. He heard whooshes overhead above the racket of the machine-guns. *Mortars.* He kept half running, half crouching as a series of explosions fell behind him. Several men screamed. *If you'd just keep up.* Twenty yards or so to his right there was another explosion and a man yelled. Bollocks, a mine. The man was still howling as he pushed on through the corn. Another burst of MG fire, but it was behind him. *Fixed lines – and I'm through.* He was nearing the edge of the field and, now, through the corn, and in the fading light of the flares, he saw coils of wire – not much, but enough.

He looked behind and saw only Trahair and White with him. Where the bloody hell were the sappers? *Damn it, damn it.*

'Stay here,' he told Trahair and White, then ran back. Another blast and another scream. Now two men were shouting, yelling in fear and shock and pain. A whoosh, a fizz, a crackle and more flares burst, this time almost directly overhead. *We need to get a move on.* The mortars would soon be upon them. Hurrying through the corn, he found Tummins and Selby crouched among the stalks. To his left, more men had stopped. *Jesus.* Grabbing Selby, he said, 'Get up, and cut that wire! Get up now unless you want to be cut to pieces by mortars!' He grabbed Tummins, too, yanking him to his feet. 'Move!' He watched them scurry forward, then ran through the corn to where one of the men was still screaming. Another whoosh above him – *mortars* – and, moments later, they were landing, thirty yards behind. Something fizzed past him and he felt a sting on his shoulder. He stumbled, then regained his footing. *Nicked by shrapnel.* The man was from C Company and had lost his foot. Several men were tending him, but around him the rest had gone to ground.

'Get up!' shouted Tanner. 'Stay here and you'll die. Move, and we'll stop these bastards and kill them instead.' He went over and grabbed a man by the shoulder, then another. 'Come on, get up! Get up! Come on! Follow me!' He looked around for a Bren gunner, saw a two-man team and, beckoning to them, said, 'Here, come with me.'

Machine-gun fire burst out again, this time closer. *They've changed their fixed lines of fire.*

Tanner hurried through the corn, the men behind him. From the light of the flares, he found Trahair and White, then saw that Tummins and Selby were lying on the ground, cutting the wire. *Good.*

'Once you've cut that wire,' he told Tummins, crouching beside him, 'we'll come through, then you make another breach.' Tummins nodded. One of the MGs was just thirty yards away, the muzzle flash clearly visible on the top of the embankment. The machine-gun was firing short bursts on a line roughly south-west. *He can't have seen us.* More mortar shells exploded behind. *Where was everyone? Had they kept up?*

Suddenly Spiers was beside him, as Tanner unslung his rifle. He could just see the top of the gunner's head. *Just, but enough.* Above, the flare was floating downwards, the light fading again. *Got to be quick.* Tanner drew the rifle into his shoulder, peered through the sight, and fixed on the top of the machine-gunner's head. The German moved. *Changing barrel?* But then he reappeared, letting rip with another burst. *One, two, three, four.* The firing stopped. Tanner breathed in, held his breath and squeezed the trigger. He felt the butt jerk into his shoulder but saw the man slump out of sight.

'Now!' he shouted, slung his rifle back on his shoulder and ran forward, towards the embankment, feeling in his haversack for two grenades. He pulled the pin of the first as he ran. Then, at the edge of the embankment, he hurled it, pulled the pin of the second, waited an instant and lobbed that over too. Spiers and the others were beside him, panting, gasping, fumbling with the pins of

317

their grenades. Explosions on the far side, the screams of men. Grenades hurtling through the air, more explosions, and then they were up, Tanner urging the Bren gunner forward. Onto the railway, the gravel crunching underfoot, indistinct shapes of men, a burst from his Beretta, several enemy falling. The Bren opened up with a three-second burst of fire and now more men were beside him. Tanner paused, saw two dead German machine-gunners and picked up the Spandau lying beside them, with a tin of ammunition.

Someone was beside him – *Trahair?* He gave him the box of ammunition, slung the Spandau across his shoulders then ran on, down the far side of the embankment. Men were calling out, bullets fizzing through the air, but the Germans knew their positions were being overrun. Tanner saw a mortar team thirty yards back, fired one-handed with his Beretta, and ran forward, firing again. Away to the left, the second MG was still firing forward, but then turned and fired a burst towards them. The tracer arced across the inside bowl of the embankment, but the bullets were high. Tanner ran forward, dropped the Spandau, unslung his rifle again, squatted down, and aimed. It was hard to see – the flares had died out – but as the machine-gunner fired again, Tanner saw the muzzle flash, adjusted his aim, squeezed the trigger, and fired, once, twice, then a third time in quick succession. He ran forward again, hugging the embankment, conscious of men beside and behind him. The air was heavy with smoke and the stench of cordite. More men were clambering over the embankment now. Tanner yelled to them, and suddenly two more flares were whooshing into the sky, fired from the citrus groves on the low slopes above them. A hiss, a crackle, and green light burst over them, casting the ground in an eerie glow. Several mortar teams were hastily clambering up the slopes, scampering into the dense citrus groves, but from the sound of it, a combination of grenades and bullets was taking a toll.

Tanner followed, calling to his men. 'Here!' he shouted, above the din. 'Here! To me!'

Shots were being fired from the slopes above. A man fell nearby. Then a burst of a sub-machine gun and rifle shots rang out. A number of Rangers answered, firing up to the slopes above.

'Come on!' shouted Tanner, scrambling onto the rising ground. He paused and looked back. Men, like dark ants, were scurrying across the open land behind the embankment. Dead and wounded lay strewn on the ground. Beyond, behind the embankment, mortar shells were still exploding. Away to the left and right, machine-guns were still chattering, barking their rapid fire, tracer pulsing across the night, and mortar shells bursting. Theirs, Tanner realized, was the only breakthrough.

There was cover now, here in these groves, and Tanner paused. Where the hell was everyone?

'Rangers!' he shouted. Then, more quietly, 'Who's here? Who's with me?'

'I am, sir,' said Trahair.

'Good man. Chalkie? Where are you?'

'Here.' A voice a few yards away.

Two more flares shot up into the air fired from

the slopes above them.

Good. They might expose those down by the railway and in the cornfield, but the groves would provide all the cover they needed from the magnesium brightness when it burst.

'Where the hell is everyone?' growled Tanner, as the green flare burst. As the scene was lit again, Tanner saw Spiers a few yards away, then Lieutenant Goodridge, a platoon commander from C Company. There were, Tanner guessed, around forty or fifty men.

Mortars were falling once more, exploding fifty yards in front of them, while enemy machine-guns further along the railway embankment to either side continued to spit bullets towards the open ground of the cornfields.

'What do we do now, sir?' asked Goodridge.

'We work along these slopes and take out those MGs from behind,' said Tanner. 'But we need more men. Where the hell are the rest?'

'A number went to ground when Merryweather lost his foot, sir,' said Goodridge.

'We need to get moving, sir,' said Spiers.

'Too damn right.' He turned to White. 'All right, Chalkie. Send a signal to Battalion HQ. Tell them to get onto the other companies and have them head for the centre of the bulge in the railway embankment. The wire has been cut and we're through. Tell them to send up A Company if necessary.'

'Right, sir,' said White, putting on his headset.

'Have we got the C Company wireless operator here?' asked Tanner. He looked around at the men, their faces green in the light of the flare,

320

eyes shadowed by the rims of their steel helmets. 'Goodridge? Do you know?'

'He was with Major Ferguson, sir.'

'Why don't I go back down, sir,' said Spiers, 'and see if I can't get some more men?'

'All right,' agreed Tanner.

'I'll take a few lads with me.'

'Good idea.'

Spiers picked four, then hurried back down the slopes to the railway embankment.

'Rangers!' yelled Spiers, from the embankment. Mortars were still being fired onto the cornfield. 'Rangers!'

Tanner watched him and his men scamper over the railway line and disappear. Then he glanced across to the east, where the Green Howards still appeared to be under heavy attack. It wasn't far. Half a mile, perhaps a little more. 'How are we doing for ammo?' he asked.

'Could do with some more,' said Goodridge, 'but I've still got a couple of grenades and a few magazines.'

Tanner saw that another of the men was squatting down, resting on a Bren. 'Well done, Tom,' he said. 'How many spare mags have we got?'

Most had one or two.

'And, Kernow,' he said to Trahair, 'have you still got that Jerry ammo tin?'

'Yes, sir.'

'Good. This is what we do. We'll stay this height on the slopes here and see if we can't cut in behind the enemy. Sounds like the Green Howards are still having a difficult time, so let's see if we can't help them. With a bit of luck,

321

reinforcements will arrive and we can win this battle. We'll leave a section here with a Bren to hold this position, though. If we hear a counter-attack developing, we'll hurry back. And if the RSM returns with more men, send 'em round. All right?' He turned to White. 'Have you got anything for me, Chalkie?'

'I've sent the message, sir, and it's been received and understood.'

'Good,' he said. 'Right then, iggery. Let's get a bloody shift on.'

At the battalion CP, Creer stood behind the signals section. Two tables had been set up and two men with radio sets before them sat at each. Messages were coming in regularly, from Brigade and from the companies in action. On one side of the barn, and at one of the tables, one signaller received the message, while the other wrote it down in pencil on the message pad. At the other table, the second pair were sending back signals in return. Next to Creer stood Lieutenant Sowerby, the regimental signals officer, and his number two, Sergeant Davenport.

'A message in from Major Tanner,' called one of the signallers, holding up a piece of paper.

Sowerby was about to take it when Creer stepped forward and took it instead. 'Let me see it,' he said. He read the message, then cursed to himself.

'What is it, sir?' asked Sowerby.

Creer shot him a glance. 'Tanner's got across the railway with a small number of men and wants reinforcements.'

'We can tell D Company and the rest of B Company to go through the gap, sir,' said Sowerby.

'But the attacks by the Green Howards and Yorks and Lancs have stalled. We don't want our men getting isolated.' Creer hovered by the wireless operators. 'Find out where B Company is.'

From the battle up ahead, the night air was still alive to the sound of small arms and mortars. Creer bit his nails. Tanner isolated was exactly what he wanted. Isolated, cut off, and taken prisoner. Or, even better, killed. But how to do that with Fauvel and Sowerby hovering about? *Play for time.*

'What about D Company?' he asked, after a minute or two. 'Any news?'

'Major Macdonald's wounded, sir. The situation is confused and the wireless operator isn't sure where all the platoons are.'

'And what about B Company? Can you contact them too?'

Creer paced again while the wireless operator attempted to make contact. He saw Sowerby glance at his watch.

'Reply from D Company, sir,' said the wireless operator. 'They're pinned down by wire and mines and coming under mortar attack.'

'Tell them to work their way towards the centre of the position,' said Creer, 'and to await further orders.'

Tanner and his men had crept around the edge of the spur and had now paused in a clearing in the groves overlooking the long, straight stretch of the railway line and towards the Green Howards' sector. MG tracer was still pouring into the open ground and mortars bursting. Another flare fizzed into the air, showering the cornfields with a bright white magnesium light. Tanner looked back up the slopes, towards Misterbianco and Etna, still towering over them. All he could see was the dark outline of more citrus groves. It was clear to him that the Germans lacked defence in depth. A bit of wire, a handful of mines, some mortars and MG teams were holding up the best part of three battalions. Behind those outer forward defences, there was very little. He imagined that mortar teams and infantry were gathering themselves together somewhere not too far above them, but they were quiet for the moment.

Where the bloody hell were those reinforcements? Now was the time to strike, while the enemy in this part of their line was disorganized and broken. Tanner had hoped men from the other companies would be pouring in through the gap by now and that they would be able to mount a significant attack. Now was clearly the moment to exploit their earlier success – leave it much longer and, chances were, the Germans would re-group and counterattack; their forward positions might be held lightly, but they were not going to leave a gaping hole in the line for long. The problem was, right now he didn't have enough men or ammunition to achieve very much. He needed those reinforcements. On the other hand, it was clear the Green Howards needed help; so did the Yorks and Lancs, and their own D Company, for that matter, but he thought of Captain

Verity and the expression on his face: apprehension, nerves. Fear. It was a big thing, going into battle for the first time, especially when it was at night and your enemy were Germans who knew a thing or two about soldiering.

'Chalkie,' he said. 'Find out what the bloody hell's going on and where our reinforcements are, will you?'

'Yes, sir,' said White.

Tanner listened as White called up Battalion. No response. A pause, and then he tried again. *Contact.*

'Hello, Sunray, where are reinforcements? Say again, where are reinforcements?'

'Ask whether they've sent A Company forward,' said Tanner.

'Has Able been sent forward to 841730?'

Tanner listened, his heart sinking.

'Wilco, Sunray, wait out.' White called off. 'I'm sorry, sir,' said White eventually. 'It seems D Company is still pinned down, B Company have become dispersed, and A Company hasn't moved.'

'Bloody hell!' said Tanner. 'That man will–' He stopped, took a deep breath, then said, 'Chalkie, call them up again, then give the headset to me.'

White did so. Tanner took off his helmet, put the headphones over his ears and the transmitter to his mouth and said, 'This is Tanner. Is the OC there?... I don't give a damn about R/T signal procedure, just put him on.' He sighed, waited, then heard Creer. 'Sir, I urgently need reinforcements. We've broken through and if we can exploit this position we can roll up the entire part of this front. But I need reinforcements now.

Send me A Company.'

Tanner listened, then ripped off the headset, cursed, and passed it back to White. *Get off the net. That's an order,* had been Creer's response. A Company would be moving nowhere. *The bastard. The bloody stupid bastard.* He sighed again, then said, 'All right. Everyone check their weapons. Keep a sharp look-out. We'll wait for Spiers, then move.' He turned to White. 'Chalkie, try and get hold of B and D Companies, will you? You can find their frequencies, can't you?'

'Should be able to, sir.'

'Good. Just keep trying.'

Spiers reappeared soon after with a further thirty men from C Company, including Captain Dawnay, the company 2 i/c.

'D Company are way over to the left,' said Spiers. 'They must have got disoriented and strayed into the Yorks and Lancs sector.'

'C Company?'

Spiers shook his head. 'I'm not sure. Major Ferguson's wounded. Not badly, but he's been sent back.'

'I'm sorry, sir,' said Dawnay. 'It was the mines. We lost several men and got pinned down.'

'Listen, Dawnay,' said Tanner, 'did you ever receive a message from Battalion to move through the gap we'd made?'

Dawnay looked at his wireless operator, crouched beside him. 'Did you, Wilkins?'

'No, sir. We were asked to give a sitrep. That was all.'

Tanner thumped the ground with his fist. 'For Christ's sake,' he said.

'Come on, sir,' said Spiers. 'Let's do what we can, eh?'

'I've spent the sodding war being held back by bloody incompetence,' he muttered. 'But, yes, you're right, Tom, let's get on with it. We've got one section still overlooking the railway. We'll send back two more. Goodridge, you can take those men. The rest of us will move in two groups. Dawnay, you take thirty men and climb a little higher, covering our flank. Wilkins and Chalkie, can you link your nets? Let's try and keep in contact.'

'Yes, sir,' said White.

'Tom,' he said to Spiers, 'you and the rest come with me. And everyone keep up, all right? Jaldi, jaldi.'

They hurried on through the groves until suddenly the citrus plantation gave way to a hundred-yard-wide strip of pasture. From here they could look down on the battle raging in the Green Howards' sector. Two more flares burst in quick succession, revealing the network of dikes, tracks and the railway line a little way back. Between the Massa Carnazza dike Tanner had seen on the aerial photographs earlier and the railway, he could see several of the enemy, ant-like figures, lugging boxes of ammunition up to a series of four machine-gun nests. Behind the railway were the mortar teams, the nearest only two hundred yards away.

He turned to Spiers and grinned. 'Pretty good view from here, wouldn't you say? Let's set up the three Brens and this Spandau and cause a bit of havoc.'

'Yes,' smiled Spiers, 'let's.'

'I'll let rip with the Spandau first,' said Tanner, 'because they'll know it's one of theirs. When that's out of ammo, we'll open up with the Brens.'

Tanner set down the Spandau and gave it a quick look over. It was hard to see much, but it appeared to be in working order.

'Got that ammo tin, then, Kernow?' he asked.

'Here you go, boss,' said Trahair, laying it beside him. Tanner opened the bi-pod, steadied the gun, then opened the feed cover. He had used both the German MG34 and the newer MG42 and had always been impressed by the engineering. They were well produced, of that there was no question. Opening the ammunition tin, he pulled out the top of the belt, found the starter tab, then placed it across the feed block and closed the cover. The ammunition belt was now firmly in place.

Lying down, he drew the stock into his shoulder, held onto the grip and pulled back the bolt until it clicked into position. He could see tracer pouring from an MG and the dark shape of two men lying on the embankment of the Massa Carnazza, as well as men carrying another ammunition box.

Tanner aimed and squeezed the trigger. Bullets spat out quicker than he had remembered, the weapon vibrating violently in his hands, and tracer stabbing through the night air. His aim was badly high, but had been enough to make the men with the ammunition box run. He fired again, this time aiming lower and saw the two men tumble and fall. Pausing again, he struggled to spot the MG closest to them on the embankment but, squinting into the shadows, saw a couple of dark shapes and opened fire again. Had he hit them? It was hard to tell.

'Kernow,' he said, 'go and tell the RSM he can open fire now.'

As Trahair scrambled across to Spiers, Tanner looked for the mortar teams, saw several faintly lit by the light of the flares and squeezed the trigger again. Tracer pumped through the air, the weapon juddered, and several men dived onto the ground, although whether that was because they had been hit or not, he wasn't sure. He paused a moment to allow the barrel to cool, then fired again, this time lower, raking the area behind the railway until, just a few seconds later, the ammunition belt was empty.

'Blimey, sir,' said Trahair, hurrying back beside him, 'that didn't take long.'

'The quicker an MG fires, Kernow, the sooner it runs out of ammo.'

The Brens had now opened up, while others were firing rifle shots. Tanner picked up his own rifle, the Aldis scope still fixed. The flares had died down now, darkness descending once more, so that it was hard to spot targets. Tanner held the rifle tight into his shoulder, watching through the scope, waiting for one of the MGs to open up. *There!* Pulses of tracer stabbed the sky. Tanner aimed towards the start of the tracer, then a fraction to the left and a little higher, and fired. The MG was silent.

Suddenly there was firing from a little further up the slope, then the familiar thud and hiss of mortars. He heard the faint whistle through the air, then three exploded in quick succession some fifty yards further up the slope. The Brens were still chattering, but now German machine-gun fire was hissing through the groves, twigs snapping, and little beds of tracer hurtled over their heads.

'Bollocks!' said Tanner. Turning to White, he said, 'Tell Dawnay to pull back.' *Jesus. We shouldn't have to pull back – not now. Not after getting this far.* He scurried, crouching, towards Spiers as more mortars exploded, this time closer. Showers of earth and grit, splinters of wood were thrown into the air, as Tanner was tugging at the men and ordering them to disappear back into the groves. Men were scampering, bodies bent low, melting away between the trees. Tanner waited for the last man, then dived flat as another mortar shell landed not thirty yards away. Lifting his head, then getting to his feet, he glanced back at the scene below. The enemy had quietened down, that was something, but whether it would last was another matter. *Bloody Creer. Bloody sodding Croaker Creer.* A renewed wave of anger coursed through him. This could and should have been a decisive victory, but instead they were running back in full retreat, short on ammunition and men. More bullets overhead and fizzing through the branches. A rifle shot rang out, then a burst from a Bren, but the enemy was not letting up. From somewhere up in the groves above, bullets and mortars were chasing their retreat.

They had broken through the German lines,

but now they would have to get back through them again. And that meant getting over the now exposed railway line.

19

Tanner halted his men two hundred yards short of where they had broken through. Wild, inaccurate machine-gun fire scythed overhead, while harassing mortar shells continued to fall. Most landed harmlessly, but then one dropped among a group of men, killing three outright, their torn bodies flung into the air. Several more were wounded; one lost most of his right leg. 'Help me! Help me! Oh, God, no!' he screamed.

Tanner hurried over.

'Christ, Christ, Christ, oh, God, no!' cried another man, standing there, looking at the carnage and clutching his head in his hands.

'For God's sake,' said Tanner, 'do you want to be any louder telling them where we are? Get a bloody grip of yourself.'

'But – Jesus!'

'Someone get him away from here,' barked Tanner. He crouched beside the wounded man, and began ripping open packets of field dressings.

'Help me, oh, my God, help me!' cried the man.

'We're going to help you, Dan,' said another man, kneeling beside him. 'We're going to get you out of here.'

'That's exactly what we're going to do,' said Tanner. 'What's your name, son?'

'It's Tredwell, sir,' said his friend.

Tredwell glanced at his leg. 'Oh, Christ, look at me! Look at my bloody leg!' It glistened vilely, a mashed stump of a thigh from which the rest of the leg hung by little more than a few sinews.

'All right, Tredwell,' said Tanner. 'We'll have you out of here in no time.' He quickly tied a field dressing tightly round Tredwell's leg as a tourniquet.

'What do we do?' said one of the others. 'His bloody leg's just hanging there.'

'Get a bloody hold of yourselves, that's what,' snapped Tanner, reaching into his haversack. He pulled out a syringe of morphine, and emptied it into Tredwell's arm. 'There you go, Dan,' he said. 'We'll get you back, don't you worry.'

Tredwell's eyelids flickered, then closed.

'Right,' said Tanner. 'He's not a big bloke. One of you is going to have to pick him up and carry him over your shoulder.'

Three more mortar shells whistled over but exploded wide. Then, moments later, a number of men were rushing towards them, bursting through the trees. Tanner felt his heart lurch, and swung his Beretta around. He was about to fire, then heard Dawnay call, 'Don't shoot!'

'Dawnay – thank God,' said Tanner.

'I'm down seven men,' he said breathlessly. 'Christ, I had to leave two of the wounded.'

'Where's Jerry now?' asked Tanner.

'Close. We need to get going. We could hear them.'

'And we're all running low on ammo. All right, but we need to get Goodridge back.' He turned to Spiers. 'Listen, Tom, I want you and Dawnay to take the men over the railway just below us here. Get over, hug the embankment, then go back into the corn through the gap in the wire.'

'All right,' said Spiers, 'but what about you?'

'I'll get Goodridge. Now go!'

Tanner left them and hurried through the groves, crouching low as he went. Nearing the tip of the spur, he slowed, looking for Goodridge and his men. 'Goodridge!' he whispered loudly. 'Goodridge!'

'Sir?' came the reply, and a dark figure stepped into the track through the groves.

'Goodridge?' said Tanner again.

'Yes, sir. I'm here, sir. It's good to see you. We heard lots of firing. To be honest, we were wondering whether we should fall back.'

'You should,' said Tanner. 'Are you all here still?'

'Yes, sir. We haven't fired a shot but–' He stopped. Above them, perhaps fifty yards further up the slopes, between the sounds of battle, they could hear voices and the chink of men moving through the groves.

'Right, go now,' said Tanner, in a low whisper. 'Hug the embankment, but cross a hundred yards back from where I've just come, then hug the other side and cross into the open through the gap in the wire. OK? Now go!'

He urged them all away and then, keeping low, moved between the trees. It was dark, with no flares now lighting their part of the battlefield.

But there was the light of the moon and the stars and that was enough to see by. Pausing, he listened. Small arms and mortars still punctured the night air away to his left and right, but in the moments of quiet, he could hear low voices. Were they getting closer? It was hard to tell.

He reached into his gas-mask case and pulled out the first of four packets of plastic explosive. The half-pound packets of TNT had come from Sykes, as had the detonators and time pencils he now took from his shirt breast pocket. Carefully, he stuck the detonators into each of the packets of TNT, then pressed in the time pencils.

Where was Jerry now? He paused again and listened, then carefully, using the shadows of the trees, inched up the slope, until he could see them. A number of men, talking in low voices, carrying boxes of ammunition and what appeared to be a mortar barrel and stand. Tanner smiled to himself, snapped the time pencil on the first pack of explosive to thirty seconds, then counted to twenty, threw it towards them and ran, hurrying back through the trees. He'd gone thirty yards when a loud explosion tore the night apart, a flash of angry orange flame lighting the sky behind him. Immediately, he snapped another time pencil and dropped it on the ground, then ran forward. Another thirty yards, and he snapped the third time pencil, this time at two minutes' delay.

He could hear shouts and screams on the slopes above him as the second explosion erupted. Glancing back, he saw flames burst around the trees setting several on fire. *Good*. The flames would give him the cover he needed. Scampering over the railway, he took out the last of the TNT, set the timer for four minutes, lobbed it over to the other side and ran, through the gap in the wire, on into the cornfield and back south, across the open ground. Not a single bullet followed him.

Standing outside the battalion command post, Creer heard the explosions and, glancing back towards the enemy lines, saw the glow of flame flicker once, then twice in the distance. Beside him, Captain Dawnay and RSM Spiers flinched and turned.

'Bloody hell,' said Dawnay.

'Those weren't mortars,' said Spiers.

Another flash of light, followed moments later by the rumble of a further explosion.

'We left Tanner there to find Goodridge,' said Dawnay. 'Christ, I hope they're all right.'

'Yes,' said Creer, stroking his chin, 'although those are quite big explosions.'

'For God's sake,' muttered Spiers. 'We needed reinforcements, sir. Where was A Company?'

'Watch your tone, Spiers,' said Creer. 'Any decision made was done with the information I had available. The attack was stalling. D Company were floundering, so too was B Company, and it seemed foolhardy in the extreme to send good after bad.'

'But you were here, sir, a thousand yards back. We were on those slopes, behind the enemy forward positions. We could see everything.'

'I'm not prepared to argue with you, Spiers,'

Creer snapped. 'I made the right decision. It's been a difficult night, I understand that, and we've lost a lot of men, but I don't want to have my decisions challenged by my RSM, is that clear?'

'Crystal,' said Spiers. A fourth flash of orange burst in the distance, followed by a low, angry roar. 'Where the hell are Goodridge and Tanner?'

'Let's hope nowhere near those explosions,' said Creer.

'I hope not, sir,' said Dawnay. 'Tanner sent us all back. He made sure we got out first, then went to look for Goodridge and his platoon.'

'He's a brave man,' said Spiers.

'Indeed,' said Creer.

'What of the others, sir?' asked Spiers. 'Where are the other companies?'

'Most of B Company have made it back to their start positions,' replied Creer. 'D Company have also been ordered to fall back to the edge of the open ground and are digging in.'

A number of men now approached the CP, emerging from the darkness beyond.

'A few more, sir,' said Dawnay.

It was Lieutenant Goodridge, leading his men in. Still short of breath, he saluted. 'I have twenty-eight men with me, sir.'

'And Major Tanner, sir?' asked Spiers.

'I don't know. He told us to head back across the open ground and that was the last we saw of him.'

'Damn,' cursed Spiers.

'At least you and your men are safe, Lieutenant,' said Creer.

'Take the men to C Company positions, Goodridge,' said Dawnay, producing a hand-drawn map. 'They're here, digging in around their start positions. I've got to speak to the IO, then I'll join you.'

Creer went back inside the CP. The signals team were still hunched over their wireless sets, canvas-cased battery packs on the floor beside them, while at another makeshift table, Captain Masters was making notes as he listened to Dawnay's breathless account of the battle. The attack, Creer knew, had been a fiasco, but little blame would be apportioned to the battalion for that. The Yorks and Lancs had completely overshot their mark, and most of one company were reported as captured. Only one company of the Green Howards had made any headway. The only breach in the German lines had been made by Tanner and C Company, but that had now been lost.

So, a bad night, yet Creer felt his spirits rising. A spark of hope had crept into his mind, one that grew with every passing minute. This time, he prayed, Tanner really had gone. Dead, or taken prisoner, he did not care, so long as he never had to see the man again. He wondered whether it was possible to hate a man more, then chuckled to himself. If the Germans had taken care of Tanner, he would owe them a debt, for sure.

Ahead, towards the enemy lines, the sound of battle could still be heard. Machine-guns barking, rifle shots, the dull thuds of shells. It was now past four in the morning, and away to the east, the first thin streaks of dawn were lightening the sky.

'Sir?' said one of the signals team, hurrying

from the barn.

Creer turned and took the message. It was from Brigade: *Bring all troops back to original positions of 0045 hours 20/7/43 with immediate effect. Dig in and prepare for further assault night 20/21.* So now it was official. Creer folded the piece of paper and put it into his pocket, then looked at his watch. *Twenty past four. And still no sign of Tanner.*

He lit a cigarette and inhaled heavily, then felt his body freeze. Up ahead, emerging through the early first light was the tall figure of a man, helmet slightly askew, a rifle on his back and a sub-machine gun in his hand.

'No!' said Creer, aloud.

Villalba, Tuesday, 20 July, 11 a.m. The column trundled up the main road that led to the town square, the tanks and half-tracks squeaking and rumbling, the barrels of the Shermans pointing resolutely forward. In his Jeep at the head of the column, Wiseman spotted the façade of the church he had last seen nearly two months earlier. Either side of him, standing in doorways or peering from windows, were Villalba's residents, Sicilian peasants watching the grand procession.

Fluttering from the aerial on his Jeep was a yellow flag with the black-stitched L, like the one he had dropped over the town almost a week before; there was another such flag on the lead Sherman too.

Wiseman gripped the steering-wheel and felt a dull ache in his stomach. His heart, he could feel, was beating just that little bit harder. Swallowing hard, he turned into the square, parked the Jeep and climbed out. Above, that blue and cloudless sky. Ahead, the honey-coloured church. Blue and gold. He squinted, the brightness suddenly overbearing. A few old men sat outside the bar. He saw several children, pointing excitedly as the tanks and half-tracks fanned out and came to a halt.

Leaning against the Jeep, the engine ticking beside him, he lit a cigarette, then saw two *carabinieri* walk towards him. As they neared, he recognized them.

'*Saluti, Maggiore!*' said the captain.

'*Saluti,*' replied Wiseman, '*ma e ora colonello.*' But it's colonel now.

The *carabiniere* captain apologized. Then, holding out his hands deferentially, he said, '*Accogliamo i nostri alleati americani.*' We welcome our American allies.

Wiseman was about to respond, when from across the square he saw a short, elderly man with a pronounced paunch ambling towards him. Don Calogero Vizzini was accompanied by several others, walking a pace behind him. Wiseman recognized Bartolomeo, Zucharini and a third man, someone he'd last seen back home in the States. As they slowly approached, Wiseman was conscious that the square had begun to fill: Villalba's residents had come out to witness a historic moment.

Don Calogero stopped a few yards from Wiseman. He was wearing the same short-sleeved shirt he had had on the last time they had met. He was holding something, which now unfurled: the folded flag Wiseman had dropped over his villa.

'*Libero, eh, Saggio?*' He chuckled. '*Libero.*' He held out his hand, and Wiseman took it and felt dark eyes boring into him from behind Don Calogero's spectacles.

'*Saluti, Don Calo,*' he said.

Don Calogero nodded, then half turned and waved a hand vaguely at the man on his right, a young, dark-haired man. '*Mio nipote.*' My nephew.

'Domiano Lumia,' said Wiseman. 'How are you? It's been a few years.'

'Yes, it has.' He grinned. 'Good to see you, Charlie.'

'And you. Don Calo has been true to his word.'

'Of course. He is a man of honour.'

Don Calogero walked over to one of the Shermans and, looking up at the barrel, patted the armour plating at the front.

'We're going to come with you,' said Lumia, 'to Palermo.'

'Good,' said Wiseman.

'Your advance has been clear so far?'

'Yes, but it seems there's still a lot of Italian troops in the Monte Cammarata area and they're not showing any sign of budging. At present they're barring our route to the west.'

Lumia smiled. 'Don't worry. My uncle has sent his agents there. By tomorrow, there won't be any more of the Assietta.'

Wiseman nodded. 'I hope you're right.'

'Of course I am. My uncle is a man of his word.' They glanced across at Don Calogero as he walked around the Sherman, beaming at the tank crew. 'So,' said Lumia, after a moment, 'now we come with you. My uncle, myself, Baldini and

Zucharini. We come with you all the way to Palermo.' They were rejoined by Don Calogero and the *carabiniere* chief.

'*Tutto e finite per il fascismo,*' chuckled the policeman, then spat emphatically on the ground. It's all over for Fascism.

They all laughed, Wiseman too.

'*Libertà,*' said Don Calo. '*Libertà in Sicilia ancora una volta.*'

'Amen to that,' said Wiseman. 'Now shall we go?'

The Yorks Rangers remained in their forward positions all day. Shelling from both sides continued. The German artillery was comparatively light but relentless, while the 5th Division's guns were more concentrated: a heavy stonk early in the morning, and another a few hours later, with desultory shelling in between. At the battalion CP, Tanner heard the shells whistling and screaming overhead, a ping-pong match of heavy ordnance. Sometimes he could even see them, a whirr of black flashing through the sky. Two waves of medium bombers attacked the German main line of defence soon after the first heavy stonk. Tanner watched the faint white mass of Misterbianco disappear behind rolling clouds of smoke. It always struck him how immensely destructive such attacks appeared, yet when the bombers had gone and the smoke dispersed, it was as though no bombs had fallen at all. The towns and villages nestling along the lower slopes of Etna were still there, and before long, the German guns were firing once more.

Enemy Spandaus and mortars also kept up a persistent presence. The men were now dug in, but if a vehicle moved, or someone poked his head above the slit trenches in view of an enemy machine-gunner, the familiar sawing sound of the Spandau would ring out, and mortars would fizz across.

And each mortar round, each burst of MG fire, was a reminder of the failure of the night attack, a failure, Tanner was convinced, that should never have been. All morning, he had been struggling to control his anger. He kept replaying his arrival back at the CP in his mind: the surprise on Creer's face, the shock of seeing him still alive. And then it had dawned on him with sudden clarity: Creer had deliberately tried to cut him off, starved him and his men of reinforcements so that they might be trapped, then killed or taken prisoner. He had sacrificed the potential success of the attack purely to get Tanner. 'I can't believe what you've done,' he had told Creer. The man had stuttered, denied it, said he'd made a sound tactical decision on the basis of the information he had at the time. But Tanner knew the truth. 'You're a liar,' he'd snarled.

This time, Tanner told himself, Creer had gone too far, but how he should deal with it, he was unsure: they were still in the front line, the battalion dug in around the previous evening's start line. It was expected they would launch another attack that night although, God only knew, their numbers were depleted. Now was not the moment to mutiny against the officer commanding because that was what it would be if Tanner,

342

Spiers and others made a stand against him. Mutiny was an ugly word.

By midday, he had still not decided what to do, which frustrated him even more: he liked to think of himself as decisive, as a man who always knew his own mind. Now, though, he was second-in-command of the battalion. He was still new to this role, while the situation in which he found himself was unlike any he had faced before.

Tanner sighed and squinted at the enemy positions up ahead – the hazy cluster of Misterbianco and, above, Etna. As ever, a small cloud of smoke hovered over its summit, a smudge of white in an otherwise endless blue. A mosquito landed on his arm and he squashed it. That was another problem: the men were getting hit by malaria – there had been half a dozen more cases that morning. He ambled into the barn, where the intelligence officer was making notes, and the signals lads were still hunched over their radio sets. Tanner lit a cigarette and headed outside again, where the headquarters men were dug in either side of the track. At least Creer was not about – he'd headed to Battalion HQ several hours earlier with some cock-and-bull story about having admin to attend to.

He glanced at Trahair, who was crouched over a Primus by one of the slit trenches, preparing some food. Seeing Tanner look his way, he said, 'I'm making tiffin, sir.'

'Good,' said Tanner, suddenly hungry. He realized he'd not eaten since before the attack.

A few minutes later the meal was ready, and Tanner joined Trahair and Spiers on the edge of the slit trench. Suddenly, a whistle of incoming mortar shells cut through the air. Flinching, Trahair jumped into the slit trench at the side. Neither Tanner nor Spiers moved.

'Watch it, sir!' said Trahair. 'Blimey!'

'Bit jumpy, aren't you, Kernow?' said Tanner. 'They were way off.'

'You'll learn, Kernow,' said Spiers.

Trahair had retrieved his mess tin and clambered back onto the edge of the slit trench when the brigadier unexpectedly arrived with Major Standish, the brigade artillery commander. Tanner saw that the brigadier had cut his arm. 'Are you all right, sir?' he asked, putting down his mess tin and hurrying over.

'Fine, thank you, Tanner. Just had a bit of a close one with a mortar shell.'

'There's a lot coming over.'

'But I'd like to think we're hitting them harder.' Rawstorne looked at Trahair and Spiers, who had set down their lunch and were now standing to attention. 'All right, at ease, you two.'

'Can I get you both some tiffin, sir?' asked Tanner.

Rawstorne glanced at Standish, then said, 'Yes, why not? Thank you, Tanner. What have you got on the go?'

'I think we can manage some Maconochie's, sir, then maybe a bit of tinned fruit and condensed milk.' He called over to Trahair. 'Kernow, fix the brigadier and Major Standish some tiffin, will you?'

'Good man,' said Rawstorne. 'Sounds delicious.' He looked towards the CP. 'Where's

Colonel Creer?'

'Actually, sir, he's gone back to Battalion HQ.'

'Never mind. You'll do, Tanner.'

'Do you want to talk in the CP, sir, or are you happy to stay here?'

'Here's fine, Tanner. Not in direct view of the enemy, I take it?'

'No, sir.'

'Well, I must commend you on your CP, Tanner,' said Rawstorne. 'I've just come from the Green Howards' and it's a little more lively there.'

'What news from them, sir? They had a hard fight last night. It was tough ground they had to cover.'

'B Company copped it hardest. You've heard about Captain Verity, I take it?'

Tanner's stomach lurched. 'No, sir. What happened?'

'I'm afraid he was wounded. Rather badly by the sound of things. He's been taken prisoner. His two i/c tried to mount a rescue, but couldn't reach him. With a bit of luck, Jerry will look after him and he'll see out the war as a prisoner, but his wound sounded bad.'

'For God's sake,' muttered Tanner. He wanted to hit something, preferably Creer, but instead turned away and rubbed his brow. *That stupid bloody bastard.*

'I'm sorry, Tanner. I know how you feel – we're all a bit shaken, to be honest. I know he was a soldier, like the rest of us, but he was also one of the finest cricketers I've ever seen. A little bit special, our Captain Verity.'

'It's not that, sir,' mumbled Tanner. 'It's just so

345

– so bloody unnecessary.'

'Excuse me, sir,' said Spiers, 'but I would like to second what Major Tanner has just said.'

Rawstorne turned towards him, a frown of irritation on his face.

Tanner sighed. 'Forgive me, sir. This is RSM Spiers.'

'Were you here at the CP last night, Spiers?' asked Rawstorne.

'No, sir,' said Spiers. 'I was with Major Tanner and a number of men from C Company.'

'I'm sorry it wasn't more successful. I know the attack was mounted in haste, and the Huns are dogged bastards in defence. It was a very tough nut to crack. Break through here, though, and the island will be ours. And break through we will.'

Spiers glanced briefly at Tanner, then said, 'I'm sorry, sir, but our attack *was* successful. We did break through the enemy lines, forced him to retreat, and cut back behind the Green Howards' sector. We should have won the day. The enemy line was there for the taking, but the reinforcements we repeatedly asked for were not sent.'

Rawstorne's brow furrowed further. 'What's this? Tanner, is this true?'

Tanner nodded. 'We broke across the railway line, destroyed their MG and mortar positions and were on the lower slopes, working our way to the east to help the Green Howards. I repeatedly called for reinforcements, and even spoke to the OC myself, but my requests were refused.'

'It was a disgrace, sir,' said Spiers.

Tanner glanced at Spiers. He'd always liked

him and had always rated him highly as a soldier. And here he was, confronting the brigadier. Spiers was telling him what he, as 2 i/c, should have been saying. *What are you so worried about, you bloody coward?* he asked himself. He thought about Verity, lying out there, wounded, then carried off by the enemy, and of Tredwell, a young lad with his leg near severed at the thigh. All because of Creer.

'Tanner?' said Rawstorne.

'Spiers is right, sir. It was a disgrace,' said Tanner. 'A criminal disgrace.' He could feel the blood rushing to this cheeks. 'Jerry's defences are thin. A few hastily sown mines, a bit of wire, then the MG nests and a few mortars. No strength in depth at all. We bloody had them beaten. Lack of ammo and support did for us, but if we'd properly got behind the Green Howards' front, Jerry would have been unable to stop us. And we should have done. A Company were never committed, as I requested. D and B Companies were never redirected to support us. Was any request made to Brigade? Was it hell. The entire KOYLI were in reserve. The whole bloody battalion!'

'All right, Tanner, take it easy.'

'Take it easy, sir? All those lives lost – and for what?'

'Tanner, calm down,' said Rawstorne. 'Now.'

Tanner clenched his fists. 'I'm sorry, sir. It's just so – it's just so wrong.' He eyed the brigadier. 'Colonel Creer had no right to refuse our requests.'

'Just what are you saying here, Tanner?' Rawstorne took a step towards him.

Tanner looked across at Spiers, then at Standish and Rawstorne. 'I'm saying, sir, that Colonel Creer is a murderer and does not deserve to wear the cap badge of the Yorkshire Rangers.' Tanner paused, then said again, 'He's a murderer.'

Rawstorne looked dumbstruck and stared at him.

'That's quite an allegation, Tanner,' said Standish.

'It most certainly is,' said Rawstorne. He paced the ground for a moment. The sun was beating down once more and the air was heavy and cloying with the stench of smoke and cordite. And death.

'All right, Tanner,' the brigadier resumed. 'You've had a hard night. A bloody difficult and frustrating night. Feelings are running high. So this is what I want you to do. I want you to consider what you've just said. As it stands, we'll be attacking again tonight, but when this fight's over and we're back out of the line, and assuming we're all still in one piece, I want you to make a decision. Either you take back what you just said and we'll make no more mention of it ever again, or you'd better have a very good reason for standing by your accusation. And I mean a very good reason. Hard evidence. Is that clear?'

Tanner nodded and felt his spirits soar. *This time I'm going to nail that bastard.*

20

In Motta Sant'Anastasia, Francesca Falcone was queuing at the bakery. School had finished, and she had Cara with her, holding onto her skirt. Guns still boomed from time to time, but the battle seemed to have calmed. She could not understand it: Nico had told her that the Allies had overwhelming numbers of aircraft, guns and men, and the way they had swept up the coast from the south had certainly seemed to support that. What was more, there was no doubt that most of the planes in the sky were Allied, not Italian or German. So what was holding them up? She had asked Kranz, who had smiled and said, 'They're a bunch of cowards and we are better soldiers than them.' She had felt that could hardly be true. If only she could have talked to Nico about it. He would have been able to explain.

Some of the townspeople had left, taking bundles of clothes up to the higher slopes of Etna, but Francesca had never considered taking such action. It was true that bombs had fallen on the town, but not many, and she had felt it was better to stay where they were, with the cellar and the sheds, and hope nothing would land directly on them. In any case, where would they go? Allied soldiers were swarming all over the plain, shells were hitting the towns along the lower slopes of the mountain and Catania was even more dangerous. And what would they eat? Where would they sleep? At least by staying in the town they could eat.

Not that there was much food. The Germans took most of the eggs, and the vegetables and fruit she had been growing. They were most scrupulous about paying her, but what did she need money for? One could only buy what was on offer in the shops and that was not very much. The official ration was just 150 grams of bread per day and sixty grams of pasta, but they had not had anything like that amount for weeks. The bombing had stopped all that; there was no fuel, no means of moving the flour around, except by cart, and the Germans and the Allies had taken most of the mules for their own use.

Francesca had lost weight. When she washed, she could see her breastbone and ribs; her breasts, once so ample, were smaller. She worried for Cara, but then every mother was worrying for her children; she was not alone.

She had just received her bread ration – less than seventy grams – and was walking towards her home, when Camprese drew alongside her and took her arm.

'What do you think you're doing, Salvatore?'

'I've been hearing things,' he said, 'about you and your German admirer.'

'You think I like having Germans in my house?'

'I don't know. Maybe you do.'

'Don't be ridiculous.' She shook her arm free.

'I've heard he's been buying you flowers, that he gives you extra rations. Apparently you've been having dinner together.'

'What rubbish! He disgusts me. But what can I do? He and his men are in my house.'

'Then come to my house instead. Live with an Italian, as an Italian woman should. Prove to me you have no feelings for this German officer.'

She stopped and slapped his face hard. 'Don't you ever talk to me like that again. I despise him! But it is my house. *My house,* do you hear?'

Camprese held his hand to his burning face. 'So, you humiliate me, the mayor of this town. You would strike me in public.'

'You deserved it, Salvatore! I don't need to prove anything to you.'

Cara began to cry. 'Now look!' said Francesca. 'Go away, Salvatore, leave me alone.'

'Be careful, Francesca,' said Camprese. 'Your German friends will be gone soon. You know what people can be like. If they thought you'd been sleeping with a German officer...'

Francesca felt tears pricking her eyes. 'Don't you dare! Isn't it enough that I have lost my father, my brother, that I have to try and survive in this – this Godforsaken place? Just leave me alone, Salvatore. Leave us alone.'

Palermo, Thursday, 22 July. It was evening as Wiseman's small column entered the city alongside another from the 3rd Division. Beside him in the Jeep, Don Calogero Vizzini sat grinning from ear to ear. Behind, in the back, were Bartolomeo and Domiano Lumia, both clutching Berettas.

A long, narrow street, lined with people cheering, *'Abasso Mussolini! Viva l'America!'* Down with Mussolini, long live America. Women were throwing flowers, handing them lemons and even water-melons. The column inched forward through the surge of people. In every town they had been greeted enthusiastically, but this was something different. This was like liberation.

Wiseman was shocked by the damage to the centre of the town. There were gaping holes where buildings had collapsed and piles of rubble strewn through the streets, yet crowds cheered them all the way. More narrow streets, of high terracotta buildings, until finally they emerged into a large piazza, at one end of which stood an imposing palace, glowing like burnished gold in the late evening sun.

'*Il palazzo dei re di Sicilia,*' said Don Calogero. '*Ora siamo i re.*' Now we are the kings.

Wiseman glanced at him and smiled. *Yes, you really are.* Don Calogero had delivered all that he had promised. The morning after their arrival in Villalba, the Italian troops on Monte Cammarata had melted away, just as he had promised they would. In every town, they had been welcomed with open arms, Don Calogero especially. Only along the coast, between the town of Cerda and the capital, had he been more cautiously received. Here, Don Calogero and his entourage, accompanied by Wiseman, had entered more protracted talks with old contacts, with wavering Fascist officials, with the heads of the local *carabinieri*.

'Many of the old chiefs are still in prison,' Lumia had explained. 'The governors and mayors here have become used to the Fascist regime. Don Calo needs a little more diplomacy.'

Wiseman had watched and listened to the discussions. Don Calogero never said much: his way had been to let Lumia and Bartolomeo do the talking, then interject at the end. A few choice words, a stare of those dark eyes, and a man who had been Fascist when he had woken that morning had become a pro-Mafia democrat once more. Charm, authority, the promise of reward and an ill-disguised threat: these were Don Calogero's tools. It had been quite something to witness.

Now the undisputed leader of Sicily had arrived at the Norman palace, the seat of the kings of Sicily. So, too, had General Keyes and General Truscott, and so too, soon, would Patton. Wiseman smiled to himself. Patton would enjoy playing king here every bit as much as Don Calogero Vizzini did.

The following morning. Overnight, two Italian generals had been captured, as had some ten thousand Italian troops. The entire city was now in American hands. Wiseman had left Don Calogero and his entourage at the palace while he accompanied Patton on a tour of the city and the harbour. The damage was even worse than he had appreciated the previous evening. Most of the harbour front lay in ruins. The stench of sewage was appalling. The population, still apparently happy to see the conquering general, were thin and threadbare, half starved.

When they met a group of US engineers, they were told that at least forty-one ships had been sunk in the harbour.

'Right now, General,' said the colonel of

engineers, as they stood amid the rubble and gazed out to sea, 'the value of this port is nil.'

'Then sort it out, Colonel,' Patton told him. 'We need it. In a week's time I want it functioning at seventy-five per cent capacity. You get whatever machinery and engineers up here you need, but this place must be open within a few days.'

As they left in their cavalcade, they saw a number of prisoners standing at the edge of a piazza waiting to be moved. They all cheered and waved as they saw them pass.

'Look at 'em,' said Patton. 'They're like the civilians – they think we're liberators.'

'Don Calo says most Sicilians are not just anti-Fascist, General,' said Wiseman, 'but anti-Italian too.'

'Your General Mafia has done well, Wiseman. I'll admit I was sceptical, but both he and you have proved me wrong. You're getting him to help with the civil-affairs people?'

'Yes, sir.'

'Good, because looking at the flea-bitten skin-and-bone folk of Palermo we're going to need every bit of help we can get. They might be cheering us now but they won't be if they aren't fed, and we don't have time to get involved with that. We've got Nazis to kill first.'

'We'll be meeting with the civil-affairs officers as soon as they get here, General. And I've already asked Don Calo to draw up a list of potential new mayors in most of the island's towns, including parts of the east still in Axis hands. That way, they can be installed just as soon as they come under our control.'

'Good idea. Is Algiers OK with this?'

'Yes, sir. All approved. I received a signal from Lord Rennell earlier this morning. He's already established AMGOT at Syracuse.'

'So Sicily will be run by the Allied Military Government and the Mafia.' Patton looked out from the command car as they passed the remains of a bombed-out church. 'As far as I'm concerned, they're welcome to it.'

15th Brigade Headquarters, the Plain of Catania, Friday 23 July, around 4 p.m. Tanner waited outside the farmhouse, as instructed, smoking and chewing his fingers. For two days, ever since the attack had been called off and they'd been moved back a mile and a half to the northern banks of the Simeto, he had been waiting for this summons, the brigadier's words ringing in his ears. He was only surprised it had taken so long, although the extra time had hardly helped. Hard evidence against Creer had been difficult to come by. Major Macdonald was gone, sweltering in some field hospital, as was Spiers, who had been struck down by malaria. It was ridiculous, Tanner thought, how they could be losing almost as many men to malaria as they had to the enemy. Sicily was a dry, mountainous country, yet they had managed to get bogged down in a stalemate in the one mosquito-infested corner of the entire island.

So two of his key witnesses had gone. He'd got Chalkie White to make a statement, but the written signals that he knew had been made that night by the wireless operators at the CP had vanished. And while they 'vaguely' remembered something of what had been said, none of them would testify to precisely what had been written down. They had received many signals that night; they just wrote them down and forgot about them; it wasn't their job to question the decisions that were made. *Yes, yes, yes, all right, I get the picture.* Even Masters, the intelligence officer, had refused to get involved. 'This is between you and the colonel, Jack,' he'd told him. 'I never saw those signals. The colonel took them. There was discussion about whether to reinforce, but I couldn't say what motivated the decision process.'

So that was it. He had a pencil-scrawled note from Chalkie White and his own testimony. And that was all. It hardly amounted to the 'hard evidence' Rawstorne had demanded. Which left him in a quandary. Press his allegations, and he would be in potentially very hot water; back down, and he and the battalion would remain stuck with Croaker Creer.

He inhaled deeply, then breathed out, watching the smoke swirl above him. *Bollocks to this.* He flicked away the stub. He would stand by what he had said. His father had told him always to stick up for what he believed, and he always had done. He was not going to back down now. If they sacked him for it, so be it; at least he wouldn't have to serve under that bastard a day longer.

'Major Tanner?'

Tanner turned to see a young staff officer standing in the doorway.

'Will you come this way?'

Tanner followed, walking through the farmhouse to a tented area at the rear. Camouflage netting covered them, the sun casting mottled shadows across the ground.

Brigadier Rawstorne was in his bell tent. There was no bed, just a trestle table, two canvas campaign chairs, a field telephone and an up-turned wooden ammunition box, with a couple of bottles and several chipped glasses.

'Major Tanner,' said Rawstorne, 'there you are.' He stood up. 'Drink?'

'Thank you, sir.'

'Scotch all right?'

'Perfectly.'

'Take a seat, Tanner,' said Rawstorne, passing him the glass. Tanner thanked him again and sat down. It was hot in the tent, and his forehead was beading with sweat.

'So,' said Rawstorne, taking a sip, 'what have you decided? You stand by what you said the other day?'

Tanner took a deep breath. 'Yes, sir, I do. I'm not certain how much hard evidence I have for you because Colonel Creer has destroyed all the written messages that were logged that night, Major Macdonald has been evacuated and RSM Spiers has malaria, but I know what happened and I'm not prepared to–'

'All right, Tanner, that's enough.'

'But, sir, I–'

'Tanner, it's enough because some interesting information has come to light.'

'It has?' Tanner's mind raced.

'It has. Furthermore, it's what I would consider hard evidence too.' He eyed Tanner, then leaned forward and picked up a piece of paper. 'If I'm honest, Tanner, I'd decided to wait for you to come and see me. I felt that if you didn't you would have decided to back down. But this morning this letter arrived. You'll be pleased to know it's from Major John Peploe.'

'Peploe? Thank God. He's alive.'

'Very much so. He's recovering on Malta and making good progress.'

Tanner breathed out heavily. 'That's tremendous news.'

'Indeed. But to the point, Tanner, to the point. Peploe has done what you have conspicuously not done, and that is write a very detailed account of the attack at Sortino. I know Peploe to be utterly trustworthy. And I have to say I'm appalled by what he says. Here,' he said passing the letter, 'I'd like you to read it.'

Tanner did so. Peploe's report had left nothing out: the Orders Group beforehand, the agreement of the plan, the late order arriving from Creer, the bombardment. Having finished reading, Tanner passed it back.

'Do you have anything to add?' Rawstorne asked.

'Only that I spoke at length to Major Macdonald, who had ordered the FOO not to fire. He had been with the FOO when he'd spoken to Creer and had run back to tell him to countermand the order as soon as he realized what was going on. Creer overruled him. Macdonald is a major, Creer a half-colonel. The FOO did what Creer ordered him to do and that was continue the bombardment.'

Rawstorne scratched his head. 'And why didn't you tell me this?'

'I tried to, sir.'

Rawstorne finished his drink. 'Another? I think I need one.' He poured two more shots. 'Now tell me about the attack the other night. Detail, Tanner, I want detail. Tell me everything.'

When Tanner had finished, Rawstorne said, 'But why, Tanner, why?'

'It goes back to India, sir.' He explained how, back then, Creer and Sergeant Blackstone had had many of the company in their pockets, but how he had refused to play ball. Corruption had been rife. 'I made matters awkward for them, but they made my life hell. Eventually Creer was posted out of the battalion and I never saw him again until last month. It was immediately clear that he wanted me out of the way. He didn't approve of men being commissioned from the ranks, thought I'd make trouble for him and that I'd show him up. I think he felt much the same about Major Peploe. You know, he's not once gone into action. I don't think he's fired a shot since we landed. There's always an excuse. He's also been whoring in Melilli and got caught out – some of the men stole his clothes. Lots of men go whoring – these things can be overlooked. But the fact remains, he did his level best to have me and Major Peploe killed, wounded or taken prisoner, and in doing so, a lot of other people suffered. The other night, his actions cost the division an important victory.'

Rawstorne stared at him, then said, 'Tanner, there's always a lot of trust involved in the army.

359

A commander can't be everywhere at all times. They can't be watching over each and every one of their men. One has to delegate and allow subordinates to get on with the job. Creer was a slightly unusual case, as he'd arrived from GHQ in Cairo with a decent report. Putting him in command of the battalion was not a decision taken lightly, but it was felt that Peploe, for all his many fine qualities, was still a little young. He has a fine service record, has been decorated several times, yet we felt he needed nurturing a little. I wasn't convinced that adding the burden of command was necessarily a good idea.' He leaned forward. 'Of course I bitterly regret that now. I'm sure Peploe would have handled the pressure with his usual phlegm.' He sighed.

'So what happens now, sir?'

'Creer will be arrested by the MPs and court-martialled. He'll be taken from the island and, I would imagine, sent back to Cairo or Algiers. Once he's gone, you won't see him again. Even if he wriggles out of the trial, his career in the Army is finished.'

'What a bloody mess, sir,' said Tanner.

'Yes, it is, and we can't undo what's happened. But we can improve the situation from now on. Tanner, you will become a permanent major and will take over temporary command of the battalion.'

'Me, sir?' He could hardly believe what he was hearing.

'You're the best man for the job. You're a fine soldier and the men respect you. At the end of the campaign, who knows? I'd like to think Peploe will return.'

'So would I, sir.'

'But for now, Tanner, the battalion is yours. I know you won't let me down.'

Tanner stood up, saluted and left. Outside, walking beneath the camouflage netting, he smiled to himself. No more Creer. That bastard had gone. But there was a knot in his stomach too. Commanding the battalion was an honour he had never imagined would be his. It would not be easy, but he would do all he could to repay the faith Rawstorne had shown in him. First of all, though, he needed a new RSM. A man *he* could trust and depend on, a man who would watch his back for him. Tanner grinned. RSM Sykes. It had a good ring to it.

21

Sunday, 25 July 1943. The shelling had been heavier that morning, the Allied guns targeting German positions with renewed vigour. More aircraft had been overhead too. Despite this, Francesca had gone to mass with Cara. She was not sure she believed in God any more but she had grown up a good Catholic girl, saying her prayers, going to mass and confession, accepting what she was told about God's mercy and the love of Jesus Christ. But could God really let these terrible things happen? Church, though, was a part of life, especially in a small town like

Motta Sant'Anastasia, and people would mutter if she did not go. At her school, church was also an important part of the children's education, and as a teacher, she knew she had to set an example.

Afterwards, as they emerged from the church, Salvatore Camprese drew alongside her. 'Francesca,' he said, 'have you heard?'

'Heard what?' she said.

'Fascism. It's all over, thank God. Mussolini has been given the boot.'

She stopped and stared at him. 'My God. Really? Are you sure?'

'Quite sure. Last night the Grand Council voted to turn command of all our armed forces over to King Victor Emmanuel. In effect, it was a vote of no confidence. He's been given the push, Francesca.'

Francesca put her hands to her face.

'You're the first person I've told,' he said, beaming at her. 'Mark my words, they'll arrest Mussolini and it'll be broadcast later today.'

'But what about you? You're a Fascist mayor.'

Camprese laughed. 'No! I may have a *tessera* but I've never been a Fascist. Well, maybe a Fascist in name, but nothing more. No, Francesca, my loyalties lie elsewhere. Believe me, I'm as happy as anyone that Fascism has gone. Mussolini – he's a piece of turd.' He laughed again.

Francesca looked at him. *So it's true. He is Mafia.*

'And I'm sorry, Francesca, for what I said the other day.' He took her hand. 'Forgive me.'

Suddenly a huge explosion erupted: a vast,

deep boom that made the town shake as though an earthquake had struck. Francesca stumbled, Cara cried out, and Camprese's eyes widened in horror. Francesca could barely think. What had happened? Where? Then a giant ball of flame was rolling and swirling high into the sky from the direction of the station, at the new town below.

'Holy Mother of Jesus!' said Camprese. 'Quick, run!'

People were screaming, diving onto the ground and running in panic, but Camprese led Francesca and Cara across the small square to her house. Inside, the Germans were shouting and Kranz barking orders. He paused when he saw Francesca. 'Are you all right, Signora?'

Francesca nodded.

'They hit an ammunition train.' He looked pale, shocked. 'A whole train of shells – all gone.'

'You'll be gone soon, too, in that case,' said Camprese. 'You know Mussolini's been kicked out? It's all over for Fascism.'

Kranz shook his head. 'You Italians,' he muttered. 'You've been nothing but trouble from the start. God knows why Hitler ever decided to help you out in Greece. He should have left you to your folly.' He took a step towards Camprese. 'You should watch yourself, Signor Mayor. Maybe we will be gone soon enough, but we're still here now, and we Germans do not like being taunted.'

Camprese smiled. 'No, Leutnant. This is my town. You're the one who needs to be careful.'

Tuesday, 3 August 1943. It had been eleven days since Tanner had taken command of the battalion. Eleven hard, attritional days in which the Yorks Rangers had remained stuck in the plain, moving positions first south of the Simeto river, then back north again. Throughout, however, there had been little chance to relax as German gunners continued to shell British positions. The Primosole Bridge, so hard-fought for, had been hit repeatedly. Sappers had patched it, strengthened it and added defences, but on at least three days it had been impassable. Three days when supplies had not been able to get through to the eastern section of the bridgehead.

And all the while the sun had beaten down, the temperature gradually rising as July gave way to August. The plain stank: of death, excrement, smoke and cordite. The men were filthy: filthy shirts and denims, filthy hair, filthy hands, filthy everything. They were covered with mosquito bites, and some had even been stung by scorpions, little black ones that were not dangerous but painful all the same. The lack of proper hygiene had led to sores and dysentery, which, along with daily cases of malaria, had depleted the battalion further. The Yorks Rangers, after just over three weeks on Sicily, were now at a little more than half strength.

This had meant some reorganization. It was not unusual: the battalion had done this from time to time throughout the past few years, when the fighting had been particularly tough. When there was a pause, new men arrived, the battalion miraculously went back to full strength, and they started all over again. With this in mind, Tanner had reduced the battalion to three companies of three platoons consisting of two, rather than three, sections each. Company Headquarters had been reduced to eight men from fourteen. He had merged D Company with B, Ferguson – now recovered from his wound – taking over command. Dawnay had been put in charge of C Company, while Ivo Macdonald, who had recovered from concussion and his slight head wound, had joined Tanner as his second-in-command. Tanner had made Sykes acting RSM, and had also brought Browner and Phyllis to Battalion HQ; Fauvel had accepted this with equanimity. 'I'll be glad to see the back of them.' He had grinned. 'I could do without Browner's endless grumbling and Phyllis – well, he's always been more trouble than he's worth.'

Morale had been low and, with Macdonald and Sykes, Tanner had thought hard about how it might be improved. The situation, he knew, was not unlike that his father had gone through in the last war, with the men spending much of their time stuck in slit trenches and being regularly shelled. The difference was the heat and disease. Static warfare like this wore the men down; they were too inactive so had more time to feel bothered by the conditions.

As soon as they were back north of the Simeto, Tanner insisted on regular patrol work, with fighting patrols at night and static patrols by day. He knew they would have to cross that ground again, and that the stalemate allowed the Germans to build up their defences, with mines and wire. By watching and sniping enemy engineers, they would make the Germans' lives more difficult, and the men would feel they were doing something, that they were improving their chances of making an easy breakthrough when their attack was finally launched. Tanner had joined several of these patrols himself, taking with him his SMLE and Aldis scope. By night, patrols would creep to the edge of the increasingly flattened cornfield, then fire flares, bathing any sapper parties in light, while Tanner and other sharpshooters would take pot-shots. He had also ordered Bren crews forward, but with the tracer rounds taken out of the magazines. They would open fire sometimes under the light of flares, at others on fixed points worked out earlier. Mortars would be sent over too.

Although rations had been occasionally inter-mittent in reaching them, Tanner had also made a point of inviting in turn each company's officers and sergeants for supper. It was, he knew, most irregular for NCOs and officers to dine together, but there was no formality involved: there was no mess here in the plain. As Tanner explained, they were being shelled together and spending their days and nights in the open together, so it did not matter if they ate together too. And so, under the draped camouflage nets of the CP, they con-sumed basic rations heated over a Primus while Tanner and Macdonald explained the latest situ-ation, told them of the progress of XXX Corps on their left and of the Americans to the north-west, and assured them the net was closing around the Axis defenders. There might have been stalemate in the plain but, Tanner promised them, it wouldn't be for much longer.

And nor was it, for now, on this stifling evening

of 3 August, the brigade were to attack once more. The wait was over.

The Orders Group had planned the assault earlier that day, and Tanner certainly felt confident that, unlike the hastily prepared attack they had made on 20 July, this time the preparation was good. It was around seven o'clock and he had called together all the officers and senior NCOs to brief them. Last time, he told them, the artillery had arrived in position only that day; they had had no time to find their targets properly. Now, though, the guns were dug in, had been working excellently with the RAF, and had clear, identified targets onto which they would be firing concentrations. It was true the battalion was at nearly half strength, but they now knew the ground, which made all the difference in night attacks. 'You've all been out onto it at night,' he told them. 'You know where the railway line is, where the dikes are, how the ground gradually rises through orange groves beyond. There will be no surprises.'

It was still stiflingly hot. Tanner could feel the sweat running down his back. The men sitting in front of him were filthy, their shirts crusted with lines of salt where the sweat had dried. The desert had been tough, but at least it had been dry and essentially clean. Here there was water and mud; hygiene had been harder to maintain. They hadn't washed properly since Melilli.

'Look, I know we're all sick to bloody death of this stinking plain,' he told them, 'but we'll be out of here tonight. The Yanks are pushing hard along the north of the island, XXX Corps are gaining ground on our left flank, and however grim it's been for us, it's been a hell of a lot worse for Jerry, because we've got loads more guns than him and plenty more aircraft. Just as Jerry gunners like firing at us, our boys have been having a good time firing at them.'

The plan, he told them, was to attack on a two-battalion front alongside the Yorks and Lancs, with 17th Brigade on their right. 13th Brigade had been temporarily attached to the 51st Highland Division, but their own 15th Brigade still had four battalions. 'The boys in Seventeenth Brigade are going to strike north towards Misterbianco, while our objective is Motta Sant'Anastasia and the lava hills around it. Then once we're there, the Green Howards and KOYLI will pass through and push on towards Belpasso.' He pointed to the various towns on the map that Sykes was holding up.

'So what happens once we reach Motta Sant'Anastasia, sir?' asked Fauvel.

'Hopefully, we get a wash and scrub. One thing's for sure – none of you'll get lucky with any *signorinas* smelling like you do.'

The men laughed.

'Speak for yerself, sir,' said Sykes. More laughter.

Tanner then outlined the plan of attack. There would be no barrage, although the artillery would continue with counter-battery fire. There would be mortar support and a number of sappers, equipped with mine-detectors and Bangalore torpedoes for mine- and wire-clearing. Each company would have its own team of sappers and would follow the gaps the sappers made.

'The most important thing,' Tanner told them, 'is to make sure we keep in line. So, when we reach the railway, we will pause there until all three companies and HQ Company are in line. We need to mutually support each other.' They would also be in regular R/T communication. 'It's going to be night,' said Tanner, 'so it'll be dark. Don't be afraid of getting on the net. We'll achieve more if we talk to each other.'

He paused, looked around. 'We might be down on numbers, but I have a good feeling about this attack. We've got lots of support, lots of ammo, we know the ground.'

'Creer's been given the chop!' called out Lieutenant Shopland.

Tanner could not hide a slight smirk. 'That's enough, thank you, Jimmy, but I will say this. I'm coming with you. I'll be fighting those Jerries alongside you. By sticking together, by fighting together, by helping one another, we'll break out of this bloody plain and Sicily will be ours for the taking.' He looked at his watch. 'We start at twenty-two hundred. Good luck.'

From her bedroom, Francesca could hear the shelling, could feel the house tremble, and could even hear machine-guns chattering away somewhere on the plain, but since there were no aircraft overhead and the siren was silent, she had not woken Cara or made any attempt to take shelter herself. Instead, and with the Germans still occupying her house, she had gone to bed at around eleven o'clock.

For a while she had lain there, staring at the ceiling, the night sky flickering intermittently as though an electrical storm was about to break. She had been terrified the first time the bombers had come but, over the past fortnight, had become strangely used to living in a war zone. It was, she thought, incredible how quickly the abnormal became normal, and how it was possible to become inured to the sound of guns booming and shells falling, even when they were landing quite close. She suddenly remembered her father mentioning much the same about his time in the last war, when he had been a doctor at the front up in the Alps. He had barely ever talked about it but he had once said he had learned to sleep through anything, even artillery fire. She could understand that now. It was evidently the same for Cara, for when she had looked in on her before going to her own room, her daughter had been sound asleep.

She must have drifted to sleep soon after because she was dreaming. Nico was there, talking to her. She was worried and scared, and he reassured her, his hand touching her cheek. But then it wasn't Nico, it was someone else, she wasn't sure who. She turned away, trying to escape, and then she wasn't dreaming but awake and conscious of someone leaning over her very close. Her heart lurched, she wanted to scream – *Who was it?* – and then another shell exploded and, in its flash, she saw it was Kranz, his face inches from hers, his hand stroking her cheek. Eyes wide, she stared at him, her brain addled with panic. His closeness was powerfully oppressive and overbearing, his touch a violation that made her cringe with fury and revulsion. She wanted to scream, but what would that achieve? She was powerless, lying there, restrained by her sheet, his greater strength obvious. And, in any case, a scream would wake Cara. If Kranz was about to rape her, she did not want Cara to witness it. *My knife*. It was under her pillow, but how to reach it? Her arms were by her sides, and he was sitting on the edge of the bed, pinning down her right side, and with an arm resting to her left, restricting her there too.

'What are you doing?' she said, hoping her voice did not betray her fear.

'I had to say goodbye.'

'You're leaving?' A glimmer of hope.

'Tonight. Now. We are pulling back.'

He stroked her face again, then ran a finger down her neck. She felt herself stiffen. *Get away from me! Get away!*

'You are very beautiful. I – I hope one day we might meet again, that...' He let the sentence trail, and pulled the sheet down, over her chest. Her heart was racing, her chest rising and falling rapidly as her breathing shortened. *Panic*. She had to stay calm. Then his hands were running down her nightdress, over her breasts.

'So beautiful,' he muttered, then pulled the sheet down further. She lay there, frozen, his hands now on her breasts and her stomach. Francesca closed her eyes, bit her lip and, tears pricking her eyes, moved her arm. She felt under the pillow and found the knife. Her heart hammered.

'Stop it,' she said. 'Please stop.'

'But this is our one chance.'

'No. Leave me. Leave me alone.' She gripped the knife in her hand.

But Kranz was not leaving her alone. Rather, he was climbing onto her bed, his hands now pinning her arms, his legs astride her.

'I'm sorry, Francesca, I'm sorry, but you are so beautiful... I may be dead tomorrow. Please...'

His grip was strong, as he leaned forward and kissed her neck and then her chest.

No, thought Francesca, tears running down her cheeks, *I can't let this happen.* She could not move her hand – it was pinned to the bed, still holding the knife under the pillow, but useless. *Utterly useless.*

'Please stop,' she said again, 'for Cara's sake. Please.'

'Stop saying that!' he said. 'You want it too... We must! This is our only chance, don't you see?'

He was kissing her chest and now her breasts, his breathing quickening, his hands tighter on her arms. *Please, God,* she thought, *help me. Help me, please.* Suddenly he let go with his right hand and began fumbling at his belt, and in that moment Francesca rammed her knee into his groin. Kranz cried out and she rammed again and now her hand holding the knife was free, and she swung it into his upper arm. The force of the blow knocked him off the bed.

Leaping clear, she saw him writhe on the floor, then struggle to his feet, pushing himself upright using the wall as a support.

'I'm sorry,' he said. 'I'm so sorry... Please

forgive me.'

She stood before him, half crouching, holding the knife, as he leaned against the wall, doubled up, gasping and clutching his arm.

'Get out!' she said. 'Get out now!'

Slowly, he staggered to the door, opened it and left.

Francesca stayed there, frozen, for several moments, her mind racing. Then she lit a lamp, went to the door and listened. Movement down below, voices, Kranz yelling orders: *'Raus, raus, schnell!'*

Slowly, she opened the door and walked out onto the landing. *Cara.* Quietly opening her daughter's door, she looked in. *Thank God.* She was there, her face peeping out over the sheet, which rose and fell rhythmically. Another clatter from below. Cara stirred, and Francesca gently closed the door again and looked down. Kranz was there, ushering the last of his men out through the front door. Then he looked up, clutched his arm and stared at her with anguish and sadness.

'Arrivederci, Signora,' he said, then was gone.

Away to the east, more shells exploded. Outside, a truck's engine opened up, the throttle growled, and the vehicle rumbled off. She waited a moment, listening, then hurried downstairs, ran out into the night and drew a bucket from the well. Filling a ewer, she stripped and, standing in the yard, as shells continued to crash and explode around the lower slopes of Etna, the air heavy with the smell of battle, Francesca scrubbed herself, weeping.

Wednesday, 4 August, around 3 p.m. Tanner was crouched beside Sykes, Captain Fauvel and a sapper lieutenant called Cartwright at the edge of a track that led up towards the town of Motta Sant'Anastasia, perched on a promontory about two miles ahead. In between lay gently rising and undulating ground, lined with small fields filled with corn or citrus groves.

They were looking at a farmhouse or, rather, what remained of it, for it had been hit several times. Half the roof had gone, and so had one side of the second floor. To their right, several hundred yards away, a German machine-gun spat a three-second burst, then another. A Bren answered.

'B Company sound a bit stuck too,' said Sykes.

Tanner sighed. 'I want a sodding bath,' he said. 'What do we reckon we're facing here?'

'A platoon, I reckon,' said Sykes. 'Two, maybe three MGs.'

'And a whole load of booby traps,' said Cartwright. He was a young man with a red face and a thin, unconvincing moustache. 'The road's bound to be mined, too, and probably the land either side.'

'I tell you, they're men after my own heart,' said Sykes.

'Well, I haven't heard any mortars yet,' said Tanner.

'True,' said Fauvel.

'And there can't be that many mines. This place obviously had artillery here until last night. All we're facing is a small defensive outpost.'

He looked at his map, then took out the aerial photograph of the land around Motta Sant'Anastasia. *Yes, there it is.* He was looking at the artillery symbol that had been drawn on the photograph. There was another near the road where B Company were also advancing. Always easier, he thought, bringing up ammunition, supplies and, of course, the guns near a road or track.

Perhaps they could simply outflank the positions. Away to their left, the ground dropped a little towards what looked like a dry watercourse.

'What do you think?' he said. 'We could keep Jerry busy here, and send a platoon round and up that riverbed. At least then we'd be opposite the open side of that farmhouse.'

Fauvel nodded. 'All right. We set up a Bren here, make sure the chaps keep taking rifle shots, then creep around, keeping out of the line of sight of that Spandau.'

'Something like that,' said Tanner. 'One more Jerry strongpoint, then hopefully into town and have a scrub.'

Behind them, A Company were waiting among the groves. Fauvel detailed a two-section platoon under Lieutenant Hewitson, informed B Company on their left and C Company waiting in reserve five hundred yards behind, then said, 'All right, sir, we're ready.'

'Good,' said Tanner. 'Stan, you and I will go with Hewitson and Chalkie White. We'll send you a signal when we're in place, Gav, then you'll open up with the Bren.'

Heading back down the slope, they reached a grass track, then cut along it until they found the riverbed. It appeared clear, so making sure they kept low, they hurried along the grassy verge beside the tumbled stones. A small reservoir, then a kink in the river, and they were scrambling up a slope, with the top of the enemy-held farmhouse just visible to their right. Some bushes. Another grove beyond; between them, the road and the farmhouse. *Good,* thought Tanner, *plenty of cover.*

Suddenly a man cried out and fell forward.

'Jesus, what was that?' cried Hewitson.

'Down!' hissed Tanner, as another bullet skimmed overhead. 'Quickly!' he said. 'Drop back down to the riverbed.'

The wounded man was gurgling, as Sykes and one of the others grabbed him and dragged him with them.

'Snowy!' said another man. 'Jesus Christ!'

'All right, calm down,' said Sykes.

The young man had been hit in the neck. His eyes were wide and wild, his legs kicking. Blood poured from his mouth and from the wound.

'It's not hit the jugular,' said Sykes, tearing open a field-dressing pack. 'Come on, you lot, bloody give me a hand here!'

'Yes, stop gawping at him and help,' added Tanner. 'What's his name?' he asked Hewitson.

'Private Jackson, sir. He's only eighteen.'

'Maybe he'll be lucky. Get four of the lads to take him back and iggery, because otherwise there's going to be more of us hit like him.' Tanner turned to White. 'Chalkie, send a message to Captain Fauvel. Tell him we've got a sniper to deal with. Chances are, we've already been reported to the farmhouse over there. Tell him to stand by for further instructions.'

'Yes, sir,' said White, pulling the radio off his back.

Tanner scurried over to Sykes, peering back up the slope behind them. 'Where d'you think he fired from?'

'That building over there,' said Sykes, pointing to the north-west. 'But one way to find out for sure.' Taking off his helmet, he drew his old seventeen-inch sword bayonet, balanced the tin hat-on the tip and slowly raised his arm. A moment later there was a loud ping and Sykes carefully lowered it again. A neat hole ran through the helmet. 'Yes,' he said. 'That's the one, judging by the line of trajectory.'

'Bollocks,' said Tanner. He pushed his helmet back and scratched his head. 'All right,' he said at length, 'this is what we'll do. I'll crawl up the riverbed with Corporal Hicks and the Bren. When I give the signal, put a couple more helmets in the air. As soon as I hear a shot, Hicks and I will dash for cover and pray we can get a clear shot at both targets.'

Sykes nodded doubtfully.

'Have you got a better plan?'

'Call in some air or artillery? Ask them to take them out?'

'Too long. It's been like this ever since we set off. Stop, start, stop, start. Bloody mines, wait for the sappers, then some sodding Jerry pinning us down. I'm fed up with it. Look, if it doesn't work, we'll call up the artillery, all right?'

'Fair enough,' said Sykes. 'You're the boss.'

A minute later, Tanner was moving up the stony riverbed, Hicks behind him. Forty yards or so further on, he glanced back. There were Sykes, Hewitson and the others. On his right, the bank climbed about ten feet, he reckoned, but there was a slight gap in the bushes that lined the slope.

'What d'you think, Hicks?' he said. 'Reckon you can scramble up there in under five seconds?'

Hicks swallowed, then nodded.

Tanner grinned. 'Good. We'll do it together, on my signal, all right? And one other thing. Take off your helmet.'

'Take it off, sir?'

'Yes – you might be safer without it. Trust me.' He looked back down towards the others and raised his thumb. Sykes waved back, then three helmets were raised slowly.

A crack of a rifle, the report ringing clearly, and Tanner said, 'Now!' Both men jumped up, ran up the bank and dived into the bushes as another bullet hissed by and Tanner felt a searing pain across the top of his shoulder.

'Damn it!' He grimaced, as he scrambled clear.

Beside him, lying in the grass, Hicks was gasping. 'Are you all right, sir?'

'I'll live,' said Tanner, wincing. He put his hand to his shoulder and saw blood. 'Just nicked me,' he said, rolling his shoulder. 'Anyway, there's a job to be done.'

They inched forward until they could see through bushes back towards the farmhouse. Tanner glanced back to check they were out of view of the sniper, then pulled his rifle off his good shoulder. He lay there and peered through the scope. He could see several men on the ground, then two on the open first floor, adjusting position, moving their machine-gun around.

'We need to be quick, Hicks,' he said, 'or our sniper chum is going to tip off the section in the farmhouse.'

At that moment, firing opened from further down the riverbed, and immediately the machine-gunners responded, firing two short bursts in quick succession.

'Won't our lads get hit by the sniper, sir?' asked Hicks.

'Nah,' said Tanner. 'Sykes will have taken them out of sight.'

No sooner had he said this than two Brens were firing from the south, peppering the far wall of the farmhouse.

Tanner smiled to himself and peered through the scope. Yes, there was the platoon commander, ordering something from below.

'Just for the moment, Hicks,' said Tanner, 'I want you to hold fire.'

'Right, sir.'

Tanner aimed, the cross-sight on the commander's head. Someone calling to him, then him leaning forward, *what was that?*, and suddenly he turned, as though looking directly at Tanner. Tanner felt his finger squeeze the trigger, felt the butt press into his shoulder and saw a spray of blood and brains as the man collapsed from view. At the same moment, the machine-gunners stopped and hastily moved their weapon, but as they did so, Tanner had a clear shot. The bolt had already been drawn back and, without moving his cheek, he carefully raised the barrel, picked out the machine-gunner and fired. He saw the man's head jerk backwards and the body slump.

'Let's go!' he said, getting up and running forward, through the citrus grove, slinging the rifle across his shoulder and gripping his Beretta, darting between the trees, Hicks beside him. Up ahead, men in panic, bullets from the south, bullets peppering the farmhouse from their left. Sixty yards, a rifle crack but the bullet wide, fifty yards, and now Tanner said, 'Fire, Hicks, from the hip!' and men were falling, scattering, as Tanner pulled back the bolt. At thirty yards, from the edge of the grove, he raised his weapon and fired. Two men fell and then he was shouting, *'Hände hock! Hände hock!'* Another two-second burst from Hicks and now the hands were going up.

'Cease fire!' yelled Tanner, as loudly as he could, then stepped onto the road, his Beretta still drawn into his shoulder. Hicks followed as they pointed to the men to move out of the house.

'Schnell!' barked Tanner. 'Go on, shift your arses!' As he stepped into the house, he said, 'Hicks, stay in the doorway, and watch them. Don't touch anything. Knowing these monkeys the place'll be booby trapped.' Several men, all filthy, lay dead, one collapsed against a broken chair, another propped against a wall. Tanner moved quickly out of the back of the farmhouse and saw several more men running through the groves beyond. Moving up the stone staircase, he took each step carefully, watching, listening.

Nothing. At the top of the staircase, he paused. There, with the floor open to the world, lay a dead machine-gunner and an MG42. Of his mate, there was no sign. Making sure he kept in shadow, he took out his binoculars and trained them on the house four hundred yards away, beyond the dry riverbed. There it was, clear as day, lit up beautifully by the sun. And there at a window, his rifle leaning on the balcony outside, was a German sniper, and he was not looking at the farmhouse but a little further south, towards, Tanner guessed, where Sykes and the others had been.

'You want to be more careful, son,' muttered Tanner, softly, as he swiftly took his rifle off his shoulder once more, briefly closing his eyes as another shard of pain coursed through him.

It took around fifteen seconds. The scope was already perfectly zeroed to four hundred yards. Raise the rifle, aim, breathe in, squeeze the trigger. Bang.

Tanner watched the German sniper fall, waited, then using the discarded MG42, sprayed the house with bullets until the belt ran out and the barrel overheated.

Another German outpost had been destroyed.

It was after six by the time they made their way up into the little town of Motta Sant'Anastasia. It had seemed almost within touching distance back at the farmhouse, but it took time: prisoners had to be sent back, B Company had to catch up, the road had to be made safe, sappers cautiously leading the way, preventing any gallop forward by the rest of the battalion.

Finally, they reached the dusty road that wound its way up to the edge of the promontory. At first, just a few children had run down the road to meet them, but as they climbed up into the town, more and more people emerged, cheering, as the exhausted troops tramped up the road. Tanner's hand was shaken and old women blew kisses.

At a small triangular piazza in the centre, they halted, some hundred and fifty men from Headquarters, A and B Companies.

'All right, boys,' Tanner called. 'Fall out, but stay here for the moment.' He looked around. Palm trees offered shade from the sun. There were steps and ornate iron benches, a shrine and a war memorial. He turned to White. 'Chalkie, get on to Major Macdonald and tell him we're at Motta. C Company are following, but we're staying put for the night. Get Echelon up here. These men need some scoff and we need them billeted.' He turned to Sykes and Fauvel. 'Right, Stan, we need a new Battalion HQ.'

'You need that wound looked at.'

'Stop fussing. We'll get a nice basha first, then I'll have the wound cleaned up. It's just a gash, nothing serious. Anyway, the MO will be here soon with Ivo and the rest of the battalion. Come on, let's go.'

With Brown, Trahair and White in tow, they climbed up to the top of the town, past still curious Italians. The road narrowed with small alleyways running off each side as it curled its way up to the church and to a small square.

'Will you look at this?' said Sykes. 'Very quaint.'

But Tanner was looking at a house just off the far side of the square – a house perched on the edge of the promontory, made of small, dark bricks, with a terracotta roof and an iron balcony that looked back over the square. It was big, solid, and had steps leading up to the main door.

'There,' said Tanner, striding towards it.

A number of Italians were watching as he walked up the steps and knocked on the door. He paused and looked around. Hurrying towards him, he saw a priest, black gown flowing, and saw him raise his hand to catch his attention, but then the door opened and Tanner turned. A tall, young woman with long, fair hair, pale almond-shaped eyes and full lips was standing before him.

'*Buona sera, Signora,*' he said, hardly able to believe his eyes.

'Good evening,' she said in English.

Tanner swallowed. 'It's you.'

22

Tanner stood on the step and stared. The woman in the photograph he had taken from the dead Italian officer was standing before him. He was certain it was her: thinner perhaps, but the hair, the eyes, the strikingly unusual features were the same. They had captivated him when he had first seen the picture among the officer's papers. What had been his name?

'What do you mean?' she said.

'I, er, nothing. I'm sorry,' he said, embarrassed to have Sykes and the others witness his discomfort.

'Your wound needs cleaning.'

Tanner shrugged. 'Yes, but it's not serious.'

A little girl now appeared, clinging to the woman's legs. Her daughter – had to be, Tanner thought. She said something and the mother replied, a burst of rapid Italian.

'My daughter is rather wary of strange men in uniform turning up on our doorstep,' she said. 'First it was Germans, now you.'

'The Germans were here, in your house?'

'Yes. Artillery. They were watching the plain, telling their guns where to fire.'

'On us.' Tanner smiled ruefully.

'I had no choice. I suppose I don't have any choice now, either.'

'I'm sorry,' said Tanner. 'We need billets, but don't worry. We'll find somewhere else.' He took a step back. 'You speak very good English.'

'I learned as a child.'

'Civil-affairs officers will be here soon, but would you consider helping us? We'll pay.'

She eyed him intently. 'A translator?'

The priest had reached them and began speaking to the woman. Tanner listened to the flurry of words, the rapid exchange.

Eventually the woman turned back to Tanner. 'He says he welcomes you and your men, but where will you go? Do you expect to be housed here? We have very little food and he is worried that your men will eat what stocks remain.'

'Tell him that we have our own rations and we

384

will do what we can to share them. British civil-affairs officers will reach the town soon and will help.'

She did so. The priest smiled and took Tanner's hand in both of his.

'Thank you,' said Tanner. 'Will you think about my offer?'

The woman eyed him again, then said, 'I think you had better come in.'

Francesca had spent half of the morning in tears. Cara had been distressed by this, but Francesca had not been able to help herself. 'I'm sorry, my darling,' she had told her. 'It's just the war. I'll be better soon, I promise.' And, in a way, she had been right: it was just the war because without it she would not have lost her brother, she would probably not have lost her father, she would not be feeling hungry all the time, she would not have been almost raped by a German. The war – it was all the war's fault.

Camprese had appeared at lunchtime, bearing some German rations. There had been a renewed swagger about him and his lips had lingered on her hand when he had kissed it. She had thought about stabbing him too. If it hadn't meant leaving Cara an orphan, she might have done it. At least Kranz had gone, clutching the wound on his arm, out of her life for ever, but Camprese was still here, still strutting about the town as though it were his personal fiefdom. Would he tire of trying to woo her and force himself upon her, as Kranz had done? She had not thought of it before, but now it was a little nugget of fear that had lodged in the back of her mind. What Kranz had done had reminded her of just how alone she really was. How vulnerable.

By the afternoon the tears had stopped. She knew she had to pick herself up and pull herself together. The war could not go on for ever, she told herself. The Germans had gone, the British would be here soon – that was what everyone was saying. Perhaps things would improve. No more bombs, no more shelling. Mussolini had fallen, and Sicily would soon be in Allied hands. Perhaps Camprese would be kicked out by the British; he had been a Fascist, after all, regardless of what he claimed now. Perhaps she would be left alone. Perhaps, she thought, she would get through this after all.

And then a tall, dark, shabby English officer had knocked on her door and had recognized her immediately. 'It's you,' he'd said without thinking. What had that meant? And then it occurred to her that perhaps he knew something about Nico – what else could it mean? Cara did not want more soldiers in the house, and neither did she, but there was something about this officer and his men that seemed unthreatening, despite their weapons and his blood-soaked shirt. They were all filthy, and they smelt, but then the whole town smelt – of refuse, dung, stale urine and sweat. And they were British: they weren't Fascists or Nazis. What was more, she told herself, they would protect her from Camprese. He wouldn't like it, her housing big, battle-scarred soldiers, and that was as good a reason as any to let them stay. In any case, she knew she had no choice. The British, like the Germans, could requisition anything they liked, yet the officer had offered to walk away, to find somewhere else, which suggested he had a good heart, that he would not try to violate her late one night.

So she had let them in.

Within a couple of hours, the rest of the battalion had arrived, with the promise of the civil-affairs team reaching them the following morning. Echelon trucks lined the main road, the via Vittorio Emanuele, which ran the length of the narrow town, while outside in the square there were several Jeeps and a fifteen-hundredweight truck, which had somehow managed to navigate along the narrow, winding road that led to the church. The troops had been billeted, most in municipal buildings at the centre and edge of the town, the companies had their headquarters in houses around the tiny square, while the Sicilians watched this sudden activity with expressions of febrile anticipation. The arrival of a battalion of nearly five hundred men had transformed the town.

At Francesca Falcone's house, Tanner was having a bath. She had lent him and his men a large tin tub, which they had taken outside. Drawing water from the well, and using his own soap, Tanner had stripped to his underpants and scrubbed himself, cleaning off weeks of grime and dust, sweat and blood. He had shaved too, heating a small amount of water in a mess tin. Trahair, meanwhile, was washing Tanner's and his own shirt and trousers in petrol, an old desert trick. The fuel got rid of the worst of the grime and, once dried, made them smell a little better.

As he sat there, on an upturned wooden box left by the Germans, his body drying alongside his clothes in the last of the evening sun, he heard Francesca call from the balcony outside the kitchen.

He smiled. 'Sorry, miss,' he said, 'not very decent I know.'

'Do you want me to have a look at your wound?'

'That's kind, but the MO will be back shortly. He's attending to some of the other men, then he'll be here.'

'My father was a doctor,' she said. 'I'm a good nurse.'

'In that case, thank you.'

'Come up when you've finished shaving.'

Sykes, who was cleaning his weapons by the sheds, whistled. The others laughed.

'Goodness, Jack,' said Macdonald, who was now having a bath, 'you're a fast mover, aren't you?'

''E's a bit of a ladies' man, is Major Tanner,' chuckled Sykes. 'Don't know why but they always fall for 'im.'

Tanner ignored them. It never paid to rise to Sykes's ribbing.

'Here, sir,' said Brown, 'do you think she's got a sister?'

'What are you suggesting, Browner?' said Sykes. 'That if she did you'd somehow have a chance?'

'I'm good-looking,' said Brown. 'I'm young. I've got prospects.'

'Really?' said Sykes. 'I think you're confusing yerself with someone else.'

'I'm more interested in getting some decent scoff,' said Phyllis.

'Siff, do you think about your stomach all the time?' said Brown.

'No,' muttered Phyllis. 'I'm just sick of bloody rations, that's all.'

''E wants some Eyetie ice-cream.' Sykes grinned. 'Some *bellissimo gelato*, that's what you want, ain't it, Siff?'

'I'd bloody love some,' admitted Phyllis.

'Then you're in luck, my son,' said Sykes, ''cos this town's got an amazing ice-cream shop. Some bloke was telling me when we first got here.'

'Really?' said Phyllis, his face brightening.

'Oh, yes. You see, the Eyeties might not have much bread or pasta or anything, but they do still have ice-cream. What d'you think they've been living off all this time? Ice-cream is a treat to us, but over here it's like, well, it's like eating bread an' dripping.'

'Well, I want to find the place,' said Phyllis.

'Oh, Siff, you're so bloody gullible,' said Browner.

Phyllis's face fell. Everyone laughed.

Tanner, having put on his still-damp denims, went into the house carrying his shirt.

'Hello?' he called.

'Here, Major,' said Francesca, emerging from the kitchen.

'This is good of you,' he said. 'It does hurt, I'll admit.'

'What happened?'

'It was only this afternoon, a couple of miles away. We were trying to clear a German outpost

389

and there was a sniper taking pot-shots. He nicked me as I dived for cover.'

'You were lucky.'

'Yes.'

'Did you get him?'

Tanner nodded.

She had put a Gladstone bag on the table, which stood open alongside a small dish of warm water. She took out some cotton wool, moistened it and began to dab at the wound. Tanner flinched. 'It's not the first scar, I see.'

'This war's been going on a long time.'

'Too long.'

'I agree.'

They were silent a moment, then Francesca said, 'Earlier, when I opened the door, you said, "It's you," as though you recognized me. What did you mean?'

Tanner had been thinking about this, about what he should say, and whether he should mention the Italian officer. There had been another photograph, he remembered. She was his sister, he thought. *She has a right to know.* He flinched again as she applied some iodine.

'Well?' she said. 'If you want me to dress your wound, you're going to have to tell me.'

Tanner sighed and rubbed his brow. 'You have a brother, miss?'

'He was killed,' she said.

'Do you mind me asking when?'

'Three weeks ago. He was a captain in the Napoli Division. Officially, he is still only missing. We had a telegram and nothing more. If you know something, please tell me.'

'What was his name, miss?'

'Nico. Niccolò Togliatti.'

Tanner nodded. 'Then it was him. I'm so sorry, miss.'

Francesca let out a small cry, and put her hands to her mouth. 'Tell me,' she said. 'Tell me.'

'We were attacking his positions,' said Tanner. 'It was dawn, first light. We'd won, almost, and I came face to face with your brother. He surrendered to me, miss. We talked, but then shells started falling down on us. It was our own guns, the barrage ordered by our battalion commander. I lost one of my very best men and one of my oldest mates was badly wounded. Lots of men were killed. I was blown God knows how far, but when it was over, I found your brother. There wasn't a scratch on him. Not one, I swear. He looked like he was asleep. At peace, I suppose. And because I'd been talking to him not ten minutes earlier, I wondered who he was and looked in his breast pocket – it's where soldiers usually keep their most precious belongings. Italians are no different. I saw his name, and I saw a picture of you, miss. There was another one – four of you, I think it was, and that was when I guessed you and he were brother and sister.' He paused. 'I wish it could be different, and I wasn't the bearer of this news.'

Francesca was quiet as she applied a bandage. Outside the men were laughing. Further away, guns could be heard in the distance; the battle had rolled north, past this corner of Sicily. But here, in this room, the air seemed suddenly very still.

'Sometimes,' she said at last, 'I dared to hope

that he was still alive, but I knew he was gone. Now I know what happened.'

'He wouldn't have felt a thing, miss,' said Tanner. 'I've seen some terrible things, and for many, death is a long and horrible process. But his... Well, as I say, he looked at peace.'

'I believe you. I don't know why. I don't even know you. But I do believe you.'

'It's the truth.'

'But why did your commander order the guns to fire on his own troops?'

'Because he was a murdering bastard, miss,' said Tanner. 'A bad man, who, thank God, has gone.'

'He was killed too?'

'No, he was arrested by our Military Police. I got his job.'

'You're done,' she said.

'Thank you, miss.' Tanner stood up and put on his shirt. 'I'm sorry about your brother and I'm sorry we've invaded your home. It's not too late for us to move, you know.'

'It is all right,' she said. 'You are not Germans.'

'Did they treat you badly?'

'Not at first. They were mostly young men, like your boys. It was their commander. He – he tried to dishonour me.'

'The bastard,' muttered Tanner. 'He tried but didn't succeed?'

'No,' she said, 'I hit him here.' She pointed to her crotch. 'And I stabbed him in the arm.'

Tanner tried to suppress a smile.

'He was not laughing, I can tell you,' said Francesca.

'Well, I can promise you have nothing to fear from me or my men. They're good lads. All the officers are honourable. We'll look after you.'

She smiled. 'How long will you be here?'

Tanner shrugged. 'I don't know, miss. A day or two. Maybe longer.'

'Francesca,' she said. 'You can call me Francesca.'

'And you may call me Jack.'

'Thank you for telling me about Nico,' she said. 'I know it cannot have been easy.'

Tanner smiled and left her.

The Germans were found early the following morning by a sapper party and some C Company men as they cleared the road north to Belpasso. Twelve of them, all shot and left lined up on the side of the road. Among them was an officer, who had had his penis cut off and placed in his mouth. With the heat, the bodies already stank. Identity tags and papers were collected and then they were buried, by the side of the road, in a long, makeshift grave.

Their identity tags and papers were delivered to Battalion Headquarters and given to Tanner by Lieutenant Cartwright.

'They did what to him?' said Tanner. They were in Dr Togliatti's old surgery, now the battalion office.

'They cut off his old chap,' said Cartwright, 'and shoved it in his mouth. I nearly retched, I can tell you.'

'Jesus, who the bloody hell would do such a thing?'

'It wouldn't be any of our lads,' said Cartwright. 'We only got here last night and those fellows had been dead longer than that.'

'Eyeties then,' said Tanner. 'But why?'

He found Francesca and told her.

'What were their names?' she asked.

Tanner looked at the papers. 'Not sure.'

'The officer was called Kranz,' said Cartwright. 'Leutnant Albert Kranz.'

Francesca gasped. 'He was the one who–' She stopped. 'They were here. They were billeted here.'

'The thing is, Francesca,' said Tanner, 'they must have been killed by Italians. I know they're the enemy, but people can't go around murdering Jerries like that. And butchering them, for that matter. If we do that, we're no better than the Nazis.'

'Talk to Salvatore Camprese,' she said.

'The bloke who thinks he's mayor?' said Tanner. Camprese had presented himself the previous evening.

'Yes,' said Francesca. 'He knows everything that goes on here. But I do not want to speak to him.'

'He's with the civil-affairs people,' said Macdonald. 'Let them do the interpreting.'

'All right,' said Tanner. 'Let's go and see him now.'

The town hall was an ornate *belle-époque* building, with palm trees outside, overlooking the war memorial.

'*Municipio*,' said Tanner, reading the marble

plaque beside the main door. 'This is it.'

He had brought with him Sykes and Captain Masters, the intelligence officer, and now they strode in. To the left of the hall, in a large, light, high-ceilinged office, Camprese was sitting behind his desk and talking to three British soldiers.

'*Buon giorno, Maggiore,*' said Camprese.

'Morning,' said Tanner. Then, to the others, he said, 'Are you the civil-affairs lot?'

'Yes,' said a neat young captain, with a trim gingery moustache and spectacles. 'Captain Bullmore. I'm the CAO for these parts.' He offered a hand. 'Major Tanner, I presume.'

'You presume right. How d'you do?'

'Very well, very well,' said Bullmore, then turned to his companions. 'These are Sergeants Lewis and Lavery of 302 Field Security Service.'

'And which of you speaks Italian?' asked Tanner.

'We all do,' said Bullmore.

'And are you staying here permanently?'

'Good gosh, no,' said Bullmore. 'I'm going to be running Misterbianco, Belpasso, this town and as far as Sferro. This is just a courtesy call, really, to speak to Mayor Camprese and see what's needed. I'll be leaving Sergeant Lavery here, though. He'll be your liaison with Camprese and the towns-people.'

'One FSS bloke? Is that all?'

Bullmore pushed his spectacles back up his nose. 'We're quite stretched, I'm afraid, Major. I shall be based at Misterbianco but I'll come over here as often as time permits.'

'So, in your absence, who will be running the

civil affairs of the town?'

'Mayor Camprese, liaising, of course, with me through Sergeant Lavery.'

From the other side of the desk, Camprese beamed genially.

'But I thought he was a Fascist,' said Tanner. 'That's what I was told.'

'Out here in the country, Major, Fascism was often worn very lightly. Camprese has been put forward to continue as mayor – no longer wearing the Fascist badge, obviously – and this has been approved by AMGOT.'

Tanner sighed heavily. 'All right, then. Can you ask him if he knows anything about the twelve Germans we found murdered to the north of the town?'

Bullmore repeated the question. Camprese shrugged and muttered something.

'The Germans were not popular. There was a lot of anger towards them. People blame them for the suffering here.'

'Does he know who killed them?'

Another shrug.

'He says the men of the town don't like their girls being chatted up by Germans.'

'Christ,' said Tanner. 'We're not going to get anywhere. He might be mayor, Bullmore, but that doesn't give him the right to play vigilante.'

'You probably won't think it's my place to say this, sir,' said Bullmore, 'but I'd let the mayor take care of things his way. We're going to have a hell of a time trying to distribute enough food, and you front-line troops have enough to worry about fighting the enemy. I agree, no one should be murdering anyone, but Sicily is different from England.'

'All right,' said Tanner, 'but I haven't been fighting this war just so little dictators like him can pile even more misery on the people we've been trying to liberate. Let him play lord of the manor, but while I'm here, he needs to watch it. If I catch him murdering anyone else, I'll string him up without a second thought.'

It was not until later that afternoon that Tanner had a chance to speak to Francesca again. He and Sykes had brought her some rations – tins of condensed milk, fruit, stew and some chocolate for Cara. Seeing them in the kitchen, he knocked on the door.

'Jack, hello,' she said. 'And Sergeant Major Sykes, isn't it?'

'Call me Stan.' He offered Cara the chocolate. Her face lit up as she eagerly tore off the foil.

'A few tins,' said Tanner, as he and Sykes placed them on the table.

'Thank you,' she said. 'Peaches in syrup. I have never tried such a thing.'

'They're not bad,' said Sykes. 'With a drop of condensed milk they're even better.'

'I want to ask you something, Francesca,' said Tanner. 'This Camprese bloke. We grilled him a bit this morning and he said the Germans had been chasing the town's girls. Is this true?'

'No, it is not. Kranz tried to dishonour me, but they barely left the houses, those men. They had no time. You should know that Camprese wants me to marry him. He argued with Kranz about it, and threatened him. I heard it.'

'But you don't want to?' asked Sykes.

'No. I despise him. He's a bully. He doesn't love me, just wants me as a prize.'

'The bastard,' muttered Tanner. 'So he murdered them. And that's why you told us to talk to him?'

'Yes. As soon as I heard of it I knew it would have been him. You will not get him or anyone else to admit it, though. I would have killed Kranz myself the other night, but Camprese had no right to do what he did. It was not his vendetta. He would not see it that way. Killing those Germans was a way of telling the town that he is still in charge. Mussolini may have gone, but Camprese is still king here. It's a warning too.'

'Don't mess with me,' said Sykes.

'Exactly. These so-called "men of honour", it's pathetic. There's no honour. Only misery. You British should stop it. The Mafia ruined Sicily once already. They ruined my family.'

'How?' asked Tanner.

'My father was a successful doctor in Palermo. He had some very rich clients, old aristocratic families, and they enabled him to take on a number of less well-off patients. He looked after the poor. My father was a good man. We had a nice house, with views of the sea and the mountains. All was right with the world. But then the Mafia asked him to join them. He knew a little about the Honourable Society, that it was corrupt and unfair, and that one day they would ask him to do something that would compromise everything he believed in. It would be a Faustian pact. He knew that so he refused.'

'So what happened?' asked Sykes.

'One by one his rich clients left him. He was threatened and once beaten up. His car was burned. His career in Palermo, where he had achieved much good, was ruined and we had to sell up. Of course, the house had to be sold for a fraction of its value because no one would buy it. We moved here, to Motta Sant'Anastasia, thanks to one of his oldest clients who felt bad – he owned the land and house and sold it to us for almost nothing. So, one bit of good fortune, I suppose. But it killed my mother. She never recovered, and within a year of moving here, she was dead. It changed my father too. He was so much fun when we were young – outgoing, caring, a good man and a good doctor. In his last years he barely spoke. It killed him too. The shame and the grief broke his heart.' She looked at them both. 'Soon after we moved here, Cesare Mori declared war on the Mafia, and by the time war broke out, he was winning too. But now, you Allies come here as our liberators from Fascism, and Salvatore Camprese is left in charge of the town.'

'He's Mafia?' asked Sykes.

'Of course!' said Francesca. 'It's like a shroud spread over the island. A big, dark shroud. We Sicilians are slaves to these people. Really, that's what it is. Slavery.'

Later, Tanner found Sykes and took him out into the square. 'I want to talk to you a moment, Stan,' he said, as they ambled towards a small metal railing near the church. From there, the view stretched up to Etna, looming over them to the north, right across the lava hills to Catania, the plain and the deep blue sea beyond.

'Bloody beautiful, isn't it?' said Sykes.

'Much better up here than down on that stinking plain,' said Tanner. He lit a couple of cigarettes and handed one to Sykes. 'I don't like that bloke, Camprese,' he said.

'Me neither,' agreed Sykes. He drew on his cigarette. 'This Mafia lark. It's just a protection racket, ain't it? I mean, we used to have gangs like that when I was a boy. You paid them a cut of what you got and they saw to it that you were all right. Fear – that's what it was all about. Making people afraid. Francesca's afraid, isn't she?'

Tanner nodded. 'And with good reason. She's a good-looking bint and she's got this Camprese joker slobbering all over her, and there's her daughter to take care of. And no bloody escape.'

'We've got to help her.'

'I know. And I feel in part responsible. That trip I did over here back at the end of May – that was to see the head of the Mafia. I didn't know it then. The Yanks were keeping him sweet.'

'Promising him the earth.'

'In return for ensuring the Italians on the island barely put up any resistance. The Yanks didn't race into Palermo by accident, you know. All the bloody Eyeties just laid down their arms and buggered off. I saw his influence at first hand, but I had no idea at the time that he was a bloody glorified gangster.'

'Well, you wasn't to know.'

'But I do now and I feel guilty. We've got to do something, Stan. But what, I don't know. I really don't.'

23

Thursday, 5 August. In the morning, Tanner was ordered up to 15th Brigade Headquarters, now camped in the foothills to the north of Misterbianco. He took Brown with him.

'Funny to think we're finally driving into this place, sir,' said Brown, as they sped in a Jeep along a narrow, straight street. 'We've been looking at it for so long, and now here we are.' Unlike Motta Sant'Anastasia, Misterbianco had been severely hit, mounds of rubble lying in gaping holes between the fine old houses that were still standing.

'I preferred it in the desert, Browner,' said Tanner. 'It was just us and the enemy and nothing in our way.' A number of children watched them pass, some waving, outsize malnourished heads on thin little bodies. Few wore shoes, most barely a shirt.

'I know what you mean, boss,' said Brown. 'I used to hate Eyeties, but then you see these poor buggers and you feel a bit different. Me and the lads have given out so much chocolate and so many boiled sweets we haven't any left.'

They sped on through the town and then were in the country again, the sun beating down relentlessly, Etna looming ever closer. Signs had been put on the roads and they soon found Brigade HQ, a collection of trucks, tents and camouflage nets in an olive grove.

The brigadier was in the office, a converted thirty-hundredweight truck, but came down the wooden steps attached to the back.

'Well done, Tanner,' he said. 'The brigade has done bloody well and your boys put up a good show. Twelve miles in twenty-four hours is pretty good going.'

'It felt slow, sir, always stopping for the sappers.'

'Still, worth their weight in gold, those boys.'

'I'll admit we only lost a handful of men in the entire operation. Which is just as well, as we're at half strength.'

'Won't be long now, though. A week, maybe two, and the island will be ours. How are you getting on in Motta Sant'Anastasia?'

'Fine, sir. The Italian mayor is a badmash, but the lads are looking a bit cleaner. They badly need new uniforms, though. Shirts, denims, underwear. We've been washing them in petrol, but they're in a bit of a state all the same.'

'Leave that with me. The build-up is pretty good now, so this should be possible. The port at Catania should be open any day now too, which will ease things even further.' They paused by a set of fold-up canvas chairs beneath an olive tree, and Rawstorne offered Tanner a seat. It was still blisteringly hot, but in the shade there was some comfort from the canopy above and the faintest whisper of a breeze. Crickets chirruped in the grass, while lizards scuttled over rocks and up the trunk of the tree.

'Just thought I'd put you in the picture, Tanner. It's been decided we're going to assault the mainland.'

'I suppose that makes sense, sir.'

'Yes. After all, there'll be no cross-Channel invasion until next year now, and we've one heck of a force in the Mediterranean. It's the airfields that the brass are interested in, though, at a place called Foggia on the east coast. If we can get our heavies over there, we can attack Hitler's oilfields in Romania and bomb the Third Reich from the south as well as from the west.'

'And we're going in, are we, sir?'

'Yes. The brigade are going to be in reserve and it was the intention to have us pull out now and start to get ready.' He breathed in heavily. 'But I'm afraid XXX Corps are finding the going tougher than they'd hoped and are getting a bit held up around Rinazzo. The Yanks are finally slowing a bit as well, now that they're up against real soldiers rather than those that bugger off at the first sight of a Sherman. So Monty's bringing Fifth Div back into the scrap. We're going to be advancing on a two-divisional front alongside Fiftieth Div around the west slopes of Etna.'

'When do we move, sir?'

'Not yet. And it will be a limited thrust just to break through Jerry's next line of defence. He's calling it the Etna Line apparently. Original, eh? Leave Echelon and Battalion HQ in Motta Sant'Anastasia. You'll get M/T as well to take you up to the front. You'll be two, maybe three days, then you can have some well-deserved rest back in Motta Sant'Anastasia. ENSA are moving into Catania, films are being laid on too. Swimming in the sea. A chance for everyone to get their strength back.'

'Thank you, sir.'

'Good man.' He sighed with satisfaction and stretched. 'Nearly there. Last over of the day, eh, then off to the pavilion for a well-earned beer. Talking of which, I'm afraid we've received some sad news. It seems Hedley Verity didn't make it. Died of his wounds at Caserta.'

'I'm very sorry to hear that, sir.'

'It's a tragedy. England's lost one of her greatest ever bowlers, and what really sticks in the gullet is that he was due to join Dempsey's staff. He'd have sat out the rest of the war in a comfortable staff job here on Sicily. I feel partly responsible, if I'm honest. Should have given Creer the chop earlier. Verity might still be alive if I had.'

With the knowledge that they would be staying in Motta Sant'Anastasia for four more days, Tanner had decided to try to get hold of Wiseman. He knew he was on Patton's staff, and before leaving Brigade HQ, he asked Rawstorne whether it might be possible to get a message to an American G2 at Seventh Army Headquarters.

'I can do that for you, Tanner,' said Rawstorne. 'Of course, you know a lot of Yanks, don't you?'

The message was simple and Tanner watched the brigade signals officer fill in the message form. It was a request for Wiseman to make urgent contact.

'What's this about, Tanner?' Rawstorne had asked.

'An operation we did before the invasion, sir. I need his advice.'

'All right, and I'll give you mine. Don't get involved.'

It was too late for that, Tanner thought, as he and Brown drove back to Motta Sant'Anastasia. He *was* involved. He'd become involved the moment he'd agreed to drop into Sicily with Wiseman and Spiro.

He wondered whether his message would ever reach Wiseman, and, even if it did, whether his friend would respond. God only knew what he had been up to, or where he was now. It might take days. For all he knew, Wiseman might not even be on Sicily any more. Maybe he was planning a drop on the mainland in preparation for the next invasion.

But Wiseman did respond, and that same day, at a little after seven in the evening, the signals team taking down the incoming message in pencil, then passing it to Tanner. *Got message. Flying to Gerbini tomorrow a.m. Will call in on you. CW.*

Good. Tanner was not quite sure, having dragged Wiseman all the way over to see him, what he was going to ask him, but it was something. If anyone knew how to play it with Camprese, it was Wiseman.

Friday, 6 August. It was around nine in the morning when Wiseman arrived. Tanner heard him before he saw him: a knock at the door, then, 'I'm here to see *Major* Jack Tanner.'

405

Stepping out of the battalion office, Wiseman grinned. 'So you're the boss-guy now!' He looked fit, clean and trim, conspicuously so, standing beside the tattered uniforms of the battalion staff.

Introductions first: to some of the men and then to Francesca.

'Ma'am,' said Wiseman, taking her hand and bowing. He grinned at Tanner and winked.

'Charlie,' said Tanner.

'Yeah, sure, we need to talk. Let's go some place else, shall we?'

'Definitely,' agreed Tanner.

Out on the square, Tanner saw the Jeep with a GI at the wheel.

'Sergeant Schwartz,' said Wiseman, putting on a pair of sunglasses and his garrison cap. 'He's a good man in a tight situation.'

'Have you had any?'

'Sure, about an hour ago when we landed at Gerbini. None of you Brits wanted to give me a vehicle, even though we'd requested one. Eventually I had to point out that a number of Jeeps there were not being used and that they were kind of ours anyway since we invented and built them. The wingco wasn't looking too convinced until Schwartz scowled at him and then he rapidly changed his tune. I tell you, Schwartz has the best scowl of any man.'

Tanner laughed as Wiseman grabbed a canvas bag from the back of the Jeep. 'Breakfast,' he said.

They walked down some stone steps that led to the groves directly below the town. Then, when they were well away from any other soul, they sat down beneath an olive tree and Wiseman opened the bag.

'Here,' he said, tossing Tanner a carton of Camels. 'I know how much you like them.'

'Thanks. I was spoiled when I was with your lot.'

'And a coupla Cokes, two Hershey bars and a tin of ham. What's not to like?' He opened the Cokes, passed one to Tanner, then raised his own. 'Cheers. You guys've been having a tough time of it, I hear.'

'We seem to be winning now.'

'Oh, yeah. We've squeezed Papa Fritz tight into the corner. Ten days max and it'll be all over. The thing that amazes me about these Krauts is why the hell they keep on fighting when they know they're beat. Why not do what the Eyeties do and call it quits when it's clear the fight's only going one way?'

'Because the Eyeties have the Mafia breathing down their necks and Jerry doesn't.'

Wiseman smiled. 'Old Don Calogero certainly lived up to his promise, I'll give him that. It was a Goddamn walk in the park.'

'You saw him?'

'Sure. Dropped a flag on his house – a kind of prearranged warning order that we'd discussed when we saw him back at the end of May – then met him in Villalba, only this time we had a few tanks and the *carabinieri* were waving us in, not pointing Berettas at our heads. Then he came with us. Christ, Jack, everywhere we went there were crowds of Sicilians cheering us. The guy was phenomenal. Even the boss was impressed and that takes some doing, as you well know.'

'What's the scale of this, Charlie?' Tanner asked. 'The Mafia? Is it the whole of the island?'

'What are you driving at, Jack?'

'Is it here, in Motta Sant'Anastasia?'

'Why d'you ask?'

'Because there's a bloke called Camprese who used to be a Fascist mayor until a week ago but now he's a non-Fascist mayor. His appointment has been approved by AMGOT. Or that's what I've been told, anyway.'

Wiseman looked thoughtful. Then, leaning a little closer to Tanner and lowering his voice, he said, 'We asked Don Calo to prepare a list of suitable mayors for the big towns. So we get to Palermo and the day after we take the place, we have this big meeting. All the top civil-affairs guys are there, including Charlie Poletti, who's now senior CAO in the city. And there's Don Calo, the self-proclaimed top man in Sicily. And he's not just got a few names, he's got names for all the towns in Sicily just about. Some are so-called Fascists, some are not. Jesus, some are in prison and have been for years under Mori's rule. And guess what happens?'

'What?'

'Every single Goddamn name on that list gets approved, there and then. I tell you, Jack, if Don Calo wasn't the most powerful man in Sicily when we first met him, he is now. There's no one to touch him.'

'But how do we know the men on his list are going to do a good job?'

'We know because, ultimately, they're answerable to Don Calo. These new mayors are going to ensure we get out of this place in double-quick time and get on with hammering the Krauts on the mainland. The sooner we hammer the Krauts, the sooner we win the war. The Mafia, Jack, are saving lives. American lives, British lives, the lives of millions of Goddamn Europeans.'

'But making the lives of Sicilians a misery.'

Wiseman shrugged. 'A small price.'

Tanner sighed and lit a Camel. 'When I parachuted into Villalba I had no idea what we were doing. I had no idea I was helping the Allies sign a pact with the devil.'

Wiseman smiled. 'A devil's pact. Well, yes, I suppose it was, if you think Don Calo is the devil. He's a rather impressive one, though, for all that.'

Tanner exhaled heavily and scratched his head. 'And what about the bastard that runs this place?'

'What about him?'

'I can't just sit here watching him lord it over these people. They're half starving and he's swaggering about the place, murdering Germans, threatening people and acting like Hitler.'

'Why not?'

'Why not what?'

'Why can't you watch him playing at Hitler?'

'Because – because it's wrong. Because I haven't fought the war for three years from Norway to Africa to see bastards like him benefit. We're fighting for a better world, not a worse one.'

'You're fighting to get rid of Hitler and the Nazis. Don't worry about places like this. Small-town redneck Sicilian backwaters. Life here has been crap for centuries and probably will continue like that. Christ, Jack, Sicily's barely out of the Dark Ages. My advice? Get the girl out, if you want, and leave Signor Mini-Hitler alone. And don't look at me all innocent. The girl's a peach. You know it, I know it, and I wouldn't mind betting Mini-Hitler knows it too.'

'So, do nothing?'

'Do nothing. I'm telling you, Jack. Keep out. In fact, I'm warning you. You're a buddy and I'd hate for anything to happen to you, but start crossing the wrong people here, and you'll find yourself in a whole load of trouble.'

Perhaps, Tanner thought, Wiseman had been right. Maybe it was best to leave the Sicilians in Motta Sant'Anastasia to their fate. In any case, Camprese kept out of their way, and there were other matters to occupy him: the arrival of new uniforms, condolence letters to write to families and wives, sitreps to read, sigint to go through. And a bit of time not doing very much. He spent two hours cat-napping in the shade, another taking Cara for a ride in the Jeep. Francesca had been teaching her English but Tanner gave her a few more words – army words like 'wallah' and 'iggery', 'char' and 'badmash', words that had mostly originated in India, then followed the men to the Middle East and the North African desert.

He was not the only one enjoying Cara's company. So, too, were the other men, especially the NCOs and ORs billeted in the sheds below. They were spoiling her, giving her chocolate and sweets, and playing games. A favourite was Sykes's coin tricks.

'Again!' Tanner heard her say.

'Blimey, missy,' said Sykes, 'you're a full-time job. All right, see this coin here... Oh, where's it gone?' Giggles from Cara. 'Oh, look, Cara, it's behind your ear! What's it doing there?' More laughter.

Later, the officers had supper together, around the kitchen table, Francesca joining them. She had offered to cook, but Tanner wouldn't hear of it. 'Our lads will do it,' he told her. 'They're used to the rations.'

Francesca was taken aback. She had never known a man to cook.

'Very well,' she told him, 'and I will provide wine.'

'You have some?'

'There's a little left. The Germans drank most of it, but I still have some. They paid for it, but I'd rather have kept it.'

Everyone had made an effort to smarten up for dinner. In fresh uniforms, shaved and groomed, their transformation was notable.

'This isn't bad,' said Macdonald, licking his lips. 'In fact, what am I saying? It's nectar, pure nectar.' He raised his glass. 'To our hostess. Thank you, Francesca, for letting us invade your home.'

'It has been an unexpected pleasure,' she said. 'And thank you to you and the other boys for being so kind to Cara. You are spoiling her, and she likes having you about the place.'

'We're keeping her entertained, that's for sure,' said Tanner. 'I've never really spent much time

411

with children, to be honest, but I've enjoyed her company today. It's been refreshing.'

'Maybe one day you'll have your own.'

'Maybe.'

'I'd like children,' said Masters. 'I've always imagined I'd have four, I don't know why.'

'I've got two already,' said Howell. 'They're rascals, the pair of them.'

'You must miss them,' said Francesca.

'Oh, I do. I haven't seen them for two and a half years. They're growing fast, my wife tells me.' He sighed, then said, 'I just hope they recognize me, remember who I am, when I get back.'

'That still seems a long way off, though, doesn't it?' said Macdonald.

'I don't know,' said Masters. 'Maybe they'll send us back after this. They might take pity on us and realize we've done our bit and that it's time for some others to do theirs.'

Tanner ate his stew thoughtfully. He'd not told them they would be going to Italy. He didn't want them thinking too far ahead yet, not when there was fighting still to be done here, in Sicily.

'It's funny, though, thinking about after the war,' said Macdonald. 'I've got my uncle's estate to run in the Dales, so that'll be it for me and the Army.'

'And I've got the family business outside Ripon,' said Masters.

'What's that?' asked Macdonald.

'It's a sawmill. We supply all sorts of timber for houses, fencing, anything, really. A good little business. Been doing well through the war, too.'

'What will you do, Jack?' asked Macdonald.

Tanner smiled ruefully. 'I don't know. My father was a gamekeeper and I grew up on the land. That's where I belong. I've started to think I'd like a little farm of my own. Whether I'd ever be able to, though, I'm not sure.'

'You'll leave the Army, then?'

'Oh, I think so. I've done enough soldiering. Seen enough killing to last ten lifetimes.' He looked down, and the men were suddenly quiet. Instantly regretting his words, he turned to Francesca. 'What about you?' he asked. 'What do you want to do?'

'Escape,' she said.

Later, around 2 a.m. Tanner had been asleep, but something had woken him. He sat up and listened. The sound of a vehicle, a truck, changing gear. Climbing out of bed, he stood by the window and listened again. There it was. A truck, definitely. A big one.

There was a light tap at the door and Tanner started.

'Yes?'

'It's me, Stan,' whispered Sykes.

Tanner opened the door. 'What are trucks doing driving around here at this time of the morning?'

'You 'eard it, then. I've seen it too. It's come up from the valley, heading for the new town by the look of things. I wouldn't have bothered, only it's American.'

'American? Here? Bit too far out of the way just to have got lost.'

'Maybe we should have a dekko.'

'Maybe we should.'

As they slipped out into the square, past their sentries, they could still hear it, rumbling slowly up the hill to the new town away to the south, but then it stopped.

Quickly, they hurried down through the labyrinth of narrow alleys. As they emerged onto via Vittorio Emanuele, up which they had tramped just a few days earlier, they heard the truck again: a slight rev of the throttle and then its low rumble.

'It's moving into position,' said Sykes.

Following the sound, they crossed to the edge of the town where the old met the new. There before them, built a little way back from the road, was a long, low, two-storey municipal building and drill yard with stores behind.

'It's the *carabiniere* barracks,' whispered Tanner.

'And look!' said Sykes. The truck was just visible in the faint light of the stars and the moon.

Keeping to the shadows, they crossed the street and moved around to the edge of the barracks yard. Crouching low, they watched what was going on. The truck had reversed towards a large shed and a group of men were unloading boxes using electric torches to help them. Tanner recognized Camprese, and one of the other Sicilians he had seen at the Municipio.

'Rations,' said Tanner. 'I'll put money on it being American rations.'

'Which they'll sell on the black market or use to bribe people.'

'Come on, Stan,' said Tanner. 'I think we've seen enough, don't you?'

Saturday, 7 August. It was a little after eight a.m., the sun already beating down from a burnished sky, as Tanner, with Masters and Macdonald, walked down the hill towards the Municipio. Camprese, they had been informed by Lavery, had now arrived. Earlier, at around five a.m., Sykes had led a dozen men on a raid on the police barracks. As they had thought, the boxes were rations, several tons of them.

Wiseman had told him not to get involved – had warned him not to get involved. Yet, as Sykes had pointed out, Camprese was unlikely to be handing out these supplies freely to the towns-people of Motta Sant'Anastasia. Rather, he would be using them to bribe and coerce, or selling them at vastly inflated prices.

Tanner knew that Sykes was right, and the decision to act had been easy, although he hadn't taken it lightly. He wished he and Sykes had not heard the truck, but they had, and he could not, would not, turn a blind eye to flagrant black-marketeering. He had always had a clear under-standing of what was right and what was wrong; dishonesty and corruption were wrong, and he would always fight them. A man should always stand by his principles, Tanner believed, even if it meant getting himself into trouble. And, by God, it had, numerous times over the years. But he was still alive. He'd stood up to men like Blackstone and Creer and look where they were now: Black-stone rotting at the bottom of the Channel and Creer languishing in the glasshouse. In any case, it was a matter of honour as well as principle. Upsetting the apple-cart with Camprese would, no doubt, cause trouble, but his conscience would be clear. A devil's pact, he'd called this alliance with the Mafia, and so it was. But he wanted no further part in it.

At the town hall, they saw Lavery smoking outside, waiting for them.

'Good,' said Tanner. 'You're here. I need you.'

'What's going on?'

'You'll see.'

Camprese looked up, startled, when Tanner opened the door. *'Buon giorno, Maggiore,'* he said.

'Tell him this, Lavery,' said Tanner. 'This morning we raided the *carabiniere* barracks and found three tons of US Army rations. Tell him we know he was there and that I would like an explanation.'

As Lavery relayed this, Camprese's expression changed. The smile disappeared.

'Come lei permette,' he exploded, standing up and crashing his hand onto the desk. *'Non aveve il diritto di fare una cosa del genere. Questo è niente a che fare con le!'*

'He says you had no right. It is nothing to do with you.'

'Tell him black-marketeering is illegal under Allied military law.'

Camprese fumed. He had been given the supplies by an American contact, he told Tanner.

'Who?' Tanner asked.

Camprese would not say.

'And what are you going to do with the supplies? Sell them? Selling US military goods is illegal.'

'He says he is mayor of this town, appointed by AMGOT,' said Laver 'He says you know nothing

416

of running a town, of looking after the people. He says you are a soldier and should stick to being a soldier and keep out of Sicilian affairs.'

'Tell him that he may have been appointed by AMGOT, but this town is still under military jurisdiction, and that while I am here, he is answerable to me.'

At this Camprese smacked the table again and swore.

'He's very angry, isn't he?' said Macdonald.

'So would you be if you'd just been as badly rumbled,' said Tanner. He turned to Lavery. 'Ask him again who provided the truck of rations. We know it was a US Army truck, but I want a name.'

Lavery repeated the question. 'He won't give one,' said Lavery, after another torrent of Italian. 'He says he's a man of honour, that this is no business of ours and that we have no right to meddle in his affairs.'

'That's all a load of cock-and-bull,' said Tanner. 'Tell him we're confiscating the lot and that we'll distribute it, for free, to the townspeople. Since he was given it by the Americans, and since he won't tell us who to return it to, that's the answer. You can also tell him I don't think it right that a mayor, a pillar of the community, a man the people of the town should look up to and admire, should be making money out of the misery of the same people it is his duty to look after.'

Lavery repeated Tanner's words. Camprese glared at him, muttered something, then spat and sat down petulantly.

'What did he say?' asked Tanner.

'He says you've crossed the wrong man, that you have no idea what you're doing insulting him and his fellow Sicilians.'

Tanner pushed back his chair, went around the desk and grabbed Camprese by the collar. He pulled the man to his feet, grabbed his crotch and squeezed. Camprese cried out in pain. 'Listen to me,' said Tanner. 'I don't like bullies and I don't like cheats, and I don't give a fig for your pathetic threats. So I'm warning you, don't ever, ever threaten me again, or I'll have your nuts boiled quicker than you can say *Società d'Onore*. Is that clear?' He squeezed tighter. Camprese nodded, and Tanner dropped him, leaving him collapsed on the floor, gasping and wincing with pain.

'I didn't know you could speak Italian, Jack,' said Macdonald, as they left.

'I can't, but I know what "Società d'Onore" means. And I know what "Mafia" means too.'

Later, back at the house, Francesca tapped at the office door and came in.

'Thank you,' she said, coming over to him and taking his hands in hers.

'For what?' he said, surprised.

'For what you did to Camprese.'

'He deserved it. I hate people like him. He's a bully.'

A smile flickered on her face. 'He will be very angry,' she said, her expression suddenly more serious. 'You must be careful.'

'I'm not scared of someone like him.'

'It's not him you need to scared of,' said Francesca. 'When you insult and threaten him, you insult and threaten all the Mafia.'

'They wouldn't dare do anything to me.'

'No, Jack, you're wrong. You don't understand these people. They'll kill you, if they can, for what you've done to Camprese.'

24

Later that Saturday morning, Lieutenant Shopland called in on Tanner. The companies had been brought in to help distribute the rations, but were discovering that none of the townspeople would accept them. Tanner had not expected this. What was it Francesca had called it? *A shroud of fear.* It was, he reflected, quite some shroud that stopped half-starved people accepting free food.

'All right, Jimmy,' said Tanner. 'Get a fifteen-hundredweight, fill it with rations, then meet me outside the town hall.'

Tanner strode back to the Municipio and found Lavery. 'Where's Camprese?' he said.

'At the bar across the road,' said Lavery. 'You've heard, then?'

'Yes,' said Tanner, 'but that's easily solved. Come on, let's go and find him.'

He was in the bar, as Lavery had said, smoking a cigarette and drinking fresh coffee, two commodities that were almost non-existent in this part of Sicily, as Tanner was well aware.

Seeing Tanner, Camprese smiled and raised his coffee cup. *'Saluti,'* he said. 'The people no want food.'

'They're too scared to take it,' said Tanner. 'Scared of what you will do if they accept.'

Camprese muttered something as he drew on his cigarette.

'He says they're not scared,' said Lavery. 'He says they know their mayor has been insulted and they do not accept the gifts out of respect to him.'

'Which is why he's going to tell them that it's perfectly all right if they do accept them.'

Camprese's smile disappeared once more.

'And you can tell him,' added Tanner, 'that if he doesn't, I'll rip his bollocks off this time.'

Five minutes later, with the truck parked beside the war memorial and with men there to help distribute the load of rations, Camprese spoke from the first-floor balcony of the Municipio.

'Amici,' he declared to the gathering crowd below, *'portare questi doni di cibo. Fatelo con la mia benedizione.'* Friends, take these gifts of food. Do so with my blessing.

'There,' said Tanner, standing behind him with his hand on his Colt .45. 'That wasn't so difficult, was it?'

The following morning, Sunday, 8 August, a message arrived early for Tanner. It was from Wiseman: *Know you are heading to front tomorrow. Please meet me today at Enna. Need your help. Please confirm. Lt Col C. Wiseman, US 7th Army.*

Tanner wondered what it was about. Another

warning, he guessed. A lesson in diplomatic relations.

'Are you going to go?' asked Sykes, after Tanner had shown it to him.

'I think I should. He came to see me when I asked him to. Why don't you come with me?'

'All right.'

'And we can take Browner and Phyllis too. Just in case Camprese's got any ideas.'

An hour later they were on their way, having received instructions from Wiseman to meet him at the Municipio in Enna at noon. With Brown driving, Tanner sat up front with his Beretta across his lap, while Phyllis and Sykes perched behind, Sykes clutching a Bren, a pack of grenades and another of ammunition.

'We don't need all this, do we?' said Phyllis. 'You said it was just an outing, sir.'

'Can't be too careful, Siff,' said Tanner. 'There's a war on, you know.'

'But there's no Jerries round here, sir.'

'You don't know that, Siff,' said Sykes. 'There might be a little pocket of hardened Nazis and Fascists who've been waiting for just such an opportunity.'

Phyllis looked at him, wondering whether he was having his leg pulled again, then decided he was. 'Nah, you're joshing me, sir.'

'Always be prepared, Siff,' said Sykes. 'Weren't you in the Scouts?'

'No, I never fancied it. I went once but it was really boring. We just sat around tying knots.'

They sped on out of the town and wound their way down to the N92, the road that bisected the island and which, in forty or so miles, would take them to Enna. With Motta Sant'Anastasia behind them and the Gerbini airfield in sight, Tanner began to feel easier. The sun continued to beat down and he took off his helmet, which was beginning to get ferociously hot, and replaced it with his dress cap, which was lighter and peaked. These were now being phased out, replaced by various berets, tam o'shanters, and the new general-service cap. Tanner hated it, and was determined to keep his dress cap for everyday use as long as he could.

The road followed the river Dittaino on their left, winding its way gradually higher towards the low mountains ahead. Tanner could not remember which unit was based at Enna, except that it had been taken by the US 1st Infantry and remained within Seventh Army's jurisdiction. They passed nothing, not a single army vehicle. The Americans were using Licata and now Palermo, the British Syracuse and Catania; there was, he supposed, no need to use this road. Occasionally, they saw a mule and cart, and peasants in the fields, harvesting what they could with scythes and rakes.

'Blimey,' said Browner, 'this place is bloody backward, isn't it? No wonder the Eyeties were so bollocks.'

'They weren't all rubbish,' said Sykes. 'Remember the Young Fascists at Wadi Akarit? And some of those paratrooper units – what were they called? The Folgore. They were a pretty tough bunch.'

'All right, but I'm just saying this place is a flippin' dump, in my book. I know they've been bashed about, but there's no running water, barely any electricity, almost no cars, peasants cutting the wheat with flippin' scythes. It's bastard hot, there's lots of sodding ants and scorpions and mossies. The people look half starved and the towns are run by arseholes like that mayor in Motta. Looks quite pretty on the face of it and old Etna up there is quite a sight, I'll grant you, but you wouldn't catch me living here. Not for all the silk in China. And, if I'm honest, I'm quite looking forward to getting home and seeing some grey skies and a bit of bloody rain.'

'Well, I'm glad we've cleared that one up, Browner,' said Sykes. 'I was worrying about what you thought of this place, but now I know.'

Brown laughed. 'What do you think of it then, sir?'

'I think the whole place is totally doolally,' said Sykes, and everyone laughed, Tanner included. 'It's a mad house.'

'Major Peploe would have liked it, though,' said Tanner. 'He'd be visiting all the ruins.'

'I'm glad he's all right, sir,' said Brown.

'D'you think he'll come back?' asked Phyllis.

'I hope so,' said Tanner.

'Don't you want to stay as officer commanding then, sir?'

'I'd happily step aside for Peploe.' He lit a Camel, then passed them round.

'Not black-market goods, I hope, sir?' said Brown.

Sykes cuffed him over the head and Brown swerved.

'Hey, what was that for?' he asked.

'Being cheeky to the major.'

'Play your cards right, Browner,' said Tanner, 'and you might be given some too. The man we're going to see is always very generous with his cigarettes, you know.'

They reached Enna in good time and, having climbed up the road that led to the strange hilltop town, found themselves speeding down a network of narrow winding streets. They found the Municipio easily enough, not least because several Jeeps and military vehicles were parked outside. It was a grand, ornate building, with four columns at the front and steps leading up to the main entrance. Telling the men to wait in the Jeep, Tanner went in alone.

Inside, there were a number of American servicemen as well as Italians, but Wiseman spotted him and called from an open office door.

'Jack, you made it! Come on in,' he said, beckoning to him.

Closing the door behind him, he said, 'Have a seat. How d'you get here? Take the N92?'

'Yes. It was a good ride. Hot, but not unpleasant with the breeze from the Jeep.'

'Great. Can I get you a drink? Coffee? Coke? Lemonade?'

'A Coke maybe, thanks.'

'Sure,' said Wiseman. 'Be back in two shakes.' He disappeared and Tanner looked around at the sparse room, with its bare desk, three chairs and whitewashed walls.

Wiseman returned. 'Here you go,' he said,

handing Tanner a bottle.

'You're not based here, are you, Charlie?' said Tanner.

'No – just a little business to attend to for a day or two. I'm usually either at AMGOT in Palermo, these days, or at Seventh Army Headquarters and CP.'

Tanner took a swig of his Coke and felt the strange carbonated liquid fill his mouth.

'Very good of you to come anyway,' added Wiseman.

'One favour deserves another,' said Tanner. 'So how can I help?'

Wiseman leaned forward on his desk and put his hands together. 'I'm going to be straight with you, Jack. Last time we met, I warned you not to meddle in the affairs of the Sicilians, but I hear that's exactly what you've done. You've humiliated Camprese, shown a lack of respect, and offended his honour. He wants you dead, Jack. He's asked his chief's permission to have you killed.'

'Christ, word travels fast around here.'

'Very fast. You have no idea.'

'I'm not scared of a jumped-up idiot like that.'

'You should be. These guys are serious, Jack, I'm telling you. And you've put me in a very difficult situation.'

'I'm sorry, Charlie, really I am, but the bloke's an arsehole. He's a bully and a murderer. He's been trying to use black-market American goods to coerce the people. Christ, he was unloading them under my nose, as though he were untouchable. As though we wouldn't mind him dealing

425

illegally in goods he had no right to have. I wish I'd never known about it, and if he'd made just the slightest effort to be a little more subtle, then maybe I never would have done. But he didn't, I found out, and I have to do what I believe is right. And before you ask, yes, he is pestering Francesca Falcone. He'll never leave her alone. He wants it all: power, riches, the beautiful girl. I don't know about other places. Maybe other Mafia mayors are cut from a different cloth. But I do know about what's going on in Motta, and much though I want to help you, Charlie, I can't sit back and let this badmash win. Ask me anything, Charlie, and I'll do it, but not that.'

Wiseman sighed and leaned back, his arms behind his head. 'All right, Jack, you win. I'll see what I can do, but don't tell me I didn't warn you. You've been a good friend, but you take these guys on at your peril. As long as you know that.' He stood up and held out his hand. 'Good-bye, Jack.'

Outside, Tanner found the others sitting across the street in the shade. 'Come on,' he said, 'let's go.'

'Did he give you any Camels, sir?' asked Brown.

'No, sorry, not this time,' said Tanner. 'But tell you what, Browner, get us back without any more swerving and I'll give you a packet of mine.'

They drove out of the town and back down towards the Dittaino valley. Etna still dominated the skyline, even from forty miles away. Tanner watched the view for a while, still thinking about what Wiseman had told him, then felt his eyelids begin to droop. The sun, the heat, the drone of the engine and the whirr of tacky rubber on the road had a soporific effect. He closed his eyes. Sykes and Brown were talking but then he stopped listening and his head lolled forward.

He awoke with a jerk as the Jeep swerved violently and shots rang out.

'Jesus Christ!' yelled Brown. They had slowed on a corner but now the Jeep was wildly out of control. More shots and a burst of submachine-gun fire, and Tanner was conscious of men either side, firing from behind rocks and scrub, bullets pinging into the metal.

'Keep driving, Browner!' shouted Tanner, as he opened fire wildly with his Beretta.

'I can't – front tyre's flat!'

The Jeep continued to swerve.

Sykes was firing short bursts with the Bren as shots continued to zip and ping around them. Then the Jeep seemed to right itself, only to slide again. This time it came off the road fifty yards from the hairpin and jolted to a halt in a ditch, Tanner cracking his head on the windshield.

'Get out!' he cried, blood already running down his face. Jumping clear, he dived into the ditch in front of the Jeep and felt Brown and Sykes land beside him.

'Where's Siff?' he said in alarm, as he wiped his face with his sleeve.

'Jesus!' said Sykes. 'Siff!' He poked his head up above the bonnet as another bullet cracked into the windscreen. 'He's been bloody hit!'

'Siff!' Brown yelled.

'I've been hit,' said Phyllis. 'I've been bloody hit!'

'Well keep your sodding head down!' shouted Tanner.

'I am! I'm keeping as low as I can.'

'Just stay there, Siff, don't move.' He crawled under the Jeep and peered back up the road. There were men either side, lying on the rising ground to the left, and in the trees on the right as the ground fell away. *How many? Eight? Maybe a couple more?*

'We've got to get Siff!' said Brown.

'No, we don't,' said Sykes, crouching low behind the radiator and fumbling in his bag. 'We've got to kill those bastard Eyeties first.'

'What've you got, Stan?' said Tanner.

'Six grenades, spare mags and some TNT.'

'All right,' said Tanner. 'Unless they've got grenades or manage to set fire to the Jeep, we should be all right here for the moment. They know we're armed.'

'So we'll throw one of the blocks of TNT onto the road, which will kick up lots of dust and grit. They'll all lie low and we dash forward with grenades and our weapons.'

'Good plan,' said Tanner, wiping his face again. Bullets continued to zip onto the road, and into the Jeep. 'Browner and I will go to the right of the road, you go to the left, Stan.'

Sykes nodded, gave them each two grenades, then lit the fuse, mouthed, 'Four seconds,' and hurled the block of TNT as far as he could. Several of the Italians shouted in panic, and a moment later the TNT exploded. Without waiting for the blast to subside, they jumped up, Tanner and Brown sprinting across the road, then crouching, away from the blast. Smoke and dust swirled into the air, a man cried out, others were coughing, and Tanner was pulling the pin from the grenade and throwing it towards the Italians. A gasp and a fleeting glance at Brown, then his finger was around the second ring, pulling the pin clear again – *count to two* – and hurling it through the air. Seconds later, a staccato of dull explosions, cries and yells, then Tanner was running forward again, firing at the shapes of several men through the smoke and dust. Pulling out the magazine, he grabbed another from his pocket, rammed it home, saw a man running away, up the hill, as across the road, the Bren sputtered and barked. Tanner aimed at the fleeing man, fired, felt the Beretta vibrate in his hands, and watched the Italian stumble and fall.

And then, suddenly, silence. As the smoke and dust cleared, Tanner counted four men dead on the cliff ledge above the road and walked over to the fifth, still sprawled on the ground, a dark pool of blood seeping out onto the dusty soil beside him.

'Browner, get back to Siff. Stan? You all right?'

'I've got four here,' said Sykes.

Tanner hurried over, clambering down the cliff overlooking the road and across to the trees where Sykes was standing, the still-smoking Bren now across his shoulder. Three were dead, one nearly so. Tanner stood over the Italian, who stared back, his mouth moving wordlessly.

'He's still alive!' called Brown, from the Jeep. 'He's been hit in the shoulder.'

Tanner looked down at the Italian once more, but the man was dying, his face a waxy white, the life force seeping away. Then he jerked and fell back, dead.

Brown was wrapping dressings around Phyllis's shoulder. 'Why were those bastards shooting at us?'

'I think because we upset Mayor Camprese,' said Tanner. He turned to Phyllis. 'We'll get you out of here, Siff, don't you worry. You've got that wadding on tight, haven't you, Browner?'

'Yes, sir.'

'I've been bloody shot,' mumbled Phyllis.

'You've been bloody lucky,' said Sykes. 'Straight through and probably missed your lung. Play your cards right, it might even be a Blighty.'

'We've got to get the Jeep back on the road and see if we can start it. Here, Browner, we need you a moment.'

The three of them moved to the Jeep and heaved. Slowly it inched out of the ditch and onto the level.

'That front tyre's shredded!' exclaimed Brown. 'No wonder I lost control.'

'What's the spare look like?' asked Sykes.

'All right. The fuel can's been hit and there's a fair few marks back here, but it could be worse.'

Sykes hopped into the driver's seat, switched on the ignition and pressed down the starter button next to the throttle. 'The moment of truth,' he said. The engine turned a few times, then coughed into life. Sykes grinned.

'Thank God for that,' said Tanner. He lowered the shattered windscreen onto the bonnet. 'It'll be a dusty ride back, but at least we don't have to walk.'

With the tyre changed in less than ten minutes, they started the Jeep once more and sped on their way, leaving the dead Italians lying where they had fallen.

'We can't let Camprese get away with this, boss,' said Sykes, as they drove east, the wind and dust battering them.

'No,' said Tanner, 'we can't.' But was it Camprese? As they drove on, a feeling of unease spread through him, a suspicion that refused to go away.

25

Monday, 9 August, late afternoon. The battalion had gone. Trucks had arrived at the edge of the town early that morning and off the men had marched, leaving the place suddenly much quieter.

'We'll be back in a few days,' Tanner had told her. 'Enjoy a bit of peace and quiet.'

'I will.' She had laughed, but in truth, she missed them already. The men had brought cheer and kindness, both to her and Cara, whom they had showered with attention, while the officers had been courteous and considerate; they had been friendly and open too, but never obsequious or lustful as Kranz had been. She had felt comfortable around those men and trusted them. They reminded her of Nico, in a way – the same kinds of conversation she had shared with her brother; the playfulness. Good, decent young men. She had enjoyed their company.

She had not been left entirely alone. Jerry Masters had remained, along with a number of the Headquarters staff, but it wasn't the same without Sykes and Ivo Macdonald. It wasn't the same without Jack.

As she walked with Cara towards the baker's, ambling slowly across the square, she thought of Tanner and wondered whether she was not falling a little bit in love with him. He was unquestionably handsome, she thought, but that was not it. Even Camprese was good-looking, and she could think of no man she despised more. Rather, it was the slightly haunted melancholy about Jack Tanner, that distant expression. Then someone would say something, and he would break into a smile. He was a serious man, but humour was never far away. And he stood up for people. He had stood up to Camprese, even though it was dangerous for him to do so; even though the Mafia had tried to have him killed. *Poor Phyllis.* She had helped Captain Howell clean and dress his wound, and then he had been driven away to hospital. Jack had been next, sitting at her table as Captain Howell stitched a gash across the top of his head. 'Scarred for life,' he'd said.

'But it's above your hair line,' she'd replied.

He'd grinned and winked. 'Let's hope I don't lose my hair, then.'

But there was something more about Jack Tanner that had attracted her. He had been the last man to speak to Nico, and he had arrived, by coincidence, or perhaps it had been Fate, at her door, and recognized her. He had told her the truth about her beloved brother. It was almost, she thought, as though Jack had been sent to her because Nico had gone. She chided herself. *Nonsense. Life is not like that.*

She looked down at Cara, happily swinging her arm as they walked.

'When will the soldiers be back, Mamma?' she asked.

'Soon, I hope, little one,' she told her. 'Soon.'

She was still thinking of Tanner when, a few minutes later, two men drew alongside her, gripped her arms, cupped a hand over her mouth and steered her with Cara down one of the narrow side alleys that fed off the street. They pushed her into a dark, empty house, shutting and bolting the door behind them.

Wednesday, 11 August, 5 a.m. About a mile ahead lay the two villages of Rinazzo and Milo, nestling against the eastern slopes of Etna, towering above them. The battalion had been on the go for thirty-six hours, and although in that time Tanner had not fired any of his weapons, they had been mortared and shelled every step of the way.

This battle was between the gunners and the sappers, as the Germans fell back ever closer to Messina. This, Rawstorne had told him the previous evening, was the endgame. 'Jerry's retreating across the Strait,' he'd told Tanner, from the seat of his still-running Jeep. 'We've smashed the Etna Line so what's left are the rearguards. It's simply a delaying action to enable as many of their men as possible to get to the safety of the mainland.'

That had meant mines and booby traps, harassing machine-guns and mortars, then being shelled by German gunners. Forward would go the sappers, protected by the infantry as Allied aircraft harried the enemy and British artillery shells hurtled through the sky in return. When the Germans stopped firing, it meant they had left the town ahead. The engineers would inch forward again, and then, as the infantry and sappers together entered the town, the German gunners would open up once more.

It would probably happen ahead too, Tanner thought. On their right, the Green Howards were about to enter Milo. The smaller Rinazzo had been allocated to the Yorks Rangers.

A brief consultation with the sappers, then on they went, A and C Companies leading, with B Company in reserve, men scurrying low along the road, while other platoons scampered across the terraces and through the trees that overlooked both villages. Tanner watched from a curve in the track that ran along the slopes and terraces above Milo, peering through his binoculars, his body tense as he waited for the sound of a machine-gun or a mine exploding.

But this time none came, and shortly after half past five, a signal arrived from A Company that they were in Rinazzo and the Germans had gone. Tanner followed with Battalion HQ, and had just reached the village when German guns opened up and the sky was alive to the sound of screeching, screaming shells. Most fell on Milo, and on the Green Howards, who had entered the town at the same time as the Yorks Rangers had taken Rinazzo.

Almost immediately, the British guns replied, pouring counter-battery fire on the German positions some two miles further up the coast. Twenty minutes later, it was over, and calm resumed.

For several hours, the Rangers remained at Rinazzo, smoking, drinking tea, eating some rations and looking at the view.

'I knew a chap who had his honeymoon here,' said Macdonald, as they sat on a stone terrace wall and gazed out across the sea towards the toe of Italy. 'Or, at least, it was near here. Place called Taormina a little further up the coast. He was a submariner. Nice chap.'

'So this is a holiday destination, is it?' asked Tanner.

'Oh, yes. It's rather well known for that. You have to admit, the coastline's stunning.'

'Now that the smoke and dust have gone, yes,' agreed Tanner, 'I'll give you that, Ivo. It's very nice.'

Then at around eleven a staff officer from Brigade arrived in a Jeep and told them 5th Division was being released.

'Message from the brigadier,' said the lieutenant, passing the note to Tanner. He waited while Tanner read: *Op Baytown being advanced to 1/9/43. Return to Motta Sant'Anastasia and await instructions. Congratulations to you and all the men on magnificent effort.*

'Thank you,' said Tanner.

'Transport will be waiting for you in Zafferana, sir.'

'All right,' said Tanner. 'That's only a couple of miles back. Tell the brigadier we'll be moving right away.'

The lieutenant saluted and left, then Tanner turned to the men around him. 'Well, that's it, boys,' he told them. 'Our part in the Sicilian Campaign is over.'

They reached Motta Sant'Anastasia in the early evening, and as Trahair parked the Jeep outside Battalion Headquarters, Tanner stepped out and looked up to see swifts circling the church, their strange cries clear in the otherwise quiet evening sky.

'Listen to that,' said Tanner, to Sykes and Trahair. 'And you know what? I can't hear any guns.'

Sykes grinned. 'Feels like we've come home.'

Tanner stretched and smiled as he looked at Francesca's house, but then the front door opened and Captain Masters appeared, his brow furrowed. *Trouble. What's happened?*

'Good to see you, sir,' said Masters, hurrying towards him.

'What is it, Jerry?' said Tanner. 'What's the matter?'

'It's Francesca,' he said, 'and Cara.'

Please no. 'What's happened?'

'They've disappeared. Two days ago. They were going to the baker's, were seen crossing the square and then they just disappeared.'

'Oh, Jesus,' said Tanner. 'What's he done to them?'

'Camprese?' said Sykes.

'Of course it's bloody Camprese,' snapped Tanner.

'We think we know where they might be,' said

436

Masters. 'Sergeant Lavery has found out from the priest that Camprese has a farm a couple of miles west of the town. Apparently, he owns most of the citrus groves around here and these buildings are where they harvest the crop.'

'This is about revenge, ain't it?' said Sykes. 'If you come after him, he's on his ground and has Francesca and Cara. If you don't, he's still got the most beautiful girl in town.'

Tanner stepped away from them, tapping his clenched fist into the palm of his other hand, trying to think. Sykes was right, he was sure of it. Why else would Francesca and Cara disappear like that? If Camprese had wanted them dead, he'd have simply killed and dumped them. And the priest had told Lavery where he thought Camprese 'might' be. If Camprese hadn't wanted them to know, the priest would not have said a word. No one would. Keeping mum was part of the Mafia code.

Think, think.

'Sir?' said Sykes.

'We need to think clearly,' said Tanner, turning back towards his friend. 'Camprese is cunning, but he's ignorant. He knows how to do things the Sicilian way, but he doesn't know much about us.'

'And he's no soldier.'

'No, and nor are his men. Most of them will be older blokes – men the same sort of age as he is.'

'It's true, there are hardly any young men in Motta,' said Masters.

'But we can't go in there in force. Do that and he'll kill them both. I'm afraid this is something

437

I'm going to have to do on my own.'

'No,' said Sykes. 'I'm coming with you. You can't do this entirely on your own. We need a small group – ask Browner and ask Mr Shopland too. They're both good men who know how to look after themselves. It's a shame we haven't got Mac. He'd have been ideal.'

Tanner nodded. 'All right, Stan, if you're sure.'

'I am. You're not the only one fond of those girls, you know.'

'Just four of us, then.'

'Sir, I'm really not sure this is a good idea,' said Masters.

'We'll be fine, Jerry,' said Tanner. 'I'm not going to be beaten by a little jumped-up Eyetie like Camprese.'

They found the farm on aerial photographs and, after studying it in detail, set out soon after. It was just past seven o'clock. The land to the west of the town undulated, rolling in long ridges, then ran roughly north–south, so they could reach the first ridge overlooking Camprese's farm on the rising ground beyond without being seen.

It was dusk by the time they were on the first ridge, but it was not until the sun had disappeared behind the mountains to the west that they dared bring out their binoculars and peer at the farm.

The buildings were little more than barns: one two-storey structure, then three sides of others, built around a square courtyard. There was no wall, no fence; the buildings themselves were the defence.

'So, what's the plan?' asked Sykes.

'I'm not entirely sure,' said Tanner. 'But I think early morning, don't you? There's almost a full moon tonight. We'll be able to see clearly enough but there'll still be plenty of shadows. We'll have to be quiet, so if there are any guards, we can take care of them and get into the buildings. Mr Shopland and Browner provide cover, nothing more.'

'Won't they hear any shots, though?' asked Brown, clutching his Thompson.

'Hopefully there won't be any, Browner. We'll use knives.' He pulled out the commando dagger that his friend Major Vaughan had given him.

'What about any distractions?' asked Sykes.

'Not unless I say so,' said Tanner. 'We've got to get them out alive, remember?'

They moved off again at midnight and by a quarter to one were in position, lying low in the groves that grew all around the farm. From their position they could see sentries, two men standing by the main entrance into the courtyard, which was a roofed archway.

'Shall I have a scout around the place?' whispered Sykes.

'Good idea,' replied Tanner.

They watched and waited. There were no windows facing out from the main building on the ground floor, but a series of four higher up, all shuttered. Sykes reappeared about twenty minutes later.

'There's no one else outside.'

'Did you spot anything?' asked Tanner.

'There are lamps on in the building to the left.

The windows are shuttered, but I could see a faint glow.'

They waited a bit longer, then Tanner looked at his watch. 'It's ten to two.'

'Dead man's hour,' said Sykes.

'All right, so this is what we'll do,' said Tanner. 'Stan, you and I will get the guards, then we'll signal to you two to move up. Take up position in the archway. If we need you, I'll shout, but otherwise don't do anything. Just cover us. All right?'

'Absolutely,' said Shopland.

'Right, Stan, let's go.'

They moved off, circling around the edge of the groves and approaching the farm from the left. As they stood flat against the wall of the left-hand barn, Tanner said, 'You go all the way around.' He looked at his watch again. 'It's nearly two now. In five minutes be ready.'

Sykes gripped Tanner's shoulder and hurried off. Tanner waited, watching the minutes on his watch.

Now. His heart was beating fast as he squeezed his finger and thumb together, pressed them to his lips and blew, making a short, low-pitched squeal, like that of a rabbit.

Forty yards away, the Italian guards muttered something.

Good.

He made the noise again, slightly louder this time, and crouching low in the shadows, saw both men turn and look towards the sound. Then one of them walked towards him. Tanner made the noise a third time, and the first man paused, then walked forward again, his Beretta in his hands. Tanner waited, watching him approach closer. *Ten yards, six, four* – within touching distance almost – and then the man paused.

A muffled sound from behind made him turn. At that moment, Tanner leaped up, pressed his hand tight around the man's mouth and thrust his knife deep into the Italian's side, piercing the kidney and killing him instantly. Taking his weight, he dragged him around the corner, then scampered to the archway, where he saw Sykes. *Good.* His friend had obviously dealt with the other guard.

They waved towards Shopland and Brown, saw them emerge from the shadows of the groves, then together they walked under the archway to the edge of the courtyard. The far side and the long, low building to the right were in darkness, but there were lamps on in the building to the left, as Sykes had warned. A low loggia extended out from this structure, while above there was an open corridor, with a flight of outdoor stone steps leading up to it at either end. Moonlight shone on this building but, Tanner thought, if they could reach the upper corridor, they would be in shadow once more.

He whispered his plan to Sykes and was about to move, when a door opened in the corner closest to them and two more men emerged. They paused, lit cigarettes, said something to one another in low voices, then walked towards the archway.

Tanner signalled to Sykes – *You take the right, I'll take the left.* Then, as the two men turned the corner, they pounced again, leaping from behind out of the shadows and killing them before they could utter more than a muffled exclamation of surprise.

'That's two less to worry about,' whispered Sykes.

'Yes, but when the others don't come back, they'll know something's up. We need to move fast, Stan. Really fast.'

He darted straight across the yard, keeping low, past the circular millstone at the centre of the courtyard, and reached the steps, paused, waited for Sykes, then hurried along what he now realized was an open store, stacked with boxes and equipment. Where was the staircase leading down to the ground floor? *Come on, come on.* Ahead was a wall and then, *yes,* there it was, a stone staircase that turned ninety degrees against the back wall of the building and led to the lower floor. Tanner could see the glow of light reaching up it, and now, suddenly, he could hear voices too. *Camprese? Yes.* Two men – or was it three? – talking, the tone urgent. Then outside, beneath them, a door opened and a man stepped out.

'Fredo! Vito!' he called.

Tanner could hear Camprese again. Then another door opened and he was shouting, *'Andiamo! Alzati, alzati!'* He heard a scream – *Francesca* – and Cara too, as she began to cry.

Sykes was watching the courtyard, and pointing.

'Fredo! Vito!' the man called again. Tanner stood beside Sykes and watched. The man had a pistol in his hand and was cautiously approaching the archway. Then he switched on an electric torch.

'Fredo?' he called again.

He disappeared from view. A moment later they heard a muffled cry.

Sykes made a line across his throat, then whispered, 'I'm going back down. If I go to the door, I can distract them while you get down the stairs.'

Tanner nodded, then carefully began stepping down the stone steps, taking out his Colt as he did so and silently pulling back the catch. At the corner, he paused and listened.

Camprese was talking in a low voice to just one other man. Where were the girls? In the room?

He waited there, listening, then heard Francesca say something.

'*Sta 'zitto!*' said Camprese. A loud slap.

'*Bastardo!*' Francesca shouted.

'*Sta 'zitto! Sta 'zitto!*' hissed Camprese.

But the exchange had told Tanner what he wanted to know: they were in the room, but away to the left, underneath the store. It meant he could go down the staircase without being seen.

He was about to move when from outside he heard a scrape of stone. *Stan.*

Camprese called something, and then someone was moving towards the staircase. It was too late to move and a moment later Tanner saw the man's shadow edging up the wall and then he turned. For a split second, the Italian stared at Tanner open-mouthed, and then Tanner lunged, this time towards the heart, and the man gasped and fell towards him, dropping his Beretta. Tanner tried to grab it, but it was dark, the man was falling heavily, and suddenly the weapon was clattering down the steps.

'Elio?' called Camprese. There was panic in his voice now, Tanner could tell. He wondered what to do. There was only Camprese left, he was certain. No doubt he was standing by the girls, a weapon in his hand. Tanner moved down the staircase and saw now that the bottom of it faced out towards the door, and that in the doorway, a few steps back and out of sight, was Sykes.

Tanner raised his pistol and pretended to fire, then pointed at Sykes, who nodded. Holding up three fingers, Tanner counted. *One, two, three.*

26

As Sykes fired his Thompson, the girls screamed and Tanner sprang clear of the staircase, both hands clutching the grip of his Colt.

'Jack!' cried Francesca.

'Cessare!' shouted Camprese, his head turning rapidly back towards Tanner. *Good,* thought Tanner. Sykes's burst of fire had done the trick, distracting Camprese for a brief moment.

Just as Tanner had guessed, Camprese had Francesca, with his arm around her neck and a pistol pressed against her temple. He could see no sign of Cara.

The fool. Tanner moved a step closer.

Francesca's eyes were wide with fear.

'Non venire più vicino o mi ucciderla!' said Camprese, his eyes darting between Tanner and the door.

'All right,' said Tanner, stopping. 'Here will do fine.' He was about twelve yards away, he reckoned. Camprese's head was well clear of Francesca's – six inches at least. Closing his left eye, he lined up the sight on Camprese's forehead.

'Francesca,' he said, 'keep calm and don't move.'

She blinked, then closed her eyes, as Tanner breathed in and gently squeezed the trigger.

With still-staring eyes, as though stunned to discover a bullet had hit his head, Camprese fell backwards with a crash, as Francesca shrieked.

'Are you all right?' Tanner asked her, hurrying over to take her in his arms. 'Did he hurt you?'

She shook her head. 'Not really. Cara!'

Sykes was beside them now. 'Where is she?' he asked.

Francesca broke free and hurried to a door at the far end of the room, opened it and Cara ran out, crying, and flung herself at her mother.

'Get her out of here! Both of you, get out quick!' Tanner told Francesca, as he glanced down at the rapidly widening pool of blood and brain spreading across the stone floor.

Francesca picked up her daughter, pressed Cara's head to her chest, and then they were all outside, in the courtyard, where Brown and Shopland were waiting for them.

'Thank God, sir,' said Shopland, seeing Francesca and Cara.

'It's over,' said Tanner. 'Now let's get them home.'

The following night, Tanner turned in early. He

445

was exhausted. The fighting in Sicily was over, Francesca had been rescued, and the thought of a few days of doing very little had made him realize how tired he was. In any case, his head hurt, throbbing oppressively. For a while he lay on the bed, staring through the open window at the milky night sky, thinking that the sooner he left this place the better. He needed to get to a proper camp before Don Calogero's network caught up with him. He would, though, be sorry to leave Francesca. He'd met a few girls over the years. There'd been a brief love affair on Crete, a longer relationship with Lucie in Cairo, and others in between, but always the war got in the way, taking him – and often them – far away. He supposed it would be the same with Francesca. She was possibly the most beautiful woman he had ever known: the almond eyes, the fair, sun-bleached hair, and the wide, full lips that lit up her whole face when they broke into a smile; he was sure he would never tire of looking at that.

He felt sorry for her. She felt trapped, he knew, and although Camprese was dead, there would be others. Another Mafia-backed mayor, and more suitors. Francesca's future did not look good. He thought about the previous night, about how, before she had gone to bed, she had thanked him and kissed him, not on the cheek, but on the lips. It was only brief, but he wished it had lasted longer. He must do something for her, he told himself. The thought of leaving her here to her fate depressed him deeply. Perhaps, he thought, he could get her a job translating at AMGOT in Syracuse. She would be paid, she would be safe. Perhaps that might be a way out for her. Perhaps. He would ask.

Tanner drifted off to sleep, then awoke as he heard a light knock on his door.

'Yes?' he said.

'Jack?'

Francesca.

'Come in.'

She opened the door, closed it behind her, then walked to his bed, pulled off her nightgown and stood there, naked, in the moonlight, before climbing onto the bed beside him.

'Francesca,' he murmured.

'I am in love with you, Jack,' she breathed, kissing him.

Tanner smiled. 'And do you know, Francesca? I think I'm in love with you too.'

As the sun rose over the sea to the east, Francesca lay with her head on his chest. 'If only every day could start like this,' she said. 'But soon you'll be gone, won't you?'

Tanner looked down at her, kissed her head, then said, 'Marry me.' He'd not thought of it until a moment before, but now it seemed so obvious.

Francesca raised her head and looked at him.

'Marry me,' he said again.

'Don't tease me, Jack.'

'I'm not. I'm being serious.'

'But how can you?'

'Francesca,' he said, 'you told me you loved me.'

She lowered her head again and held him more tightly. 'I do. God knows, I do.'

447

'I love you too. So let's get married. If you marry me, I can get you a job in Syracuse working for us. You'll be safe there. I've got some money put away, so you can leave the house and sell it later if you wish. When I'm posted home, which will happen eventually, you can come too, with Cara. If anything should happen, you'll get my pension and you'll get my money and you'll still be entitled to live in Britain if you want to. After the war, we can get a little farm somewhere in Dorset or Devon – it's beautiful there. Not so hot, mind, but lovely. There's no Mafia, it's calm and peaceful, and I'd look after you and Cara. We could be happy. I've no other family, you know. It would be just us. Orphans from the war. Survivors, you and I, living happily ever after.'

Francesca said nothing.

'I'm serious, you know,' he said at length. 'Please say yes. You'd make me very happy. I'm not a Catholic, it's true, but you said you weren't sure you believed in God.'

She lifted her head and he saw now that there were tears running down her cheeks.

'I think I might have begun to believe in Him again,' she said, laughing through the tears.

'I know it would be a big step, but you said you wanted to escape. You can escape with me.'

She laughed and kissed him again, repeatedly. 'I want to, Jack, I really do, but you must give me a little time. I need to talk to Cara. She likes you, I know, but...' She let the sentence trail.

'I understand,' he said. 'But I'd always look after you both. You have my word.'

Friday, 13 August. Wiseman arrived at Battalion Headquarters midmorning, and found Tanner cat-napping among the olives below the house.

'So this is what you do off-duty. Get the zeds in while your men do all the work.'

Tanner got up and rubbed his eyes. 'Why are you here, Charlie?'

'The chief's in bed with a fever, so I decided I'd come and see my old pal. Actually, I've got to go to Syracuse. C'mon, I've got some things for you. Can you spare me an hour?'

'I should think so,' said Tanner.

He followed him out onto the square. 'No Jeep?' he said, looking around.

'I left it outside of town. I get fed up driving through these narrow alleys. Anyway, it's good to walk sometimes.'

They crossed the square and took the steps down to the olive grove where they had talked before. Finding a quiet spot, Wiseman took out his satchel and threw Tanner another bottle of Coca-Cola. Tanner caught it, but when he looked back at Wiseman, he saw the American had produced a pistol and was pointing it straight at him.

Tanner sighed. *Damn it all.* 'So it was you.'

'I did warn you, Jack.'

'I thought you were my friend. I thought your warning was out of concern for my safety.'

'And so you are and so it was. Nothing's changed on that score, believe me. I hate to do this, I really do, but there's too much at stake.'

'Why?' said Tanner. 'We've won, haven't we? What do we care whether we piss off the Mafia now?'

449

'Because without the Mafia Sicily will collapse. There will be riots, there will be violence. There will be a whole load of trouble. They hold the key to controlling this island. We've got the rest of Italy to sort out, a much bigger, more complicated task. The last thing we want to have to do is waste money and manpower controlling Sicily. And your actions, Jack, have pissed them off in a big way, let me tell you.' He nodded towards Tanner's Colt. 'If you wouldn't mind, Jack. Careful.' Tanner passed it to him; it wasn't cocked and he knew he had no chance of firing first.

'Where are we going?' Tanner asked him.

'Don't you worry about that. Now, I've a vehicle a little way from here. It's not far. You lead, Jack.'

Tanner wondered how he might disarm him, but Wiseman was too far behind. *Perhaps in the Jeep. Jesus.* Wiseman. *My friend.*

But when they reached the road, there was no Jeep. Instead there was a military Ford light sedan, and sitting at the wheel was an Italian, dark-haired, about thirty, Tanner guessed, with a Beretta beside him.

'Get in the back, Jack,' said Wiseman.

'So we'll go for a drive, somewhere remote, I suppose.'

'I'm afraid so, Jack. Trust me, I'm sorry. I'm really sorry. But it's out of my hands.'

They drove off, leaving Motta Sant'Anastasia behind, then dropped down towards the plain, pulled off the road and went down a narrow track between yet more groves.

'Here,' said Wiseman, as the car came to a halt.

450

'This time, Jack, it really is goodbye. It's been good knowing you.'

Tanner stared at him and at the pistol still pointing at his stomach. The Italian opened the door. 'Out,' he said in English.

Tanner got out.

'Walk,' said the Italian.

Tanner did so, praying that these really were not going to be his last moments. For the first time in his life, he'd believed he had a future. He'd been fighting this long, terrible war because he was a soldier, it was his job, and because he had accepted that Nazism and Hitler were blights on the world that needed defeating. He had believed it was a moral crusade and that the Allies had right on their side. Sicily had made him question that. But suddenly the prospect of a life with Francesca and Cara had been offered to him and it had given him a reason to keep going, to keep fighting, because the sooner it was all over, the sooner he could be with them. For ever. She was going to marry him, he knew she was.

'All right, stop.' They were among the trees, the car hidden from view.

Tanner stopped and turned, so that he was facing the man, the pistol pointing at his stomach so close the barrel was almost touching his shirt.

'On your knees,' said the Italian.

Bugger that. Tanner swung his left arm up and knocked the Italian's arm clear. The pistol fired, high and wide, as Tanner swung his right fist into the man's face. The blow, delivered with all Tanner's strength, rammed the Italian's nose back into his skull. A moment later, he collapsed onto the ground, dead.

Grabbing the pistol, Tanner hurried through the groves to the edge of the track behind the sedan. He could see Wiseman, still sitting on the back seat, smoking, flicking ash from the open window. Crouching low, Tanner scurried silently across the grass behind the car, then moved around so that he was below the window of the rear door. There he waited until he saw Wiseman extend his hand again to flick away the cigarette. As he did so, Tanner grabbed the arm, breaking the bone against the edge of the car door.

Wiseman yelled in pain as Tanner stood up and swung his fist through the open window. He felt Wiseman go limp, so opened the door and caught him as the American's unconscious body fell towards him.

Laying him on the ground, Tanner felt his pulse. *Good. He's alive.* Quickly, Tanner searched him. He found a second pistol in his pocket, a small Walther, and a knife, both of which he took. From the leg pocket on his denims, he pulled out a field dressing, made a sling for Wiseman's broken upper arm, tied the uninjured wrist tightly to the American's belt, then lifted him into the front passenger seat.

He was about to get into the car himself when he heard a vehicle pull off the road and saw a Jeep coming towards him.

'Stan,' he muttered.

'Blimey, there you are!' shouted Sykes, leaping out. Tanner grinned. With him were Brown and Trahair. 'What the bloody hell's going on?'

'I'll tell you on the way. Tell Trahair to take the

452

Jeep back and you and Brown can come with me.'
'On the way where?'
'Villalba.'

Sykes told him he had seen him wander off with
Wiseman and had been worried. He knew Wiseman was a friend of Tanner's but a few things
didn't add up as far as he was concerned. It had
seemed to him that Wiseman had to have been a
prime suspect for the ambush on the way back
from Enna.

'The thought had crossed my mind too,' admitted Tanner. 'I hoped I'd got it wrong.'

Sykes had followed, and had seen Wiseman
leading Tanner away. He had immediately run
back for Brown and Trahair. They had all jumped
into the Jeep and hurried after them.

'How did you know which way we'd gone?'

'I saw from the town. You were heading south
but then turned off. I couldn't find the turning,
though. Not at first. Then we saw the tracks in
the dust. There's not many cars around here, as
you know. I was worried we'd be too late.'

'You almost were, but my Italian assassin made
the mistake of letting me get close.'

'So you were able to knock the pistol clear?'

'Yes.'

'Kill him?'

Tanner nodded.

'So why Villalba?'

Tanner told them about the drop into Sicily
back in May, and about Don Calogero. And he
explained about Wiseman's role and the Allies'
use of the Mafia.

'Jesus!' whistled Sykes, when Tanner had finished. 'So why are we going to Villalba? Shouldn't we go back to Motta and lie low?'

'No,' said Tanner. 'Don Calogero holds the key. He's the head man. I need to see him.'

Beside him, Wiseman stirred, then cried out in pain.

'Holy Jesus Christ!' he muttered, then glanced at Tanner. 'Jack? Christ, Jack, what are you doing here? Aren't you dead?'

'No,' said Tanner. 'But this is the end of it, Charlie. I'm sick of this. Use the sodding Mafia for all I care, but I want them off my back.'

'I'm not sure that's possible, Jack,' muttered Wiseman.

'Course it is. We just need to ask the right person, which is why we're driving to Villalba.'

'Jack, it was Don Calo who ordered you dead.'

'What?' said Brown, from the back. 'And now we're going to see him?'

'Relax, Browner. It'll be fine.'

They reached Villalba soon after four o'clock and drove straight to Don Calogero's villa. Untying Wiseman's arm, Tanner told Sykes and Brown to wait by the car.

The door was opened by Bartolomeo and Wiseman spoke to him.

'I always knew you could speak Italian,' said Tanner.

They were ushered in, Bartolomeo looking at both men suspiciously.

'It's good timing,' said Wiseman, as Bartolomeo disappeared. 'He's had his siesta.'

454

After a few minutes, Bartolomeo reappeared and led them into the same room where they had had their first audience with Don Calogero. He looked much the same: short-sleeved shirt, braces, dark trousers and glasses perched on his nose.

'I'm trusting you, Charlie,' said Tanner. 'No – I'm warning *you* now.'

Wiseman waved his good hand. 'OK, OK,' he said, then spoke to Don Calogero.

'Tell him,' said Tanner, 'that it is out of respect for him that I have come here. Our enemies are the same enemies: the Nazis. Tell him I have been fighting the Nazis for three long years and I am ready to fight them some more, but I cannot if he has me killed.'

Tanner watched as Wiseman spoke. Ahead, perched on his chair, Don Calogero sat with an implacable expression on his face.

'Tell him I'm sorry if I insulted him. It was not intentional. My grievance was with Salvatore Camprese and him alone.'

Again, he listened as Wiseman relayed his words.

There was silence for a moment, and Tanner was struck by how still the room had become. Then Don Calogero cleared his throat.

'*Lei è un uomo coraggioso.*'

'You are a brave man,' said Wiseman.

'*E io rispetto il fatto che siete venuti qui.*'

'And I respect the fact that you have come here to see me.'

'*E hai ragione. Hai un altro nemico da combattere.*'

'And you are right. You have another enemy to fight.'

'*Si può andare. Non saranno danneggiati.*'

'You can go. You will not be harmed.'

Tanner breathed out heavily with relief. '*Grazie*,' he said. '*Grazie mille*.'

Don Calogero bowed his head, then turned to Wiseman. '*Saggio, si è fortunati ad avere solo un braccio rotto, credo.*' He chuckled.

As they left, Tanner turned to Wiseman. 'Why does he call you Saggio? He used that name before, last time I was here.'

'It's Italian. *Saggio* means "wise man". But it's also because he knows I'm Italian, Jack.'

'You are?'

'My parents are. Sicilian, in fact. From Mussomeli, just down the road from here. Came over to New York in 1918. I was seven. I was in trouble as a kid, so when I applied to join the Army, I changed my name. To sound more American.' As they stepped outside, Wiseman turned to him. 'I'm glad you're not dead.'

'So am I,' said Tanner. 'But when we get back, Charlie, I don't want to see you again.'

Tanner married Francesca Falcone five days later, on 18 August 1943, in the church across the square, with Sykes as his best man. It was the day after the Italians surrendered the island. An understated wedding. Tanner didn't care. In fact, he was glad. He'd asked the brigadier for permission, which had been given, not that he'd needed it at his age. Even the priest had left his religion unquestioned.

Francesca had agreed to marry him when he returned from Villalba. 'It won't be easy,' he told

456

her. 'I'm going to have to go and fight again, but when it's all over, we can start a life together. A proper life together. And I'll look after you always. I promise you that.'

Later as they lay in bed, Tanner realized he had never felt happier in his life. He wished he could be with her like this for ever, but that, he knew, could not be. Soon they would be invading mainland Italy, and the fighting would begin again. But one day, Tanner thought, the war would be over. *And I'm going to be there when it is.* He kissed his wife. The thought of her would keep him going.

Historical Note

Even now, and despite numerous books and other exposés on the subject, the workings of the Mafia are shrouded in myth. What is not in doubt, however, is that during the years of Fascist rule, Mussolini made it a priority to stamp out the Mafia, sending to Sicily a particularly tough and uncompromising Fascist governor called Cesare Mori. During his time on the island, Mori arrested some eleven thousand suspected Mafiosi, and restricted Mafia influence to a few isolated pockets deep in the interior, such as that of Villalba. Mori left the island in 1929, claiming the Mafia was finished, but over the next fourteen years, the organization continued to function, although they never reclaimed the position they had had before Mori's arrival. Then the Allies landed, Fascism was overthrown and power handed back to the Mafia, since when their influence has continued.

Don Calogero Vizzini was very much a real character, lived in the house in Villalba as described in the book, and was leader of the Sicilian Mafia until his death in 1954. His influence remained strong, even during the years of Fascism, and there seems to be little doubt that he cut some kind of deal with the invading Allies. Just what this deal was, and to what extent it was he and his associates who persuaded so many Italians to throw down their arms during Patton's lightning drive to take the western half of the island, remains shrouded in mystery. Among the stories – and one that Don Calogero certainly cultivated – was that a yellow flag with the letter L stitched in black was dropped by an Allied plane on Villalba. And, according to the myth, the L did not stand for *libertà* but 'Luciano' – Lucky Luciano, the pre-war American-Italian mobster. Some claimed that Luciano was freed from prison, where he was still serving time, and sent on a clandestine mission to Sicily, others that he gave advice and re-established links with the Mafia on behalf of the US intelligence services from his cell. Sadly, there is no written evidence that proves either was true. Plenty did claim the flag was dropped for Don Calogero, however, and that when American tanks reached the town on 20 July, the old Mafioso climbed aboard.

He was away from Villalba for six days, helping to pave the way for the US advance and then, after the fall of Palermo, ensuring that his fellow Mafia leaders took most of the plum posts as AMGOT began facing up to the difficulties of imposing military rule on the island. It was true that Don Calogero provided the list of men recommended to take over as mayor in many of the island's towns, and that they were largely accepted; some were even released from prison to take up their new posts. Such was the poverty of most Sicilians, and so bad was the problem of distributing food and getting the bomb-damaged cities back on their feet, that the Allies accepted

Mafia collaboration would make life considerably easier. But it was a devil's pact in many ways. Many Sicilians would feel they have been paying the price for that collaboration ever since.

Although Tanner's exploits and those of the Yorks Rangers are fiction, the framework of events was much as described. After quick gains in the first days of the invasion, Eighth Army did become bogged down in the Plain of Catania, while XXX Corps to the west also struggled against a determined and mostly German defence along what was known as the Hauptkampflinie, that is, at the foot of the lower slopes of Etna. The hard battle for Primosole Bridge also happened much as described. Very real, too, were 15th Infantry Brigade and 5th Division, the former led by Brigadier Rawstorne. He had fought through and survived the First World War, then briefly became a first-class cricketer, winning a cap for Lancashire. Also real was the great Hedley Verity, one of the finest bowlers ever to have played for Yorkshire and England. Joining up at the start of the war out of moral conviction, he was mortally wounded in the night attack on 19/20 July, as described, and suffered a tragically protracted death as he was put on carts and trucks, boats and trains to a hospital in Caserta on the Italian mainland. He could have survived, but lack of proper medication and the onset of infection did for him, sending ripples of shock through Eighth Army and beyond. He is buried in the Commonwealth War Graves Commission cemetery at Caserta.

Motta Sant'Anastasia is a real place, perched on a rocky outcrop among the lava hills beneath

Etna. However, there is no record that the town had a Mafia mayor at that time and, in reality, it took a few months for Mafia control of the island to really take grip. Not only were a large number of Mafiosi released from prison, but the chief civil-affairs officer of Palermo, an American called Colonel Charles Poletti, was horribly corrupt, had strong Mafia ties, and later, in 1944 when he took over the civil affairs of Naples, went into business with Vito Genovese, one of the most notorious and unsavoury American-Italian gangsters around. Their black-market profiteering, while thousands were being killed and wounded at the front, and with many Italians literally starving, was an abomination. But, to a large extent, the Allies had only themselves to blame.

As ever, I need to say a few thanks to a number of people who have helped along the way: Oliver Barnham, Dr Peter Caddick-Adams, Professor Rick Hillum, Bill Scott-Kerr, Mads Toy and all at Transworld, Patrick Walsh, and last but not least, Rachel, Ned and Daisy.

The publishers hope that this book has given you enjoyable reading. Large Print Books are especially designed to be as easy to see and hold as possible. If you wish a complete list of our books please ask at your local library or write directly to:

Magna Large Print Books
Magna House, Long Preston,
Skipton, North Yorkshire.
BD23 4ND

This Large Print Book for the partially sighted, who cannot read normal print, is published under the auspices of

THE ULVERSCROFT FOUNDATION